"It's like we'r̶e̶ ̶m̶a̶r̶r̶i̶e̶d̶, Cooper. Only without any of the good stuff. Like sex."

He had to admit that up until the night before, he'd never really thought about Kara and sex in the same sentence. But now, he wasn't so sure.

"You want us to have sex?"

"Of course I want sex. But I want more than that, too." Sighing, she said, "I want a husband, kids. A home. I just got so comfortable that I didn't notice that I wasn't getting anywhere."

"What's so bad about comfortable?" he demanded.

"Nothing," she said. "If that's all you're looking for, then comfortable is great. But it's not enough for me. Not any more."

He knew that once she'd made up her mind about something, that was it.

And the thought of losing Kara hit him hard.

Pregnant with the First Heir
by Sara Orwig

ᗡ ᔇ ᕮ

Olivia's eyes half-closed in a sultry expression that took Matt's breath away.

"Let's get this out of the way between us, right now…" he said softly, leaning closer.

She slanted him a sensual look that set his pulse pounding. He slipped his arm around her waist and heard her gasp. She was soft, warm, all curves. He took his time, giving her a chance to pull away or protest.

Somewhere in the depths of his being, he knew he was crossing a line, going against everything he'd sworn to do. But he couldn't resist, even if he knew in his heart that he was opening himself up for unending trouble.

Even if he was damned for it, he was going to kiss her…

Strictly Lonergan's Business
MAUREEN CHILD

Pregnant with the First Heir
SARA ORWIG

MILLS & BOON®

Desire™

*First published in Great Britain 2007
Harlequin Mills & Boon Limited,
Eton House, 18-24 Paradise Road, Richmond, Surrey TW9 1SR*

The publisher acknowledges the copyright holders of the
individual works as follows:

Strictly Lonergan's Business © Maureen Child 2006
Pregnant with the First Heir © Sara Orwig 2006

ISBN: 978 0 263 85016 1

51-0507

*Printed and bound in Spain
by Litografía Rosés S.A., Barcelona*

STRICTLY LONERGAN'S BUSINESS

by
Maureen Child

MAUREEN CHILD

is a California native who loves to travel. Every chance they get, she and her husband are taking off on another research trip. The author of more than sixty books, Maureen loves a happy ending and still swears that she has the best job in the world. She lives in Southern California with her husband, two children and a golden retriever with delusions of grandeur.

To my "other" mother – Mary Ann Child

For everything you've given me.
For everything you've been to me.
I couldn't love you more.

One

"It's really easy," Kara Sloan told herself, giving her own reflection a narrow eyed glare in the rear view mirror. "He opens the door, you say 'I quit.'"

Right.

If it was that easy, she'd have said those two little words six months ago. Heck. A *year* ago.

The minute she'd realized she'd made the huge mistake of falling in love with her employer.

The trouble was, every time she was anywhere near her boss, Cooper Lonergan, her brain shut down and her emotions took over. One look from the man's dark brown eyes and she turned into a puddle of goo.

She still wasn't sure how this had happened.

Heaven knew she hadn't planned it. She'd been the man's assistant for five years, and for four of those five, everything had been great. They'd had a comfortable friendship and easy working relationship. Until it suddenly dawned on her nearly a year ago, that she was in *love* with him.

And ever since that day, she'd been miserable.

She couldn't even get mad at Cooper for not noticing that her feelings had changed. Why would he? To him, she was as familiar a sight in his life as the dark red leather sofa in his living room at home. And just as comfortable.

This situation was her own fault. She'd changed the rules and he didn't even know it. She was in love and he was in like.

Not a good thing.

"Which is *why*," she said sternly, still meeting her own wide green eyes in the rental car mirror, "you have to quit. Just suck it up, face him down and say it."

She inhaled sharply, blew out a breath and nodded grimly. She could do this. She *would* do this.

Muttering darkly, she swung her legs out of the car, slammed the door and then stared up at the big yellow Victorian farmhouse Cooper had rented for the summer. It looked...welcoming, somehow. As if the house had been waiting for her.

Silly, but she was sorry she wouldn't be staying. Sorry she'd have to leave and go back to New York in just two weeks. There was something about this place that 'spoke' to her.

It sat far back on a wide, manicured green lawn and several old shade trees surrounded the structure. Window panes glinted in the morning sunlight, fresh flowers in terra cotta pots lined the porch, their bright summer colors dazzling in the morning light.

She inhaled sharply, deeply, enjoying the scents of freshly mowed grass and the hint of the ocean, just a few miles away. Kara had always considered herself a city girl. Happy in Manhattan, she loved the rush and crush of the crowds, the blaring symphony of horns and shouted insults from the cabbies who drove as if every mile made was a personal victory.

But, she thought, there was something to be said for this, too. The quiet. The color. The lazier pace.

No point in getting used to it, though.

Her three inch heels wobbled slightly on the crushed gravel driveway, and she thought that was only appropriate. Hadn't she been off balance around Cooper all year? Besides, if she'd had any sense, she'd have traveled in jeans and sneakers. But no…she'd had to look *good* when she saw him. Not that he ever noticed what she was wearing.

Gritting her teeth, Kara silently admitted that Cooper wouldn't notice if she had shown up naked.

Which, she reminded herself sternly, was *exactly* why she had to quit her job. It was just too hard. Too miserable to be in love with a man who only saw you as the world's most efficient assistant.

"My own fault," she muttered, turning her back on the house to walk to the rear of the car. She pushed a button on the rental car key ring and the trunk slowly opened like a coffin lid in an old Dracula movie.

They worked well together, had a lot of laughs, and Kara had had the satisfaction of knowing that she did her job so well, he couldn't get along without her. Then she'd messed it all up by changing the rules.

She wasn't even sure when it had happened. When she'd stopped looking at Cooper like an employer and started having X-rated dreams about him. He'd slipped up on her. Sneaked under her defenses. Damn it, he'd made her fall in love with him without even trying and didn't even have the decency to *notice*.

That's why she had to quit. Had to get out while she still could. It was, as her best friend Gina had put it just the night before, *a freaking emergency*.

Gina had taken her out for drinks and given Kara the pep talk that apparently was considered the best friend's duty.

"You know darn well that man is never going to change."

"Why should he?" Kara challenged, stabbing the olive in her martini as if it were an alien out to take over the world. "As far as he's concerned everything is great. Fabulous."

"Exactly my point." Gina blinked at her, lifted one hand to signal the bartender for another round, then turned back to look at her friend again. "He's been in California what? Three days?"

"Yesss…"

"And he's called you like a hundred times already."

True. Her cell phone, always on so that Cooper could get in touch with her whenever he needed to, had been ringing with alarming regularity. Kara checked her watch. Twenty minutes since his last call. He was due. "I work for him."

"Oh, it's way beyond that, Kara," Gina said, leaning across the glossy bar table until her long blond hair brushed the polished surface. "Last time he called, the man asked you how to make *coffee*. He's thirty something and can't make a cup of coffee without your help?"

Kara laughed. "He's thirty one and he can too make coffee. It's just terrible."

Gina was not amused. Shaking her head, she sat back. "You did this to yourself, girlfriend. You made yourself indispensable."

"That's a *bad* thing?" Kara reached for her fresh drink and turned her attention to the new olive.

"It is when Cooper Lonergan sees you like a well-programmed robot." Gina took a gulp of her apple-tini and then waved the glass in the air. "He doesn't see *you*. He never will."

"That's harsh."

"But true."

"Probably."

"So," Gina demanded, "What are you going to do about it? Stick around until you're old and alone and wondering what the hell happened to your life? Or get out now while you still can?"

And *that*, Kara thought now, reaching into the trunk, is the million dollar question. She knew Gina was right. Heck, she'd known the truth for the last year. She had no future with Cooper. At least, nothing beyond what she had now. And that just wasn't enough.

Not anymore.

A crisp, cool wind with the scent of the sea on it, swept across the yard, set the leaves on the trees dancing, and tossed her dark brown hair across her eyes. She plucked it back, blew out a breath and grabbed up both her suitcase, the small carry-on bag she'd filled with fresh bagels from Cooper's favorite deli, the gourmet coffee he couldn't write without, and five bags of marshmallow cookies.

The man had the palate of a ten-year-old. She smiled to herself, thinking, as she always did, that it was kind of cute how Cooper had to have his favorite cookies on hand at all times.

But she caught herself an instant later. Not cute. Annoying. Right.

Nodding to herself, she pledged that the minute she saw Cooper, she'd give him notice. Two weeks.

He could hire someone temporarily for this summer in California, then when he went home to Manhattan, he could find a more permanent replacement.

As for Kara, the sooner she got back to New York and what was left of her life…the better.

Grim determination fed her steps as she started toward the big house at the end of drive. With every wobble of her heels, she told herself over and over, *It's just a job. You can find another, better one. You don't need Cooper.*

She'd almost convinced herself when the front door flew open, the ancient screen door slapped against the wall of the house and Cooper Lonergan stepped out onto the wide front porch.

Tall and lean, he was wearing his New York uniform of black pants and black shirt. His features were sharp, angular and his black hair, just long enough to touch his shoulders, flew about his face like a dirty halo. His dark eyes glinted in the sun and when he smiled, Kara felt it deliver a solid punch to her belly. Probably had more impact because he didn't really smile all that often. But brother, when he did…

The man was mouthwatering.

Damn it.

"Kara!" He took the five steps down to the yard in two long strides and crossed to where she was still standing, dumbstruck by the force of her own emotions. He swept her up into a brief, hard hug that lit up her insides like Times Square on New Year's Eve, then let her go so abruptly, she staggered back a step.

"Thank God you're here."

A brief flash of something that might have been hope darted through her. "You missed me?"

"Boy, did I," he said. "You have no idea. I made coffee this morning and it pretty much tasted like I think motor oil with a dash of cinnamon would taste."

Right. Hope dissolved into reality. Of course he hadn't actually missed her. When she took her three weeks of vacation every year, he didn't miss *her*. He missed the convenience of having her around. Why should this time be any different?

"Please tell me you brought real coffee and my cookies."

She sighed, accepting the truth. "Yes Cooper, you too tall four-year-old. I have the coffee and I brought your cookies."

"Excellent." He ignored her jibe, just as he pretty much ignored her, Kara thought. Then he took her suitcase from her and started for the house. "Did you get the dry cleaning for me, too?"

"It's in the trunk."

"And bagels. Oh God, tell me you remembered the bagels."

She shook her head and kept pace with him. Ten seconds with him and she fell into the old, familiar pattern. What had happened to her vow? Where had her backbone gone? Why wasn't she looking into those dark chocolate eyes of his and telling him that she quit?

She took a breath and almost groaned. He even *smelled* delicious.

"Yes, I remembered the bagels," she muttered, disgusted with both of them. "When in the last five years have I *not* remembered?"

"Never," he said with a quick wink that weakened her knees even as it stiffened what was left of her resolve. "That's why I can't live without you."

Words spoken so easily, so lightly. She knew it meant nothing to him, but if they were only true, what those words would mean to her.

Cooper ushered Kara into the house, standing back to let her pass in front of him. Her heels clicked against the wood floor and she flipped her long, dark brown hair back over her shoulder as she turned in a circle to look around the room.

He took his first good look at the same time. Sure, he'd been there three days already, but he'd spent most of his time in the master bedroom, sitting at a makeshift desk, working.

Well, *trying* to work. In reality, he'd played about three thousand games of solitaire. Which wouldn't help him meet the deadline that was already flying at him.

"It's a great place," Kara said, studying an old brass chandelier hanging in the center of the living room.

He glanced around, noting the big, overstuffed

chairs in faded cabbage rose upholstery. A braided rug covered most of the scarred wood floor and the pale yellow walls looked bright and cheerful, even to him. The property management company who'd leased the place to him had done a first-rate job keeping the old house in shape.

"People say it's haunted."

She whipped around and stared at him, her green eyes wide and fascinated. "It is?"

He nodded. "When I was a kid, I spent every summer here in Coleville with my grandfather and my cousins." Memories rushed in, nearly strangling him with the force of the accompanying emotions. He pushed them down, deliberately shut the door on the feelings rising in him as he said, "We'd ride our bikes over here at night and watch this house, tell each other scary stories and wait to see something otherworldly floating by." He shrugged and smiled. "We never saw a damn thing."

"And since you've been here…?"

"Nada."

"Well that's disappointing," Kara said.

He smiled at the whine in her voice. No matter what, he could always count on Kara to see the same possibilities that he could. As a horror novelist, he'd really enjoyed the idea of renting the same haunted house that had fascinated him as a kid.

But he should have known that the only ghosts he'd find this summer were those in his own past. Instinctively, Cooper cut that thought off neatly. He wasn't going to go there.

"Anyway," Cooper said with a shrug, "It's only a couple of miles from my grandfather's place, so it was handy."

"Oh! How is your grandfather?"

"Long story. But he's actually fine."

"But his doctor said he was dying…"

"Like I said," Cooper repeated, not really wanting to go into it all at the moment. "Long story. First, tell me what took you so long to get here. I expected you yesterday."

"I told you it would take three days to close up your condo and take care of all the details—"

"You're right, you did. Just felt like a really *long* three days. You're the best, Kara. Have I given you a raise lately?"

"No," she chided.

"Put that on your list—" he cut her off before she could say anything else. "The important thing is you're here now."

She smiled at him and Cooper added, "With you here, I can finally work. I'm telling you, I haven't had a decent meal since I left home."

Her smile slowly faded.

"The grocery store in Coleville doesn't deliver, so you'll need to make a trip over there to stock up." He picked up her suitcase and headed for the stairs. "I'll put your bags away. You're in the room across from mine. It's big, got a nice view of the fields. We have to share the bathroom, but we'll work it out. You could make up a schedule and—"

"Cooper!"

He paused, looked back at her and sent her another one of those rare, genuine smiles. "It really is good to see you, Kara. And it's okay. I know what you're gonna say."

"Really?"

"Absolutely," he said. "I feel the same way. Good to have things back to normal."

Two

A few hours later, Kara had been to the grocery store, had a chicken roasting in the oven and had even managed to arrange for a fax machine to be delivered and set up first thing tomorrow.

Cooper was upstairs working and down here, in the square, farmhouse style kitchen, Kara was wondering what the heck had happened to her plan.

She hitched one hip against the worn, Formica countertop and folded both arms across her chest. Wearing her favorite pair of faded, nearly threadbare jeans, a pale blue T-shirt and wonderful, comfortable sneakers, she shook her head and said aloud, "You're a wimp, Kara. A spineless wiener dog. A disgrace to assistants everywhere."

Late afternoon sunlight slanted through the curtained window, making lacy shadows on the round, pedestal table and the gleaming wood floor. Kara watched as a soft breeze ruffled the curtains, sending those shadows into a lazy dance.

Walking across the room, she pulled out one of the captain's chairs and plopped down onto it. Bracing her elbows on the table, she stared out through a gap in the curtains at the rolling back lawn that stretched out to a wide green field. Then she heaved a dramatic sigh of complete disgust. Oh, she wasn't disgusted with Cooper so much as she was with herself.

Back to normal. Abruptly, she shifted in the chair, leaned back and stretched out her fingertips. Her nails tapped against the table like a frantic heartbeat. "Not his fault he fell right back into the same pattern we've been in for years. You *knew* this was going to happen, Kara. The question is…why didn't you quit?"

But she knew the answer to that already. Because one look at Cooper and her fantasies took over. Her reasonable, intelligent, logical brain went right to sleep and into Fantasy Land.

She'd imagined it all so perfectly, her dreams were even filled with the dialogue her brain had provided. And sitting right there at the kitchen table, she indulged herself yet one more time. She'd walk into a room, a stray beam of sunlight would strike her just so and...

Cooper glances up. His gaze meets hers. And for one, heart-stopping moment, the two of them are lost in the suddenly discovered rush of love.

He crosses the room to her, cups her face in his big, wonderful hands and says, "My God, Kara. How could I have been so stupid? How could I not have seen the real you for so long? Can you ever forgive me?"

And Kara smiles, reaches up to cover his hands with her own and says, "There's nothing to forgive. It's enough that we're finally together. I love you, Cooper."

He whispers "I love you, too," just before he kisses her with more passion than she could have imagined.

"Right," she muttered now, coming up out of her daydream like a drowning diver frantically breaching the water's surface to find air. "*Nothing to forgive?* What am I? An idiot?"

Yes, she thought. An idiot in love with a man who was clueless enough to not even notice what was right in front of him. A man who would *never* see her until it was too late.

A sigh swept through the room.

Kara jolted upright and twisted her head from side to side, glancing around the empty kitchen, futilely trying to find the source of that heartbreaking sound. But there was nothing. She stiffened, waiting for it to come again. It didn't. There was just a sunny kitchen, empty but for her. Chills snaked along Kara's spine and tingled at the base of her neck.

A ghost?

Cooper did tell her the house was supposedly haunted. But then he'd also said he hadn't felt a thing in three days.

"Imagination," she whispered, standing up slowly, carefully. She chuckled softly, and pretended that her laughter didn't sound quite as shaky as it felt. Swallowing hard, she rubbed her hands up and down her arms, dispelling the sensation of every nerve in her body standing on end.

Then, blaming the weird feeling on her own day-dreaming, Kara shut down her brain and finished getting dinner ready.

Cooper spent his day with a murderous demon.

His mind raced just a few beats ahead of his fingers, furiously typing at the keyboard. He knew what he wanted to capture. What he wanted his reader to feel. What surprised him was that this was the first piece of decent writing he'd managed to accomplish since arriving in California. It felt good. Good to be lost in his own imagination. Good to be caught up by the characters forming on his computer screen.

Good to let go—however briefly—of the memories that had been choking him for three long days.

*A silent shroud of snow covered the walkway
to the old hotel, but David hardly noticed. The
cold seeped into his bones, down to his soul and
a ribbon of dread slowly unwound in the pit of
his stomach. His shoulders hunched against the
icy wind, he shuffled his steps, reluctant to
approach, as if every cell in his body was trying
to warn him to stay away...*

Cooper finally lifted his fingers from the
computer keyboard and leaned back in his desk chair.
He knew exactly how the hero of his latest novel felt.
Hadn't he himself only reluctantly returned to Coleville? Wasn't every cell in *his* body still telling him
to get the hell out?

But he was trapped for the summer. No getting out
of it. He'd given his word to his grandfather, and a
Lonergan never went back on his word. Even to
sneaky old men who lie to their grandsons about
being at death's door on a skateboard.

Not that he was pissed off about that, he assured
himself. He was glad Jeremiah wasn't dying. Glad
the old man was as healthy and apparently, as
slippery as he'd always been. But damn it, Cooper
hadn't been back to Coleville in fifteen years. And
if Jeremiah hadn't pulled one over on him, he
doubted he ever would have returned.

It was too hard. Too many memories, constantly

fluttering through his mind like swarms of gnats—annoying and impossible to ignore.

His screen saver flicked on, a haunted house complete with bats, ghosts and vampires. Usually, that was enough to motivate him to get back to writing. To delve into whatever story he had going. Today though, he ignored the animated cartoon drawing filling the screen.

From downstairs came the clank of pans and the rush of water through old pipes. The scent of something delicious wafted up the stairs and he took a deep breath, enjoying not only the mingled aromas of garlic and sage, but the realization that Kara was right downstairs.

Damn, it was good having Kara here. And for more reasons than her cooking abilities.

Since arriving in Coleville for the first time in fifteen years, Cooper had never felt so alone. Sure, his family was right down the road a couple of miles, but here, in this house, he lay alone at night and felt emptiness crowding in on him.

Ordinarily, he liked being alone. In New York, he spent most days working, avoiding the phone, the doorbell, and e-mail. Kara kept the world at bay, affording him plenty of time to lose himself in his stories. When he needed a distraction, the city was just beyond his doorstep and there were any number of women he could call.

Here though, the quiet reigned supreme. There

were no hustling throngs of people. No loud crash and scream of cabs darting in and out of vicious traffic. No sirens or street peddlers. Just the quiet—and too much time to think.

Pushing his chair back, Cooper stood up and walked across his bedroom to the window overlooking the front of the house. He wasn't seeing the neatly tended yard, or the shade trees, or even the green field sweeping down the narrow two lane road toward his grandfather's ranch.

As he had the last three days, he looked beyond, to a lake he couldn't even see from here. He'd thought that renting a house a couple of miles away would be enough. That not being able to actually *see* the water would make being here easier.

But he should have known better.

Hell, he'd been living in Manhattan for years, and every night in his dreams, he saw that lake. Every day when he sat down to write the horror novels that had given him fame and fortune, he saw that lake. Saw again how that summer day fifteen years ago had become a nightmare.

If he closed his eyes now, it would all come racing back. The feel of the sun on bare shoulders. The rush of laughter from his cousins. The sigh of wind in the trees. The splash as he and his cousins had taken turns jumping for distance into the icy water.

The numbing shock that followed.

So he didn't close his eyes, but the memories clung to the edges of his mind, taunting him, pushing at him. He reached up, scraped one hand through his hair, then rubbed his eyes as if he could rub away the images that felt as though they were burned on his retinas.

"Hey!"

Startled, he spun around and found Kara standing in the open doorway staring at him. Heart pounding, he shook his head and scowled at her. "Trying to give me a heart attack?"

"It wasn't on the schedule for tonight, no," she said and stepped into the room, still watching him curiously. "Everything okay?"

No.

"Why wouldn't it be?" he hedged and turned his back on her to walk back to the desk and his laptop. He never left the lid up when someone else was around. Call it superstition or whatever, he didn't like anyone getting a peek at what he was working on.

"Well, because I called your name three times and you didn't hear me."

"I was…thinking," he said and at least it wasn't a lie.

"New book giving you trouble?"

"Yeah." His fingertips smoothed over the gray lid of the computer as if caressing the words hidden inside. "At least, it was. Until today." He forced a smile as he looked at her. "You must have brought me some luck."

"Uh-huh." She crossed the room, threw the curtains back and opened the window. A cold sharp breeze raced into the room as if it had been crouched just outside, waiting its chance. "So, translation is, you didn't work before because I wasn't here."

"Right." Cooper watched her as she wandered the room, efficiently tidying up the space, folding the old quilt at the foot of his bed, straightening a framed landscape, then turning to the desk, where she shuffled papers into neat stacks.

He felt calmer just watching her. Damn, Kara was good for him. She always had been. Her voice, her even temper, her cool logic, her no-nonsense way of looking at the world was exactly the right leash he needed to keep him grounded.

"So I'm guessing," she said, glancing at him with a knowing gleam in her eye, "that means you killed me horribly again."

One corner of his mouth quirked into a half smile. God, she knew him better than anyone ever had. Part of the fun of being a writer was being able to kill off whomever happened to be bugging you at the time. And when Kara wasn't around, it was lowering to admit just how lost he felt without her. Hence the catharsis of killing off a secretary/assistant in one of his stories.

"How'd I die this time?" she asked, planting both hands on her hips. "Drowning?"

"I told you before," he said, his voice going as stiff as his spine. "*You* never drown."

"Okay," she said, lifting both hands in mock surrender. "Sheesh. Just asked."

"Right. Sorry." He pushed one hand through his hair again and willed the tremor inside into stillness.

In every one of his books, at least one character drowned. But it was always someone Cooper didn't like. Someone he thought the readers wouldn't be too invested in. Death by drowning was something Cooper could never take lightly. Not with his memories. Not with the past that was always so close.

"You sure you're okay?"

"Yeah," he said, nodding as if to confirm his own word. "I'm fine. Did you come up here for something in particular?"

"Dinner's ready."

He glanced at the window. The sun was just setting. Turning his gaze back to her he asked, "This early?"

"Shoot me, I'm hungry." Shrugging, Kara headed for the door and said over her shoulder, "You can wait till later if you want to."

"No," he said, sweeping his gaze around the room that without her suddenly seemed way too empty. "I'll join you."

"Great. You can open the bottle of chardonnay I got at the market."

He chuckled as he followed her downstairs.

"Mmm. Chardonnay from Al's market in Coleville, California. Can't wait."

"Snob."

"Peasant."

Kara was still laughing as they walked into the kitchen. She took a seat at the table and watched him as he grabbed the wine and the bottle opener. They'd already settled back into the familiar routine. And damn it, it felt good. And right.

God, she would miss this so much when she left. And she *had* to leave. That was more apparent by the moment. They'd become too comfortable together.

He sat down and his long legs bumped into hers. Kara felt a flash of something hot and dazzling skyrocket inside, and only just managed to keep from yelping.

Naturally, Cooper didn't notice.

While he poured clear, straw colored wine into the pink antique glasses she'd found in a cupboard, Kara looked around at the homey old kitchen. The cabinets were painted white, the appliances looked as though they were new in the fifties, and the windows overlooked a huge backyard lined by ancient shade trees.

It all should have been…soothing somehow. Cozy. Instead though, Kara felt a sensation of…waiting. She hadn't heard anything weird since that sigh earlier in the afternoon and she'd almost convinced herself that hadn't really happened.

"This smells great," Cooper said, helping himself to a serving of chicken, potatoes and fresh broccoli.

"You know you could have found the grocery store yourself," Kara pointed out, taking a sip of her wine. Cool, tart, wonderful.

"Oh, I did," he said, reaching for a slice of wheat bread from the plate in the center of the table. "I bought coffee and a couple boxes of doughnuts. Oh," he added, "and a few frozen burritos."

"Pitiful." And somehow, cute. How twisted was she?

"We go with our strengths," he said around a bite of chicken. Then his dark eyes closed and he sighed, obviously in pure heaven. "At home, I can call a restaurant. Here—let's just say that the Burger Hut doesn't deliver." He swallowed and groaned. "Man, Kara. I owe you. Big."

She didn't want him to owe her.

She wanted him to *love* her.

But she might as well wish for a ten pound weight loss and a spanking new wardrobe by morning. Neither wish was going to happen.

Outside, late afternoon slid into twilight, the sky softly darkening. Inside, a familiar, comfortable silence settled between them and Kara found herself taking mental pictures that she would be able to pull out and look at later—after she left.

At that thought, her gaze landed on Cooper and a twinge of regret pinged off her chest, bouncing off her heart, leaving it feeling bruised. She hated the notion of walking out of Cooper's life, but at the same time, she had to, if she ever expected to get a life of her own.

Still, she wanted to enjoy what time she did have with him, so she pushed those thoughts to the back of her mind and asked, "So, what's the story on your grandfather?"

He grabbed his wineglass and took a long drink. Then he eyed the liquid in surprise. "Pretty good."

"Uh-huh," she said, sensing a stall tactic. "Talk."

"Right." While he ate, he told her the story of Jeremiah's tricky maneuvers to get his grandsons back home for the summer. Not only had Jeremiah faked a bad heart, he'd even convinced his own doctor to go along with the deception. He'd worried them all, just to get them to come back to Coleville.

"That's terrible," Kara said.

"Yeah," Cooper agreed, taking another bite of chicken. "Jeremiah's a wily old goat. But this was pretty low. He scared the hell out of us."

"No," Kara said, glaring at him because he couldn't see what she was trying to say. "I *meant* it was terrible that your grandfather felt as though he had no choice but to coerce his grandsons into a visit."

"Huh?" His dark eyes fixed on her in confusion.

"How could you all do that to him, Cooper?" She set her fork down on her plate and the quiet *clink* it made sounded overly loud in the suddenly still room.

The silence only lasted for a moment or two.

"*We* didn't do anything," he pointed out defensively, waving his own fork at her for emphasis.

"That's the point," she said, taking a gulp of wine and letting the icy liquid slide down her throat to form a nice warm ball in the pit of her stomach. "You didn't do anything. None of you."

"Hey."

"You said you haven't been back here in fifteen years, Cooper."

"There were reasons."

"*Reasons?* For breaking an old man's heart?" Sympathy welled inside her and along with it came anger. "You went away and stayed away. The poor man. No wonder he was desperate enough to lie."

He sighed and sat back in his chair, gripping his wineglass as if it were a life rope. "You're right."

"What?" She thunked the heel of her hand above her right ear. "I mean, excuse me?"

"Funny," he acknowledged with a nod. "But you heard me. I know we were wrong to stay away so long. Trust me, it wasn't easy on any of us, either. Don't you think we missed Jeremiah? Don't you think it was hard for us to stay away?"

"Then why?" she whispered, leaning on the table to watch him carefully. "Why did it take you so long to come home for a visit?"

"Because, Kara," he said softly, shifting his gaze from hers to the surface of the pale wine in his glass.

"As hard as it was to stay away, it was even harder to come back here."

There was something distant about Cooper. As if he had emotionally taken one giant step back from her. As if he were deliberately trying to shut her out. And it hurt. They'd been close for five years. She'd thought they were, if not lovers, then at least friends.

"Cooper…" she waited for him to look at her. As stubborn as he could be, she kept quiet, counting the ticking seconds as they passed before, at last, his gaze lifted to hers. Those dark brown eyes looked shadowed by old pain and instantly she felt an answering ache inside her. "What could be so important that it would keep you from someone you love for so long?"

He took a sip of wine, swallowed, then set the glass carefully onto the table as if afraid it would shatter.

"Sometimes love's just not enough, Kara." He sighed, scraped one hand across his face, then forced a smile that did nothing to ease the shadows in his eyes. "Sometimes love is the problem."

An icy draft slipped through the kitchen, twining itself around Kara, reaching out for Cooper and then holding them both in a chill embrace.

"Whoa," Cooper said as Kara shivered, "these old places really let in the cold." He stood up and started across the kitchen. "I'll close the living room windows."

The cold eased away and Kara sent a disquieted glance around the empty room. Old houses were drafty, yes. But Cooper's errand was a fruitless one. She'd closed the windows herself an hour ago.

Three

Kara woke up with a jolt.

Heart pounding, lungs heaving, she shook off the last of the nightmare still clinging to the edges of her mind. She swallowed hard and grabbed at the quilt pooled at her waist in an effort to steady herself.

She couldn't remember what she'd been dreaming. Couldn't remember what had chased her from that dream into wakefulness. All she *did* know was that goose bumps were racing up and down her spine and air was still hard to come by.

Then she heard it.

Sobbing.

Someone in the old house was crying as if their

heart was breaking. The sound lifted, rising, filling the house with pain that was nearly tangible. Then an instant later, the sobs quieted, becoming a whisper that Kara strained to hear.

Mouth dry, heartbeat frantic, she tossed the quilt back and swung her legs to the floor. The polished wooden floorboards felt cold against her bare feet, but she hardly noticed. She moved to the door, determined to follow the desperate sobs to their source.

Fear tugged at her insides, but curiosity was stronger. Grabbing hold of the icy brass knob, she opened her door, stepped into the hallway and stopped dead. The sorrow filled wails rose again, and with them, the small hairs at the back of Kara's neck.

Moonlight filtered in through the arch-shaped window at the end of the hall, painting a pale silver glow on the walls and the faded carpet runner stretched down the center of the hallway. Outside, trees danced in the wind and their shadows dipped and swayed wildly.

Kara could have sworn she jumped three feet, straight up, when the door across from hers suddenly swung open. Heart in her throat now, she grabbed hold of the doorjamb as Cooper appeared on the threshold. His long black hair mussed from sleep, he glared at the empty hallway, then at her.

"What the hell is going on around here?" he demanded, voice raw.

She had to swallow hard before she could be sure

her voice would work. He wore dark red cotton drawstring pants that hung low on his hips and the hems stacked up on his bare feet. In the moonlight, his sculpted chest looked as if it had been lovingly molded from a sheet of bronze and Kara's palms itched to touch it. Touch him.

"Kara?" He waved one hand in front of her face to get her attention. "Hello?"

She shook her head, told her hormones to take a vacation and snapped, "Get your hand out of my face, Cooper."

"You zoned out on me."

"I did not *zone out*," she argued, though she was pretty sure she had. Heck, one long look at Cooper, fresh from bed, was enough to conquer the strongest of women. And Kara had already admitted to being a spineless wiener dog.

The sobbing rose again, swelling up from below the stairs like a slowly inflating balloon taking to the sky. And a new set of goose pimples ice-skated up and down Kara's arms.

Cooper turned his head and stared at the head of the stairs for a long minute, before turning his gaze back to her. "Tell me you heard that."

She huffed out an anxious breath. "Oh, yeah."

"Good."

"*Good?*" she repeated. "What's *good* about that?"

"I thought I was dreaming it," he whispered, stepping further into the hall and throwing another glance at the stairs. "Then I figured it was a hallucination. But if we're both hearing it, then that means it's real." His voice dropped even further and he leaned in close so she could hear him above the mournful weeping that seemed to be dripping from the walls. "And if it's real, then somebody's trying to pull something funny."

Kara swallowed hard. Cooper's breath came warm against her cheek and she had to fight to concentrate on what he was saying instead of the way he made her feel, leaning in so darn close. Closing her eyes briefly, she gulped at air then asked, "Who would think this kind of thing is funny?"

He shot her a look. "My cousin Jake for one, but as far as I know he's still in Spain." Then he smiled. "Mike Haney."

"Who?" Kara followed him quietly, walking right behind him as he started down the center of the hall toward the stairs.

He turned around quickly and she nearly yelped.

"Shhh..." he said, dropping both hands onto her shoulders. "Mike Haney's an old friend. We all grew up together. My cousin Sam told me he saw ol' Mike in town the other day. And trust me, this is *just* the kind of thing Mike would think up."

She didn't think so. But then, her brain wasn't really working on all cylinders at the moment. His big hands, with those talented, long fingers, held her firmly and felt so warm on her skin. Everything inside her hummed with an electrical sort of awakening that couldn't be quenched—even by the goose bumps that were still rippling along her spine.

Focus, Kara, focus.

"Cooper—"

"Stay here," he warned, lifting one hand to hold up his index finger like he was signaling a recalcitrant puppy to sit.

"Excuse me?"

He scowled. "Kara, will you just stay here while I go down and beat the crap outta Mike?"

"No, I'm not staying here," she said and waved a hand, silently telling him to get going and she'd be right behind him. "What? Are we in a 1950s movie? Big strong man leaves the little woman behind while he stalks off to danger?"

He snorted. "The only one in danger around here is Mike Haney."

"That sobbing does *not* sound like a guy."

He looked about to argue, so she added, "Besides, what if you're wrong? You think I want to be up here all by myself? No freakin' way."

The crying continued, rolling on and on, lifting and falling like waves cresting on the shore, then sliding back out to sea. The very air seemed thicker, heavier somehow and Kara—for just a second and who could really blame her—almost wanted to be in that old movie. Hiding under a bed while Cooper went to check things out.

Then a terrible, wrenching moan swept through the house and Kara's heart twisted in empathy.

"Stay behind me," Cooper muttered, starting down the stairs at a dead creep, carefully putting one foot gently down before moving the other.

"No problem there," she murmured and stayed as close to him as his shadow at high noon.

He reached behind him, grabbed her hand in his and held on tight. Kara clung to him like he was the last eighty percent off sweater at a clearance sale at Bloomie's.

At the bottom of the stairs, the sound was all around them, reverberating off the walls, the floor, the ceilings, until it seemed to echo over and over again.

"Cooper…"

"Come on…"

His legs were a lot longer than hers, so Kara practically had to trot to keep up with him as he sprinted for the main parlor.

"It's centered there," he whispered. "You hear it? Louder the closer we get."

And now that they were almost on top of the sound, Kara wondered why in the devil she'd wanted to come down here to investigate it in the first place. If it *was* a friend of Cooper's, then there was nothing to worry about. And if it *wasn't?* Oh, she so didn't want to think about that at the moment.

"Ready?" He glanced at her as his left hand curled around the brass knob of the parlor door.

"No."

He shot her a wicked grin that quieted her fear and stirred up other, far more interesting things. She nodded jerkily. "Fine. Just open it."

He did. Throwing the door wide open, Cooper dragged Kara into the room behind him.

Instantly, the sobbing stopped.

Moonlight slanted through the wide front windows, illuminating the tiny room like someone in heaven was focusing a spotlight on the place. Deep shadows crouched in the corners, but when Cooper flicked on the overhead chandelier, they disappeared. Kara and Cooper were alone in the room.

Loosening his grip on her hand, Cooper stalked around the perimeter of the small, old fashioned parlor. He pulled back the drapes at either side of the windows and even opened an old armoire, as if expecting to find Mike Haney and a tape recorder, crouched inside.

When he found nothing, he turned around and looked at Kara. "Okay, I admit it, I'm stumped."

Kara wandered the room more slowly, touching the little china dog on an end table, smoothing her fingertips across the fringe on a lampshade. Thoughtfully, she asked, "You said the place was haunted, right?"

Cooper frowned, folded his arms across his chest and watched her. He'd been so sure that either Sam or Mike was at the bottom of this night's little spookfest. Hadn't they all enjoyed scaring the crap out of each other when they were kids? And what better thing to do to a horror writer then give him his very own personal ghost?

But if his cousin and friend were behind it, where was the proof? Of course, he'd have to give the room a thorough going over in the morning, but at the moment, he couldn't figure out how that voice was pumped through the whole damn house and then cut off in an instant.

"Just because I didn't find Mike hiding in here," Cooper said, "doesn't mean there's a ghost in the house."

"Uh-huh."

She didn't look convinced. As she wandered around the room, studying the spines of the worn leather books tucked into a bookcase, Cooper studied her. He hadn't noticed before—now, he couldn't imagine why not—but, Kara's sleep ruffled dark brown hair hung in unruly waves to her shoulders. The summery, pale green silk nightgown she wore had thin straps and dipped low across her breasts before skimming a surprisingly taut, tempting body and ending just beneath the curve of her behind. Her legs were bare and her toenails were painted a brilliant scarlet.

Heat slammed into him and Cooper whooshed out a breath in reaction. His gaze locked on her as she stooped down to inspect a book on a lower shelf and he caught himself hoping she'd simply bend over.

Man.

Where the hell had that come from?

In the five years he'd known and worked with Kara Sloane, Cooper could honestly say he'd never once been slapped with the notion of tossing her over his shoulder and throwing her onto the nearest bed.

Now, it was the only thought in his fevered mind.

"Are you okay?"

"Hmm?" He shook his head and scowled even more fiercely when he found her watching him curiously. Great. Could she tell he'd been wondering if she was wearing anything underneath that nightgown? "Of course I'm okay. Why wouldn't I be?"

"No reason," she said, in a tone that clearly contradicted her words, "you were just…looking at me weird."

He forced a laugh that grated his throat and sounded overly loud. "No I wasn't."

"Yeah, you were."

Smooth, Cooper. Really smooth. He stabbed both hands through his hair and gave it a tug while he was at it. Anything to distract him from the thoughts that were now racing uncontrollably through his brain. Kara in that nightgown. Kara *out* of that nightgown. Geez.

"Didn't mean to," he said with a careless shrug, "it's just, you look…different."

"*Different?*" She folded her arms beneath her breasts, thereby pushing them high enough to peek over the top of that low scooped neck.

Cooper felt what was left of the blood in his brain rush southward.

"Never mind," he muttered and turned to check all the windows, making sure the latches were closed. *Keep busy. Don't think. Don't...*

"Different how?"

He glanced at her over his shoulder and immediately turned back around. She was suddenly looking *way* too good. And his own body was starting to get *very* appreciative. "Leave it alone, will ya?"

"Nope. *Different how?*" Amusement colored her voice and Cooper winced.

Sighing, he admitted stiffly, "The nightgown."

She chuckled and he turned to look at her, keeping his gaze locked with hers, for his own peace of mind.

"My nightgown? Honestly, Cooper," she said, skimming her hands along the silky fabric barely covering her. "It's not like I'm wearing black lace."

Mmm. A picture burst into life in his mind and he enjoyed it far too much.

"Besides," she added, "I was sleeping. What? Did you really think I wore high heels to bed?"

Yet *another* interesting image filled his brain and left him inwardly groaning. Seriously. Between the weird noises and the new visuals of Kara, he was probably going to be awake all night.

He blew out a long breath and determinedly shifted the subject away from Kara's nightgown. "We're not going to figure out what's happening tonight and I'm too tired—" translation, *horny*, "—to talk about this anymore. Let's just forget about it and go back to sleep."

The smile slid off her face as her gaze swept the quiet, empty room. "You think it'll start up again?"

"I sincerely hope not," he muttered and led the way out of the room. He heard her walking behind him, the soft fall of her small bare feet against the floorboards. At the foot of the stairs, he started taking them two at a time. No way was he going to climb those stairs behind Kara.

The view would kill him.

The next day, as Kara sat beside Cooper in his enormous SUV, she was still enjoying the sensation of having finally won his attention. However briefly it had lasted. She'd seen his face the night before. Watched him watch her and though she knew nothing would come of it, she'd relished the few moments when he'd looked at her and really seen her.

Of course it wouldn't happen again.

Without the quiet intimacy of a shadow filled house in the middle of the night, everything was back to normal. Cooper, kind but distracted, Kara, wishing things were different.

He'd avoided her all morning. When he came down for coffee, he'd simply nodded at her, then filled a thermal jug so he wouldn't have to face her again. She'd heard his fingers flying across the keyboard, but except for that constant sound, whispering in the background, she might as well have been alone in the house. Well, just she and whoever had done all the crying the night before.

And now, though he was sitting less than a foot away from her, he still wasn't talking. Instead, he kept his gaze locked on the road and determinedly away from her.

She simply could not go on like this forever.

She wanted a man to love her. She wanted children before she was old enough to be a grandmother.

Slanting a look at him now as he steered his car into the driveway of his grandfather's ranch, she watched as his features tightened. His dark eyes narrowed and a muscle in his jaw twitched as if he were gritting his teeth.

What was it? Why was he so reluctant to be here? To see an old man she knew he loved?

And why wouldn't he tell her?

The SUV sailed smoothly over the rutted road with hardly a bump to the occupants. Cooper drove around behind the edge of the house and parked the car under the shade of a giant tree that looked as though it had been there since the beginning of time.

Wind scuttled across the open yard, lifting dust and tossing it into tiny tornadoes while it fluttered the laundry dancing on the clothesline. Ancient shade trees lined the property, swaying in that same wind, sliding in from the nearby ocean.

There was a small guesthouse at the edge of the yard and even from a distance, Kara could see the sunlight glinting off shining window panes. Pansies in shades of deep purple and blue tumbled from a window box near the tidy front porch and a grape-vine wreath with a tiny Welcome sign attached hung on the door.

About a hundred yards from the main house, a barn stood proudly, its double doors standing open, inviting visitors into the cool, shadowy interior.

But the house itself caught Kara's attention. It was old and proud and wide. It sprawled across the land like a lazy old man stretched out for a nap. Stone pillars guarded the four corners of the house and bright red and white geraniums crowded the outside edges of the structure. It looked, Kara thought, permanent. Cozy.

Apparently though, it looked like something else entirely to Cooper. Shutting off the engine, he pulled the keys from the car and jangled them in his palm for a second or two.

They'd been invited to his grandfather's house for lunch, but never had a man looked less willing to go inside a relative's home.

Finally, Kara asked, "Are you okay?"

"Fine," he said shortly. "Why?"

"I don't know," she answered, "because there's enough tension rolling off of you right now to make diamonds out of charcoal?"

He sighed and leaned back, unbuckling his seat belt but making no move to get out of the car. Turning his head, he looked at her for the first time that morning. In his eyes, Kara saw a tumult of emotions that appeared and disappeared so quickly, she couldn't identify them all.

And for the first time since she'd known him, she was worried about Cooper. There was something here. Something that was tearing at him.

"It's not something I want to talk about."

Intrigued, and a little unsettled, Kara unsnapped her own seat belt and shifted in her seat to look at him. "But if there's something I should know before I meet your family…"

He smiled briefly, the slightest curve of his lips and then it was gone again. "Don't worry," he said, opening the car door. "They don't want to talk about it, either."

Four

Cooper watched his cousin Sam wink at his new fiancée Maggie and felt a twinge of something suspiciously like envy. Which didn't really make any sense at all, because he'd never wanted the whole "wife and family" thing anyway. And yet…

Lunch had been awkward, despite Jeremiah's repeated attempts to keep everyone talking, laughing. Cooper had been uneasy from the moment he'd stepped into his grandfather's house. For some insane reason, he'd kept waiting for a sixteen-year-old Mac to come running into the room—and when he didn't, the pain roared through Cooper, as hot and fresh as it had been fifteen years before.

Now that he was outside, sitting in a lawn chair at the back of the house, Cooper at least felt as though he could breathe again. But the memories here were just as thick. Still watching Sam, in the chair beside him, he blurted suddenly, "How can you do it?"

"Do what?" Sam reluctantly tore his gaze from Maggie, hanging damp sheets on the clothesline.

"Be here," Cooper said, clutching his beer bottle in one tight fist and sweeping his arm out to encompass the ranch. "*Live* here."

The smile in Sam's dark eyes dimmed a bit as he took a sip of his own beer before answering. "Wasn't easy at first," he admitted. "So many memories."

"Exactly." Cooper sighed with relief. Good to know he wasn't the only one wrestling with the images of the past. "Just sitting here, I can see us all clearly, playing over the line."

Sam smiled sadly as he, too, thought about those days. "You remember when Mac hit the home run through Gran's kitchen window?"

Cooper chuckled. "And it landed in her pot of spaghetti sauce? Who could forget?" The memories took hold of his throat and squeezed. To ease the tension, he added, "By the way, you should have had that ball."

"Right. It was miles out of my reach."

"Too lazy to jump for it," Cooper said, and took another sip of cold, frothy beer.

"Mac always could hit a ball like a bullet."

"Yeah." The beer suddenly tasted flat, bitter. "Damn it, Sam, I keep expecting to see him. Hear him."

"I did, too, at first," Sam said softly. "Then I realized Mac's gone. He's not here, Cooper. He's not hanging around trying to make us all feel bad about what happened."

"He doesn't have to," Cooper muttered and stood up, because he couldn't sit still another minute. Knots formed in his guts, his throat tightened and his mouth was suddenly dry. "God. Every day of my life I remember. And I feel bad. Guilty."

Sam looked up at him, understanding shining in his calm brown eyes. "There's no reason to."

"No reason? Mac *died*." Cooper kicked at the dirt and watched pebbles skitter. "While we stood there like morons, Mac *died*."

"We were kids, too," Sam reminded him and pushed his hair out of his eyes, when the wind blew it across his face.

"Yeah," Cooper said stiffly, "but we didn't die at sixteen."

And just like that, he was back there. On that long-ago summer day.

Playing one of their favorite games, the four cousins had lined up along the ridge above the ranch lake. One at a time, they ran and jumped in, while the guys on the bank timed them. You got points, not only for how far out you could jump, but for how long you stayed underwater.

Jake always won.

Mac though, had been determined to be the winner this time. He had outjumped Jake by a mile and Jake was seriously pissed. But to win, Mac had to stay underwater longer than he had, too.

Sam had the stopwatch and Cooper and Jake stood on either side of him while he timed Mac's turn. Jake got madder by the second, sure his best time was going to be beaten. Cooper hooted with glee that one of them had finally taken Jake down.

When Mac was underwater two minutes though, Sam started worrying. Wanted to go in after him. Cooper urged him to give Mac a few more seconds. Make sure Jake lost for a change.

And God, even now, Cooper could feel the wind in his face, the sun on his back. He heard Jake's muttered cursing and the note of worry in Sam's voice. Most of all though, he heard himself saying, "Don't be such an old woman, Sam. Mac's fine. He'll come up in a second."

Except he never did.

The three of them had—at last—jumped into the icy water after Mac and they'd found him. On the bottom of the lake. They'd dragged him out, tried mouth-to-mouth, but Mac was gone. The doctor said later he'd broken his neck in the fall and unconscious, had drowned.

And nothing since that day had ever been right again.

Cooper had avoided this ranch like the plague

ever since. Hell, they all had. Punishing themselves and each other. Now he was here again and damn it, he could hardly draw a breath without strangling on it.

Sam stood up and took a white-knuckled grip on his beer bottle. "Do you really think you have to remind me of what happened? Do you honestly believe that Mac's death hasn't chased me through the years as hard as it's chased you?"

In the cool shade of the old oak where they'd once played on a tire swing, Cooper stared at his cousin and saw the same torment in his eyes that he faced every morning in the mirror.

"No." He shook his head. "No, I don't. It's just…" he looked around, at the yard, the house, the barn, and felt the memories pulling at him as strong as a riptide. "I don't understand how you got past it. How you can live here and not choke on every breath?"

"I couldn't at first. Hell, I had my plans all laid out." He laughed shortly and took another drink of beer. "I was going to stay the summer, since Jeremiah had tricked me into giving my word—"

Cooper nodded wryly, since he, too, was caught by the same wily old man.

"—then," Sam continued, "I was going to hit the road again. Get as far from Coleville and the memories of Mac that I could."

"So what happened?" Cooper asked, then held up one hand. "Never mind. I know what happened."

He shot a glance at Maggie, now in a desperate tug-of-war with a golden retriever puppy over a wet pillowcase. "I like her, by the way."

Sam grinned. "Thanks. Me, too." His smile faded as he added, "It wasn't just falling in love with Maggie though. It was finding a way to make peace with Mac." His gaze locked on the woman he loved as she laughed, dropped to the ground and gathered the tiny dog to her chest. "Maggie helped me do that. Helped me see that Mac wouldn't want us torturing ourselves forever."

Cooper didn't know if he agreed with that or not, but he was willing to admit that the belief had certainly helped Sam. "Special woman."

"Beyond special," Sam said quietly. "She's everything."

Envy swept through Cooper again and was just as quickly brushed aside. After all, he wasn't interested in loving anybody. Too much risk came with love. Too high a chance at pain. And he'd already had enough pain to last a lifetime.

No. The only romance he was interested in, was the kind he wrote about. The kind he gave whatever hero and heroine he was dealing with in his latest book. And when he wrote their "happily ever after," his readers didn't know or care if he believed in it or not.

But unthinkingly, his gaze drifted to the edge of the field, where Kara walked with Jeremiah.

* * *

"It's good to have Cooper back home," Jeremiah said as he followed Kara's gaze to the two men standing beneath the oak tree at the far end of the yard.

"I can't believe he stayed away so long."

"They all had reason," he said on a sigh. "Or so they thought. Which amounts to the same thing, really."

Kara turned her gaze on the older man. His skin was leathery from a lifetime spent outdoors. Only a fringe of gray hair remained on his head, but his dark eyes, so much like Cooper's, sparkled with intensity.

She liked him a lot. Just as she liked Sam and Maggie. Kara had spent most of the afternoon trying not to be jealous of the other woman as she talked excitedly about her wedding plans and her pregnancy. In just a few weeks, Sam and Maggie would be getting married and moving into the main ranch house together.

Sam was taking over the local doctor's practice and Maggie was finishing school and…Kara's life felt emptier with every word Maggie had spoken. Terrible, she thought, immediately ashamed of herself. She should be happy for them. And she was. They seemed like perfectly nice people. But wasn't it only natural that she'd be just a little bit sorry for herself?

What did she have to show for her life?

A nicely balanced checkbook? A good apartment

and a tidy savings account? She was nearly thirty and beyond her mother, who made a point of calling at least once a week to remind her that she wasn't getting any younger, Kara had no one to care about. Or to care about her.

Something was definitely wrong with this picture.

She walked alongside Jeremiah, but only half listened as he talked about the ranch and what he and Sam were planning for it. Instead, her brain raced and though she didn't much like the decisions it was reaching, she had to admit that they were the right ones.

She'd put off quitting when she knew Cooper was having a hard time getting his latest book going. But she wasn't doing herself any favors by stretching this out. Better to just suck it up and make the move.

Her gaze shot to Cooper again, standing in the shade, laughing at something Sam had just said. And while her heart broke a little, she filled her mind with these pictures of him. Etched them into her brain so that years from now, she'd always be able to see him as he was today.

Then mentally, she started packing.

"Man, you're a great cook," Cooper said, leaning back in his chair at the kitchen table and grinning at Kara.

"Thanks, but steaks? They don't exactly require gourmet training."

"I've burned enough of 'em in my time to know that it takes a knack."

Kara shook her head. "Cooper, you are the only human being I know who could actually burn water."

"Sad, but true," he admitted and didn't look the least bit ashamed of himself. "I don't know what I'd do without you, Kara," he said and stood up to carry both plates to the sink. "Seriously," he went on when she didn't say anything, "you're the best."

"That's nice Cooper, but—"

He set the plates into the sink with a clatter. "You know though, you don't have to cook while we're here. You could hire someone locally to come in and do the cooking and cleaning."

All she had to do now was work up the nerve to tell him he was going to need not only a cook and a maid—but a new assistant. "Now that you mention it—"

A knock on the back door interrupted Kara and Cooper paused in clearing the table to go and open it. His grandfather stood on the porch, holding a foil covered plate.

Cooper grinned at the older man. "Didn't we just see you a few hours ago?"

"Sure did," Jeremiah said and pushed past his grandson without waiting for an invitation. Right on his heels came the puppy, its claws scrambling for traction on the old wood floor. It shot across the room, then put on the brakes and slid into the underside of the cabinet.

Jeremiah chuckled. "Told Maggie I'd take Sheba there for a walk and she loaded me down with a plate of her chocolate chip cookies to bring you two."

"Cookies? Always welcome," Cooper said, already reaching for the plate. "Oh, you can come in too, Jeremiah."

The older man laughed and stepped inside, taking a seat at the kitchen table. He reached out to pat Kara's hand and whispered, "Don't suppose you could spare an old man a cup of coffee? Maggie's got me drinking that decaffeinated stuff at night. Like to kill me."

"You bet," Kara said, pathetically grateful for the interruption and the chance to stall a few more minutes. *Why* couldn't she tell Cooper she was quitting? *Why* couldn't she bring herself to leave him? It was the right thing to do and she knew it. So why was it so hard?

In a few seconds, Cooper had the rest of the table cleared and Kara poured three cups of coffee.

The puppy lay under the table, contentedly chewing on the laces of Cooper's sneakers.

"So," Jeremiah said after a hearty sigh with his first sip of coffee, "you two see any ghosts yet?"

Cooper laughed and took a cookie for himself. "Haven't seen anything, but did hear something last night. Crying."

"More like sobbing," Kara corrected and cradled her own cup of coffee between her palms as if to ward off a chill she knew was coming.

"Yeah?"

Cooper laughed at his grandfather's eager expression. "Don't get excited. It's more likely somebody's playing a trick on us than it is for there to be a ghost in this house."

"Hell, boy," Jeremiah scoffed, "you write scary stories for a living and you don't believe in ghosts?"

Cooper's expression hardened. "Not the kind who make noises in old houses."

Kara watched as Cooper, in a heartbeat, distanced himself, even though he hadn't budged from his chair. It was as if he'd taken an emotional step back and she was clueless about what had caused it. But as she always did, she stepped in to help him out.

"Do you know anything about this house?" Kara asked, dissolving the taut silence and shifting his grandfather's attention from Cooper to her.

The older man sighed heavily, then gave her a small smile, as if to say he knew she was trying to smooth things over and he appreciated it. He gave her hand another friendly pat, took a sip of his coffee and said, "Everyone around here knows the story of this old house."

Cooper didn't say a word, so Kara urged, "Tell me."

Jeremiah nodded. "It was back during the gold rush era," he said, his deep voice slipping into storytelling mode as if he were born to it.

As he painted a vivid picture of the times, Kara

realized that Cooper had inherited his gift with words from his grandfather.

"Weren't many ranches here then. Most of the land was still owned by Spanish dons who weren't real happy about the yankees streaming into California by the boatload." He looked around the kitchen, took a sip of coffee and continued. "This house was built by one of the first to find gold. Bought the land from the local don, built this place and brought his wife out from back east. They had one daughter and when he died, he left the house to her—who, as young women will, fell in love with a scoundrel of a man."

"Oh, this doesn't have a happy ending, does it?" Kara murmured.

"If it did, it wouldn't be a ghost story, now would it?" Cooper took a drink of coffee and leaned back in his chair, his gaze fixed on his grandfather, sitting across from him.

Jeremiah ignored him and focused instead on Kara. "Oh, the young man loved her, but he was ambitious. He wanted to make his fortune more than he wanted to settle down. He left for the gold fields, promising to come back for her."

"He didn't?" Kara's heart hurt for the long-dead woman.

"She waited here for him," Jeremiah said, "for two long, lonely years. Desolate, she stood at the parlor window, crying for her lost love while she watched the road, hoping for a sign of him."

Pain swelled inside Kara and she could almost feel that poor woman's misery shivering in the air around her. Outside, the wind kicked up, spattering the window panes with dust and pebbles. A frigid puff of air scuttled through the kitchen and beneath the table, little Sheba growled, low in her throat.

"She died," Jeremiah said softly, almost reverently, "of a broken heart."

Cooper snorted.

Kara glared at him.

Jeremiah ignored him completely. "Without the love of her life, she simply couldn't go on."

Kara felt, rather than heard, a sigh.

"Every tenant since then never stays long in this place. It's not a happy house. Shame, really," Jeremiah said.

"What happened to her young man?"

The older man looked at her. "He finally did come for her, a few weeks after she died. But he was too late."

A shutter slapped against the side of the house and Kara jumped, startled.

Cooper laughed. "God, Kara, you should see your face. Jeremiah really got you going on that story, didn't he?"

His grandfather scowled at him, gray brows beetling. "Boy," he growled, sounding a lot like the puppy still restive beneath the table, "don't you think love is worth dying for?"

Cooper shook his head, got up and went for the coffeepot over on the counter. He refilled everyone's cup, then returned the pot before answering. "Jeremiah, the moral to that story is simple. Love isn't worth it."

"You got it all wrong, Coop," his grandfather said with a slow shake of his head. "Love is the only worthwhile thing there is."

Kara's heart sunk as she listened to the two men argue over the value of love. Emptiness opened up inside her and she felt a cold that went down deep into her bones. Her instincts had been right. Cooper would never love her. Never see her as anything more than an uber-efficient assistant and a pretty good cook.

It didn't matter how long she put off her decision, nothing was going to change. So what was the point of hanging around and torturing herself?

None.

An hour later, Jeremiah and the puppy were gone and the two of them were alone in the kitchen again. Working together, Kara dried the dishes as Cooper washed them. The silence was companionable, the task ordinary, and she knew there would never be a better time to say what she had to say.

"Cooper?"

"Yeah?" He turned to hand her another plate.

"I quit."

Five

"Very funny." Cooper gave her the plate and chuckling, turned back to the dirty dishes. "But don't joke about stuff like that."

"I'm not joking, Cooper."

"You'd better be, because you can't quit."

"Yes, I can. I just did. Consider this my two weeks' notice."

Cooper shut off the water and turned to face her. Her dark brown hair was pulled back from her face and held by one of those clip things that opened like an alligator's jaws. In the overhead light, her big green eyes were shadowed as she looked at him, and there wasn't so much as a hint of a smile on her face.

A solitary thread of worry slithered through him.

"Is this about the ghost thing? And the crying last night? Because if it is, don't worry about it—I swear it's just somebody playing a dumb joke."

"It's not about the crying, or the ghost story. It's about us."

Now he was really confused. "*Us?* What about us?"

She tossed the yellow-and-white striped dish-towel onto the counter, then folded her arms under her breasts, tipped her head to one side and glared at him. "You don't get it at all, do you?"

"Apparently not."

"So typical."

"What'd I do?"

She unfolded her arms, slapped her hands on her hips and said, "Nothing. Ever. Just nothing." Before he could speak, she held up one hand for silence, took a deep breath and said shortly, "Never mind. Let's just say that I'm quitting because we can't keep going on like this."

"Like what?" Why did he suddenly feel like he was speaking Greek in a Chinese restaurant?

"Like we are, Cooper."

"What's wrong with it?" And why was she suddenly not making any sense to him at all?

"It's like we're married, Cooper. Only without any of the good stuff. Like sex."

Instantly, the memory of her in that pretty silk nightie popped into his brain and set fire to a completely different part of his anatomy. He had to admit that up until the night before, he'd never really thought about Kara and sex in the same sentence. But now, he wasn't so sure. "You want us to have sex?"

Kara blew out a frustrated breath, reached up and tugged the clip from her hair then shook her head and rubbed at the spot where it had been. All of that thick, dark brown hair flew about her face in soft waves and made Cooper want to reach out and comb his fingers through it.

Hey, maybe sex was a good idea.

"Of course I want sex. But I want more than that, too." Sighing, she said, "I want a husband. Kids. A home. I've been working for you for five years and all I've got to show for it is a nice savings account and a few new recipes."

"So you've been miserable working for me? Is that it?"

"No, that's not it at all. Just the opposite, in fact," she said irritably. "I got so comfortable that I didn't notice that I wasn't getting anywhere."

"What's so bad about comfortable?" he demanded, suddenly realizing that she might just be serious about quitting. Her eyes shone with regret, but there was no going back with Kara. He knew that already. Once she'd made up her mind about something, that was it.

And the thought of losing Kara hit him hard.

"Nothing," she said, "if that's all you're looking

for, then comfortable is great. But it's not enough for me. Not anymore."

"Hold on," he countered, feeling his heart jolt in his chest. "This is all coming out of the blue for me, Kara. As far as I knew, everything between us was working great."

"Well sure," she snapped, throwing both hands high and letting them slap to her sides again. "Why wouldn't it be great from your point of view? I take care of everything for you. I pay your bills, talk to your editors, handle your publicity, pick up your dry cleaning…you can't even make a decent pot of coffee on your own."

"Hey!" Insulted, and not just because most of what she said was true, Cooper stared at her like he'd never seen her before. In the five years they'd been together, Kara had always been calm, cool, reasonable. This Kara had sparks flying from her eyes.

Which he was just twisted enough to actually think sexy.

"It's not entirely your fault," she conceded. "God knows, I worked hard at making myself indispensable."

"Did a good job of it, too." Cooper tried a smile out on her and felt a quick stab of disappointment when it didn't warm her eyes. "How about a raise? Would that make you feel differently?"

"No!" Frustration ringing in her voice, she said loudly, "It's not about the money, Cooper. It never was."

He reached for her, but she took a quick half step back. "Kara, you can't quit. I need you too much."

"That's exactly why I have to go!" She inhaled sharply, deeply and blew the air out again in a rush. "Don't you get it? If I keep acting like your wife, I'll never get to really *be* one."

Those sparks in her eyes were flashing like warning lights at the edge of a cliff. And Cooper was bright enough to back off fast. "You're tired. Why don't you sleep on it and we can talk about this in the morning when you're calmer?"

"Grrrrrr…" Kara tugged at her hair again and shouted, "I'm perfectly calm."

"Yeah," he assured her, keeping a wary distance between them. "I can see that."

"Honestly Cooper, you can be the most infuriating man…" She turned on her heel, stomped across the kitchen and marched into the living room. Just before she turned for the stairs, she stopped dead, turned her head and fried him with a look. "Just so you know. I'm not going to change my mind. I *am* quitting."

Then she stomped up the stairs, managing to sound like an invading army, which just proved to Cooper that she was too upset to be making major decisions. He walked to the doorway and winced when she slammed her bedroom door. She'd feel differently in the morning.

He could talk his way around Kara.

She'd see reason.

So why, he wondered, was he suddenly so worried?

When the sobbing started in the middle of the night, Kara was already awake. The muffled crying seemed to weep from the walls, surrounding her in a sea of pain that was strong enough to bridge the centuries. Cold crept through the bedroom and sighed around Kara.

Despite what Cooper might like to think, this was no joke. And Kara knew she should be terrified. Should be running screaming from the old house, putting as much distance between her and the ghost as she possibly could. But she didn't feel *fear*. She felt…compassion.

Sitting up in bed, she rubbed her bare arms as tears welled up in her eyes. Empathy for the long-dead woman filled her and Kara realized that she and the ghost had a lot in common.

Okay, not *a lot*.

After all, Kara was still alive.

But the ghost had waited for love until it was too late—Kara had waited, too, hoping that Cooper would see how good they could be together. The sobbing woman had allowed the longing for love to kill her. Kara wouldn't make the same mistake.

"I'm so sorry," she whispered, glancing around the shadow-filled room as tears rolled unheeded down her cheeks. "I'm sorry for both of us."

* * *

Cooper, wide awake and trying to work, jolted as the sobbing began. Already, he was on edge since he hadn't been able to write a single coherent sentence since Kara had told him she quit. All he could think about was her. And how in the hell he could convince her to change that stubborn mind of hers.

The crying was just what he needed as a distraction. He jumped up and headed for his bedroom door. Yanking it open, he stepped into the hall and paused, waiting for Kara to appear as she had the night before. In his mind, he saw her again, hair tumbled about her face, that silky nightgown and all of her bare, tanned skin. But her door didn't open. Did she not hear the crying? Unlikely. She was simply trying to avoid him. That simple truth jabbed at him and he scowled at her closed door. Damn it, how could she quit? How could she walk away from him?

Cooper muttered darkly, then headed down the hall alone, following the crying as it seemed to float through the house. He didn't care what Jeremiah said, Cooper didn't believe in ghosts and he was going to find the damn joker behind these nightly visits.

He didn't bother with turning on the lights, finding his way with no problem, since moonlight filtered through the windows. The wood floor cool beneath his bare feet, Cooper moved soundlessly through the house, determined to put an end to this ghost stuff once and for all.

Only last night, he thought, he and Kara had been in this together. And a part of him missed having her with him. Missed the feel of her hand in his as they slipped through the shadows. Missed the sense of…teamwork, they'd always shared.

Damn. How could she *quit?*

Pushing that furious thought out of his head, he concentrated instead on the mournful cries reverberating around him. The night before, when Kara had been with him, the sobs had led them to the parlor. Tonight, the terrible crying took him to the front door.

Smirking to himself, he muttered, "Trick me into opening the front door? Bet Mike Haney's crouched on the porch laughing himself sick over this."

Grabbing the brass doorknob, Cooper threw the door open, expecting to come face-to-face with some practical joker.

But no one was there.

He took a step forward and stopped dead.

A wall of icy cold blocked the doorway.

Cooper sucked in air like a drowning man. His heartbeat jumped into a frantic beat that felt as though it was going to burst through his chest. Chills snaked along his spine. His throat squeezed shut and his mouth went dry.

The cold was immovable. Solid. As if it had always been there.

Around him, the sobs grew harsher, louder, more desperate.

Moonlight spilled onto the lawn, spearing through the trees, laying down lacy patterns that dipped and swayed in the wind.

"Mike Haney's not behind *this*," he whispered, scrubbing one hand across his face as his heartbeat slowly returned to normal.

This was no joke. The wall of cold was too real to be ignored or explained. He watched as his breath formed tiny clouds of mist in front of his face. Nope. No joke. This was yet another ghost.

The too late lover?

The cold pressed forward, trying to enter. Trying to get into the house, even if it had to go through Cooper. He felt the pressure against his chest as if someone were pushing him. The small hairs at the back of his neck stood straight up as the sobbing in the house became a moaning wail and then nearly a shriek of desperation fueled by fury.

It was one thing to *write* about ghosts. It was totally another to actually *live* with one.

"Is that what this is all about?" he asked, not really expecting an answer. "She's been waiting for you and you're finally trying to get into the house?"

His breath misted. Chills raced up and down his spine, but he fought off the instinct to close the door. If he could solve this ghost problem, maybe the long-dead lady would stop crying in the night. So instead, he opened it wider, stood back and waved one arm in silent invitation. "Come on then. Come find your

woman and apologize or whatever it is you're trying
to do and—"

The door was snatched free of his grip and
slammed closed with a force that rattled the
window panes.

Cooper blew out a breath and looked around the
suddenly silent room. The cold was locked outside,
the crying ghost was quiet—and apparently pissed
off—and he was just as confused as ever. According
to Jeremiah, this ghost had been waiting for her lover
for a hundred and fifty years. Now that he's come she
won't let him in?

Women.

"He's the most stubborn man on the face of the
planet," Kara said grimly and snapped a green bean
neatly in half.

"Believe me," Maggie said with a quiet smile. "I
totally understand."

"No, you couldn't possibly." Kara pushed up from
the table set under the oak tree in the backyard of
Cooper's grandfather's ranch. She'd come to talk to
Maggie, Sam's fiancée, because frankly, she was
going a little stir crazy.

The last few days had crawled past.

Cooper wouldn't talk to her. Wouldn't even *acknowledge* the fact that she'd quit her job. Whenever
she tried to talk to him about arranging for a temp
until he could find someone permanent, he only gave

her a patient smile. He wasn't listening. Wasn't taking her seriously.

Heck, she was going to have to actually leave to convince him she meant business.

"Trust me," Maggie said as she leaned back in her chair and stretched her legs out in front of her. "I think stubborn is a Lonergan family trait."

Kara shook her hair back out of her face as a quick wind kicked up out of nowhere, carrying on it the scent of the sea. She took a deep breath, blew it out and made a concentrated effort to calm herself.

It didn't work.

Lifting one hand, she rubbed her aching eyes. The headache that had been creeping up on her for hours was now in full bloom and every muscle in her body hurt. It was lack of sleep, she knew. Had to be.

The ghost had been in fine voice the last three nights. And every night, Kara sat in her room alone, listening to a long-dead woman cry for her lost love. It was as if the ghost were trying to tell Kara something. Warn her. *Don't let this happen to you,* she seemed to be saying.

"Are you okay?"

Turning around to look at the other woman, Kara swallowed hard, forced a smile she didn't feel and said, "Yes. I'm fine. Just...tired."

"The ghost?"

Kara smiled again. "You don't have any trouble believing?"

"No." Maggie stood up and walked to Kara's side. Dappled shade from the tree swept across her face in a lacy pattern. "Love's the strongest emotion there is. Why shouldn't it be able to linger long after we've gone?"

"I feel so bad for her," Kara said, "it's not just hearing her. I can feel her pain. Her sorrow is so profound, so all encompassing that—" What? That she was beginning to think the ghost was trying to communicate with her? Kara shook her head at her own crazy thoughts and chuckled. "Though I could really use some sleep."

"You sure you're only tired?" Maggie's dark gaze fixed on her with concern. "You sort of look feverish. I could take you into town, have Sam give you a checkup."

Kara's stomach turned and she sucked in a gulp of air to steady it. She didn't want to see a doctor. She just wanted to go. To leave Coleville and Cooper behind so she could start the big plan of getting over him.

"Honest. I'm fine." She tried another smile and added, "I actually came over here to ask you for a favor, Maggie."

"Sure, what is it?"

"I told you that Cooper won't admit that I quit my job?"

"Uh-huh."

"Well, I've decided the only way to prove it to him is to just go."

"You're leaving?"

"I have to," she said firmly, not really sure if she was trying to convince Maggie, or herself. But did it matter? "I wanted to give him two weeks' notice, but he's not listening to me, so what's the point? Anyway, until I can arrange for a temporary assistant for him, Cooper's going to be on his own—and he'll probably starve if someone doesn't remind him to eat occasionally."

"You're worried about him."

"Only natural," Kara said, trying to shrug off Maggie's words. "I've been running his world for five years. Without me, he's going to be lost." Just as she would be without him. "So I was wondering if you'd mind checking up on him once in awhile. You know, just…make sure he goes grocery shopping for more than frozen burritos?"

Maggie watched her for several long seconds and Kara wanted to squirm under the woman's steady regard. Finally though, Maggie said, "I'll be happy to—if you answer one question for me."

Kara sighed. "What is it?"

"Why don't you tell Cooper that you're in love with him?"

Surprised, Kara thought briefly about denying the truth. Then, looking into Maggie's understanding gaze, she figured, why bother? Rubbing at her forehead again in an attempt to quiet the pounding just behind her eyes, she said softly, "Because he doesn't want to know."

"But loving him, can you really walk away?" Maggie asked, reaching out to lay one hand on Kara's forearm.

"I have to," she said, wishing things were different. "While I still can."

Cooper was waiting for her.

Twilight filled the kitchen. Candles on the old table stood straight and tall, their flames dipping and swaying in the breeze. From the living room came the quiet, smooth sound of old jazz playing on the stereo. Everything was set. He had dinner made—even he could make pasta—and a bottle of wine open and breathing on the table.

Over the last few days, he'd done a lot of thinking—mostly because he hadn't been able to do anything else. He couldn't concentrate enough to write and couldn't talk to Kara without her talking about leaving him. This afternoon, he'd decided on a plan of action.

She walked inside, closed the door, then turned to face him.

Cooper looked her over, head to toe. Her dark brown hair had been tossed by the wind and her green eyes glittered in the reflected sunlight. She wore denim shorts, a pale yellow tank top and white sandals. She looked...*beautiful*.

Why had he never really noticed before? When had he become the kind of man who didn't pay attention to the people around him? Had he really become so secluded that he didn't even take notice of the woman who kept his entire life running on schedule?

"What's wrong?" she asked.

"What?"

"What's wrong, Cooper?"

"Nothing." He shook his head, told himself to quit with the self-analysis and get down to the plan. "Nothing's wrong."

"Good." She sniffed the air. "You *cooked?*"

"Contrary to popular belief, I'm not a complete moron."

"Pasta?" she asked, giving him a half smile.

"With chicken this time."

"Ah, innovation." She smiled a bit, then asked, "What's this about?"

He stepped up close and laid both hands on her shoulders. She looked up into his eyes and something inside Cooper clicked. He didn't know what the hell it was, but it was there and it was…important.

Don't think about it now, he told himself.

"What're you doing, Cooper?"

"I've been thinking."

She gave him a half smile. "I'll alert the media."

"Ha-ha." He pulled her closer and enjoyed the hell out of the look of surprise that flickered in her eyes. "I think I figured out what the problem is between us—"

She huffed out a breath. "You mean the problem where I quit and you don't believe me?"

"No, the other one."

"There's another one? This should be good."

"I think so."

"Okay, tell me," she said, squirming a little in an attempt to either get closer or move away—he wasn't entirely sure which.

"It's unrelieved sexual tension, Kara," he murmured, his gaze moving over her face before settling briefly on her mouth, her full bottom lip and that top lip that she always chewed on when she was worried about something.

Like she was doing now.

He smiled. "Why don't you let me chew on that lip for you?"

She went perfectly still and blinked up at him. "Are you *serious?*"

He pulled her hips tight against him so she could feel just how serious he really was. Her green eyes went wide and she huffed in a quick breath. His gaze dropped to the swell of her breasts, barely visible over the edge of her tank top.

A rush of need, much stronger, hotter, deeper than he'd expected, pumped through him and he drew her even closer, dipping his head to hers. She fit perfectly against him and he wondered why he'd never noticed that, either. And wondered why the hell it had taken him so long to come up with this plan.

She wanted him, he could see it in her eyes. He wanted her too. So what could be simpler than having each other? And once they'd had sex, she'd quit talking about leaving and things could go back to normal.

Brilliant.

"Well?" He lifted one hand to smooth her hair back from her face, then trailed his fingertips along the line of her jaw. She shivered and he smiled. "What do you say we get rid of all this tension?"

"I should warn you, I'm feeling pretty tense," she said, slowly sliding her hands up his chest until she could hook her arms around his neck. "This could take awhile."

He smiled and brushed his mouth against hers, once, twice, experiencing a surprising jolt of something hot and amazing each time. Then he met her gaze and promised, "Work, work, work."

Six

Kara's head was spinning, the headache behind her eyes was pounding and even her stomach wasn't very happy.

But all of that paled into nothingness the minute Cooper's mouth came down on hers. It was everything she'd been dreaming about…and so much more.

She sighed into him and gave herself up to the spiraling sensations unwinding inside her. He parted her lips with his tongue and she gasped at the sensual invasion. Their tongues met in an erotic dance that began smoothly, softly and quickly escalated into erupting need.

His arms came around her waist and he held her

tightly to him. So tightly, she felt his erection against her abdomen and her muscles quivered in anticipation. She'd wanted this, needed this for so very long, she could hardly believe it was finally happening.

Maybe she shouldn't give into the urges clamoring inside her. Maybe she should back up, step out of his arms, end this moment of fantasy. But the instant that thought raced through her brain, she greedily shut it down.

He slid one of his hands up her spine to cup the back of her head, fingers spearing through her hair. She moaned and leaned into him, taking more, giving more.

One corner of her brain screamed at her to be logical. Rational. To *think* for heaven's sake.

But she didn't want to think.

Not anymore.

Now, all she wanted, was to *feel*.

It didn't matter that she was a little woozy, that her headache had already begun slipping back up on her or that her stomach was none too steady.

If she had *bubonic plague*, she wouldn't have been too sick to have sex with Cooper. Not after she'd spent so much time over the last year imagining it, dreaming about it.

And oh boy, so far, it was *way* better than her dreams.

He tore his mouth from hers and dropped his head to the curve of her neck. His teeth and tongue slid over her flesh, sending ripples of something hot and delicious crashing through her.

His breath hot on her skin, his voice came muffled, strained. "Dinner can wait. Let's go upstairs."

Upstairs.

To a bed.

Oh, boy.

Once he stood back from her and took her hand to lead her from the kitchen, Kara's brain woke up with a new set of warning signals. *You're planning to leave. You've already quit. Is this really the right thing to do? Won't this only make it even harder for you to live without him?*

Probably, she acknowledged to the voice in her brain she was seriously starting to hate. But loving him, could she really not take the opportunity to have him for herself? If only for one night?

Not a chance.

He hit the stairs at a dead run and pulled her along in his wake. Kara stumbled a bit, but kept up, her much shorter legs having to move twice as fast. At the landing, he made a sharp right turn to his bedroom and when he'd pulled her in behind him, he slammed the door, enclosing them both in the big room.

A soft breeze rippled the curtains over the windows and the spicy scent of geraniums, mingled with the richer scent of summer roses, filled the air. She hardly noticed. All Kara knew was that Cooper was looking at her as she'd always wanted him to and nothing else mattered.

His dark eyes shone with a fire Kara had never seen before and it was all for her. It didn't matter that he didn't feel for her what she did for him. Not at the moment anyway. All that mattered now was this minute. This room. This man.

Cooper reached for the hem of her pale yellow tank top and in one smooth, practiced move, pulled it up and over her head before tossing it onto the floor.

"Gorgeous," he murmured and as Kara swayed unsteadily, he undid the front clasp of her bra and pushed it off her shoulders. His hands cupped her breasts and when his thumbs and forefingers tweaked her nipples, Kara heard a groan and only belatedly realized it had come from her.

Abruptly, his hands dropped to her waist. He scooped her up, tossed her onto the bed, then stood looking down at her with a smile. "Can't think why we never did this before, Kara."

"Me neither," she said, lifting both arms in welcome.

He grinned, reached down and pulled her denim shorts off, then paused a second or two to admire her white lace thong. "Man, if I'd known you were wearing something like that under your sensible clothes, I swear, it wouldn't have taken me five years to see it."

That nagging ache behind her eyes dulled a bit as she enjoyed the rush of his admiration.

She'd wanted this so long, hoped for it, dreamed

about it, that she wanted to remember every second. Every feeling. Every image. She wanted to imprint on her brain the sensation of Cooper's hands on her skin. She wanted to commit to memory the rough sound of his voice and the hot flash in his eyes.

Oh, she wanted it all.

For one night, she wanted it all.

Delicately, Cooper slid his fingers beneath the fragile elastic band of her thong and slowly, sensually, slid it off, caressing her thighs, her calves, as he went.

Kara chewed at her top lip and shifted impatiently on the quilt covered mattress. She watched him with hungry eyes as he quickly tore his own clothes off and then loomed over her on the bed.

He was simply amazing.

Body sculpted by the gods, his skin was bronzed, and her fingers itched to caress him. Reaching up, she smoothed her palms across his chest and over his shoulders and he sucked in a breath through gritted teeth at her touch. Then he dipped his head and took first one of her hardened nipples into his mouth and then the other.

Dizzying sensations rocked her and she held onto him as if it meant her life. Arching into him, she sighed breathlessly as his mouth worked her flesh into a tingling mass of nerves. His hands kept moving, sweeping up and down the length of her body, exploring, caressing, stroking. Wave after wave of desire crashed inside her, leaving Kara a whimpering mass of need.

Cooper shifted over her, raising his head just enough to kiss her, to take her mouth with a hunger that matched her own. His left hand dropped to her center and his fingertips slid across her damp folds, sliding back and forth with a sure, tender touch that spiked her desire into a frenzy.

Rocking her hips into his hand, she sighed into his mouth as he dipped his fingers deep within her. He used first one, then two fingers, to tantalize her, to push her to the very brink of climax—only to pull her back, demanding she stay hungry.

"Cooper," she whispered, tearing her mouth from his long enough to snatch at desperately needed air. "Cooper, I need…"

"So do I, Kara," he murmured, looking down into her eyes. His breath came in short, sharp gulps as he watched anticipation crest and recede on her features. "Let me watch you go over."

"No," she said, twisting her head from side to side, and smiling, though it cost her. "No, I want you. Inside me. Now. Now, Cooper."

"You're killing me, Kara," he said, dipping his head long enough to steal a kiss and taste her need.

She managed a short laugh, then lifted both hands to cup his face, even as his thumb brushed across a most sensitive nub at her center. "Oh, not yet. Definitely, not yet."

He swallowed hard and pulled away from her. Kara wanted to drag him back instantly, but she watched him reach over to the bedside table and yank open the drawer. He pulled a box of condoms out, then tore the package apart, grabbed one foil packet and quickly took care of the necessities of sex in the twenty-first century.

In seconds, he was back, touching her, stroking her, moving to position himself between her thighs. She moved with him, eager now to feel him inside her. To feel him take her deep and fast and hard.

While his fingers worked that one tender bud, he pushed his body into hers, and Kara gasped as she stretched to accommodate him. Her body awakened in a series of sparkling jolts of awareness. He rocked his hips against hers, pushing deeper with every thrust.

"Cooper..." She tipped her head back, into the mattress, closed her eyes and concentrated solely on the amazing sensations peaking inside her. She smiled, gasped and smiled again. "So...good. So...good."

"Let go, Kara," he said, pushing himself deeper into her body, shuddering with the force of his own all encompassing need. For the first time in his life, Cooper felt connected to the act of sex. To the wonder of it. To the incredible sense of expectation crowding at the edges of his brain.

He fought for control—despite knowing he wouldn't find it. He'd never before so lost himself in the moment. Never experienced this rush of tenderness and passion so completely commingled before.

And staring down into Kara's passion glazed green eyes, he knew that nothing would ever be simple between them again. Yet he couldn't bring himself to care.

He needed to hold her closer, deeper. To feel himself sliding so deeply within her that they would be locked together. Groaning, he leaned back, sitting on his heels and drawing Kara up with him, until she was on his lap, legs at either side of him, impaled on his body.

Her head fell back as she held onto his shoulders. His hands at her hips, he lifted her, moving her up and down on his body, drawing her up and down his length until neither of them could breathe. Until the passion was so thick in the room they were strangling on it.

He felt it when her climax rushed in. Knew the exact instant when she finally released the tension within and rode the first wave of completion.

Her body arched and she swiveled her hips on him, taking him even deeper. "Cooper! It's too much!"

"It's not," he told her brokenly. "It's not too much."

The air around them seemed to sigh, echoing softly in a tender whisper.

Their eyes met and locked and Kara's fingers dug into his shoulders as she groaned, trembling against him.

And holding her tightly to him, Cooper at last allowed himself to follow. Then when the tremors eased and the electricity arcing between them shimmered to an end, Cooper rested his forehead on her shoulder and tried to keep his thundering heart in his chest where it belonged.

Seconds ticked past, with the only sound in the room, their labored breathing. Then long before Cooper was willing to move, Kara shifted in his grasp and murmured, "Uh-oh."

"Hmm?" He tightened his grip on her and felt his body stir again. Sucking in air, even he was surprised by just how quickly he needed her again.

"Cooper," she whispered, "let me go."

"Not yet." He lifted his head, looked into her eyes and gave her a smile. "I kind of like you just where you are."

She shook her head, and inhaled sharply through her nose. "I need to—"

"Hey, I need something too and—"

"*No.*" Eyes suddenly wild, she clambered off his lap, pushed off the bed and staggered hurriedly out of the bedroom to the bathroom off the hall. She slapped the door open and in seconds, Cooper heard her being violently ill.

Frowning now, Cooper followed her into the bathroom and stood in the open doorway. As the first bout of sickness left her gasping for air, leaning back against the edge of the tub, he said, "You know, if this is a comment on my lovemaking skills, I want you to know I've never had this particular complaint before."

Clearly miserable, Kara swept her hair back out of her face and muttered thickly, "Go away, Cooper."

"Are you okay?" he asked, going down on one knee.

"*No* would be the short answer," she said, then gulped, "oh, no…"

Kara gripped the edges of the toilet and wished she could just open a hole to the center of the Earth and fall into it. How could her world go from glorious to miserable in the space of a couple minutes? And oh, *why* did she have to be so sick in front of Cooper?

"Take it easy," he whispered from just behind her. He held her hair back and soothed her with muttered nonsense as she turned inside out.

When she could take a breath, she tried again. "Cooper, if you care anything about me at all, you'll go away. Leave me to my misery in private."

He actually had the nerve to chuckle. Vaguely, she heard water running in the sink and then he was back, holding a cool damp cloth to her forehead while she was sick. And when she was at last finished, wanting only to curl up on the deliciously cold bathroom floor, he scooped her up in his arms and carried her back to the bedroom and to his bed.

Head pounding, mouth feeling like she'd been

sipping a sewer and a raceway for goose bumps forming on her spine, Kara wished absently that she were alive enough to enjoy being carried. But at the moment, that was simply beyond her.

She did try one more time to slink back to her own room. "Cooper, I just need to sleep," she said, trying to push up from the mattress on arms that suddenly felt too weak to support her.

"And you're going to," he said, helping her into a bathrobe and pulling the quilt out from under her, then draping it across her still form and tucking it tenderly in.

Damn it, he was being *nice*. And she was too weak and humiliated to protest. Apparently, the Fates had quite a sense of humor—and the joke was on her. She'd wanted him forever and it wasn't until *now* he paid attention. Now when she finally gets him into bed, she has to end the interlude by worshipping at the porcelain altar.

God.

Maybe she was weak enough to die.

"You're burning up," Cooper said, resting his hand on her forehead briefly.

"No I'm not," she argued, "I'm *freezing*." She burrowed deeper under the quilt and made a conscious effort to keep her teeth from chattering.

"Right. Okay. Stay put. I'm gonna call Sam."

"Sam?" She shook her head and looked up at him. He stood there beside the bed in all his naked glory and Kara couldn't even bring herself to care. She really was sick.

"He's a doctor. He'll know what to do."

"I don't need a doctor. Mortician, maybe."

"Funny." He grabbed his jeans off the floor and tugged them on, not bothering with the button fly. He scraped one hand through his hair and headed for the door. "I'll be back."

An hour later, Sam and Cooper stood in the kitchen. The candles he'd had burning when Kara came home had long since guttered out in their own wax puddles. The pasta was cold and congealed in a bowl on the table and the lingering scent of garlic still seasoned the air.

"You're sure she's okay?"

"Trust me," Sam said, snapping his black leather bag closed. "It's the flu. Kara will be fine in a couple of days. Just make sure she rests and gets lots of fluids."

"That's it?" Cooper demanded, glaring at his cousin. "You go to medical school for God knows how many years and the best you can do is *take a nap*?"

"Hey, you called me for my professional opinion, remember?"

"Right." Cooper blew out a breath. He didn't like this. He liked Kara up and annoying him. Ordering him around. Seeing her so weak and tired and…sick, worried him. "So should she eat anything?"

"Not till tomorrow at least. Then light stuff. Chicken soup, crackers." Sam studied him for a minute or two, then shook his head. "I can arrange for a nurse to come in and take care of her if you want."

Cooper's gaze snapped to his. "No. I'll do it."

"You sure?" Sam's voice was disbelieving and who could blame him?

Cooper couldn't remember a single time in his life when he'd voluntarily put himself out for someone else. Man. What did that say about him?

That he was a miserable, selfish jerk. Which he already knew. Hell, since that summer fifteen years ago, he'd done his best to keep a safe distance between himself and the human race. It had started deliberately. He even remembered making the choice to pull back, not only from his cousins, but from his parents, his grandfather, his friends.

Then after a few years, that distance had become a part of him. A part of his life that he'd grown so comfortable with, he'd never tried to change. Safer that way. Easier.

Until now.

But this was different.

This was Kara.

"It's not rocket science, Sam," he snapped, shoving both hands into his jeans pockets and rocking on his heels. "I can take care of the house and one sick woman."

"Okay," Sam nodded, eyeing him speculatively,

as if he wasn't quite sure Cooper meant what he was saying. Then he shrugged. "Maggie will probably want to come over tomorrow to check on her anyway, though."

"She doesn't have to, but thanks."

"Now, I'm going home." Sam turned for the back door, opened it, then stopped, looking at Cooper over his shoulder. "And while you're at it, you ought to get some rest, too. You look like hell."

Cooper shrugged off Sam's suggestion and once his cousin was gone, set the teakettle on the antique stove and turned on the burner. Rummaging through the kitchen cabinets, he located a coffee mug, then finally unearthed the jasmine tea bags that Kara had bought her first day in town.

Hitching one hip against the counter, he stared at the kitchen windows and the night crouched just beyond the circle of lamplight. He caught his own reflection in the glass and admitted that Sam had a point. He *did* look like hell. Worry etched itself into his eyes and bracketed his mouth.

Not too surprising. Of *course* he was worried about Kara. She was a part of his life. And tonight, she'd become an even bigger part.

A draft of cold air slipped past him and he shivered. Still staring at the glass, while the water in the teakettle began to stir, Cooper noticed a flash of movement. A white, shadowy film that moved across the glass and then disappeared.

He straightened up slowly and only absently heard the low pitch of the teakettle beginning to hum. He looked around the empty room and wasn't even surprised when he heard a heavy sigh reverberate around him.

The teakettle began shrieking, the sound driving into his head like a nail. He took the two steps to the stove, shut the fire off and flipped the cap off the kettle to end the noise. He poured a steaming stream of water into the cup, instantly releasing a flowery aroma.

While the tea steeped, he searched through the pantry for a couple of soda crackers. Despite what Sam had said, he figured Kara might be hungry and he wanted to be ready. When the tea was ready and the crackers on a small plate, he picked them up and looked around the room again.

"You still here?" Weird. Talking to a ghost. Weirder still, he was half expecting an answer. When nothing happened, he headed out to the stairs. At the door to his bedroom, he stopped. In the soft puddle of light from the bedside lamp, Kara lay, sound asleep.

He walked into the room, set the tea down on the dresser and placed the crackers alongside it. Then Cooper took a nearby armchair and dragged it to the side of the bed. He sat down and felt another cold chill brush along his shoulders and he stiffened reflexively.

Whispering into the quiet room, he said, "I'd appreciate it if you could skip the crying tonight. Kara's sick and she needs to sleep."

For several long moments, nothing happened, and then Cooper felt the chill in the room slide away, as if it had never been. Nodding to himself, he settled into the chair, got comfortable and prepared for a long night of keeping watch over Kara.

Seven

The cold was a living wall, surrounding him, devouring him. David felt it taking small bites of his heart, his soul. Helpless to stop it, he could only observe helplessly as the cold slowly, inexorably, eased into every corner of his being.

But there was something more, too. Something less substantial than the cold and yet far more insidious. Like an oil spill, it filled him, an inky blackness that was slowly obliterating who he had been before he'd first entered the hotel.

Worse, he couldn't fight it.

A scream slashed through the silence,

tearing it as a sharp blade would rend fragile
silk. And...and... Damn it.

"Then what?" Cooper said aloud as he flopped
back against the chair and glared at the screen of his
laptop computer as if the machine itself were deliberately sabotaging him. A scream? Who the hell
screamed? And why?

Usually, he worked through his books by the seat
of his pants, believing strongly that if he ever sat
down and plotted the thing out, scene by scene, he'd
suck the heart of it out. The immediacy. And besides,
he sort of enjoyed being surprised by whatever his
characters got into.

But now...he couldn't think. Couldn't concentrate on his book because he couldn't stop thinking
about the woman upstairs, lying in his bed. Sitting
in a chair in his bedroom, he'd managed to doze off
a couple times during the night. But every time Kara
moaned or sighed in her fevered sleep, she'd brought
him right out of it again.

His eyes felt like two marbles rolling in sand.
Lifting both hands, he rubbed them, making the ache
more pronounced. Then he braced his elbows on the
tabletop and cupped his face in his palms. How was
he supposed to come up with a fictional horror story
while he was so concerned about Kara? Should the
flu really be this hard on a person? Shouldn't she be
feeling better by now?

Kara wouldn't drink any of the tea he brought her. Turned green at the offering of soda crackers and only spoke to tell him to go away.

As a nurse, he was a bust.

Or maybe Sam was a quack and she needed something more than rest.

Pushing up from the chair at the kitchen table, he stalked out of the room, across the living room and up the stairs, his long legs taking them two at a time. He turned for his bedroom and knocked quietly before opening the door.

Kara turned her head on the pillow to look at him as he entered. In the sunlight, her skin was too pale and lavender shadows lay beneath her eyes. She looked exhausted.

"Cooper, at least let me go back to my own bed."

"No," he said, giving her a smile she didn't want. "You're not getting out of that bed until you can do it without racing to the bathroom."

She tugged the quilt up to her chin and sulked. "I'm not a child," she pointed out.

"I remember," he said.

She groaned and pulled the quilt up over her face. Voice muffled, she said, "Oh, God, don't."

"Don't what?"

"Remember." She weakly pushed the quilt back down but closed her eyes as if she couldn't bear to look at him. "Put the whole night out of your mind. I have."

That stung more than he would have thought

possible. Amazing how much difference a few hours could make. Last night, he'd held her in his arms, locked himself inside her body and felt her quickening response. Today…they were like two polite strangers.

The easy camaraderie they used to share was gone. Friendship splintered by sex. Sex she didn't even want to think about. Great. By changing their relationship, he'd hoped to convince her not to quit. Now, it was starting to look like he'd only accelerated the process. Hell, she was lying there in his bed and already further away from him than she'd ever been. Disgusted with himself and the situation, he said, "I'm going into town. Pick up a few supplies."

"Good. Go away."

"Won't be gone long," he said, paying no attention to her crabbiness. "I'm going to ask Maggie to come sit with you. Make sure you stay in that bed."

Her eyes opened so she could glare at him briefly. "I'm not an infant. I can survive on my own for a couple of hours."

He ignored her tone, figuring a person was allowed to be crabby when they felt like hell. He always did. And the last time he was sick, he remembered suddenly, Kara had been at his side the whole time. He'd never questioned it, never even really taken the time to *appreciate* it. *God, what an idiot.* "Trust me, I don't think of you as an infant. But Maggie'll be here anyway."

"I don't need a sitter. I just need to get well."

"You will."

"When?"

"Okay," he said smiling, "now you're starting to sound like a baby."

"I can't help it," she snapped and flopped her arms down on top of the quilt. Her fingertips idly played with a loose thread. "I hate being sick and I don't want you taking care of me."

"You've been taking care of me for years," he reminded her. "Consider this payback."

"A debt." She sighed. "Great. Perfect."

Now what had he done? "I'll be back in awhile."

"Apparently, I'll be here."

He left her then and went to call Maggie.

"This'll be good for him," Maggie said, smoothing the fresh linen case on the plumped pillow behind Kara's head. As she moved along the bed, tugging at the quilt, she walked through a slash of sunlight that gilded the lighter streaks in her dark hair. Smiling, she glanced at Kara. "Maybe what Cooper needs is to feel needed."

Kara wasn't so sure about that. In the years she'd known him, he'd made a point of never being indispensable to anyone. He never had relationships that lasted more than a few months. And until this summer, he hadn't even seen his family in years.

He wanted to be needed?

No, Kara didn't see that. She'd always thought that Cooper did everything he could to keep from being needed.

"He's making me crazy," Kara admitted as her stomach did another wild pitch and roll. She slapped one hand to her abdomen and swallowed hard, determined to get through the rest of the day without ending up on her knees in the bathroom. Inhaling deeply, determinedly, she said, "He hovers. He brings me tea I can't drink and crackers that make me want to heave. And then he just sits there and stares at me. And I look *hideous*."

Maggie chuckled then sat down in the chair beside the bed. "Apparently, Cooper doesn't agree. He's worried about you."

She'd like to think so, but reality kept rearing its ugly head to keep her from delving into fantasies best left alone. "It's not worry," she said on a sigh. "He said he's just paying me back for all the years I've been taking care of him."

Maggie shook her head, disbelieving. "Did he actually say that?"

"Yes. And," Kara added, "he feels bad for me because I got so sick right after—" Oops. No point in turning this little chat into a confessional.

But Maggie was too quick to be fooled. A pleased smile curved her mouth as she leaned back and lifted her feet to cross them on the edge of the bed. "Ah...so you finally managed to get him to *notice* you?"

Kara sighed again, this time in disgust. "Oh yeah. He noticed all right. Hard not to notice when the woman you're making love to suddenly has to make a break for the bathroom."

"Oh no." Maggie winced in sympathy. "Right in the middle?"

She shook her head. "Right after. In the middle of what was looking to be a truly great afterglow."

"Oh," Maggie said dreamily, "I do love the whole glow part."

"I wouldn't know," Kara said. "My glow was cut short."

"So, next time will be better."

"Next time?" Kara repeated on a disgusted groan. "There won't be a next time. He saw me sick as a dog. Held my head. Please. Any man who has to live through that is never going to look at that woman with passion again."

Maggie laughed.

Kara scowled at her. "So happy to give you your morning chuckle."

"Well come on, Kara." Still grinning, Maggie nudged her with her foot. "You think couples never see each other at their worst? Trust me. I'm sick every morning and every night, Sam's right there, pulling me in close and…" She cleared her throat. "Well, that's not the point."

"No you're right. It's not. That's completely different. You're *pregnant,*" Kara said, pointing an accusatory finger at her. "With Sam's child. Of course he's still sexually attracted to you. He *loves* you."

"Yeah," Maggie said with a contented sigh, "he really does. Are you so sure Cooper doesn't love you?"

Kara snorted and tugged a little harder at the loose string on the quilt, wrapping the thread around her index finger until the tip of it turned purple. "Love didn't have anything to do with it. At least not on his part. Trust me Maggie, I wish you were right. I wish he did love me. But he doesn't."

Another sigh wafted through the room. This one was deep, tormented, heartfelt. It came from nowhere. And everywhere.

Maggie dropped her feet to the floor and shot straight up in her chair, like someone had shoved a steel rod down the back of her tank top. "Was that...?"

Kara looked around the room and shrugged. "I'd introduce you but I don't know her name. So I'll just say, Maggie, meet our ghost. Ghost...Maggie."

He really had to get out of the frozen food section more often.

When left to his own devices, Cooper usually snatched up whatever edible looking frozen dinners he could find and called his shopping finished. Today, he'd gone up and down every aisle, the produce section and even the meat counter. Amazing really, what was out there.

He stacked a dozen grocery bags in the trunk of

his SUV, and slammed the lid shut. Then he looked around the quiet main street of Coleville and for the first time, really felt as though he'd come home.

Not much had changed and a part of him was grateful. Stupid really. He'd been avoiding this place for fifteen years because of the memories and now he was relieved to find it much as he'd left it.

A cool, sharp wind flew in off the ocean, dispelling some of the summer heat as Cooper walked toward the drugstore on the corner. Two kids rattled past him, surfing the sidewalks on skateboards whose wheels growled in their wake. An old woman lifted her suitcase-sized purse and shouted at them, but the kids didn't even slow down.

Cooper was still smiling to himself as he opened the door and heard the familiar clang and jangle of the old-fashioned bell over the door. God, when he and his cousins were kids, they'd been in and out of this store all summer. Candy bars, ice cold sodas and comic books were all he'd needed back then to make him happy.

And just for a second, Cooper wondered why life had to get so complicated.

He wandered through the aisles, nodding and smiling to the few people he passed. A refrigerated cabinet held a selection of flowers and before he could think twice about it, Cooper had the thing open and was reaching inside. Roses? He grabbed up a big bouquet of yellow roses, took a sniff, then stopped to think about it.

Did Kara like roses? He didn't know. And why the hell didn't he know? Five years they'd been together and he didn't know if she liked roses? He scowled down at the tight, colorful buds, then let his gaze sweep the interior of the case. There were a few mixed bouquets and a selection of carnations, daisies and some weird looking purple flower he couldn't identify.

"This shouldn't be so hard," he muttered, shifting his gaze from one bunch of flowers to the next as refrigerated air puffed out around him.

"Cooper Lonergan, shut that door! You think I'm paying to cool off the inside of the store?"

He jumped, startled and spun around to look down into Mrs. Russell's beady black eyes. The old woman had been a hundred and ten when Cooper was a boy, so he could only guess that she really had been an evil witch. Because she was still alive—and looking no friendlier than she had back in the old days.

"Sorry Mrs. Russell," he said and stepped back, still clutching the roses as he shut the glass doors. "Just trying to make up my mind."

She frowned at him and scuttled past toward the cash register behind the front counter. "Well, do your thinking with the door closed."

"Nice to see you, too," he muttered.

"Horrifying, isn't she?"

Cooper turned to face a tall pretty woman with

pale blond hair and deep blue eyes. She had a wire basket over one arm and a knowing smile on her face.

"Ah, yeah," he said, trying to figure out who she was. She looked at him as if he should know her, but for the life of him, he couldn't figure out how. "But then she always was."

The blond cast a quick glance to make sure Mrs. Russell was out of earshot before saying, "I think she's still holding a grudge against you and your cousins for the Fourth of July fiasco."

He smiled just thinking about it. Funny, he hadn't remembered that in years. He, Jake, Sam and Mac, eager for a little early celebration, had pooled their money and bought some illegal bottle rockets. They hadn't actually *planned* to launch one of them into the Russells' shed and burn it down.

Still smiling, he recalled, "And then Jeremiah made us spend the next three weeks building her a new shed."

"You got off easy," the blond said. "I was grounded for a month."

Cooper narrowed his gaze on her and just for a minute or two, the last fifteen years fell away and he saw her as she had been then. Tall and skinny, with wide blue eyes that were always locked on Mac. "Donna? Donna Barrett?"

"Hi, Cooper," she said, "it's good to see you again."

He swept her into a hard hug, then jumped back

as the bouquet of roses dripped water on her shoulder. "Sorry about that."

"No problem. I heard you and Sam had come home."

"Yeah. For the summer anyway. Jake's coming, too."

"All of you together again." Her voice went wistful, and her gaze dropped to the basket on her arm.

"Almost all of us," he said, knowing that Donna's thoughts were centered on Mac. And why wouldn't they be? Donna and Mac had lived in each other's pockets that last summer.

She'd become an unofficial part of their little group not just because the rest of them liked her, but because if they hadn't included her they wouldn't have seen much of Mac. In fact, the day Mac died, was only one of a handful of days Donna hadn't been with them. If she had been, maybe things would have been different. Maybe they wouldn't have waited so long to jump in after him. Maybe…

Silence stretched out between them as taut as an overextended rubber band as both of them drifted through the past, facing their regrets. Finally, he spoke up again, scrambling for something to say. "I heard you moved out of Coleville right after—"

Great. Perfect. Nice job, Cooper. Think of something else to say and go right back to that summer. But Donna played along.

"Yeah. I went to live with my aunt. In Colorado. Stayed there and went to school and now, well…" she shrugged and swept her hair back from her face. "It was time to come home." She waved one hand at the roses, now dripping water all over the linoleum. "So, hot date?"

He laughed uneasily. "No. Just trying to find flowers to bring to a…friend." *Friend?* Weak word. But what other word would do? *Lover?* Did one night together make them lovers? Not if Kara was to be believed. She was already trying to find a way to wipe that incident from her memory and his.

"She'll love them."

"You think?" He stared at them as if expecting them to change color or something. "All women like roses, right?"

One blond eyebrow lifted. "We're not interchangeable, Cooper."

"I know, I just meant—hell." He didn't know what he meant. Never before had he been so at a loss as to how to treat a woman. But Kara was different. She had a place in his life. She was…special.

Right. So special he didn't even know if she liked roses or not.

Well, he could solve that problem at least, he told himself and opened the refrigerated door again. Grabbing up all of the other bouquets, he figured that the one sure way to get Kara's favorite flower, would be to buy all of them.

"Making a statement?" she asked, laughing.

"No," he said, resisting the idea—even the vague hint of the idea—that he might be trying to win someone's heart. That wasn't what this was about. This was about being nice to someone he…cared for. About wanting to make Kara feel a little less crappy. "Just buying too many flowers," he said firmly.

From outside, a car horn blasted three or four times in short, impatient bursts. Donna threw a quick look over her shoulder at the wide windows overlooking the street. Then she turned back to Cooper, and said, "It was good to see you, but I've really got to run."

"Everything okay, Donna?" She looked…nervous all of a sudden.

"Fine." She hurried to Mrs. Russell at the cash register. "I hope your friend likes her flowers."

"Yeah, me, too." Thoughtfully, he watched her leave the store, and hurry to a pickup truck. There was someone in the passenger seat, but thanks to the sun's glare on the windshield, Cooper couldn't make out who it might be.

Then shaking his head, he told himself to forget about Donna Barrett. Whatever she had going on in her life now, he wished her well. But he had a sick woman at home and he didn't want to keep her waiting.

"Six bouquets?" Kara asked, astonished as Cooper carried in the last bunch of purple irises and set them across from her on top of the dresser.

He shrugged, shoved both hands into the pockets of his black slacks and said, "I didn't know—" he caught himself and started again. "They were all nice."

Kara smiled in spite of the disappointment she felt. Five years of knowing him, working with him every day and he didn't even know this one small thing about her. "You didn't know what kind of flowers I like."

He frowned and pulled one hand free long enough to stab his fingers through his hair. In a disgusted grumble he admitted, "No, I didn't. I did know you like flowers, though."

"Uh-huh." Thank God, her stomach had stopped its rumbling and spinning. Otherwise the combined scents of the fresh flowers would have had her running for the bathroom again. Now, it was just giving her a headache.

But he looked so pleased with himself, it was hard to burst his bubble.

"It was sweet of you to think of it," she said finally, trying to let go of her old dreams and see him as he really was. Did it matter that he didn't know what kind of flower she liked? Wasn't it more important that he'd thought of the act at all? "Thank you, Cooper."

He beamed at her, then reached for the shopping bag he'd dumped unceremoniously at the bedroom door. "I brought these, too. And stared Mrs. Russell, the old bat, right in the eye while I paid for them."

"What are you talking ab—" she broke off and smiled as he pulled five magazines from the bag and laid them on the bed beside her. Magazines about fashion and hair and gossip, he'd picked up exactly what he thought a woman would read. "Thanks, they're great."

"So how about soup?" he asked in a coaxing voice, "I bought chicken and stars."

"You don't have to fix my dinner, Cooper. Why don't you just go out and get something for yourself."

"Get something?" He managed to look both proud and insulted. "I bought steaks at the market and I'll be cooking my own dinner."

"Really?"

"I'm not completely useless, Kara."

"I never said *useless,*" she corrected. "I believe the word I used was *hopeless.*"

"Is that right?" He moved around the edge of her bed and straightened the quilt laying over her. "Well, I not only grocery shopped, but I did a couple of loads of laundry—did you know you can overfill a washing machine?"

"How big a mess was it?"

"The floors are clean."

"Cooper…"

"And, I even did some ironing."

She stared up at him, amazed and just a little sad. "You ironed?"

"Not for long," he admitted with a shrug. "The

plastic cover on that ironing board in the pantry? Why would they want you to put something hot on a covering that can melt?"

"You didn't."

"I'll buy a new iron," he said, brushing aside his little domestic disaster.

"Cooper," Kara said softly, "why are you doing all this? Really."

He stopped, looked down at her and gave her one of those smiles that could turn her inside out in a heartbeat. "Because I want to. Now, about that soup?"

Kara nodded, but didn't speak because she was just a little bit afraid that her voice might break if she tried. She watched him leave the room and when he was gone, she shifted her gaze to stare up at the late afternoon sunlight playing across the beamed ceiling. The scent of fresh flowers surrounded her and from somewhere in the room came the softest of sighs.

Not only was Cooper surviving without her...he appeared to be thriving.

Eight

"How're you holding up?" Sam set his medical bag onto the kitchen table and gave his cousin a stern look.

Morning sunlight shone in the room and Cooper squinted against the brightness while he cupped a full coffee mug between his palms. Lifting it for a sip, he shuddered at the taste and made a mental note to ask Kara *again* how to brew a decent pot of caffeine.

"I'm great," he said tightly, then dropped into a kitchen chair before he fell down. He felt as though he hadn't slept in weeks. "Now why don't you tell me about the patient you actually came here to see."

Sam shook his head and wandered over to the coffeepot. Grabbing down a cup from the cabinet, he filled the mug, took a sip and grimaced. "How can anybody screw up coffee this badly?"

"It's a gift," Cooper said, bracing one elbow on the table. "How's Kara?"

"She's fine. Probably better than you," Sam said, leaning back against the counter. "Did I mention that you look like hell?"

"Thanks." He took another gulp of coffee—not because he was getting used to the taste, but because the caffeine was the only thing keeping him awake. "She's okay? Really?"

"Yeah. I told you before, it was just the flu." Sam checked his wristwatch, took another sip of coffee, then choked it down before setting the almost full cup aside. "She's tired and weak, but she'll get better. Give her a couple more days to rest up. Keep her on light foods, a bland diet."

"Bland I can manage," Cooper muttered.

"Maggie would be happy to come over and help you out."

"No," he said. "I can take care of Kara. I want to."

"Hmm." Sam walked to the table, sat down opposite Cooper and stared at him thoughtfully.

"What?"

"Nothing. This is just interesting. I've never known you to have a domestic side."

"Cute." Cooper leaned back in his chair and said with a choked laugh, "Hell, Sam. I had no idea there was so much to do every day. I don't know how the hell Kara does it all. She never gets shook. Always has things organized. And never so much as has a nervous breakdown. Seriously, I haven't been paying her nearly enough money."

"I'm sure she'll be glad to hear that," Sam mused.

Cooper didn't even hear him. "I've spent so much time on the phone, dealing with my editor and agent and publicist, not to mention trying to get Kara to eat some soup and do laundry without flooding the place, I haven't written a word in two days."

"Or slept?"

Wryly, Cooper smiled. "Yeah. I've been sitting in a chair beside Kara in case she wakes up and needs something."

"Uh-huh." Sam shifted in his seat, threw one arm across the back of the chair and smiled to himself.

"Whatever you're thinking," Cooper told him, "forget it."

Sam drummed the fingers of his left hand against the tabletop. "Okay. If you don't want to talk about Kara, then why don't we talk about you?"

Cooper groaned inwardly. He was in no shape to be analyzed and Sam definitely had that "look" in his eyes. The look that said, *I know what your problem is and I have the solution.*

"Sam," Cooper said softly, "take pity on an exhausted man. Give me a break."

"You've been here for a few weeks now," Sam

said softly, completely ignoring Cooper's plea. "As far as I know, you still haven't been out to the lake."

Cooper's grip tightened on the handle of the mug until his knuckles went white. Fatigue pulled at him, but he stiffened despite the slump in his shoulders. "No, I haven't. Don't plan to, either."

Sam looked disappointed, somehow. "Damn it, Cooper. You can't keep hiding from that day."

Something squirmed in his guts and Cooper fought the urge to shift uncomfortably in his chair. "It's worked for me this long."

"You're here," Sam said quietly. "You came all the way to Coleville. Why not take it the rest of the way?"

"I came for Jeremiah's sake. I'm not here to relive the past." Deliberately, Cooper released his grip on the coffee mug and sat back in his chair. "I was in town the other day," he said, noting that Sam looked irritated by the change of subject. "I saw Donna."

"Barrett?" Surprised, Sam stared at him for a long minute. "I didn't know she was in town."

"Apparently, she's moved back."

"How's she look?"

"Good. But that's not my point," Cooper said, pushing his coffee cup away from him and leaning both forearms on the table as if he couldn't quite hold himself up straight in the chair without support. "I saw her and instantly, my mind went back to that summer. I could feel the sun. Smell the ocean." He sighed.

"Hell, Sam, I could have sworn I actually heard Mac laugh. It was all so close. Just by seeing Donna."

"Cooper…"

He looked into Sam's eyes and shook his head solemnly. "No. I buried the past, Sam. And I'm going to keep it buried."

Sam watched him for a few long seconds then sighed. "It's not buried, Cooper. It's with you every damn day. And until you face it—face *Mac*—you'll never really be free of it."

After Sam had gone, Cooper sat alone in the sun drenched kitchen and felt cold pressing in on him. Whether it was the ghost in the house or the ghosts in his own mind, Cooper acknowledged the truth. He didn't deserve to be free of the past.

He deserved to be haunted.

Kara pushed herself weakly into a sitting position against the pillows propped up on the headboard of the bed. She was finally starting to feel alive again. Barely. At least her stomach had stopped churning every few minutes. But she also felt like a slug. She hadn't even been able to work up the energy to crawl into the shower.

"How you feeling?"

She snapped a look at the doorway. Cooper stood there, leaning one shoulder against the doorjamb. Hands in his pockets, one foot crossed over the other, he looked tired. And impossibly good.

The last couple of days had been so hard. Not only feeling like death, but being so close to him. Having Cooper sit up at her side all through the night and knowing that he wasn't doing it because he loved her, but because he felt he owed her.

He pushed away from the door and walked toward her slowly. Kara grabbed at the quilt covering her and pulled it up higher, covering her chest, wanting to pull it up over her head. She knew what she must look like. She'd caught a brief glimpse of herself in the bathroom mirror earlier and had yelped in fright.

"Kara?" He waved one hand back and forth in front of her face. "You're zoning again."

"I didn't zone. I'm in a coma."

"Pretty chatty for a coma."

"Was there a reason for this visit?"

Twin black eyebrows lifted. "Should you still be this crabby now that you're getting better?"

"Cooper…"

"Relax. I only came to see if you felt well enough to try a shower."

She blinked at him, trying to dislodge a sudden, extremely clear image of the two of them, naked, wrapped together under a stream of hot water. His hands, slick with soap, sliding over her body, dipping between her legs, stroking, while his mouth…

"Kara?"

She came up out of the fantasy and gave herself a mental kick. Oh, sleeping with him had been a *big* mistake. Now she knew what she'd be missing for the rest of her life. And in her heart, she knew damn well there wasn't another man alive who would ever compare to Cooper Lonergan.

But the simple truth was, he wasn't hers and never would be. Might as well get used to that fact.

"I heard you," she said and threw the quilt back. Cool air hit her bare legs and she shivered. "And the answer is yes. I'm definitely willing to give it a try."

"Hey, not so fast," he cautioned, moving in to grab one of her arms as she jumped to her feet.

"I'm fine," she said, "I can do this myself—" She swayed unsteadily and leaned into his hard, muscled chest. The room did a nasty little tilt and she closed her eyes to steady herself. "Okay," she acknowledged a few seconds later, "maybe I could use a little help."

"You've been flat on your back for nearly three days, Kara." He wrapped one arm around her waist and Kara could have sworn she felt five separate stabs of heat from each of his fingers.

"You haven't had any food in your system," he reminded her. "So take it easy until you get your strength back, okay?"

His voice was tight, and she was pretty sure she heard his heart pounding out a frantic rhythm. Kara wasn't sure if it was worry or desire causing the jump in his blood pressure but decided to go with worry. Since that thought was less likely to break her heart.

Patting his chest, she straightened up, backing out of his embrace and then took a single step, wishing her legs didn't feel quite so wet-noodley. Her head spun crazily and her vision went a little fluffy at the edges.

"Whoa. Interesting sensation," she whispered just before Cooper scooped her up into his arms.

"Okay, we'll do this another way." He cradled her close and Kara indulged herself. Laying her head on his shoulder, she inhaled the scent of him—soap, shampoo and the spicy zing of his aftershave.

Her stomach wobbled, but it had nothing to do with the flu. It was simply the effect Cooper had on her. Only now, it was worse than ever before because she knew what it was to have him inside her. To feel his mouth on her skin, his hands on her body. She knew the shattering sensation of climaxes rippling through her system and the brush of his breath against her neck.

And oh, she wanted it all again.

Even knowing that it was going nowhere.

That he would never love her.

She wanted him so much, everything in her yearned.

"You okay?" he whispered, his breath dusting the top of her head.

"Yeah," she insisted firmly. "Just a little light-headed is all."

He left the bedroom, walked down the hall and stepped into the bathroom. The walls were a cool green and the old tile floor was laid in a pattern of green-and-white checks.

"You want me to help you?" he asked as he set her down onto her feet.

"No," she said, though her mind was screaming *yes!* No point in making this even harder on herself. Her shower fantasy burst once again into full bloom in her brain, and the images it produced left her nearly breathless with a hunger that shook her right down to her bones. But she steeled herself against it, and met his gaze squarely. "I'll be fine."

He didn't look as if he believed her. But still, he backed up toward the door. "I'll be close if you need me. I'm gonna change the sheets on the bed."

Kara blinked. "You are?"

Scowling, Cooper said, "You know, I wish you'd quit looking at me like that."

"Like what?"

"Like I'm performing a miracle or something whenever I do something around here. I *am* capable of a few things."

She smiled at his insulted tone and tried to smooth his ruffled feelings. "Of course you are, it's just—"

"I know." He held up one hand to stop the rest of her explanation and gave her a half smile. "I've never done it before. But then, never really had to, did I?"

"No," she mused, thinking about how she was usually the one taking care of him. She'd worked so hard for so long to make herself indispensable to him, it had never occurred to her that maybe she'd done too much. "I guess not."

He nodded and stuffed both hands into his jeans pockets. "Oh yeah, you didn't have another nightgown that I could find, so I put one of my T-shirts in there for you to wear while your nightgown gets washed."

She glanced down and saw his neatly folded white T-shirt. He'd even thought of this. She'd been in her nightgown for nearly three days now and she could hardly wait to get out of it. "More laundry?"

He shrugged and smiled. "Think I'm getting the hang of it."

"Thanks," she said, "for thinking of it."

"No problem," he said, backing the rest of the way out of the bathroom. "And if you get dizzy again, while you're taking a shower, for God's sake, sit down."

"I will."

He stopped. "Maybe I should just stay in the room with you, just in case…"

Oh, that's all she needed.

"Go away," she said, laying one hand on his chest and pushing him out of the room.

She closed the door and leaned back against it for a long minute or two, trying to keep from opening it again and inviting him inside. Then she heard his footsteps moving off down the hall and she sighed. In disappointment or relief…she wasn't sure.

Then shaking her head, she peeled off her nightgown and headed for the shower.

* * *

In the darkness, Cooper sat alongside the bed and watched Kara sleep. Moonlight spilled across the mattress illuminating her in a silvery light that made her already pale skin glow like fine porcelain. Her eyelashes were long and lay curved on her cheeks in a smudge of darkness that was vulnerable as well as tempting.

He sucked in a breath of air and blew it out again while leaning forward, forearms braced on his thighs. He couldn't seem to stop watching her and he wondered why he'd never noticed before just how beautiful she was. She sighed and shifted in her sleep, the quilt sliding down, baring her shoulder and the plain white T-shirt that covered her.

Damn, who would have thought a woman could look that good in a man's shirt? He could still see her, coming out of the bathroom. The hem of the T-shirt hit just beneath her bottom, baring her long, lean legs to his gaze. Her hair, freshly washed and dried, drifted around her shoulders in thick, tempting waves and her eyes, though still shadowed, looked clear for the first time in days.

His fingers itched to stroke her skin again as memory after memory rushed into his brain, crowding it with the images and sounds and scents of their lovemaking. Only a few nights ago, she'd opened herself to him and he'd discovered a depth and passion he hadn't expected.

His body stirred, tightening with a hunger that clawed at his insides until he wanted to howl with need. And he called himself all kinds of a bastard for wanting her when she was so clearly exhausted.

He leaned back in his chair and then jolted upright when an unearthly howl erupted from the bowels of the house. Jumping to his feet, he stared around the room, but it did no good. The wailing came from nowhere and everywhere. It seemed to seep from the walls as if even the house itself were keening in misery.

"Damn it," he muttered, swallowing past the knot lodged in his throat. It had been a couple of days since the ghost had made itself known. Cooper had almost begun to think that it had decided to leave them the hell alone.

Now though, it was back and louder than ever.

Another heartrending wail sobbed around him, sending a chill washing through him. Outside, a wind kicked up out of nowhere, rattling the window panes. Bits of dirt and pebbles were thrown high, pinging off the glass like eager fingers tapping, tapping, demanding entry.

The temperature in the room dropped suddenly and as the sobbing continued, cold gathered. Cooper moved closer to the bed, standing with his back to Kara, so that he stood as a sentry, between her and the growing cold.

Even as he did it though, he fought down a sharp laugh. What the hell could he do to a ghost? What

he should do was grab up Kara and get her somewhere...else. But he'd be damned if he was going to
be chased out of his own house by the psychic
energies of one long-dead woman and her erstwhile
lover.

"Get out," he muttered thickly, and the sobbing
throbbed in the air.

"Cooper?"

He spun around to find Kara sitting up in bed,
pushing her hair back out of her eyes and looking
around the empty room.

"She just started up," he muttered, glaring at the
shadows as if trying to intimidate the spirit into silence.

Another howl was his answer. The sound rippled
along his skin, and lifted the hair at the back of his neck.

"She's lonely," Kara whispered.

"She's *nuts*," Cooper countered.

A disembodied moan whined around them.

Kara reached for his hand and pulled him down
onto the bed beside her. He sat down, back braced
against the headboard and pulled her in close, if only
to keep her warm in the bone numbing cold.

"She shouldn't have waited for him for so long,"
Kara said, her voice almost lost in the weeping.

Cooper shook his head, amazed that they were
sitting in the dark, discussing the feelings of a
woman long dead. "Hell, she'd waited two years.
Maybe she should have waited a little longer. He *did*
show up finally."

"Too late," Kara reminded.

"It didn't have to be too late," he said, raising his voice to be sure even the ghost heard him. "If she hadn't curled up and died, they could have been together. He's outside the house right now and she *still* won't let him in."

Kara looked up at his profile in the darkness and tried not to make too much of his words. The problem was, she wanted to believe that he was trying, subconsciously even, to tell her to not give up on him.

But if she started believing things like that, she'd only be setting herself up for the same kind of misery that haunted the woman trapped in this house.

Better if she did what that woman had not done.

Give up on the dream and move on.

Nine

Kara reluctantly woke up from the most erotic dream she'd ever experienced, to silent darkness. Apparently the ghost had given up for the night.

So what then had woken her?

An instant later, she knew. In her dream, Cooper's hands had moved over her body with smooth deliberation, caressing, stroking, driving her toward a climax she knew would be soul shattering.

Now that she was awake, she realized the dream was real. Cooper lay right behind her, spooned up along her back. At some point during the night, he'd undressed, because the heat from his naked body rushed into hers and she felt the hard, solid length of his erection pressing against her behind.

Yet even that delicious sensation was trumped by the feel of one of his hands cupped between her thighs. Damp heat pooled in her center and her breath staggered past a knot of need lodged in her throat.

Instinctively, she parted her thighs for him, silently asking that he touch her more surely, more deeply. Closing her eyes, she shifted against his hand, delighting in the frisson of sensations that swept through her in a rush. His fingers moved on her, dipping into her warmth, sliding over the tender, sensitive flesh.

She sighed and his name came out on a groan. "Cooper…"

"Right here," he whispered, bending his head to the curve of her neck, nibbling, licking.

"Yeah," she said breathlessly, "I got that…"

He smiled against her skin, then nibbled a little harder. "Sorry I woke you."

"No," she said, "you're not." Smiling, she gulped in another breath as his fingers continued their gentle invasion.

"Okay," he admitted, "I'm not."

She rolled over onto her back and stared up into his dark eyes. While she watched him, he dipped one finger and then two inside her and she swallowed hard, loving the feeling of him touching her so deeply. When her nerve endings stopped frying, she managed to ask, "What're you doing, Cooper?"

In the pale wash of moonlight, she saw one dark eyebrow lift. "I would have thought that was obvious."

She sucked in a breath as he shifted his grip on her and stroked a nearly electrically charged nubbin of flesh.

"Yes," Kara choked out a laugh that was just the tiniest bit hysterical. "I guess I meant, *why?* Why are you…we…" she lifted her hips, arching into his hand, "…oh, boy, that really feels so good."

"Yeah," he murmured, dusting a hard, brief kiss on her mouth. "It really does."

Fighting to maintain, to hold onto some semblance of her dignity—which Kara was beginning to think was way overrated—she shook her head on the pillow and demanded, "Is this some sort of sympathy thing?"

"What?"

"You know," she said, pausing as his fingers once again plumbed her depths, pressing, stroking. "Wow, you're good at this," she said even while her brain shrieked at her to think.

"It's a gift," he said, kissing her again, drawing the tip of his tongue along her bottom lip.

Deliberately, she focused her splintering concentration even while her hips rocked, setting a rhythm she ached to give herself up to. "But Cooper—I don't want a pity orgasm."

"Huh?"

"I've been sick and you want to make me feel better and—"

"You're crazy," he said, his voice filled with wonder. "I never knew that about you."

"I'm not crazy," she countered, trying not to notice that he was rubbing that sensitive spot again, "I'm just not interested in a 'poor little Kara, let's give her a ride' night."

His hand on her stilled, his palm pressed tight against her heat. "What're you talking about?"

"Come on, Cooper," she said, fighting to keep from begging him to rub her again. To stroke her inside and out. To push her over the edge into those fireworks she remembered so well from their one night together.

Her hips moved again, seemingly of their own accord. Apparently her body was smarter than she was. It didn't care why he was offering up an orgasm, it just wanted one.

But Kara ignored the tantalizing rush of sensation. Fought to keep her mind focused on what she knew to be true. To keep her from allowing him to do something that would mean nothing to him and, therefore, little to her.

Shaking her head, she met his gaze and said it, plain and simple. "You saw me sick as a dog, Cooper. You can't be feeling attracted to me after that disgusting display, so this has got to be some warped sense of a good deed—or—I don't know."

"You *are* nuts," Cooper said, spearing his fingers

up into her damp heat again, groaning as her head tipped back into the pillows.

"Cooper…"

"Look at me," he ordered thickly, his voice a raw scrape of sound. When her gaze was locked with his, he said, "I've been wanting you for days. I even wanted you when you were sick. Hell, there you were, bent over a toilet and all I could think about was what a cute behind you've got. How twisted is *that?*"

Kara ground her hips against his hand. "Really?"

"Really." He stroked her inner folds, driving her to the brink of desperation, only to pull her back from the edge and taunt her toward it again. "And," he said, dipping his head to claim a kiss, "I know you're still exhausted. Haven't had a good night's sleep in three nights, and am I letting you rest? Nope. I'm waking you up and hoping to hell you want me as badly as I want you."

"Really?"

"Will you stop saying that?" He dropped another kiss on her mouth, ran the tip of his tongue across her lips.

"Right," she murmured, expelling a long breath on a deep groan.

"So? Are you with me here, Kara? Or should I let you go to sleep?"

"Who needs sleep?" she asked breathlessly, opening her thighs for him, reaching up to wrap her arms around his neck.

"I was so hoping you'd say that," he admitted, dipping his head to nibble at the line of her throat as she tilted her head back, deeper into the pillow.

Kara finally stopped thinking.

Stopped questioning his motives.

And gave herself up to the pure pleasure swamping her.

Again and again, his clever fingers worked on her body even as he slid farther down and used his free hand to push up the hem of the T-shirt she wore. When her breasts were bared to the moonlight, he took first one hardened nipple into his mouth and then the other. Over and over, he suckled her, drawing on her skin as if trying to sip her being into his.

Dizzying sensations jolted through her and Kara could hardly keep up with them all. It felt as though her entire body were on fire and she encouraged the flames. She wanted them hotter, brighter. She wanted to be engulfed in the heat that was Cooper.

Shifting over her, he moved down her body, trailing damp kisses along her flesh. She grabbed at him, trying to pull him up for a kiss. To feel his mouth on her own. But he neatly avoided her grasping hands and settled himself between her thighs with an anticipatory sigh.

Opening her eyes, she looked at him and her breath caught. In the wash of moonlight pearling through the windows, his dark eyes gleamed with temptation and his tanned, hard body shone like marble.

"Cooper…"

"Shut up, Kara," he whispered with a smile. Then he lifted her hips off the mattress, slung her legs over his shoulders and covered her heat with his mouth.

She shrieked.

Kara heard her own voice ricocheting off the walls, but she couldn't care. Couldn't do anything but feel.

His lips, teeth and tongue took her higher, faster than anything ever had before. She fisted her hands in the sheet beneath her, trying desperately to keep that one little grip on sanity as her brain fractured in a wash of fiery sparks.

He suckled her here, too. And while his mouth did amazing things to her, he managed to slide one finger into her depths, doing to her from the inside what his mouth was accomplishing on the outside.

"Too much," she whispered brokenly. "All too much. I can't. Cooper, I can't—"

He chuckled and her eyes went wide even as her body stiffened at the approaching climax. She felt it build at a fever pitch and wondered absently if she'd survive. Then she knew she didn't care. She would risk anything to feel this. To have this man in this moment.

That one sensitive bud at her core felt as though it were electrified and when Cooper lapped at it with the tip of his tongue, Kara shrieked again. His big hands cupped her behind and held her steady as she shouted his name and rocked her hips wildly in his grasp.

Releasing her death grip on the sheets, she reached for him and as a raw, charging fury raced through her body, she held his head to her and watched him as he took her over the edge.

Her body still trembling, still humming with the incredible power of her orgasm, Cooper knew he couldn't wait another moment. He had to be inside her. Had to feel her body surrounding his, feel the internal tremors as her muscles fisted around his length, squeezing him dry.

Heart pounding erratically, Cooper laid her down onto the mattress and stretched out a hand to the bedside table. Blindly, desperately, he yanked the drawer open and didn't even blink when it fell free of the table and landed upside down on the floor. He couldn't care about anything. Not now. Not after tasting her surrender. Not after holding her while a storm crested within her.

Not after experiencing Kara's climax with a force stronger than anything he'd ever known.

His only thought now was to feel it again. To be inside her when it came, to push himself so high and so deep within her body that the climax they would share would be incredible.

"Cooper…?"

"Just a minute." He scrambled off the edge of the bed, tossed the drawer to one side and grabbed up one of the foil packets that had fallen out. Quickly, he unwrapped it, sheathed himself and was back on the bed. His only regret was that he had to wear the damn condom in the first place. He wanted, more than anything, to feel her slick warmth on his skin. To feel the matchstick heat of sensation that could only come from two bodies, sliding together, unprotected from each other.

But he was too smart and too concerned for Kara to take that kind of chance.

Her arms opened to him as he rejoined her on the bed and he kissed her, taking her mouth while the taste of her body was still with him. His tongue swept inside her mouth, exploring, stroking, silently demanding.

And she gave as good as she got.

Their tongues met in an erotic dance, twining together, twisting, caressing until neither of them could draw a breath without a struggle. Her hands dropped from his back and tugged at the fabric of the shirt she still wore.

Groaning, Cooper eased back up and in one quick movement, had the shirt up and over her head and tossed into a heap on the floor.

"Better," she said, lifting her head from the pillow to claim his mouth again. She nibbled at his bottom lip and he felt an answering tug of need deep in the core of him.

"Gotta have you," he whispered, his lips moving over hers hungrily. Not enough, his brain shouted.

Not nearly enough. He wanted to taste every square inch of her body. Wanted her beneath him, over him, under him. He wanted her every way a man could want a woman and when they were finished, he wanted to do it all again.

And again.

"Yes," she said, moving to accommodate him as he shifted, kneeling between her legs.

He entered her with one swift thrust and she gasped at the invasion. Cooper paused, throwing his head back, staring blindly at the ceiling, concentrating solely on the lush feel of his body embedded in hers. But in an instant, need crowded within him and pushed him onward.

Bracing his hands at either side of her head, he rocked his hips against hers. She lifted her legs high, helping him to go deeper. He bent his head, tasted her nipples, rolling his tongue across their pebbly tips, one after the other. His hips pistoned, her sighs and moans echoed his. She tossed her head from side to side on the pillow. Licked her lips.

The sight of her tongue, darting across her parted lips enflamed him and Cooper bent to meet it. Then, staring into her eyes, he watched as flames erupted within her. Watched as passion glazed the surface of her deep green eyes and sparkled with the rush of completion.

He felt the clawing, clamoring ache within and fought to hold it off. He wanted it to last. Wanted this moment to never end. And in fact, the only reason he finally gave into his own release was because the only way to do this over again was to allow the climax to happen.

Her body erupted beneath his.

She called his name, her voice breaking.

And an instant later, Cooper groaned and followed her into the abyss.

Hours passed as they found each other again and again. Every muscle in Kara's body ached—and yet, she'd never felt more complete. More satisfied. Cooper had taken her in every way possible, she mused and in return, she'd taken him a couple of times, too.

And now, with the first streaks of dawn blurring the sky into a slow blossom of rich color, she lay in the circle of Cooper's arms and fell into an exhausted sleep…and a shared dream.

Cooper held her hand and Kara felt the warm strength of his fingers curled around hers. They stood in the parlor of the old Victorian—not as it was now, but as it had once been.

A piano stood in one corner of the room, sunlight streaming through the window to dance across the ivory keys. A paisley shawl was draped across the gleaming top of the piano and atop it, were a dozen or more framed, sepia-toned photographs. A black-

and-white cat was curled up in an overstuffed chair and at the wide front window, a woman stood.

Outlined in gilded light, she stared out the window at the road beyond, as if watching for someone. One hand to her mouth, she wrapped her other arm around her waist as if trying to comfort herself, when there was no comfort to be found.

Her quiet grief echoed in the room, and her tears looked like diamonds in the light. She kept watch, waiting for the lover who had promised to return. She walked from window to window, hope and fear keeping pace, her steps muffled on the carpets beneath her feet. Somewhere, a clock chimed out the hour and the woman's shoulders hunched with every soft gong.

Kara felt the woman's misery as if it were her own. Even the house itself seemed to throb with the pangs of the woman's agony. Time stood still, in this one little bubble of memory. For decades, the woman had been trapped—by her own pain and desperation and there didn't seem to be an end coming.

Kara looked up at Cooper and saw his eyes flash with pity just before a shutter dropped over them, locking her out.

She felt, as well as sensed, his withdrawal.

And in her sleep, Kara clung to him, afraid somehow that he would slip away from her and she would be left—like the crying woman—waiting for a love that would never be.

* * *

Cooper woke up first, half surprised to find that the dream was gone. Kara lay curled against him, her small hand on his chest. He covered it with one of his own, then reluctantly, let her go.

How had they shared that dream?

How had they been pulled into the ghost's pain and made to feel it with her? And how could he have forgotten, even for a second, the lessons he'd learned so long ago? Seeing the ghost as she'd once been, a young, beautiful woman who'd lost everything because she'd ventured to love, had reminded Cooper love meant pain.

Frowning, he eased out of the bed, stubbed his toe on the drawer, still laying on the floor, and bit back an angry oath. Staring down at the naked woman lying in his bed, something inside him turned over and he almost wished things could be different. But he knew, better than most, that they couldn't.

As if she felt his gaze on her, Kara woke up. Stirring languidly, she opened her eyes to meet his and gave him a tentative smile.

"Did we just—"

"Dream?" he asked, then nodded tightly, uneasy with the reborn feelings crashing around inside him. "Yeah, we must have."

"But how?"

"I don't know," he muttered and grabbed up his jeans off a nearby chair. He had to get out of that room. Had to keep from looking at Kara, or he'd slip. He'd forget about lessons learned and ghosts and old pains and lose himself in the arms of the woman who was, he suddenly realized, *way* too important to him. He couldn't let that happen, he told himself sternly, because he'd learned at a very early age, that to love only invited disaster.

"I'm going downstairs. Make some coffee."

"Cooper?"

He shook his head and chanced a quick look at her. Instantly, he realized his mistake. Love shone in her eyes and that terrified him. His heart went hard and cold in his chest and his throat tightened until he wasn't sure he'd be able to breathe.

He turned his back on her, because he couldn't look at her and not want her. Heading for the door, he grabbed hold of the brass knob, turned it and paused, door partially opened. "I'll bring you some coffee and maybe some eggs. I think you're well enough now to have some solid food."

"Okay," she said, her voice filled with questions he couldn't—wouldn't—answer. "But Cooper, we have to talk about—"

He shook his head and stepped out of the room. "Nothing to talk about, Kara. Dream's over. Time to wake up."

Ten

Two days later, things were still strained between Kara and Cooper. But actually, she thought, *strained* wasn't the right word. After all, he'd only reverted to normal.

He was back to being the closed off boss she knew so well. Distracted, preoccupied, Cooper spent most of his time locked away in his makeshift office. She heard the tapping of his fingers at the keyboard, but rarely saw him all day.

They still had dinner together in the kitchen, but there was no lighthearted chitchat. No teasing, no laughter. Nor was there any hint that their night of lovemaking was still haunting him as it was her.

The long nights passed slowly, Kara's only company, a ghost with whom she was beginning to think she had far too much in common.

"Serious thoughts?"

Kara looked up as Maggie approached and found a half-hearted smile to offer. "Very," she admitted and shifted her gaze to Cooper, standing on the opposite side of his grandfather's yard, talking to Jeremiah and Sam.

If he felt her gaze on him, he didn't let her know. He stood slightly apart from the other two men, as if keeping a careful distance even from his family. It broke Kara's heart, but she didn't have a clue how to fight it.

Maggie eased down onto the chair beside Kara's and stretched her long tanned legs out in front of her. She cupped her right hand over her still flat abdomen as if stroking the tiny child nestled within. "Oh, the shade feels great. I swear it's at least ten degrees cooler under this tree."

"Mmm-hmm." Kara was only half listening. Most of her focus was on Cooper. The heat rippled the air and made his image waver slightly as if he were already no more substantial than a dream. She squelched a sigh as she realized she couldn't even imagine her life without Cooper in it. But she would have to find a way to move on. Still, she couldn't look away from him. She'd made up her mind to finally leave him and now, all she had left were these unguarded times when she could look at him and store up as many mental snapshots as she could.

"You haven't told him that you love him, have you?"

Kara shot Maggie a glance, then shook her head. "No. There's no point. Trust me, it's not something he wants to hear."

"Maybe it's something he *needs* to hear, though," Maggie insisted, lifting her hair off her neck and then twisting it into a ponytail with a rubber band she tore off her wrist.

Kara would like to think so, but even knowing that Maggie meant well, the other woman didn't know Cooper as well as Kara did.

"Sam was the same way," Maggie continued, her voice softening as she shifted her gaze to where the three men stood talking. Sam and his grandfather were laughing at something and Cooper, aloof and alone, stood watching.

"What do you mean?" Kara asked, more to be polite than from real interest.

"I think what happened to Mac affected all of the cousins," Maggie said. "I know it's haunted Sam all these years, so I'm sure Cooper and Jake feel the same way. I mean, if you think about it, they were all only kids. And to have your cousin die like that…right in front of you…it must have been terrible for all of them."

Something cold slithered through Kara as she slowly swiveled her head to look at the woman sitting beside her.

Maggie caught her expression and read it correctly. She winced. "You didn't know any of this, did you?"

"No." God, it hurt to admit that. She'd been closer to Cooper than anyone else in his life for the last five years and he'd never said a word. Never let her in. Never gave a hint that there was something so horribly traumatic in his past. Here then was the reason for his withdrawal from life. For his refusal to let anyone past the walls he'd erected around his heart.

"I'm so sorry." Maggie reached out and laid her hand on Kara's. "I never would have said anything, but I assumed you knew."

"It's not your fault," Kara said, fighting the swell of regret and disappointment rising inside her.

"God, I'm an idiot."

"Tell me," Kara urged quietly.

"I don't know…" Maggie shook her head and looked as though she wished she were anywhere but there at the moment.

"Maggie, I have to know."

The other woman sighed, glanced at the men across the yard, then back to Kara. "Yes, I think you do."

While she talked, Kara's heart sank further. With every word she heard, the connection she'd felt to Cooper unraveled just a bit more. Like an old tapestry being torn apart, the fragile threads of their years together disintegrated. Tears filled her eyes, not only for the boy Cooper had once been and the tragedy of that long-ago summer day…but for the man he was now because of it. For chances lost, dreams crushed.

And Kara finally admitted the hard truth that she'd resisted for so long.

Cooper would never allow himself to love her.

Cooper watched Maggie and Kara, sitting in the shade of the old oak tree and wondered what the two women were talking about. Meanwhile, Jeremiah's and Sam's voices rattled in his ears, but he wasn't really listening. It was as if he was standing behind a glass wall. He could see them, but he was apart from them.

Hell, he'd been apart from everything for days now. Since he and Kara had shared that dream. Memories clouded his brain all the time. Whenever he closed his eyes, he saw Mac's face. He remembered that summer day fifteen years ago and how he'd vowed that he would never lose someone he loved again.

And the secret to that was to never love.

Caring too much was simply an invitation to pain.

That was why he'd cut himself off from his grandfather and his cousins. Losing Mac had hit him hard. As a kid, you think yourself immortal. Invulnerable. Learning differently had cut him nearly in two. Then his parents had died not long after that summer, reinforcing his decision to keep himself separate from any kind of closeness.

All he cared about now were his books. The imaginary people he interacted with on a daily basis. When one of them died, it didn't tear him up. Didn't rip out his heart and soul and leave it battered and bloody on the ground.

But then there was Kara. The feelings she pulled from him terrified him, plain and simple. A humbling thing for a man to admit, but there it was. He didn't want to care, damn it. And he resented like hell that she'd awakened something in him that had been long—and safely—dead.

And as much as he wanted to stalk across the yard, pull Kara from her chair and drag her home to bed…he knew that road could only end in pain.

So he stayed where he was. On the outside, looking in. Every night, he lay awake in his bed, afraid to sleep for fear of seeing Mac die again. And he couldn't lose himself in Kara because he knew he couldn't give her what she wanted and this way, though it cost him, he was able to spare Kara any more pain than was necessary.

He wasn't a complete idiot. He'd seen that happy little glow in her eyes the morning after they'd loved each other half to death. The shine of joy and pleasure and the dream of tomorrow had all been written there in her expression.

And he knew damn well that ignoring her now was hurting her. But how much better to be hurt now than devastated later? If he let her believe that there could be a future for them only to back away? No. It was better this way.

Not easier.

Better.

"What do you think?" Sam asked, snapping his fingers in front of Cooper's face.

"What?" He scowled at his cousin.

"Jeremiah and I were talking about re-doing Gran's old sewing room as a nursery," Sam said, and the tone of his voice said that this wasn't the first time he'd said it. "I asked what you thought."

"I think it's none of my business," Cooper pointed out and looked away from the slow head shake of disapproval his grandfather sent him.

"You're a big help," Sam muttered. "What the hell's wrong with you, anyway?"

"Not a damn thing," he said, disgusted that he'd let his own feelings be seen so easily. Starting for the house, he asked, "I'm going for a beer. You two want one?"

"Yeah," Sam said.

"Not for me." Jeremiah lifted his still half-full bottle in explanation.

"Fine." Cooper stalked across the grassy yard and headed for the house as a dying man in the desert aimed for the only oasis for miles. He just needed a little space. Some time alone. Some time to get away from everyone who was watching him in either hope or disappointment.

He couldn't give any of them what they wanted. Didn't they see that?

As he hit the front step, he paused to listen. The low growl of a motorcycle engine cut through the air and halted Jeremiah and Sam's conversation. The deep rumble of power rolled toward them, heralding the approach of a man who could only be Jake, the last Lonergan cousin.

Beer forgotten for the moment, Cooper stood stock-still and waited.

Sheba, the puppy who thought of herself as a Great Dane, set up a barking, howling discord to alert everyone just in case they hadn't heard the same noise she had. Then the little dog ran to Jeremiah and cowered behind his overall-clad legs as a huge motorcycle, chrome gleaming, prowled into the yard.

Sam and Jeremiah were there in seconds, leaving Cooper to study the situation from a safe distance. Jake turned off the engine and climbed off the bike, one hand extended to Sam. Jake's long black hair fell down the middle of his back in a ponytail. He wore a white T-shirt, black jeans and scuffed black boots that looked as though they'd walked to hell and back. A United States Marine Corps tattoo colored Jake's right bicep and two days' worth of beard shadowed his jaws. He yanked off wraparound sunglasses as he grinned at Sam.

"Good to see you, man."

"You, too. Nice bike."

"It rides," Jake said with a shrug, then turned to grin at his grandfather. "Jeremiah. You're looking a lot less dead than I expected."

"Good to have you home, boy," the older man said and swept his last remaining grandson into a fierce embrace.

Maggie and Kara were headed across the yard toward the commotion when Jake turned to look at Cooper. "There's the World Famous Author," he said, his tone putting the words in capital letters. "Read the last one. Scared the hell outta me."

Cooper smiled and walked the few steps toward his cousin. "Thanks." Then he held out one hand and as his cousin grabbed it, he said, "It's good to see you, Jake."

The Lonergan boys were together again.

Was he the only one feeling Mac's absence so intensely?

"Same here." Then Jake's dark eyes lit up as he spotted the women. "And who are the gorgeous ladies?" he asked, a well-practiced smile on his face.

"Cut your engines," Sam said, laughing, as he grabbed Maggie into a tight hug. "This one's mine."

"Well then," Jake continued, not even missing a beat as he stepped up to Kara and gave her a wink, "That leaves you and me. Unless…" he turned to look at Cooper, a question in his eyes.

Everything in Cooper yearned to knock Jake back a step. To drape one arm around Kara's shoulder and announce that she was *his*. But he couldn't do it. Not to her. Not to himself.

Instead, he forced himself to shrug and said, "Jake, this is Kara. My..." Did she take a breath and hold it? Waiting to see how he would introduce her? Could anyone else in the yard feel that near tangible tension that suddenly sprang up between them? Or was he imagining more than was there? "...assistant," he finally finished and then he watched as the expectant light in Kara's eyes flickered out.

Coolly then, as if she and Cooper hadn't just shared a knowing look, she gave her hand to Jake and smiled up at him. "It's a pleasure to meet you. Cooper's told me nothing about you."

Jake took her hand and threaded it through the curve of his arm. "I can take care of that," he said and gave her another wink. "As soon as I get some food in me. It's been a long ride."

"Hell, yes," Jeremiah shouted enthusiastically, as if trying to fill the sudden, yawning void that had opened up in front of them. "We've got steaks in the fridge. Sam, fire up the grill and Maggie, how about you and Kara do up some potatoes?"

"No problem," Maggie retorted and slipped out of Sam's grasp with a quick kiss. Then as she passed Kara, she asked, "Mind helping me out?"

"Not a bit," Kara said smoothly and stepped away from Jake.

As she walked past Cooper, he caught her scent

on the air and inhaled deeply. He whispered her name, not sure what it was he wanted to say—or even if there was anything he could say that would make things less awkward between them. All he knew was, he had to try.

But if she heard, she paid no attention. She deliberately passed him by, as if he weren't even there.

And wasn't that what he wanted?

Kara wanted to cry, but damn it, she wasn't going to.

She'd done this to herself and she knew it. That knowledge though, didn't make this any easier to take. She'd set herself up. Let herself dream idle fantasies about Cooper and how it could be for them.

But the simple truth was, Cooper didn't want her. A couple of nights between the sheets—no matter how fabulous they'd been—didn't make a relationship. And she wasn't willing to settle for anything less.

Now, after talking to Maggie and spending the evening watching Cooper avoid being drawn into stories about the old days, she knew there was no more hope. He hadn't only pulled away from her, he'd also shut himself away from his own family.

"What're you doing?"

Cooper's voice came from behind her and though it startled her, she didn't turn around to look at him. Instead, she picked up her yellow blouse from the bed, folded it neatly and tucked it into the open suitcase in front of her.

"I'm leaving."

"What?" He stepped into the room, walked to her side and stared from the suitcase to her. "*Now?*"

"Yes, now." She swallowed hard, inhaled sharply and blinked furiously, to keep any tears at bay. She wouldn't cry in front of him. Wouldn't let him see that her heart was breaking.

"Were you even going to tell me?"

She glanced at him. His mouth was grim, lips pressed tightly together. "Of course I was, Cooper." She reached past him for the denim skirt she'd brought with her and never wore. Folding it neatly, she laid it into the case. "Besides, I already gave you my two weeks' notice, remember?"

"Yeah, but—" He stalked to the end of the bed, then came right back again. "I didn't think you meant it."

"Now you know."

"Damn it, Kara…" He shoved both hands through his hair then pushed them into the back pockets of his jeans. "What's this really about? I know you like your job, so—"

"Cooper," she said on a sigh, "you know darn well what it's about."

"It's about us, then." He nodded stiffly, pulled one hand free of his pocket to scrape it across his face. "It's about the other night and that dream and the damn ghost and—"

Kara shook her head, grabbed up the last of her blouses and tucked it away. "This has *nothing* to do with the ghost and *everything* to do with us. Well, me, really."

"Kara," he said softly, voice filled with regret, "I just can't give you what you want."

Oh, she knew that. Felt it. Deep in her bones. And she wanted to weep with the knowledge. But that wouldn't do the slightest bit of good.

"Cooper," she said softly, lifting her gaze to his. "Why didn't you tell me about Mac?"

He backed up a step and stared at her for a long minute. "Where did you—oh. Maggie."

"Yes, Maggie."

"She shouldn't have told you."

"You're right," Kara said quietly. "You should have."

He shook his head firmly, shutting out her statement and the remote chance that she might be right. "It was a long time ago."

"No," she argued. "For you, it was yesterday."

He sucked in a gulp of air. "I don't want to talk about this."

"I know that, too," she said and walked to him. Laying both hands on his arms, she felt the tension in his muscles. Felt the rigid self-control he was drawing on and her heart hurt for him. "It wasn't your fault, Cooper. It wasn't anyone's fault."

He blew out a breath. "You don't know."

"Maggie told me what happened."

"She wasn't there. Neither were you."

"You were a kid, Cooper."

He stepped out from under her touch and the shutters were back in his eyes, closing her out. "So was Mac."

The tips of her fingers still hummed with warmth as if she could still feel his skin beneath hers. But there was no point in pretending any longer. There would be no future with a man who couldn't see past his own pain to the promise of something beautiful.

Still, she had to try to help him. One last time. "There was nothing you could have done. Maggie told me that Mac broke his neck when he jumped in."

Cooper actually flinched at her words as if they were a physical blow. He swallowed hard and jerked a nod. "He did. He was trying to beat Jake and his jump did it. But he had to stay underwater longer, too."

Kara tried reaching out for him, but he shook his head firmly. "You wanted to know, well here's what Maggie couldn't tell you," he said tightly. "Sam wanted to go in after Mac. He was worried. Jake was pissed off about losing, but I was *glad*." He slapped one hand against his chest as a choked off, harsh laugh shot from his throat. "I was *happy* that Mac was staying under so long. Glad Jake was finally getting beaten. *I* talked Sam into waiting longer. If I hadn't..." his voice trailed off. "We'll never know

now. We might have saved him. If I'd just gone along with Sam and jumped in after Mac, he might still be alive. So don't tell me you understand. You couldn't."

"No," Kara said softly, empathetic pain rippling through her in response to the torment she read in Cooper's eyes—heard in his voice. "I can't know what you feel. What your regrets are. But I do know that Mac wouldn't want you torturing yourself forever over something that can't be changed."

His mouth worked as if he were grinding his teeth. "I loved him like a brother. And he died while we all stood there like morons."

"You didn't know."

"We *should* have known," Cooper countered quickly. "Should have felt it. And we didn't. And the misery of that day is still with me. I won't love somebody like that again, Kara. I won't risk it."

"I'm so sorry," she said as one stray tear escaped the corner of her eye and trickled down her cheek. "For Mac. For all of you." She inhaled sharply and added, "And I'm sorry for us."

Then she turned, walked back to the bed and closed her suitcase. She zipped it shut, the sound overly loud in the strained silence. Picking it up, she slung her purse over her shoulder and turned for one last look at Cooper.

"I'm going to your grandfather's. Maggie said I could stay in the guesthouse until my flight tomorrow night."

"You don't have to leave."

"Yes," she said, "I really do."

She walked to the open doorway and paused on the threshold to look back at him again. His gaze was locked on her and she wished desperately she could know what he was thinking, feeling. But Cooper had become too adept at hiding those feelings from everyone—including himself—to give anything away now.

"Be happy, Cooper," she said, then turned and walked away.

Eleven

Cooper was still standing where she'd left him, dumbfounded by the fact that Kara had actually gone, when he heard the front door open, then swing shut behind her. Silence pounded through the old house like hammer blows. He couldn't believe it. Kara. Gone.

Her image still fresh in his mind, he saw the hurt in her eyes and closed his own in a futile attempt to make that vision disappear. Instead, it became more clear.

"Damn it," he whispered into the empty room, feeling more alone than he ever had before. "I'd love you if I could, Kara. But it's too late for us."

Instantly, icy cold dropped onto the room as if an invisible blizzard was blowing through. Wind whistled around him, punching at him, driving him toward the doorway. His hair lifted in the swirling, chilly blast and he grabbed the doorjamb and hung on.

Throat tight, heart pounding, he looked around the bedroom in disbelief. A roar rose up with the wind and became a wild, frantic moan of pain. Framed pictures lifted off the walls and sailed in a wide, frigid circle. The overhead light flickered on and off in a frenzied flash like a strobe light in a nightclub. The mirror over the dresser shattered and reflective shards snapped into the room, landing on the floor in a tumble of jagged pieces.

Cooper let go of the doorjamb and braced his feet, leaning into the overpowering wind, determined to stand his own against the fury of the ghost. He stared at the mess and shouted to be heard above the wind, his breath misting in front of his face. "Knock it off! I don't owe you anything, you know!"

The wild keening became louder still and raised goose bumps on his flesh. His stomach dropped and he swallowed back a knot of pure adrenaline pumping through him. The painful, throbbing moan seemed to slice into his soul with an agony that was too deep for description.

And still the wind howled, pictures whirled in ever tightening circles and frost formed on the inside of the windows.

"She's gone and I can't stop her!"

More wailing, higher pitched, frantic.

The walls trembled and the wind screamed.

"I don't take orders from ghosts," he shouted, still trying to make himself heard. But even as those words sounded out in the room, a part of his brain argued with him.

Didn't he take orders from ghosts?

Wasn't everything he did because of Mac's ghost? Or at least the memory of him and what had happened so long ago?

Confusion rattled him and he staggered against the force of the cold battering at him. Was he really so different from the ghost trapped in this house?

Like him, hadn't she given up everything because of her own pain? Hadn't she spent the rest of her life, locked away in grief? Even in death, she stayed determined to shut out even the spirit of the man who was still trying to reach her.

She was so caught up in her own misery, she wasn't able to see a way out. Not then. Not now.

And suddenly, his own possible future stretched out in front of him and that, more than the ghostly cold, chilled Cooper to the bone.

"No," he muttered, shoving both hands through his hair and feeling the ice on his own fingertips. He wasn't like this trapped ghost. His situation was different.

But was it?

He'd cut himself off from love to protect himself from more pain. Kara had tried to get in, past the walls he'd put up around his heart and he'd shut her out. Hadn't this ghost done the same damn thing?

Wasn't she *still* doing it?

The wind abruptly died and the whirling pictures dropped to the floor with a clatter. The cold eased back and rivulets of water traced through the suddenly melting frost on the glass, as if the house were crying.

As the temperature in the room climbed back to normal Cooper stood stunned, like a survivor of a battle, and tried to make sense of his own thoughts.

Before it really was too late.

When a vehicle pulled into Jeremiah's yard an hour after she'd gone to bed, Kara sensed that it was Cooper. She lay awake, staring at the ceiling. She refused to get up and go to the window. Refused to look at him one more time, knowing that if she did, her resolve to leave would only weaken.

And she couldn't allow that.

Couldn't spend the rest of her life, waiting for Cooper to wake up and see that he had a right to live. To love.

So she burrowed under the quilt and willed herself into a restless sleep.

Cooper pounded on the back door of his grandfather's house. He glanced across the yard to the darkened guesthouse and fought the urge to go over there. To pound on the door and demand that Kara let him in.

Desperation ticked inside him like an over-wound clock. Turning back to the door in front of him, he pounded on it again, hard wood stinging his knuckles. He felt a tightly coiled spring inside him and wondered what would happen when it finally snapped.

When the door flew open, he staggered back a step and damn near fell off the back porch.

"Are you *nuts?*" Sam demanded, glaring at Cooper in the harsh glow of the porch light. "What the hell are you doing waking me up?"

"I need to talk to you." Cooper ignored his cousin's temper and pushed past Sam into the lamp lit kitchen. His sneakers squeaked on the linoleum as he paced a frantic route back and forth between the sink and the refrigerator. Stabbing his fingers through his hair repeatedly, he tried to shake loose the tumbling thoughts rolling through his brain, but he just couldn't make sense of them.

Which was why he'd come to Sam.

Sam had been there that day.

Sam knew what Cooper was living with because he had to live with it, too. But somehow, Sam had made it past the ugliness of that one day fifteen years ago. He'd made peace with Mac and Cooper desperately needed to know how he'd done it.

The door closed and Cooper looked at his cousin. Wearing only a pair of drawstring pajama bottoms,

Sam leaned back against the door, folded his arms across his bare chest and demanded, "What the hell is wrong with you, Cooper?"

"Nothing," he muttered, then corrected himself. "Everything."

"I'm gonna need more," Sam demanded, then headed to the fridge. Pulling out a jug of orange juice, he walked to a cupboard, took out two glasses and poured each of them a drink. Taking a sip, he said, "And keep it down, will you? Maggie spent most of the night heaving her guts up and she needs the rest."

"Sorry," Cooper said automatically, holding the small juice glass cupped in both palms. "But I had to see you."

"Okay," Sam said, picking up on the desperation wafting off Cooper in thick waves. He sat down at the table, pointed to a chair and said, "So here I am. Talk."

Cooper ignored the chair. He couldn't have sat still at the moment if his life had depended on it. Instead, he took a gulp of the OJ and said, "How'd you do it?"

"Do what?"

"Get past what happened to Mac." Cooper's gaze fixed on Sam in a steady stare. "I know you, Sam. You've spent the last fifteen years just like I have— just like Jake has. Avoiding family. Avoiding each other. All because of what happened that day."

Sam's gaze dropped to the glass of juice. "Yeah. I did."

"So what changed?"

He lifted his gaze again and shrugged. "I found Maggie."

"And just like that you could open up? You could change who you were?"

"Hell, no," Sam said, slumping back against the chair. "I didn't want to change. Didn't want to love her. Didn't want to stay here," he said, waving one hand to encompass the house, the ranch and all of Coleville. "But damn it, Cooper, I was tired of running from Mac."

"Is that what we're doing?" he asked thoughtfully. "Or are we running from what we didn't do that day?"

"A little of both, I think," Sam said. "Sit down, Cooper."

Slowly, Cooper sank onto the chair but kept his gaze fixed on his cousin. Quietly, he said, "Kara's leaving."

"I know."

"Of course you know," Cooper said with a strained chuckle. "She's *here.*"

"And are you letting her go?"

"I can't stop her." It tore at him. Everything in him wanted to leave this house, march across the yard and pound on the door of the guesthouse until she let him in. He wanted to bury himself inside her and let her warmth wrap around him.

But how could he do that?

"You're an idiot."

Cooper's gaze snapped back to Sam's. "Thanks. I feel better."

Leaning forward, bracing both arms on the tabletop, Sam shook his head and said, "You shouldn't feel better. Kara's leaving and you're not doing anything to prevent it. You should feel horrible."

"I do," Cooper admitted. "But damn it, how can I love her? How the hell can I do that after Mac?"

"What's Mac got to do with it?"

"You're a great one to say that."

"Right. Okay. I get it. But I got past that," Sam said. "I almost lost Maggie. Almost lost the child we made together." He shook his head slowly, in disbelief, as if even *he* could hardly understand the man who'd made so many bad choices. "Do you really think Mac would have wanted that? Do you believe Mac wants us all to suffer for the rest of our lives?"

"No, I don't," Cooper said grudgingly. God, he could still see Mac so clearly in his mind. Forever sixteen years old, his eyes shining with mischief, his wild laugh punching the air as he challenged his cousins to one daredevil stunt after another.

Mac had loved life so much. Had squeezed every drop of fun out of every damn day he'd had. He'd hate knowing his cousins had pretty much resigned from life because of him.

"But how do you get past the fear?" Cooper asked quietly, studying the surface of the orange juice as if it had the secrets of the world etched on top. "How do you let yourself love somebody that freely again without being terrified of losing it?"

"You don't," Sam said, just as quietly. "The fear's always there. I can't even imagine losing Maggie. The thought of it terrifies me."

"Comforting."

"But the love's always there, too," Sam told him. "And without that, all you've got is the fear. That's an empty way to live, Cooper."

"Yeah."

"So, if you came here looking for advice...here it is." Sam stood up and looked down at him. "Make peace with Mac. Lay the past to rest so you can have a future."

"I don't know that I can."

"If you can't..." Sam said, "If you're willing to let Kara go out of your life because you're too scared to let her in—"

"Yeah?"

"—Then you don't deserve her anyway." He picked up his orange juice, drained it, then set the glass on the kitchen counter. "Turn off the light and lock the door when you go."

Cooper knew the way to the lake.

Could have found his way there blindfolded.

Time ticked past though as it took him more than twice as long to walk the distance as it should have. Every step felt as though he were dragging his feet free of mud. His brain knew he had to go back to the lake—face what had happened so long ago.

But his heart ached at the thought of it.

Fifteen years had passed, but the land hadn't changed much. He slowly climbed the ridge in the pale wash of moonlight and in the distance, heard the high-pitched howl of a coyote serenade. A soft, cool wind with the taste of the ocean on it, swept across the open fields and tugged at Cooper's hair. He turned his face into it and paused long enough to settle the frantic race of his heartbeat.

He'd never intended to come back here. To this place. Never thought he'd be able to.

And as he made it to the top of the ridge and looked out over the dark water, dappled in moonlight, he felt the years pass away. Once again, he was sixteen, standing with his cousins at the top of the world.

He felt the sun, hot on his bare shoulders. Heard Jake cussing a blue streak because Mac had out-jumped him. Listened to Sam chuckle as he carefully studied the stopwatch, timing Mac's underwater stretch. And heard himself saying *Give him another few seconds, Sam. He really wants to beat Jake. And I want him to. Mac's okay. Stop being an old woman.*

Wincing now, Cooper stared out at the spot where Mac had landed that last time. And he kept staring, as if he could see through the water to where they'd eventually found Mac, stretched out on the bottom of the lake—already dead.

They'd tried CPR. They'd tried pushing the water from Mac's lungs.

But they were too late.

And they'd lost not only Mac that afternoon, but their own innocence and sense of invincibility.

"Mac?" Cooper's whisper came low and strained, as if that single word had been squeezed out of his throat grudgingly. "You still here?"

The wind pushed at him playfully and in his mind, he heard laughter. Mac's laughter. Cooper spun around, half expecting to see the tall, lanky kid striding up the ridge to join him.

And the disappointment at finding himself all alone was staggering.

Still, remembering the furious temper of the ghost he'd left behind at the Victorian, Cooper wondered if Mac's spirit was trapped at the lake. Was he here, even now, waiting for his cousins to come back and—*what?*

"What could you be waiting for? To hear us say we're sorry?" he asked the wind. "What good would that do?"

Toward the east, the sky was beginning to lighten into a soft violet, heralding the coming dawn. Hours must have passed since he'd left the ranch house. Amazing that he'd been walking for so long.

He lifted his gaze from the rippled surface of the lake to the star-studded sky overhead. "We *are* sorry, you know. For all the good it does. You died too young, Mac. And we miss you. All of us do."

Shaking his head, he admitted, "God, I've relived that day a thousand times. Over and over again in my mind, I've replayed what happened. And every time, I save you." His voice broke and his gaze dropped, back to the lake, where his young life had shattered so completely.

"I want you to know that, Mac. Every time I remember that day, we save you." He choked out a laugh and rubbed his hand across his face. "Of course, we didn't when it really counted...God, I wish I could change it. Wish I could bring you back. Or hell, even talk to you. I've missed you so damn much."

A freshening wind slapped at him again, throwing his hair across his eyes and he found himself smiling in spite of the knife-like pain twisting inside him. Was the wind Mac's way of telling him to stop beating himself up over the past?

Or was that just wishful thinking?

Hell, up to a few weeks ago, Cooper had never really believed in ghosts. Now, he was convinced that something of who you were survived death. It wasn't a complete end. Maybe death really was just a bend in the road, beyond which we can't see. Maybe there's more out there than any of us have ever imagined.

God, he hoped so.

Hoped Mac was having a great time wherever he was. But could he move on, knowing that those he'd left behind were all still trapped in reruns of that summer day?

Cooper had never known pain like he'd experienced that day fifteen years before. Because he'd deliberately avoided it. By never allowing himself to love that freely, deeply, he'd kept himself free from pain—but he'd also hidden away from real joy. He'd lived a half life—safe but alone. Hell, Mac had lived more in sixteen years than Cooper had in thirty-one.

He'd locked himself away from life in some self-appointed penance for something he couldn't have changed. He'd felt guilty being alive when Mac was dead. And maybe, he thought, if something of Mac lingered in this place, maybe it was because none of his cousins had been able to let him go.

He'd hate to think that.

The three of them—Cooper, Sam and Jake—had all grieved in their own way, but they'd all shared at least one trait. They'd stayed away. From here.

From memories of Mac.

Yet, there'd been so much more to Mac than that one last day. And instead of focusing on those memories, they'd all chosen to relive the tragedy over and over again.

What a waste.

What a pitiful way to remember a boy they'd all loved.

Suddenly exhausted as emotions churned inside, Cooper dropped onto the grassy ground, drew his knees up and wrapped his arms around them. In the moonlight and the still chill of the night, Cooper felt the ice around his heart shatter and fall away. The cold he'd lived with for so long began to melt and he drew his first easy breath in fifteen long years.

Stretching out on the dewy grass, Cooper closed his eyes and felt the exhaustion of the complete release of tension seep through him like a rising tide. The aches and misery of years washed away, leaving him with only the memories of the good times they'd all had.

Of the summers that would live forever.

Of the boy who'd died too young, but had lived a lifetime in sixteen short years.

And in his mind, he saw Mac again. Young and laughing. Running up the ridge and leaping out into the lake—fearless, joyful.

Cooper smiled and whispered, "Thanks, Mac."

Twelve

Cooper woke with a jolt.

Sunlight streamed into his eyes and he squinted instantly in self-defense. A moment or two of complete confusion rattled through him. Where the hell was he and how did he—

The lake. He sat straight up and stared down from the ridge at the dark blue water below. Sunlight skittered off the surface, twinkling like downed stars.

He rubbed his eyes and stood up, stretching aching muscles. Not the most comfortable place to spend the night, he thought, but at the same time, it had been the best sleep he'd had in fifteen years. He'd finally come to terms with Mac.

Sorrow balled in the pit of his stomach, but this was a sweet sadness for something long missed. Not the lurch of guilt and pain that had so long been a part of his life.

"Kara was right," he said aloud, then shot a quick look at his watch. *Kara.*

She was leaving and he had to stop her. Had to try to make her see that he wasn't a complete loss. That he'd finally found a way to look ahead. To look into his own future and when he did, all he saw was her.

Then, as if Mac were standing right there beside him, he heard his cousin's voice say, *What're you waiting for? Go get her.*

Grinning, Cooper turned around and started running toward the ranch—toward Kara.

"Thanks for the ride," Kara said, reaching into the backseat to pull out her suitcase.

"Not a problem," Maggie told her and closed the door for her. "But are you sure about this? You've got a long day of just sitting at the airport waiting for your plane."

Kara inhaled sharply, deeply and glanced around at the people jostling for space at curb side check-in. Then she shifted her gaze back to Maggie. The woman stared at her with sympathy in her eyes, and though Kara appreciated the thought, she really didn't want to acknowledge it. And, if she'd spent the day at the ranch, she'd have been faced with that sympathy all day. Not only from Maggie, but from Sam and Jeremiah and even Jake.

And, there was always the chance that Cooper might drop by the ranch house. No. It was better this way. She'd rather spend the day at the airport than risk running into Cooper one more time.

"Don't worry about me," she chirped, putting a little too much cheer into her voice, "I've got a good book and a pile of magazines to read."

Maggie nodded as if she understood every thought that was racing through Kara's mind. "Okay. But if it's okay with you, when I get back to the ranch, I think I'll give Cooper a good hard kick."

Unexpectedly, a sheen of tears bristled at the backs of her eyes and Kara smiled tightly. "Thanks," she said and instinctively leaned in for a hug. Then before she could change her mind, she grabbed hold of the suitcase handle and headed for the terminal.

"Kara!" Cooper pounded on the door of the guesthouse, then moved to the front window. Stepping through the jungle of geraniums planted before it, he cupped his hands on the window glass and peered into the dark house. "Kara, damn it, open the door! I need to talk to you!"

Nothing.

"What the hell are you up to?" Sam called out from across the yard.

Cooper spun around. "I'm looking for Kara. Where is she?"

Sam leaned one shoulder against a porch post and lifted a cup of coffee for a sip. "She came here to get away from you, Cooper."

Pushing through the geraniums that fought him every inch of the way, Cooper stomped across the grassy dirt and stood at the bottom of the steps, glaring at his cousin. "Don't get in the middle of this, Sam."

"Get in?" Sam countered with a sneer, "You're the one who *dragged* me in, remember? Weren't you just here last night complaining to me?"

"Yeah," he admitted. "I was." Scraping one hand along the side of his head, he pushed his hair back then let his hand drop in disgust. "But things're different now. I—" He shut up suddenly and demanded, "Where is she?"

"She's gone."

"Gone?" Panic bubbled up in his throat but Cooper swallowed it. "What do you mean, *gone?*"

"What's all the shouting about?" Jeremiah demanded, stepping out onto the porch beside Sam. "Oh, Cooper. It's you."

"Yeah, it's me."

Sheba hurtled out the back door, squeezing through the legs of the two men to throw herself joyfully at Cooper. Bounding at his legs, she yapped and barked and ran in dizzying circles around him in a bid for attention. Cooper was too focused to notice.

"Man, can't a guy even get any sleep in the country?" Jake's grumble rolled over the puppy's gleeful barking in a growl of complaint. "I've slept in train stations quieter than this place."

"Great." Cooper threw his hands high, then let them fall again. "Everybody here now?" Narrowing a look at Sam, he demanded, "Where's Kara?"

"Why should I tell you?"

Jake grabbed Sam's coffee and took a long gulp. "Hey, get your own."

Jake ignored him, only mumbling, "Tell him where she is, already, huh? And somebody shut that dog up."

"Still a prizewinner in the morning, aren't you?" Jeremiah snapped, then said, "Sheba! Cut it out."

The puppy immediately quieted and plopped her butt onto the ground beside Cooper, all the while managing to still wag her tail and squirm in place.

"Damn it Sam, tell me," Cooper said, ignoring the others. "Please."

Sam studied him for a long minute before making up his mind. Finally though, he nodded, took his cup back from Jake and looked at Cooper. "Maggie took her to the airport. She went early I think, to avoid seeing you again."

Cooper winced as the truth of that statement hit him like a slap. God, he'd been an idiot. The question was, was it too late to make up for it?

"Thanks," he said and headed for Jeremiah's beat-up ranch truck. "I'll bring the truck back later."

"Boy," Jeremiah shouted, taking the first couple of steps. "Wait up a minute there. I've got something I've got to say to the three of you and—"

Cooper never even looked back. "It'll have to wait, Jeremiah." He opened the truck door, climbed inside and fired up the engine. Slamming the door shut again, he threw the car into Drive, punched the gas pedal and muttered, "I've got something way more important to say. I only hope she'll listen."

"Hey!" A security guard shouted as Cooper parked the truck in front of the terminal and bailed out. "You can't leave that thing there!"

He didn't have time to move it. Didn't care enough to worry about it. His brain was focused on one thing. Kara. She was all that mattered now.

She was *all.*

"Have it towed," he shouted back and hit the automatic double doors in such a hurry they didn't have time to swing open for him. He'd worry about the truck later. Pay the fines, whatever.

Right now, he had to find her.

His gaze swept the crowd. People. Too many people. The noise level was immense. Kids cried, parents soothed, teenagers up against a wall, kissing goodbye as if facing Armageddon. Huge suitcases rolled across the gleaming linoleum, their steel wheels growling a warning at anyone in their way. A disembodied voice shimmied through the speaker system, but the words were garbled, as if the speaker was talking around a mouthful of marbles.

Cooper's gaze swung back and forth, searching every face. Stalking through the crowd, pushing through the congested terminal, he checked the television screens for arrival and departure times and located the gate that Kara's plane would be using.

He sprinted down the long, narrow passage, slipping in and out of the crowd, mumbling apologies, but never stopping. Never slowing. His heart raced and his brain moved even faster. One speech after another rose up in his mind, was considered, then rejected. He had to make her see. Understand.

Had to make her *believe*.

But how?

Just outside security, his gaze shifted quickly over the people standing in line until he found the one face he'd been searching for. Kara. She stood alone, staring into space.

His heart twisted in his chest and he swallowed hard. This was it. And if he blew it, he'd never forgive himself.

Hurrying to her, he stopped right in front of her and waited as she slowly lifted her gaze to his. He saw surprise and pleasure light up her eyes before those emotions were extinguished and buried under a sheen of regret.

He felt the solid punch of her pain as if it were a blow to his midsection, but he couldn't let it stop him. "I've been looking for you," he said inanely.

"I left the ranch early so I wouldn't have to see you again," she admitted.

"Yeah, I figured that out. And I don't blame you," he said. Reaching for her hands, he held them in both of his and tightened his grip when she would have pulled free. "Don't. Kara, please. You've gotta listen to me."

Hope lit up her eyes briefly, then was gone again in a wink. But the fact that it had been there at all, gave Cooper reason for a little hope himself.

"I really think we've said everything, Cooper."

"Not by a long shot," he argued, then fixed a steely stare on a businessman type who wandered up to take his place in line behind her. The man got the message and scuttled off quickly.

"Fine," she said. "Say what you came to say and then go, okay?"

"I'm an idiot."

Both of her eyebrows lifted. "Interesting start."

He gave her a half smile and squeezed her hands briefly. "There's more."

"I'm listening," she said and he could see her take a deep breath and hold it.

Shaking his head, Cooper searched for the right words but couldn't find them. "Damn it, I'm a writer.

I should be good at this. But now, when I need them the most, the words aren't there."

Hope was back in her eyes and just a hint of a smile was on her mouth. "Give it your best shot."

"Okay." Nodding, he said, "I'll say the most important part first and work back around to it again later."

She nodded, waiting.

"I love you."

She sucked in a gulp of air and tears began to glitter in her eyes. Panic jolted inside him.

"I don't want you to cry," he said desperately. "I wanted to make you happy. Make *us* happy."

"Then keep talking," she urged.

"You were right," he said, figuring every woman loved to hear that—especially when it was true. "I should have told you about Mac. Hell, I should have found a way to deal with that pain a long time ago. But I didn't. Because it was easier to hide from it. To hide from everything. Everyone."

She squeezed his hands. In support? Sympathy? He didn't know, so he kept talking.

"I hid from life for so long, Kara," he said, "I'd forgotten what real joy was. What life could be like. But the last week or so with you reminded me. I know we've been together for a long time, but here, it was different. In Coleville, we were really *together,* together. You know?"

"Yeah, I know what you mean."

"Good. Good." He nodded and fought for breath.

That voice over the loudspeaker came again and all over the airport, heads cocked to listen, to try to understand the garbled words. The security line moved forward.

Cooper and Kara ignored it.

"I went to the lake last night."

"You did?" Understanding lit up her eyes and highlighted the banked tears about to fall.

Cooper talked faster, hoping to forestall them.

"I did. I talked to Mac. Discovered something else you were right about. It wasn't our fault. And Mac doesn't blame us."

"Oh, Cooper..."

"I think he wants us to be happy," he was saying, feeling the truth of his words as they poured from him in a rush. "I think he expects us to live the kind of life he would have if he'd been given the chance. And Kara, I want that, too."

"I'm glad."

"Good," he said smiling, "because you're pretty much integral to my plan."

"I am?" Her fingers curled around his and he lifted their joined hands to kiss her knuckles.

"Oh, you really are. I love you, Kara. See? Told you I'd get back around to the most important part of this."

"I'm liking it so far."

He swallowed a knot of emotion so huge it threatened to choke him, but still he found a way to say,

"I never thought I could love this much. But I do. You're everything to me, Kara. And I want the chance to prove it to you."

"Cooper..."

He spoke fast, half afraid she'd shut him down before he could finish. "No, listen. I won't let you go without a fight, Kara. If you get on a plane, I'll follow you. If you move, I'll go wherever you do. I will spend the rest of my life proving to you just how much I love you. If you'll just give me that chance."

Kara's heart swelled in her chest so that she could hardly draw breath. This was everything and more than she'd ever hoped for. And oh, she wanted to believe. She looked into Cooper's eyes and read the very emotions she'd so hoped to see. But she had to have more.

She wasn't prepared to settle for less than everything.

"I love you, too, Cooper," she said.

"Thank God," he murmured, shoulders slumping in relief.

"But..."

"There's a but?"

She smiled at him. "I won't settle for being your assistant or live-in lover. I want it all, Cooper. I want to be married. I want kids. A family."

He gave her a grin that nearly knocked her off her feet. "Of course we'll get married. And we'll have dozens of kids!"

"Dozens?"

"That part's negotiable," he acknowledged, then added, "and you won't be my assistant anymore. We'll hire someone else."

Kara shook her head and leaned in for a long, lingering kiss. "Nobody butters your toast but me, Cooper."

He sighed and drew her into the circle of his arms. "Now that sounds like a plan." After a quick hug, though, he pulled back and said, "Come on. I'm taking you back to the house. We've got a lot of making up to do."

"Now *that's* a plan," she said, throwing his own words back at him.

They had to take a cab, since Jeremiah's truck had indeed been towed. But Cooper promised to ransom it... *later*.

He carried her up the short flight of steps to the front door, but before he could open it, the heavy wood door swung open in invitation. Tightening his grip on Kara, Cooper cautiously stepped into the foyer and stopped dead.

Warmth spilled through the old house and sunlight seemed to spear in directly through the walls, making the whole place brilliant with a hazy, golden glow as unearthly as it was beautiful.

"What?" Cooper whispered.

"Shh..." Kara urged, smiling. "Listen."

Cooper held his breath and waited. Then he heard the soft, musical sound that Kara had.

A young couple, laughing with unrestrained joy. Together at last.

Epilogue

The truck had been bailed out of the storage yard, Kara's already checked suitcase would be returned as soon as it reached New York and she and Cooper had already made quite an effort at starting their first child.

After dinner at Jeremiah's, the family sat around the kitchen table and waited for the older man to make the announcement he'd called them all together for.

At last, he stood up, and looked from one grandson to the other. "I can't tell you boys what it means to this old man to have you all home again." Then he smiled at Kara and Maggie in turn. "And to have you two in my family, makes me gladder than you'll ever know."

Kara reached for Cooper's hand and her heart skipped when he folded his fingers around it.

"But beyond missing you all," Jeremiah said, "there was another reason for getting you back here this summer."

"You're not going to try the 'I'm dying' thing again, are you?" Jake asked.

"Nope." Jeremiah had the grace to flush and in the overhead kitchen light, his eyes sparkled with something that looked a lot like expectation. "This is the God's truth. And I decided to wait until all three of you were here together to tell you."

"C'mon, Jeremiah," Sam urged, dropping one arm around Maggie's shoulders. "Spill it before you bust."

"Right then. Donna Barrett's back in town."

"I know," Cooper said. "I saw her at the drugstore. Hell, I'm the one who told you guys. So if that's your news, Jeremiah, it's a little late."

The old man scowled at him. "There's more. She didn't come back to town alone. She's got Mac's son with her."

* * * * *

Maureen Child's SUMMER OF SECRETS
comes to an end with
Satisfying Lonergan's Honour,
available in July 2007.

PREGNANT WITH
THE FIRST HEIR
by
Sara Orwig

Dear Reader,

What happens when a determined, "take-charge" male clashes with an independent, "mistress-of-my-own-destiny" woman?

I wanted to explore two strong-willed people who had opposing goals and dreams. What happens when they charge head-on into each other's lives? Each one has plans for the future that are changed totally by the other person. Sparks fly, burned away in the fiery attraction that develops between them and ignites passion.

Pregnant with the First Heir introduces the Ransome family, Matt Ransome, the oldest son, and Olivia Brennan, a woman with no family. I couldn't resist writing about that hard, cynical male who hides his soft heart until a woman comes along who can dissolve the barriers and win his trust and love.

Family dynamics are always interesting to me. The majority of my books involve families in the background of the story, and *Pregnant with the First Heir* launches THE WEALTHY RANSOMES series about two Ransome brothers and their younger sister.

So, dear reader, please turn the page and enter the world of Matt Ransome and Olivia Brennan, who are getting ready to meet for the first time and toss each other's world into upheaval.

Best wishes,

Sara Orwig

OFFICIAL OPINION POLL

ANSWER 3 QUESTIONS AND WE'LL SEND YOU
2 FREE BOOKS AND A FREE GIFT!

0074823 |||||||||||||| ||||||||| ||||||||

FREE GIFT CLAIM # 3953

YOUR OPINION COUNTS!

Please tick TRUE or FALSE below to express your opinion about the following statements:

Q1 Do you believe in "true love"?

"TRUE LOVE HAPPENS ONLY ONCE IN A LIFETIME."
○ TRUE
○ FALSE

Q2 Do you think marriage has any value in today's world?

"YOU CAN BE TOTALLY COMMITTED TO SOMEONE WITHOUT BEING MARRIED."
○ TRUE
○ FALSE

Q3 What kind of books do you enjoy?

"A GREAT NOVEL MUST HAVE A HAPPY ENDING."
○ TRUE
○ FALSE

YES, I have scratched the area below.

Please send me the 2 FREE BOOKS and FREE GIFT for which I qualify. I understand I am under no obligation to purchase any books, as explained on the back of this card.

D7EI

Mrs/Miss/Ms/Mr _____ Initials _____

BLOCK CAPITALS PLEASE

Surname _____

Address _____

_____

Postcode _____

Visit us online at
www.millsandboon.co.uk

**THE READER SERVICE™
FREE BOOK OFFER
FREEPOST CN81
CROYDON
CR9 3WZ**

NO STAMP
NECESSARY
IF POSTED IN
THE U.K. OR N.I.

SARA ORWIG

lives in Oklahoma. She has a patient husband who will take her on research trips anywhere from big cities to old forts. She is an avid collector of Western history books. With a master's degree in English, Sara has written historical romance, mainstream fiction and contemporary romance. Books are beloved treasures that take Sara to magical worlds, and she loves both reading and writing them.

With many thanks to Melissa Jeglinski and
to Jessica Alvarez.

One

She was born to please a man.

The auburn-haired waitress behind the wooden counter had lush, come-hither looks. Her pouty lips promised sexual gratification. The sensual way of moving her ripe body made a man think of hot sex. Judging by her flat stomach, it was difficult to believe that she was three months pregnant. Her cutoffs revealed long, shapely legs that added to her appeal. At ten o'clock on a July Saturday night, male customers in the smoke-filled Texas honky-tonk constantly watched her move around the room. Matthew Ransome was certain that Olivia Brennan was so accustomed to men staring at her that she wouldn't wonder about his glances.

In the red T-shirt and cutoffs that was her uniform at Two-Steppin' Ribs, she waited on a customer in a nearby booth. Three musicians played country-western music while boot-scooting couples circled the dance floor. Even though he occasionally chatted with passing friends, Matt's attention remained focused on Olivia.

In the time since he had arrived and ordered his rib dinner, slowly eating and sipping one cold beer, Matt had watched half a dozen men hit on her. Some touched her, taking her hand or her wrist, patting her rear. She twisted free, or shaking her head, sidestepped groping hands, and he guessed she was being asked either to go out after work or—judging from the rough crowd—to have sex. He was surprised by her solemnity. She rarely gave more than the most perfunctory smile, not at all what he had imagined about her.

Matt watched locals he knew—Pug Mosley, the manager of the honky-tonk, openly flirted with her and several times during the evening let his hand brush her bottom. Once she spun around, telling him something. He grinned, shrugged and said something in return before he walked away in his usual swagger.

Fighting the urge to step in when Pug talked to Olivia, Matt intended to keep his approach to her low-key.

From what he had learned about her from the Fort Worth private detective he had hired a week ago, she wasn't dating anyone and there hadn't been a man in her life since Matt's brother Jeff. Matt found that difficult to believe except he had great faith in his P.I. With her body and mane of unruly auburn hair, she looked sexy and wild, like a woman with many partners.

Jeff could get mixed up with some shady people and seldom had there been a woman in his life that he had brought home. Including Olivia, who was carrying Jeff's child.

Nearing midnight, another local drifted to Olivia, just as obviously flirting with her as other men had. And received the same reception that was so cold Matt could discern her response without hearing a word of her conversation. Since she had been unreceptive to every man in the place, Matt reassessed his opinion of her as easy. He had never seen a female his younger brother couldn't charm, but Matt was beginning to wonder if Jeff was one of few men with whom she had ever had a relationship. Matt's opinion of her climbed a notch.

A small voice inside Matt insisted that he walk away now and never look back. Logically, he knew he should forget Olivia Brennan, but he couldn't any more than he could stop breathing.

Finally, after midnight, she was alone, standing behind the counter with no one around her. Silently warning himself he was seeking a hell of a lot of trouble, he slid out of the booth and circled the dance floor, crossing the room beneath revolving ceiling fans.

When he stopped in front of her, she looked up at him, turning the full force of big green eyes on him. Even in the dim light of the honky-tonk, he was mesmerized, and for a moment, she seemed as ensnared as he.

Attraction, as hot and tangible as a lightning flash, burst between them. The bar and people around them vanished from Matt's consciousness while he focused totally on her. Desire aroused him, a startling need to explore every inch of her ripe body and her sensual mouth. Once again, he knew why his brother had been attracted to her and why every man in the place seemed aware of her. She exuded a blatant sexuality that was all the more powerful up close.

While seconds passed, she stood as still as he did. Then, inhaling deeply, she turned her head, and the eye contact was broken.

As she started to walk away, Matt regained his wits.

"Wait—" he said. When she paused, he held out his hand. "I'm Jeff's brother Matt."

Her eyes narrowed. "I'm sorry about your brother," she stated coolly without taking Matt's hand. Once again, she moved on.

"Wait a minute. I want to talk to you," Matt said, catching up with her. "When do you get off work?" As silence stretched between them, even in the dim light, he saw the flash of fury in the depths of her eyes.

"Look, Jeff and I parted ways a while back," she said. "I don't know why you found me, but there was no longer anything between Jeff and me. You and I have nothing to talk about." Her words poured out swiftly in a throaty voice that was as sexy as everything else about her.

"There was a baby between you," Matt reminded her. "A baby that you and I will both be related to and need to talk about," Matt continued as his insides coiled in a knot. "I'm the uncle, so you give me a few minutes."

She bit her full underlip with even, white teeth and her mouth tempted him to forget the object of why he intended to talk to her.

"I can't guess what you want. Words won't do you any good," she insisted, shaking her head. "I'm through with your family. I don't want to see any of you." Suddenly she leaned closer, lowering her voice. "If you think I'm giving up my baby, you can forget it!" She turned her back and started to walk away.

Momentarily taken aback, Matt stepped in front of her, blocking her way. "I'm the baby's blood relative. You can't dismiss me like that. I want to talk—when and wherever you agree to. If you don't consent, we'll discuss the baby in a court of law. Take your pick."

Glaring at him, she visibly bristled. As she inhaled deeply, he was aware of the strain of the red shirt across her lush breasts. "I don't get off here until two in the morning when we close," she said.

"I'll wait. I promise you, we're going to have a discussion."

"All right. Two o'clock in the parking lot," she said in a level tone of voice even as her eyes sparked with fury.

"Fine. In the meantime, you can bring me some coffee. I'm in a booth on the other side of the room."

Nodding, she walked away and he couldn't keep from watching the sway of her hips.

She turned and slanted him a look over her shoulder, catching him watching her. He clamped his lips together. She had to be aware of the effect she had on men. At least she hadn't been coming after him for money which had surprised him because as soon as he learned about the pregnancy from Jeff, that's what he had expected.

"Damn, Jeff," Matt said under his breath, anger and pain mingling as he thought about his reckless younger brother whose wild lifestyle had caught up with him when he'd died climbing mountains in the Himalayas.

Matt dallied over the cup of coffee until it was obvious that closing time approached. As he stepped to the cash register, Olivia lingered to take his money.

"You can wait out front," she said, giving him another blast of her mesmerizing green eyes. Her low, seductive voice glided hotly over his every nerve. "Employees park in the back and when I'm finished closing, I'll drive my car around to the front. Our chat has to be brief. It's late, and I've had a long day."

He nodded. When he stepped outside, he heard the lock click in the door behind him as it shut. Yellow light from a tall lamp shed a bright glow over the graveled lot. Beneath a sliver of July moon a south breeze tugged at locks of his black hair.

Wondering how long it would take to close, Matt strolled behind the wooden building. Brown paint peeled in spots and the big blue trash bin overflowed with cartons and bottles. Another light on a tall post shone over the graveled area. Three ancient cars with assorted dents and scrapes were parked in the back. Matt's jaw tightened with disgust when he looked at the empty lot. Beyond the circle of light was a field with a grove of scrub oaks. Without security of any sort, the lot was no place for a woman alone at two in the morning.

Matt waited while the employees locked up, dimmed the lights and left, two women and a man coming out at the same time. As the burly man started toward Matt, Olivia caught his arm and said something to him. Giving Matt a long look, the man walked to his car. While the man and woman climbed into separate cars and drove out of the lot, Matt strolled over to Olivia. She stood with her hands on her hips.

"Jeff and I split. I don't think you and I have much to talk about."

"You're carrying his child. He told me and he was certain the baby was his."

"This is his baby, all right," she said. Her face was bathed in light, and Matt could see the fire dancing in her eyes and hear the anger in her tone which heightened his own irritation over her uncooperative attitude.

"Look, I'm related to your baby. Jeff told me you don't have any family and you're on your own. I want to help you."

"Thanks, but no thanks. You don't owe me anything, and I'll take care of my baby," she declared stiffly with a toss of her head that sent her thick mane swirling across her shoulders.

"Why make it more difficult for yourself and for the baby?"

"Jeff didn't want any responsibility for his child. Far from it. His exact words were: 'I don't want to ever know or even see your kid,'" she flung at Matt, and pain stabbed him. "He told me I should have been more careful. He was right there. I don't want any part of anything or anyone connected to Jeff!" she exclaimed firmly and turned to walk to her car.

Matt bit back angry words. It hurt badly to hear that Jeff had denied his child. Jeff hadn't told him that, but then, his kid brother would have known how Matt would react to such news.

Matt hurried ahead of her and blocked her from getting into her car.

"Get out of my way," she said.

"I want to talk. Surely you can give me a few minutes."

She inhaled deeply, and he resisted letting his gaze lower to her full breasts, but it was an effort.

"All right, for only a few more minutes." She crossed her arms over her middle and raised her chin and he knew he was in for a fight.

"This baby will be the only one of the next generation in my family."

"You can't have children?" she asked.

"I'm not a marrying man. I'll never marry anyone."

"That didn't slow your brother down. And he didn't care if this baby was the last of your family. Blood relations didn't seem important to him," she said, and Matt could easily hear the bitterness in her voice. Her fists were clenched, and he realized instead of a rift between Jeff and Olivia, Jeff had created a bottomless chasm. She was all but shaking with fury.

Matt fought to bank his own anger that she was being so almighty unreasonable when he offered help that she seemed to desperately need.

"As I recall, there were several of you—a brother, Nick, a sister, Katherine. Can't they produce grandchildren?"

Matt shrugged. "Perhaps someday, but who knows? Nick and Katherine are on the wild side and not likely to settle down soon."

"Like Jeff," Olivia said with bitterness in her voice again.

"None of us is as wild as Jeff was," Matt snapped. "Jeff took whatever he wanted and indulged himself. He thought he was invincible, but it turned out that he wasn't."

"Look, I'm trying to help—"

She shook her head. "No, you're not. You want something. If it's my baby, forget it. And don't think you can go to court and get my precious baby. I'll fight you every inch of the way."

"Will you listen to me?" he said patiently, and she arched her eyebrows.

"I'll listen, but you're on limited time that's growing shorter."

Matt wanted to shake her. Instead, he nodded. "I'm sure you don't make much money as a waitress here. I want to take care of you and the baby financially."

"I don't need your help. End of conversation. You have no claim on me. If you want to go to court over it—go. Since you're not the father, you won't have a strong case. They would give a father rights, but an uncle? I'm willing to take that chance. You stay out of my life. Your brother was a jerk! Now get out of my way."

She slid into her car, slammed and locked the door. The engine rumbled to life with a persistent knock. She backed up, swung in a circle and drove away, crunching gravel beneath the tires.

"Dammit!" Matt swore and clenched his fists. He strode angrily to his pickup, climbed in and headed toward Rincon, Texas where he knew she lived on the fringe of town.

He would try to talk to her one more time before he called his attorney. Little stubborn witch!

Jeff disowned the baby. Matt gritted his teeth as he reflected that most of his life he hadn't understood his kid brother. Without a doubt, the feelings had been mutual. Matt knew his single parent father had done the best he could, but he had been too indulgent with all of them. Jeff, the youngest, he had spoiled rotten.

Matt drove through the neighborhood of small frame houses with dented, ancient cars parked in front yards and lawns high with weeds. When he reached her darkened house, he discovered that Olivia had not come straight home. She might not be coming home tonight at all.

In disgust, he wondered if she had taken up with a man. He shrugged away the unwanted notion, reminding himself that there hadn't been any mention from the P.I. of a boyfriend. Tonight she had given the cold shoulder to every man in the honky-tonk.

He slowed and parked in front of the house. In the next block he saw a man stumbling along the sidewalk until he turned and disappeared inside a house.

Olivia's car approached and turned into her drive that was no more than a gravel path. When she stepped out of the car, she picked up a grocery sack and walked toward her house, merely glancing at him when he emerged from his car.

"We've talked," she said when he caught up with her. She brushed past him and climbed rickety steps, crossing the porch to unlock her door. Matt followed and held the screen door. He stood close enough to get a strong whiff of the odor of cigarette smoke trapped in her hair.

She looked up at him. "You're not welcome here. I've said all I need to say to you."

"Listen. You're carrying a Ransome. I want to help you and you damned well need support. Stop being so stubborn and listen to what I have to offer. For all you know, you could be turning down a million bucks."

Her eyebrows arched. "Am I?" she asked, startling him at her change in temperament because he thought he heard amusement in her voice.

"Let's go inside and talk," he answered. She gave him a level look and he wondered if she was going to send him on his way, but she shrugged and entered her house, leaving the door open behind her.

He followed her into a small, frame house that had to be nearly a hundred years old. White paint had peeled from the cracked walls, revealing a coat of dark blue paint. The furniture was threadbare and looked older than he was, yet there were some green plants and a few touches that contrasted with the dilapidation.

She tossed her purse on the sofa, set down the sack of groceries and motioned to him. "Have a seat."

"How long have you lived here?" he asked, looking around and sitting on an overstuffed chair covered in a faded, flowered slipcover. A blanket was thrown over the sofa and he suspected it hid holes.

"Almost a year now."

Leaning forward, he rested his elbows on his knees while he watched her kick off her shoes and rub her foot.

"I know you're going to school. You don't have any family. You work in a dive and you reek of cigarette smoke. The bar can't be healthy for your baby or you."

"I'm trying to get another job that pays at least as much as the one I have. I don't have the skills or the wardrobe for an office job," she said, thrusting out her chin defiantly. "Pay is higher at Two-Steppin' Ribs because the bar is out in nowhere."

"How many hours are you taking this semester?"

"Two classes—six hours. I'm in pre-law."

"You're a sophomore, aren't you?"

"I think you already know the answer. And you're thinking that a sophomore is not much for someone who is twenty-two, but it's the best I could do," she replied, curling her long legs beneath her and settling in the corner of the sofa. His gaze slid along her legs. He tried to keep his thoughts on his mission, but he was responding to her physically in a manner that shocked him.

"All right. Here's the deal," he said. "I'll send you to school. You quit that job and move out to the ranch with me—"

"No way! I'm sure you think I'm easy, but I'm not climbing into bed with you to get my tuition," she said, flinging the words at him and standing.

"Sit down," he said with such ice and authority that she did. "I don't want your body." Even as he said the words, a devilish urge made him too aware that he was lying to her as far as what his body desired. Yet he could control himself and good sense kept telling him that he shouldn't want her physically. She would be pure poison. He didn't want to get involved emotionally with any woman.

"I'll pay for your school, let you quit that damn job," he repeated, "take care of you and the baby. I'll pay your medical bills—"

"No one is that filled with benevolence. What do you want out of this generous offer?" she asked in a cynical voice.

"Stop fighting me," he said, gazing steadily into her green eyes and thinking that every inch of her made a man think of sex. "I want to know my niece or nephew. I want to make sure this baby is taken care of in the manner he or she should be. I don't want your body," he reaffirmed, trying to avoid looking at her lush body and failing annoyingly to stop thinking about it. "I want to know your baby. I want to see you able to take care of yourself and the baby. I can pay for your education. In turn, this Ransome will become part of our family. Dad has had one heart attack already. I want him to know his only grandchild."

"If you want your father to have a grandchild so badly, you should rethink your stance against marriage."

"I married once and never again for me," Matt replied grimly, refusing to discuss the matter further.

"What happened? She didn't like your bossy arrogance?"

He banked his irritation and ignored her question. "Your baby will be the only Ransome in the next generation. My dad isn't getting any younger and he desperately wants a grand-child. I think he's given up on all of us, but now, with your baby, his hopes are rekindled."

As Olivia bit her lip, Matt couldn't resist looking at her mouth.

"Look, dammit. What are you holding onto here besides your independence?" he asked. "This isn't a castle. Your job is tough and tiring and pays little. You work in an unhealthy atmosphere. Men hit on you, and I can imagine what they're saying to you—"

"And you won't hit on me?" she asked in a sarcastic tone.

"No, I won't," he said flatly, trying in vain to shove erotic images of her out of his mind. "You know you're an attractive woman, but you're like a relative," he said, while an inner voice laughed and he wiped his perspiring brow. When had the temperature in the small room climbed so high?

"What do you want?" she asked. "You look like the straight-arrow, determined, accustomed to getting-your-way type."

"I want to take care of my dad and our ranches—we own three. No commitments beyond my family and our ranches. I want my dad to get to know his only grandchild. Pretty damn simple," Matt snapped, thinking it should not be complicated, but it was. He was playing with dynamite right now by bringing her into their family.

"I suspect there's more to it than my baby."

"I swear I'm telling you the truth."

"I know I work in a bad place and I'm looking for another job," she said, waving her slender fingers at him. "I'm holding on to my independence because that's all I really have. I don't want to have to depend on you and I don't want to have to repay you for favors."

"If it reassures you, we can put my offer in a contract. I don't want anything physical," he repeated. "I'll pay for your school and all your expenses and your baby's. I'll pay you a lump sum up front so you're not beholden to me for money. You don't have to repay any of it."

"That sounds too generous. I know you can't understand someone holding such a value on independence, but it's important to me. In spite of what you say, I can't believe there aren't strings attached to your offer."

"Listen. I'm trying to give you the help you need to become

completely independent. In exchange, I want to know my brother's child That's all there is to it."

She glowered and inhaled, and he looked down as her full breasts strained against the fabric. When he glanced up, she frowned.

"It's difficult to be convinced that you really want to know this baby—or that your father wants a grandchild badly—when Jeff so totally denied us and was emphatic he didn't want anything to do with my baby."

"None of us knew Jeff's attitude. My guess is, his reaction was to get out of his responsibility, which was typical of my younger brother."

"So what happens later when I want to move on?"

"We'll work that out when we come to it. I hope you'll stick around until you finish your education. Maybe by then you'll like us and trust us enough to stay close permanently. Do you have long-term plans?"

"I intend to finish school and get a job. I still say, you could marry again if you want kids so all-fired much."

"There is already a baby coming who is a Ransome. I'm not going to turn my back on a child who has Ransome blood. I have to keep reminding you—your baby is my relative."

Matt stared at her while she glared at him and the clash of wills was tense, but along with the contention was a sexual undercurrent of desire. Sparks danced between them, and Matt was certain she felt the same attraction he did.

Instinctively, he knew the appeal was as unwanted to her as it was to him. Trying to control his insistent lust, he made a stronger effort to think only of the future and a baby he wasn't going to surrender without the fight of his life.

"If I give you a sum of cash up front and promise to pay your expenses, you won't feel dependent on me. I'll repeat—we can sign a contract."

"I don't want to get involved with Jeff's kin," she insisted and he wondered if she had a clue how much he was willing to give her to change her grim conditions.

"Possibly my offer will help with your decision. We'll set up a trust fund for your baby. I'll cover your expenses and you'll have room and board at the ranch. Plus how's a hundred thousand dollars paid to you, half now, half in six months?"

Two

Olivia stared in disbelief at Matt Ransome as the princely sum stunned her.

"For that much money, you want me, body and soul, plus my baby," she replied curtly as she stood. "Get out!"

"Sit down," he ordered in the cold, quiet voice he had used before that sent a chill down her spine, yet made her feel that the last notion on his mind was her body. She sat.

"I keep telling you that I can have our attorney draw up a contract. If you want, you can meet my family and talk to them."

Barely considering his family, Olivia nodded stiffly while the amount of money spun in her thoughts. The sum dazzled her. Unable to stop herself, she speculated about the classes she could take, the freedom she could have, the dreadful job that she could leave. It was more money than she could ever earn at the bar. Her heart pounded, her palms had grown damp and it was an effort to resist accepting his offer blindly and instantly. She realized silence was stretching between them and he was waiting patiently.

"You're very different from your brother," she remarked.

"I hope to hell I am," he said.

She had seen Matt Ransome at the rib place hours before he had spoken to her. She had never met him, but she had seen him once when she was with Jeff and he had told her that Matt was his brother. Matt had none of Jeff's easy charm or happy-go-lucky ways. He was perhaps a couple of inches shorter, more broad-shouldered, handsome in his own way with the same dark blue eyes and thick lashes. Matt's hair was black. Jeff's had been brown.

That first moment of a close encounter with Matt Ransome had disturbed her. She had to admit that she'd had a physical reaction to him that she'd never had with Jeff or any other man. She didn't know why, either, because Matt Ransome was too forceful, too determined to get his way to suit her. He was all business, but that first moment of looking directly into his blue eyes while he gazed back at her, had taken her breath, held her totally and had steamed with sexual tension. For a few seconds, she was certain that he had been locked into the same jolting awareness that she was.

Now here was his proposition that she still found difficult to believe from a man who disturbed her physically in a way no other man ever had. With most men, she had always felt in control. But Matt Ransome demolished that sense of power. She didn't like to acknowledge it, but she had to admit to herself that she was drawn to Matt in a purely physical way. She couldn't explain why and she didn't want to be. She never again wanted to be involved with a Ransome.

At the same time, Matt's offer was tempting beyond belief, but she wasn't rushing into an agreement. She had given her trust to Jeff and he had trampled it.

She cocked her head to one side to study Matt. "You know for the money you're offering, you could adopt a child."

"Since this baby is a Ransome, I intend to take care of it and I want to get to know him or her. Do you know what you're having?"

"It's too early. I haven't decided whether I want to know or not."

"We'll say a prayer for a girl. The males in this family haven't turned out so good."

"I'll think about your offer," she said coldly, standing. "It's time for you to go."

He stood. "Look, you can mull it over, but you know you need what I'm offering. In the meantime, you should move out of this neighborhood. Come stay at the ranch tonight."

"Tonight?" Again, he startled her. "I can't possibly—"

"Of course you can," he persisted. "I'll bet you don't have more than two suitcases of stuff. Do you rent this furnished or is this your furniture?"

"I rented it furnished. Look, if you're taking charge of my life, then that settles it, I'm not going," she said, hoping her voice was forceful and trying to keep her gaze from roaming down his long legs or across his broad chest.

"I'm trying to improve your situation," he stated patiently. "What's holding you in this place?"

Her face grew hot and she glanced away, unable to meet his direct gaze. "Nothing," she admitted. "Except you're a stranger."

"Not a total stranger. You knew Jeff, so you know a lot about me. You're not safe here. This isn't a healthy place for an ex- pectant woman. You don't need to be alone and you could be a hell of a lot more comfortable. All right?"

Annoyed, she shook her head. "You're taking charge. Back off and give me some room. I'll think it over. I'll come out in the morning and we can discuss your offer more."

He inhaled and looked as if he were trying to cling to what little patience he had. "All right, but resign and get away from the secondhand smoke. At least think of your baby."

"I do think of my baby."

"If you'll get a pencil and paper, I'll give you directions to the ranch."

She glared at him and knew he held his annoyance in check. She didn't like him taking over, yet it was for the best. If she moved to the ranch, she knew she would be making a commit- ment from which it might be difficult to shake free.

She didn't like Matt's forceful ways. Maybe that's why Jeff had had such a rebellious nature.

"I'm beginning to understand why your brother was like he was."

Anger flashed in Matt's blue eyes. "My youngest brother wouldn't take responsibility for anything."

She realized she had touched a nerve. Dropping remarks about Jeff, she hurried to get a pen and paper. As Matt wrote directions to his ranch, she looked at his well-shaped hands, his thick, slightly curly eyelashes and straight nose. A faint dark stubble showed on his jaw.

"After knowing Jeff, who could not be relied on, I find it difficult to trust you," she admitted.

"I'll keep reminding you, I'm not like Jeff," Matt replied quietly. They stood only inches apart and he had focused on her with that intensity he had the first time they had made eye contact. Her insides got butterflies and her gaze lowered to his mouth while she wondered what it would be like to kiss him.

When she looked up to find him gazing at her mouth, her heart missed a beat. She drew herself up. "I want one point clear—you're a take-charge person. If I move to your ranch, you agree now that you won't try to run my life."

"I wouldn't think of it," he answered with sarcasm as the fiery clash of wills continued to snap between them. "But I am going to speak up when you do things that might endanger the health of your baby."

"Right now, you can forget about ever trying to take my baby from me."

"I know a child needs its mother. I don't want to jeopardize that relationship as long as you are a loving mother. Your family has a history of neglect and abuse."

"I'm not like my parents," she snapped while anger made her hot. "My folks drank, were into drugs. They were verbally abusive. They neglected me as well as themselves and were irresponsible and it killed them. I couldn't wait to get away from them," she said flatly. She studied him for a moment. "You know a lot about me. Especially for having just met me. More than Jeff knew, I think. How'd you find out so much?"

"I wanted to know about you before I started dealing with you. I hired a P.I. to check into your life."

Her displeasure heightened that he would have her background checked, but then she knew if she were making the offer he was, she might do the same.

"You don't approve, do you?" he asked.

"No, but I can understand why you wanted to know about my past. I'll think about your offer to move into your home," she said, knowing she should accept eagerly, but she was loath to relinquish her independence.

"We won't get in each other's way. It's a big house. Also, fall enrollment is open at the university in Fort Worth." He reached into a back pocket and withdrew brochures and a catalogue. "Here, you can look at these," he said and placed them on a table. "You can become a full-time student and graduate sooner," he said.

"You've been planning this for a while. How far from Fort Worth is your ranch? I've forgotten what Jeff told me."

"Thirty miles. Not far. You can commute easily."

They stared at each other, and she wondered if he intended doing what he said. She had been surprised by men before, so if Matt Ransome didn't live up to his part of their bargain, she could deal with it. She knew he lusted after her. It showed in the way he looked at her, but his control was evident also. She had the feeling that he didn't like her at all. She suspected he didn't approve of much his younger brother had done or the women Jeff had known. Matt Ransome would have seemed like ice, real straight and arrogant, except for the smoldering looks he gave her. What astounded her was the effect he had on her. Since Jeff, she had been immune to men, but she wasn't immune to Matt. He made her pulse race, her breath catch. She didn't want to react that way to him and she knew he didn't want to respond to her, so whatever kind of chemistry there was brewing between them, it was unwanted and hopefully would evaporate.

"Are we finished for tonight?" she asked, wanting him out of her house.

"I don't think you're safe here. Anyone who wants to break into this place can do so easily if they have an ounce of skills. Do you want me to stay here? I can sleep in a chair or on your sofa."

She smiled, amused by his offer of protection. "Thanks, but no thanks. I've been taking care of myself for a long time. My dad died five years ago. My mother died two years later and I've taken care of both of them since I was twelve years old. We lived in a lot tougher neighborhoods than this. That's one reason I moved here. Cheap rent and a better area, although I'm sure it doesn't look suitable to you. One more night here is nothing to worry about."

He stared at her and she wondered if he was going to insist she let him stay. It was obvious that he disapproved of her. He probably thought she was easy. If he got to know her, he would find out he was wrong in that judgment. The last thing she wanted was to be a live-in girlfriend, going from one brother to the other.

As they gazed at each other, that searing awareness flashed between them. In spite of all her intentions to keep a wall between them, it was impossible to resist reacting to Matt. Right now her heart raced. Perspiration had broken out on his forehead, and he seemed as riveted as she was.

Inhaling deeply, he spun away to cross the room to the door. She trailed after him, pausing a few feet from him. "I gave you my cell number. Call me if you need anything," he said.

"Thanks," she replied.

"Don't worry. You'll be glad if you say yes," he said. He opened the door and strode outside. She followed, watching Matt Ransome climb into his car and drive away.

When she stepped back inside, she looked around the shabby room. By accepting Matt's offer, she could take care of her baby, get her education, live in a safer place. She was scared to celebrate because she hadn't been to the ranch yet, nor had she spent a night under the same roof with Matt Ransome. Was he leveling with her and telling her the truth? Was his sole interest in the baby?

"I hope so," she said quietly, looking around at her few possessions. She would be glad to leave this house. It would take less than a couple of hours for her to get all her possessions packed.

She switched on a bedroom light, looking at the nondescript bed and the dresser, a chest of drawers that didn't match and a torn braided rug on the floor. As she got ready for bed, she thought about Jeff Ransome. She had enrolled in a two-year college, working in a café until she had gotten the job at the Two-Steppin' Ribs. It paid more so she put up with the smoke and the leering men, but from the start, Jeff had been different from the others.

Tall, brown-haired and handsome, Jeff had gone to the Ribs to gamble. There was a high-stakes poker game in a back room that was invitation only and the night she'd met him, Jeff had been part of it. After closing he had hung around and asked her to go out with him.

Since she was twelve years old, she had known that she attracted males. Early on, she had learned to try to keep a wall around herself, but when she met Jeff Ransome, he had charmed his way past her defenses. She had been unable to resist his charismatic personality.

As Olivia pulled on cotton pajamas, gathered up the school catalog and brochure and climbed into bed, her thoughts went back to Jeff. He'd been the second man in her life, which she knew he hadn't believed. She'd had a wonderful time with him until she discovered she was pregnant. They had used birth control, but she had gotten pregnant anyway.

From that moment on, Jeff was through. And then a month ago he had left for a trek in the rugged Himalaya mountains where, in a daredevil climb, he'd had a fatal fall.

Olivia gazed into space, mulling over Matt Ransome's offer. She had to accept, but as much as possible, she wanted it on her terms, not his.

She opened the catalog and turned to the section on prelaw, her major, and for the first time allowed herself to think of the windfall Matt Ransome was providing. If only it was exactly as he said and there were no hidden agendas, no strings attached and no unpleasant surprises ahead for her. She could move to the Ransome ranch and quit her job! In the early hours of morning, the whole offer seemed surreal, and she suspected that as soon as she settled on the ranch, Matt would want to sleep with her. He was appealing, sexy and generated sparks in her the way no other man had.

Forget it, she told herself, knowing she would not go from one brother to another. "If I accept his offer, I vow I won't have sex with Matt Ransome," she said aloud, trying to stop remembering the tingles she had when she gazed into Matt's blue eyes.

Forcing her thoughts off Matt, she wondered about her future and his offer. Was there anything she could do to get Matt's proposition more on her own terms?

The next morning her palms were damp from nervousness as she drove through an open gate and passed a sign announcing the Ransome ranch. In minutes she turned a bend in the ranch road. Ahead spread houses, a barn, a corral, pens and outbuildings. A pumping windmill stood near a stock tank filled with water.

When she drew closer, she looked at an intimidating, sprawling stone ranch house with a shake shingle roof. It was surrounded by immaculate, lush green lawns and a profusion of flowers in well-tended beds that all proclaimed the wealth of the owner. She had never lived in a house that looked as grand as this one. Swallowing hard, Olivia couldn't imagine herself suddenly part of the Ransome family.

A rail fence enclosed the yard and two live oaks gave inviting shade that failed to calm Olivia's nerves. On the porch the hanging pots of yellow bougainvillea, scarlet gaillardia and purple impatiens added a dreamlike feeling. This could be her new home. She couldn't fathom it.

Adding to her jittery nerves and disbelief, Matt Ransome came striding outside. In a white T-shirt, jeans and western boots, he looked muscled, tough and electrifying. Without saying a word he created a high voltage magnetism. The sight of him did nothing to calm her nerves.

He motioned her where to park in front of a six-car garage. When she climbed out, she was conscious of her cutoffs and her white T-shirt.

"Hi there," Matt said in a deep voice as he took a box from her car. In his T-shirt that revealed sculpted muscles and his tight jeans, his sensuality jumped a notch. One look in his eyes confirmed that the sexual appeal between them burned as hot as ever. When she stepped out, she looked up to see him gazing at her waist.

"You don't look pregnant," he said.

An inner voice told her to keep everything impersonal with Matt, but she couldn't do what she knew she should. "I guess it's because I'm tall," she replied breathlessly, mindful of how close he stood. She barely knew what she said to him. He should move away. She should step aside. Instead, she gazed up at him while her heartbeat continued to accelerate.

Silence between them carried sparks. When his attention lowered to her mouth, her pulse drummed. As he gazed at her, the blatant, scalding desire in his eyes heated her.

"No physical relationship comes with this package," she repeated.

"It damn well doesn't," he replied, sounding half angry. "I don't ever want to get involved again except in the most superficial manner. You and I absolutely don't need entanglement between us."

"That's something we can agree on. It would help if you'd move away."

Something flickered in the depths of his eyes before he leaned around her to pick up another one of her boxes.

"I'll get your things and then I'll show you around. Have you quit your job?"

"No, I haven't. I figured whatever we decide to do, I'll work tonight."

Matt straightened up and she saw the hard look back in his features. He shook his head. "You quit today. You don't owe them anything and you shouldn't be there one more hour."

"I thought you weren't going to meddle in my life," she said, trying to curb her temper.

"Where the baby is concerned, I'll interfere. That nightclub isn't healthy. They'll manage without you."

"Look—"

"No, you look," he said quietly. "The bar's atmosphere isn't healthy. They're going to get along without you. If we have a deal, part of it includes you taking care of yourself and your unborn baby."

Where sexual tension had spun tightly between them only moments ago, now friction set sparks flying. She glared at him, yet she suspected she would get nowhere if she argued the rest of the day.

"Why do you want to wait tables so all-fired badly?" Matt asked her.

"I don't. That isn't it."

"There you are."

She put her hands on her hips. "I'm here tentatively. We haven't agreed on what we're going to do. I haven't accepted your offer. We need to discuss it before you start taking complete charge."

"Let me show you around, let you select your room and then we'll sit down and see if we can't come to terms," he said, lifting the last box and putting it under his arm. "Tomorrow I'll introduce you to everyone who works here. Mrs. Marley is the housekeeper and cook. You'll meet her at the end of the week. She's here two days a week. Fridays, she cooks. Saturdays, she cleans. My dad lives down the road from me. She's at his house Monday through Thursday."

Olivia nodded.

"Wait a minute," Matt said and set a box on her car. Following Matt's gaze, she watched a tall, sandy-haired man approach and shake hands with Matt.

"Olivia, this is our foreman, Sandy McDermott," Matt said easily. "Sandy, meet Olivia Brennan who will be staying with us a while."

"I'm glad to meet you, Sandy," she said, extending her hand and smiling.

"Happy to meet you, Miss Brennan. Glad to have you here."

"It's Olivia, Sandy. Call me Olivia."

Sandy nodded. "Nice meeting you, Olivia," he said, turning to talk to Matt. Olivia listened while they discussed cattle and a world she didn't know. Matt was quick and decisive and more relaxed than when he was dealing with her. As soon as Sandy told them goodbye and left, she and Matt headed for the house.

She was aware of Matt walking close beside her. Her jittery nerves kept her on edge, and she wondered what she was getting herself into.

Once again Matt took her arm and she drew a deep breath. She hadn't known him twenty-four hours, yet his slightest touch set her ablaze. She couldn't fathom the chemistry. She had known other handsome, decisive males and she had had no trouble dealing with them and no difficulty ignoring them. Until now. Even Jeff with all his charm had never carried the electricity of a bolt of lightning the way Matt did.

She wondered again what she was getting into if she accepted Matt's offer that was a windfall in her circumstances. She was heartily glad to be out of the bar and away from lustful men. At the same time, she wanted this bargain to be partially on her terms. Her queasy nerves jangled when she thought about her plan and her requests. She had no idea how Matt would react. The knowledge was constantly with her that she was taking a risk by making her own demands because if she accepted his offer and he did what he said and kept his bargain, her life would improve beyond her wildest dreams.

He held the door, following her inside an enormous kitchen with oversize windows. Sunlight streamed into the room that held maple cabinetry, granite countertops, a marble floor and maple furniture. The floor-to-ceiling windows overlooked a patio and a pool with sparkling blue water.

"This is beautiful," she said, unable to keep a breathless tone of awe out of her voice. "It doesn't look like what I imagined."

"Jeff and I must have created the wrong impression."

Her gaze flew to him and heat flooded her cheeks. Embarrassed by her reaction, she bit her lip.

"You probably thought we lived in a cabin with mounted heads and gun racks and the sort."

"No," she denied halfheartedly and then shrugged. "Maybe something like that," she admitted.

"C'mon. Let me show you this wing of the house." He took her arm lightly, yet the contact sizzled, and as they crossed the kitchen, her surroundings paled in comparison to the man beside her.

From the hall he led her into a family room and her awe returned at the sight of a twenty-foot-high cathedral ceiling, a massive stone fireplace, luxurious tan leather furniture and pictures of landscapes.

"This is a dream!" she gasped and her face flushed. "You can tell I've never lived in a house like this," she said.

"Well, now you do," he said. "It's comfortable. Across the hall are the living and dining rooms," he said, taking her arm again as they returned to the hall. "On the other side of the kitchen is a utility room, exercise room and my office. The bedrooms are in the opposite wing. Other than my bedroom, in the southeast end of the house, you can have whichever bedroom you want."

As he led her through a workout room, a media room and his office, the elegant furnishings overwhelmed Olivia. It was a dream-come-true moment to think she would live in this palace. She realized Jeff and Matt weren't the ordinary cowboys she had imagined they were. The house reeked of money and power and she wondered whether she could hold her own and govern her baby's future against the Ransomes' wishes.

"We'll have a decorator help you with the nursery." Matt's words jolted her back into awareness of the moment.

"I won't be here forever." Olivia gave him a startled, wide-eyed look.

"That's all right. You'll return to visit and bring the baby."

"You're so certain!" she exclaimed, yet now she realized part of the source of his arrogance and assurance. Growing up in a home like this, how could he be anything except confident?

"Shouldn't I be?" he asked, looking blandly at her.

Olivia stopped to face him, a frown creasing her brow. "Our lives are so different."

"It doesn't matter, Olivia," he replied easily. "We'll be related to the baby and we'll want to see him or her through the years. It'll save you money to live here until you finish your education."

She merely nodded and returned to thinking about her future while she looked at more rooms in a house that dazzled her.

"How's this for you?" he asked later, leading the way into a bedroom that took her breath and she could not imagine living in it.

She stood in the room large enough to contain the house she rented. The room was plush beyond her wildest dreams. It was ample for a king-size bed with a bronze headboard, a massive mahogany chest, bookshelves, a wide-screen television, a maroon sofa, a rocking chair and assorted tables. The decor was maroon with accents of white and beige and an oriental rug partially covering the gleaming plank floor.

She knew she wasn't hiding her amazement. She reminded herself that it was premature to celebrate her newfound fortune, her future prospects or this house that could possibly become her home. In the next few minutes, she knew, it could all disappear from her life as swiftly as it had entered.

The time had come to present her conditions.

"This is beyond anything I had imagined," she said softly, turning to face him. Her pulse drummed. She wanted to learn how earnest he really was about this whole proposition. "Shall we discuss our future and terms of a contract?" she asked, the words *our future* causing her insides to clench.

"Sure," he replied, giving her a long, speculative look that made her feel he knew her every thought. "Let's get a drink and sit in the family room."

They walked in silence back to the kitchen and she watched, barely aware of what he was doing while her pulse beat faster and her nervousness increased. At the last minute she vacillated between an overwhelming desire to accept his offer unconditionally and reap the fortune, or risk her demands that would either cause him to send her packing or solidify her prospects and fortune.

Finally, they were seated in the family room at a polished oak game table with tall, frosted glasses of ice and lemonade and a plate of cookies in front of them. She couldn't eat or drink anything. Aware that her entire prospects hung in the balance, she inhaled deeply to calm down.

"You've had time to think it over. You're here on the ranch. Does this mean you'll accept my offer?" he asked.

His blue eyes cut into her like shards of a glacier. He was formidable and determined, but she clung to her course. It was time to see how much he would commit to what he wanted. She took a deep breath and raised her chin while she locked her hands together.

"You're being very generous," she said, still awed by his offer and filled with trepidation over what she was about to demand from him for her part. "I have a counteroffer to make to you."

Fire flashed in the depths of his eyes and a muscle worked in his jaw. She suspected he was bracing for her to ask for more money.

"All right. Name your conditions and price," he said, grinding out the words. "How much Ransome money do you want?"

"You've made an overwhelmingly generous offer, but if you're truly committed to protecting this baby and raising it as a Ransome, then I want you to give my baby the Ransome name. I want a paper marriage, an in-name-only marriage that we can later dissolve." Her heart thundered so loudly that she could barely hear herself speak. "In other words, will you marry me?"

Three

Stunned, Matt stared at her. "You want me to marry you?" he repeated in amazement.

"Yes, if you're so determined to make my baby a part of your family. It'll be the same conditions you've already given me, plus marriage. This way, you're more committed. My child will legitimately be a Ransome as it should have been all along. You'll do the honorable thing that your brother would not do."

Matt stared at her. Anger and shock rocked him that she would put one more demand on him when he had given her an offer that was magnanimous beyond anything she had ever known in her life. Then he noticed her white knuckles and her hands doubled into fists. Perspiration dotted her brow and worry glazed her green eyes.

Suddenly he could see her viewpoint and why she wanted legitimacy. In the future marriage would truly tie Jeff's child into the family.

Yet it would bind Matt to Olivia in a manner he never intended. For an instant heat flashed in him at the thought of marriage to her. On a purely physical level he speculated about her shapely, naked body in his arms. With lightning speed the image aroused him.

He forced his thoughts back to business and a contract with her and a paper marriage. A marriage in name only.

"We can dissolve it as soon as I get my law degree," she added.

Could he stay under the same roof with her and keep his hands to himself? He had planned to do just that before she had come up with the proposal.

"You want it all," he said quietly, and she flushed, her cheeks turning a bright pink.

"No. I don't want sex with you," she answered bluntly. "You know it wouldn't be a true marriage. Not in any manner. But you can see that if you really want what you've been telling me, it would give my baby more protection and give me a better deal."

"Hell, yes," he snapped. "You could sue me for divorce and half of everything I own."

"You said we'd have a contract. We'll have a prenuptial agreement that will list terms as both of us want them. You can have your lawyer draw it up."

Matt was impressed. She was taking charge of part of their bargain, making some shrewd demands and she once again surprised him. He rubbed the back of his head. She had him in a corner and she knew it. He didn't want to marry her, not even a fake, paper marriage of convenience because that would be legally binding.

But if he backed out on marriage, she might refuse his deal and the baby would go out of the Ransome family.

"And you still want all the rest I've offered—the education, the cash, the trust fund for the baby?"

"I want the education and the trust fund. I'd like some cash so I can go to school full time, but if I live at the Ransome ranch, I think you could cut the amount of money in half or even less if you want. As soon as I finish my education, we can dissolve the union. I don't intend for it to be permanent."

"I've got to think about it. I hadn't planned on marriage," he said and watched her let out her breath and unclench her hands. She raised her chin.

"I didn't think you'd do it." She stood and sighed. "You were better than your brother, but it's not good enough. Since you're not interested in my terms, I'll keep my independence and move on."

"You'll be walking out on a fabulous future that's a whole hell of a lot better than you're doing now or can do. You're selling your baby short by turning down my offer."

"Perhaps, but I'm not the one who wants something here," she said. "If you're willing to commit to this baby, I want the whole deal—I want support and legitimacy and some of the things your brother should have given me." She shrugged. "I'm accustomed to tough times. You can take it or leave it."

He gazed into green eyes that were fiery and unyielding and he was certain she wasn't bluffing about turning down his offer. He believed every word she said and it increased his anger that she was being so foolish, yet at the same time, he couldn't keep from appreciating her determination to get more for her child. And deep down, Matt knew she was right. He might have done the same thing himself, had he been in her place.

"Sit down," he ordered quietly, his anger growing. "I didn't say I wouldn't do it. I simply want to think about it like you wanted to consider my offer last night."

She sat and he stared hard at her. She stared right back at him and he felt tension coil.

"I'll talk to my attorney about it," Matt finally replied, buying some time before he made any kind of commitment. "In the meantime, call and quit your job and settle in. I'll introduce you to people who live and work on the ranch."

"Until you come to a decision, I'm not leaving a job that pays better than most around here. I'm going to my room to get ready to go to work."

Matt stood and watched her walk away. He wanted to grab her and shake her and he had never felt that way with a woman before. Not even Margo before she walked out on him. Olivia Brennan got to him as no one ever had.

What was worse, was that steady, fiery sexual awareness of her, a hot attraction that kept his nerves on edge. Marry her!

His whole being wanted to yell never, but then he thought about what he would be tossing aside. He was certain she would walk right out of his life and at any point in time, she could move far from Texas. She had no roots, no ties except going to college and right now she was between semesters. Right now, she could move away without much disruption in her life. Her college credits would transfer.

"Dammit!" He pushed back his chair with a scrape and crossed the room to call the family attorney.

He presented the problem swiftly, asking questions about a prenuptial agreement, keeping his eye on the clock. While part of him listened to the lawyer speaking, part of Matt's attention was focused on hearing Olivia return.

Matt finally replaced the receiver and stared at the phone. As he suspected, marriage, even a paper-only union, would be far more binding than the bargain Matt had intended to strike with Olivia. But it could be dissolved, and he could put stipulations to try to protect himself from later demands. It didn't mean she wouldn't sue or take him to court and he would have to fight her later. On the other hand, the baby would legally be a Ransome.

Matt rubbed the back of his neck and swore under his breath. He didn't want to get bound to her. Not Olivia or any other woman.

He heard her in the hall and he crossed the family room in quick long strides. In the kitchen he caught up with her and she glanced at him as he strode into the room.

"Wait a minute!" he snapped.

Her brows lifted in question as he crossed the room to stand with only inches separating them. "I called our attorney and talked to him," Matt declared. "Marriage is a hell of a lot more commitment than you're asking me to make."

"You are the one who wants my baby in your family, remember?"

"I'm considering what you want. Call in sick tonight. You can miss one night and still keep your job."

"I can, but I don't see any reason to. I'm going to work. I need every dollar I can earn."

"I've offered you a damn good deal."

"Indeed, you have, but I told you that I want it all," she said softly. She had on her tight red T-shirt and short cutoffs.

"Hell, I'll pay your salary for tonight, but you take sick leave," he ordered, annoyed that she was uncooperative. He was as angered by her demands and stubborn will as he was by his own heated response to her.

She stared at him a moment and he thought she was going to still refuse. Instead, she nodded and crossed the room to the phone, hanging her red vinyl purse on a hook by the door.

She asked for another woman and spoke softly, turning her back to Matt, but he heard her tell her friend that something had come up and she wouldn't be there tonight.

"You could have told her you were sick," Matt said as soon as she replaced the receiver and turned around.

"I'm not sick. Kira will think of some excuse for me, no doubt. I don't think you have a very high opinion of me," she remarked. "I'm sure you think I'm cheap and easy and not too bright."

"I'll admit that I might have thought that at one time, but the P.I.'s report changed my opinion. You don't have any men in your life now. Your grades are top-notch. My opinion of you changes almost hourly. You constantly surprise me."

"The same as you astound me. So did your brother. To my misfortune, I misjudged him in too many ways. I'll never trust a Ransome again like I did Jeff."

"You want to marry a Ransome," Matt reminded her.

"That is purely a business arrangement for both of us." She took her purse off the hook. "I'm going to unpack my things, shower and change before you show me around. I'd just as soon not meet people dressed like this."

He nodded and watched her start out of the room. At the door she turned back to look at him. "Unlike Jeff Ransome, you can trust me. If I give you my word, I'll keep it." She left, and he heard the soft slap of her sneakers in the hall.

"I'll be in my office," he called after her and headed down the hall, wanting to talk to his attorney again.

Olivia closed the door to her new bedroom, walking around the room and touching the furniture lightly. She shook from pent-up nerves and her proposal to Matt Ransome. To demand that the man who owned this mansion marry her—it took her breath with its presumptuousness. How could she be that brash and calculating? Yet it would give the world to her baby.

Her proposal of marriage had jarred Matt. It wasn't what he had expected or wanted, yet he was considering it. She could detect a grudging respect growing in him.

She paused in front of an elegant rosewood-framed mirror and looked at herself. Her riot of red hair always gave the impression of a wanton woman. Her breasts were full, adding to the attraction to males. She ought to cut her hair and buy fake glasses. With the money—if she made a deal with Matt—she would be able to afford to get her hair fixed and buy new clothes.

She frowned at her image. She shouldn't think about where or how she would spend one nickel of his money. She didn't have a deal yet with Matt, and they might not ever have one.

With her proposal, had she opened it up for Matt to take control of her child? That question nagged at her. If they married, he would legally have rights and she was certain he would have all sorts of opinions on how Jeff's baby should be raised and what schools it should attend. Never would she be able to pack, divorce Matt and walk away as easily as she would if she simply accepted Matt's money offer.

At the thought of relinquishing control of all decisions concerning her child, her stomach knotted. On the other hand, giving her baby the Ransome name and making him or her an heir would offset letting Matt into their lives. And from what she could see, Matt seemed to truly want what was best for her child.

She had never had a decent home life. She glanced around

the splendid bedroom and knew she would be giving her off-spring the best.

And Matt? How long could they resist the sizzling physical attraction? She didn't want to ever love another Ransome, another untrustworthy male and in this case, an arrogant, controlling one. Yet even now when Matt was away from her, she was hot and breathless merely thinking about him. It was a volatile chemistry she didn't have with other men and it might make living under the same roof with him a challenge. Seduction was unwanted, but would she be strong enough to resist the attraction, she wondered.

Could she be uncompromising and walk away if he rejected her proposal?

She couldn't answer her own question. She thought of the money he offered, the chance for her to get through school quickly, then care for herself and the baby. How could she walk away from all that? Would it be horribly unfair to her child to turn her back on Matt's offer?

Yet she suspected if she didn't walk away, he would never come back with acceptance of her proposal. And she wanted the Ransome name and all that went with it.

Her gaze drifted around the room again and the thought of her baby being part of the fortune of this family took her breath! She strolled to the window and looked out at grounds that were well tended. Beyond them acres of range land stretched to the horizon. The wealth of the place was so foreign to her, she might as well have been in another country. Would Matt consider running the risk of letting her lay claim to some of what he owned?

Matt wrote out a hasty prenuptial agreement, trying to think of all the things he wanted to put into the document so he would be prepared when he saw his attorney.

His mind kept jumping to Olivia, remembering watching her and touching her. He groaned and rubbed the back of his neck. He had known her less than twenty-four hours and he couldn't get her out of his mind.

Disgusted with himself that he couldn't stop thinking about her, Matt went to look in the desk in his bedroom for a copy of the prenuptial agreement he'd had with Margo. They had married young and both had come from wealthy families so they had drawn up a prenup agreement, but when they parted, there had been no hassle over money. With her tremendous salary and her family's money, she cared nothing about demands on Matt. She simply wanted out of the marriage to pursue her career.

In the hall Matt passed Olivia's closed door and thought about her in the shower, water pouring over that lush body and down her long legs. He groaned and walked faster, suspecting he should go work out and burn some energy. A whole evening with Olivia was going to be hellish temptation.

"Matt—"

He turned as she opened her door and stepped into the hall. Her shirt was pulled out of her cutoffs and partially unbuttoned, the open V giving a tantalizing glimpse of heart-stopping curves and cleavage.

"I can't get the hot water faucet to turn," she said. "Is it broken or am I doing something wrong? I can't imagine the plumbing breaking in this castle."

"Oh, hell. Sorry, I forgot. I've intended to get that fixed. And the plumbing does break on occasion," he added with amusement. "I'll get a wrench. It won't take more than a minute to repair it. Or you can move to any of the other occupied bedrooms."

"I'll wait if you don't mind repairing it."

He left to get pliers, a washer and a wrench and returned to her room, taking a deep breath before he went inside. She stood by the window, and he hoped she stayed out of the bathroom.

The scent of her perfume hung in the air and he tried to ignore it and think about water and pipes. As he leaned over the tub, working on the faucet, he swore because he hadn't taken care of the plumbing before she arrived or remembered it and put her in a different bedroom.

In minutes the faucet functioned again, and he picked up his wrench and pliers. As he started out, she entered the room and they almost collided. Taking her arm, he steadied her. "Sorry, Olivia," he said.

She looked up at him and again, he was ensnared in wide, thickly lashed green eyes. Desire rocked him and her eyes half-closed in a sultry expression that took his breath. He placed one hand on the doorjamb beside her and leaned closer. When she inhaled deeply, his gaze lowered and then returned to her full lips. Hemming her in, he could feel the heat from her voluptuous body, detect the come-hither fragrance she wore.

"We can find out now and get this out of the way between us," he said softly, leaning closer.

Her eyelids drooped a fraction as she slanted him a sensual look that set his pulse pounding. He slipped his arm around her waist and heard her gasp. She was soft, warm, all curves. He took his time, giving her a chance to pull away or protest or whatever she wanted.

Instead, when she placed her hand on his forearm and gazed up at him with a hot look, his body responded. If he was damned for it, he was going to kiss her.

With a seductive look from her, he was hard, wanting her, wanting to plunder her swollen lips, to taste and explore and see what a storm he could stir in her. Never had he seen a woman who looked more ready for sex.

Somewhere in the depths of his being, he knew he was crossing a line, going against what he had sworn he would avoid. With the temptation of a Pandora's box, he couldn't resist even if he knew in his heart that he was opening himself up for unending trouble.

As he leaned closer, she tilted her head up. Her breath was sweet and she was soft in the curve of his arm. His mouth came down on hers, opening her lips, his tongue sliding inside her mouth. Hot and wet, his kiss demanded more. He wanted to discover her sexually and his kiss and his body pressing hers was the fiery beginning.

She wrapped her arms around his neck, leaned into him,

molding her soft curves against him as she kissed him in return. Her tongue played over his, stroking and stirring his blinding need.

His rational thought had been lost back there when she first pressed against him. He tightened his arm around her, pulling her closer into his embrace, leaning over her and taking her searing kisses, letting go the pent-up longing he had controlled until now.

His pulse roared, drowning out other sounds, and he thought she would melt him with her scalding kisses. Why was she so different? he wondered. His heart thudded and he was in flames while below his belt he was rock-hard. He pulled her up tightly against him as his hand slid down her back and then trailed over the enticing curve of her bottom.

Her softness fanned the fire that consumed him. He ached to drown in her softness and unleash all her promised passion.

Grabbing a silky handful of her hair, he held her. When her hips twisted against him, he groaned.

Their kiss had escalated and spun out of control, seconds becoming minutes, time lost in need. She was too hot to handle, yet too desirable to release. Danger, danger ran through his thoughts, but he paid no heed. He never wanted to stop kissing her, kisses that were etched in his memory. Kisses that bound him to her in spite of all his reluctance.

Dimly, he became aware of her hands pressed on his chest, lightly pushing against him.

With an effort he opened his eyes, looking down at her to see her watching him. He released her and she stepped away, her gaze raking over him. "That was pure lust," she whispered.

"There was nothing pure about the past few minutes," he retorted, breathing heavily, seeing her gasp for breath as much as he did.

"I wasn't going to do that," she said, shooting him a torrid glance and then snapping her mouth closed.

"It's not going to happen again," he said, grinding out his words, hating his loss of control. His insides churned because emotionally, he hadn't wanted to kiss her. Physically, he lusted to have her in his bed with her naked body against him. "I don't think either one of us intended that kiss to happen, but it did and it seemed inevitable. Now it's over and done and we can forget about it," he said, wondering if he was trying to convince himself. In a lifetime, could he forget her kisses?

"That wasn't what I intended," she repeated in a low voice.

"There's some chemistry that we both gave in to, but it doesn't need to happen again."

She gave him a level, direct look. "So you're sorry you kissed me."

"You know I'm not, but we'll go back like we were."

When she nodded and closed the door, he let out his breath and shook his head. Why had he kissed her? Every shred of common sense told him to keep his hands to himself.

Burning with desire, he stormed down the hall. The fire in her kisses had been even more than he had expected. And his thoughts seethed about her marriage proposal and the prenuptial agreement, because now he felt differently about her demands and expectations.

Their relationship had just changed. Whether she knew it yet or not, his feelings toward her had intensified. How easily she could wreck his peaceful life! His reaction to Olivia was lust. Lust and anger and he needed to keep tight control of both emotions. He promised himself he would never let down his guard with her again. After Margo he would never trust a woman. Margo had taken his heart and stomped it to a million pieces. He didn't ever want to risk his heart with another woman.

He charged into his bedroom and slammed the door, crossing to his desk to open a drawer and once again get the prenuptial agreement from his marriage. Margo had made no demands on him. She had wanted out of the marriage and between her job and her family, she'd had all the money she could possibly want so there had been no problems there. The only problem had been that he had thought he was in love with her and he suspected she had only briefly been in love with him.

Looking at stipulations, he pored over the agreement some more and jotted notes while he wondered how many of his demands Olivia would accept.

Thinking about Olivia, he paused. She was honest, intelligent and shrewd. Had Jeff had a clue about what she was really like or had he simply seen her as a gorgeous, sexy woman?

Matt knew his brother well enough to know the answer to his question as swiftly as the question had risen—Jeff wouldn't get beyond sex.

Matt dropped his pen. He did not want to marry Olivia and damned if he would! After the poverty she had lived in, he couldn't imagine that she would walk away from the comfort and luxury he was offering.

While a plan formed in his mind, he stared out the window. He would give her two days of fabulous living—fly her to Houston, buy her a fancy wardrobe and shower her with jewelry and clothes she had never been able to afford. He would wine and dine her at places that would impress the most hardened sophisticate. Then see if she still wanted to reject his offer when he turned down her marriage proposal.

He picked up his phone to call and change his appointment with his lawyer. Next he called to get the Ransome corporate jet ready.

He strode down the hall and knocked on her door.

"Just a minute," she called. She swung the door open to face him. She stood with a towel wrapped around her and looking at her was as jolting as getting socked in the middle and having the wind knocked out of him.

Her slender shoulders were bare and the white towel was a contrast to her creamy skin. The towel was midthigh and all he could think about was only a towel covered her naked body.

While heat flashed through him, his heart thudded. He wanted to reach for her, remove that towel and pull her into his arms. Memories of her kisses fanned the flames that consumed him and for an instant, he was tongue-tied.

Her hair tumbled over her shoulders and she still had a few

drops of water that sparkled on one shoulder. She had been sexy in the T-shirt and cutoffs. In a towel, she was gorgeous.

He realized he was staring and she shifted impatiently. "Yes?" she asked, tilting her head.

"Get dressed," he said, hating the husky scrape in his voice. "I've made arrangements for a plane and I'll take you shopping in Houston so we can get you some new clothes. You'll need them. We'll eat there tonight and then we can fly back here or get rooms there."

"You're not doing this to postpone having to reach a decision about my proposal, are you?" she asked.

"Partially," he admitted, suspecting it wouldn't fool her if he gave her any other answer. "We're making big, life-changing decisions about our futures, though, so what will a twenty-four hour postponement hurt?"

"It might get me fired from my job if I don't show up two nights in a row."

"You can be back by tomorrow night," he answered.

She stared at him while she seemed to be mulling things over and finally she nodded. "I can be ready in ten minutes," she said and closed the door.

He stared at the closed door and still saw the image of her in the white towel. He wiped his brow. How was he going to cope with her under his roof for the next several years? He wanted the baby close, but if every encounter with Olivia was like the last two, he would be a basket case in no time.

Matt charged back to his room to call his favorite hotel and reserve adjoining suites. He made dinner reservations and then hurried to shower and shave and get dressed to go.

Ten minutes later he entered the family room to find her waiting. His gaze raked over her, taking in her denim skirt and simple, sleeveless white cotton blouse and sandals. He suspected what few clothes she owned were practical and cheap. There would be no way she could afford anything fancy or expensive unless she had the good fortune to find it in a secondhand shop. Even so, the sight of her made his pulse accelerate and he still had to fight the urge to want to touch her as he squelched images of her without the denim skirt or white blouse.

"I've never flown before," she said.

"Good! You'll like it," he answered, taking her arm and steering her out of the house and toward his car. He wanted to dazzle her and make her want to stay so badly that she would give up all thought of marriage.

They drove in silence to Meacham International Airport in Forth Worth. As they approached the waiting plane, her eyes were larger than usual. She was pale and silent, gazing with awe in her expression at the sleek jet awaiting them.

In a short time they were buckled into their comfortable seats with Olivia near a window. She seemed overwhelmed and he hoped her life was changing forever today and she would never want to go back to the poverty and hard life she had known in the past.

The moment they sped down the runway and then lifted into the air, she flashed him a brilliant smile that set his heart pounding. "This is fabulous!" she exclaimed, and satisfaction shot through him. Hopefully, in forty-eight hours he would be able to tell her no to marriage and she would cave in to his terms. All her awe and pleasure over the trip were only beginning— he could imagine how she would feel after two days of lavishly showering her with whatever she wanted. He smiled in return.

Four hours later, his satisfaction had increased. He swam laps in the hotel pool while he waited for Olivia who was getting her hair cut and styled. He had dinner reservations and after the first hour with her he had left her to shop on her own.

He glanced at his watch and climbed out of the pool to dress for dinner. She had seemed as overwhelmed by the hotel as she had been by their flight. Matt smiled grimly. He didn't want to deal with her about anything, but at least now it would be on his terms and not hers.

No one could live like this for two days and then go back to a grinding job at a rough Texas honky-tonk.

He dressed in a navy suit for dinner. He had helped her

select a simple black dress for dinner tonight, a dress with a price that had made her eyes grow round with wonder.

Matt knocked on the door of her suite and waited. The door swung open and Olivia smiled at him.

Once again, she stunned him and threw him off guard. Drawing a deep breath, Matt stared at her.

Four

"**G**ood evening," Olivia said with far more assurance than she felt. At the sight of Matt, who was handsome, commanding and appealing in an immaculate white shirt and navy suit, her qualms faded momentarily to be replaced by a jump in her pulse.

Matt's gaze drifted over her in a thorough assessment that was as provocative as a caress. "You look sensational," he said softly.

"Thank you," she replied, knowing they were treading dangerous ground. She reminded herself that he was a Ransome with all the complications of being Jeff's brother. Her smile faded and she inhaled, fighting that irresistible draw she experienced around Matt.

In spite of her wariness, she couldn't keep from being pleased by the admiration in his expression. She was certain that his compliment had been sincere. Earlier, she had hardly known herself after the hairstylist finished. Her hair was cut, the sides brought up and looped on her head, the rest tumbling down her back. Instead of the simple black dress Matt had selected, she had found a dark blue one she liked that had a low-cut, draped back and was sleeveless with a skirt that stopped inches above her knees. She loved the cool silk lining that was smooth against her skin when she stepped into it.

"Ready to go?" he asked, and she nodded, picking up her purse.

"So is this a truce, more or less?" she asked as they headed to the elevators.

"Might as well be," he answered easily, yet she had a suspicion his animosity toward her had changed little. "You've moved into my house and we'll be together a lot from now on so we might as well get along."

She smiled disarmingly at him, yet she couldn't get rid of her suspicions that his sudden change in attitude hid an ulterior motive. Whether it did or not, she intended to enjoy the evening. She was with a handsome, sexy man, going to an elegant restaurant and she was dressed in the most gorgeous, expensive dress she had ever owned. Tonight she was Cinderella. She would enjoy herself until the clock struck twelve or whatever happened to burst her bubble.

Today, his kisses had rocked her. Remembering caused her lips to tingle. She hated that he had stirred feelings she thought were long dormant.

His kiss had plundered and all that pent-up desire that burned in the depth of his blue eyes had poured into his kiss and demolished any resistance she might have had. Tonight she would be even more susceptible to his charm.

As they left the hotel and climbed into a limousine, it came to her what he was possibly doing—giving her a taste of a life-style she had never known, but soon would be able to afford if she accepted his offer.

Anger flashed at the realization of his motive. Of course that was what he was doing! His smiles held all the threat of a crouching tiger. In his own way, Matt was fighting for what he wanted. Yet she couldn't blame him, because she was doing the same with her threat to walk if he didn't accept her terms.

They rode in the back of the limo across from each other and she smiled at him.

Desire blazed in his eyes, cutting across the battle between them. While she watched, he reached into his pocket. "I bought something for you today," he said, handing a small box to her.

Surprised, she glanced at the box and then at him. She was tempted to throw it at him for what he was doing, but then she reminded herself that he was trying to win her over to agreeing to his offer just as much as she intended to persuade him to consent to her proposal.

She opened the box. Nestled inside was a gold, diamond-studded bangle. Catching the light, the diamonds sparkled. "It's beautiful!" she gasped, momentarily forgetting his motive or her caution, because she had never dreamed of owning such a piece of jewelry.

He reached over to pick it up. Taking her hand in his warm, strong fingers, he slipped the bracelet on her slender wrist.

"Thank you! It's absolutely gorgeous!" she exclaimed, her emotions churning because all at once, she was both thrilled to receive the jewelry from him and at the same time, she was annoyed. Beneath those warring emotions ran an undercurrent that saddened her that the gift held no meaning whatsoever. It was simply a beautiful bribe.

"There's something to go with it," he said, smiling at her, and her heart skipped a beat. His bone-melting smiles were irresistible, so her guard came up again because she knew she was treading on dangerous ground. In icy clarity, she realized that with this Ransome her heart was more at risk than it had been with his younger brother.

Matt withdrew another small box and handed it to her. If his motive hadn't been so underhanded, she would have been dazzled. As it was, she gazed at him solemnly, telling herself she could still refuse his offer. Cinderella for a day. She could turn her back on this and survive. But it was beginning to nag at her whether if she did, and lost her big gamble, would she be cheating her baby of a better future?

She opened the box and gasped again. Even when she knew it would hold another beautiful, expensive bauble, she stared at the golden necklace with a diamond pendant that matched her bracelet.

In a smooth movement, he slid onto the seat beside her. "Turn around," he said, taking the necklace from her hand.

When she turned her back, his warm fingers brushed her nape. Reaching behind her head, she held her hair up while he fastened the necklace and then she faced him. He sat close enough that their thighs touched and his blue eyes bore into her, causing her heart to race.

"Thank you. They're both beautiful."

"You're what's beautiful, Olivia," he said softly, brushing a stray tendril of hair away from her ear.

He was only inches away and desire, like heat lightning flashed, holding them locked in the moment. When his gaze lowered to her mouth, she thought he surely could hear her heart pounding. She should move, but it was impossible. She fought the urge to slip her arm around his neck and pull him the last few inches, to draw him close and lose herself in his hot kisses.

"I thought we both agreed we weren't going to do this," she said, as much to herself as to him. She closed her eyes and turned away.

He slipped onto the seat facing her. Even while hot desire still burned in the depths of his blue eyes, the tight clamp of his jaw reflected a tense, angry look in his expression.

"You're right. We'll eat and then get the hell back to the ranch," he said, looking out a window.

"Regrets for bringing me here?"

His head swung around and she braced against the force of his gaze. He shook his head. "Not at all. You should have this. Before long, one way or another, you get a tidy sum of money to buy whatever clothes or car you want. You might as well get some things now."

She bit back her reply when the limo stopped at the front door of a restaurant.

Even though the sun was still above the horizon, tiny lights twinkled in the bushes while large lights shone on tall pines. As she emerged from the limo, Matt took her arm.

They were led through the restaurant past a dance floor where couples already circled to piano music. The waiter seated Matt and Olivia at a table on the patio near a splashing fountain. Brightly colored lanterns were glowing overhead and red roses filled crystal vases on each linen-covered table. In the festive ambience with Matt at her side, Olivia bubbled with excitement.

Their waiter appeared, placing thick black folders with the menu in front of them. Olivia opened hers. She glanced at Matt who was reading his menu and then she looked down at her own. The dishes sounded exotic and the prices astounded her.

"I can't believe we're eating anything as expensive as these dinners," she said.

"The food here is very good," he said. "Do you like lobster?"

She shrugged. "Actually, I've never eaten lobster so I have no idea whether I'd like it or not."

"I suggest you try it and then you'll know."

"The daredevil Ransomes who will always try the un-known," she said quietly, thinking about Matt and Jeff.

"Life is exciting."

"Maybe from your perspective. From mine, life is survival."

"It doesn't have to be from now on," he said smoothly waving his hand to include their surroundings and she was aware again of the clash of wills between them. "My offer will open all the doors for you," he added.

"Marriage wouldn't be real and it wouldn't be permanent," she reminded him and they paused when the waiter appeared.

After they had ordered, she gazed across the table at Matt. "The clothes are beautiful, the jewelry breathtaking and my first flight was thrilling. My first limo ride was unforgettable. But you're not going to hold me with the life you're dangling in front of me now," she said softly. Something flickered in the depths of his eyes. Otherwise there was no reaction from him except an arch of his eyebrow.

"Don't lose sight of the fact that if you turn down my offer, you'll be taking all sorts of opportunities away from your baby. Do you want to raise a child in a neighborhood like you grew up in, instead of the Ransome ranch or a house you can afford in a prosperous neighborhood with a suitable school? You've got to think for two. It's not only you," he reminded her quietly, and her anger soared.

"Dammit, I'm taking that into consideration, but I'm not selling short of what I know my baby should have," she said, hurting because Matt was right. Pain was tight in her chest, and she fought back tears that startled her since she rarely ever cried. His accusation had been on target and hurt badly. But she wanted the Ransome heritage locked in for her baby. "You'll commit to a point and then it stops."

"It's a damn generous commitment, I'd say," he retorted.

"I'll do something to stay out of bad neighborhoods. There are some acceptable jobs out there that I can do and I'll find one. I've gotten farther now than all the odds indicated I would."

"That you have. But don't sell the baby short to try to get me to marry you. Jeff wouldn't, and I'm not going to either."

His words stabbed into her, deepening her hurt. "That's your answer?" she asked, wondering if he would abandon her on the spot. She held her breath while fear chilled her.

"No, it's not my answer. I believe you'll walk so I'm still contemplating the future. I'm not deciding something that important without giving it a lot of thought. Now, on that note, try to enjoy the evening."

"Oh, right," she answered, yet his reply rekindled her hope.

"I mean it," he said in a softer voice. "Had we met under other circumstances, we both could probably enjoy the next few hours. Neither of us will take decisive action tonight, so relax."

"That's a tall order," she remarked.

"It's simple." He stood and came around the table to take her hand. "We'll get away from our problems. Let's dance."

"I can't dance," she said.

He shook his head. "You've got two feet and you can move, so you can dance. I'll show you," he said, ignoring her protest and leading her inside to the dance floor. Her heart drummed as she looked at couples moving so easily together.

"I really can't dance. I never did get around to learning and most of my life has been spent studying and working and trying to survive."

"That's going to change," he said, pulling her into his arms. "Just move with me," he said, holding her lightly. Their proximity was volatile, and every nerve in her body quivered with awareness. As his thighs brushed hers, her desire flamed. His hand held hers against his chest.

She stepped lightly on his toe and almost stumbled, but his arm tightened around her and he held her. "Sorry. I told you—" she said.

"Don't worry. You're a feather and it doesn't matter," he said, interrupting her. "I'm holding you so you're not going to fall," he added in a husky voice.

In minutes it became easier to follow his lead. Even so, when the music stopped she stepped back. "End of first lesson. Let's sit the next one out."

"Fine," he said, taking her arm to lead her back to their table.

When they were seated, over glasses of water and tossed green salads, she paused to study him. "You know a lot about me, but I know very little about you. Jeff was a party boy—he seldom mentioned his family or background."

"He probably talked about himself and his wild exploits. My kid brother and I weren't much alike. At least, I've always hoped we weren't because Jeff was damned irresponsible. What do you want to know about me?"

"Start with telling me about your family," she asked, curious about him because whenever she had approached the subject of family with Jeff Ransome, he had talked about himself.

"There's my dad who has heart trouble and isn't in good health, but he still wants to be in charge and that's why I have my own house. The big house is down the road a ways."

"The big house!" she exclaimed. "I can't imagine one much larger than yours."

"Oh, yes. Bigger, fancier. All it needs is a moat around it and we'd have a castle. I'll take you to see it and meet Dad soon."

"So where do the other family members live? Tell me about Nick and Katherine."

"We're all close in age. I'm thirty-two, Nick is thirty-one and Katherine is twenty-eight. Business is Nick's first love. He's CEO of Ransome Energy and under Nick's control the family oil business has tripled in size, gone public and continues to grow. Nick thrives on making deals."

"Is he married?"

"No. Nick isn't the marrying kind. He's almost as wild as Jeff was, but not quite. Nick is reliable—there's the big difference."

"What about your sister?"

"Katherine has a home in Dallas and one here on the ranch. Nick has his own ranch near ours. She's single and she's a graphic artist, but she specializes in murals. At the moment she's painting one for a museum in Chicago. She's quite good."

"So how long were you married?"

To her surprise his eyes clouded over. "Two years. Margo preferred a career to marriage. Her family is wealthy, so she didn't need the money from the career, but she wanted everything else that went with it."

"What does she do now?"

"She's a news anchor in L.A. now. I suppose in the beginning, I could have gone with her if I'd been willing to leave the ranch and leave Texas, but I have my own agenda and didn't like the idea of tagging along wherever her career led her. Her career is first in her life."

"So you still love her?"

"No, I'm over Margo, but that was a bad time when we divorced. It wasn't what I'd planned."

"And what happened to your mother? Is she no longer living?"

"I don't know," he answered with a cold tone. "When we

were little kids, she walked out on us. There was another man and she married him, but it didn't last a year." Matt's brows arched. "You haven't heard any of this before?"

"No," she said. "Jeff really did focus solely on himself. In spite of that, he was charming and entertaining and drew friends like a picnic drawing ants, but then you know about him. So tell me about your mother. You didn't finish."

"My dad raised us. We've had no contact with her which is the way she obviously wanted it."

"That's dreadful. Do you even know where she lives?"

"No," he said, a shuttered look coming to his expression. "None of us want any contact now that we're grown and she certainly hasn't wanted any since she disappeared out of our lives."

"Sorry."

He shrugged. "That's the way I've grown up. I don't think about it any longer."

"So you're the cowboy in the family who loves the ranch."

"Yes. I get away occasionally. I like to ski and to escape from the ranch. Occasionally, I go to the tropics. We own three ranches, this one, one in Wyoming and one along the California coast and we're buying one we've leased in Argentina."

"As in South America?"

"Right. It's the best ranch of all. It's the one I prefer."

"And Jeff helped you here?"

"Jeff worked with me when he wasn't off gallivanting around the world. He couldn't possibly have settled and worked in an office like Nick is doing. You'll meet my family soon."

"And they approve of your offer to me?"

"Sure. Everyone is interested. A new Ransome in the family would be damn good."

"Seems to me, among the three of you, one of you could produce a grandchild."

"There's already a grandchild on the way." His gaze swept over her. "Have you felt all right?"

She nodded. "Fine. Not even any morning sickness."

"You definitely are pregnant."

"That's a statement and not a question, isn't it? I'm sure you checked that one out and you know who my doctor is."

"Sorry about checking up on you, but I had to be certain."

The waiter brought their lobster dinners. After the first bite, she looked up to find him waiting and watching her.

"It's delicious. You want me to like eating lobster. You want me to cultivate a taste for exotic food."

"I don't know that lobster is exotic. Every grocery store carries them, but I'm glad you like it," Matt answered.

"It's another sales pitch," she said, touching her diamond pendant and knowing that he was doing all in his power to get her to accept his offer and forget her proposal.

"Ma'am, I'm a plain ole cowboy," he drawled, and she had to laugh.

He gave her a wicked look. "Olivia, you're doing your own share of bribery with your smile that seduces and befuddles. You want me to succumb and accept your proposal and you're stooping to as much bribery as I am," he said softly.

"My smile seducing and befuddling?" she asked in mock disbelief, for a moment letting go worries and enjoying his company, bubbling inside because he was flirting.

"You know what you're doing," he said, inhaling deeply and she flashed him another merry smile, wishing she could befuddle him enough to get him to agree to what she wanted.

"Yes! So may the best man—or woman—win!" she exclaimed, holding her water glass up in a toast to him.

Eyes twinkling, he touched her glass with his. "You're on. But then this battle is already under way."

"And you're flirting shamelessly," she said. "Besides the gifts and dinner and clothes and the evening out."

"All my weaponry pales beside yours—your face, your body, your smile, that dress, your legs. You have the edge and you know it."

"Whoo!" She fanned herself. "I didn't know you'd noticed," she purred, enjoying flirting with him. "You have armor that protects you totally. You are shielded and immune."

"Forget dinner. Let's dance," he said, coming around the table to take her hand to lead her to the dance floor. After a few minutes he looked down at her. "You've gotten the hang of it. You're very good at this."

She laughed. "Your flattery overwhelms me! Wait until I step on your toe again."

"I mean it. You're doing fine. Don't you like this?" he asked in a silky voice.

She slanted him a look. "You're flirting again."

"So what's wrong with that? No harm done. You're a beautiful woman and a sexy one. Why shouldn't I flirt?"

"Don't expect it to lead you anywhere."

"Where did you think I want to go?" he asked.

She shook her head and laughed again. "Don't tell me you don't want me in your bed."

"I'll tell you one thing I don't want in my life—any emotional complication. Judging by your demands, I don't think you want any in your life."

"I definitely don't. Not with a Ransome, thank you."

"I take it you and I will never have a handshake deal, even if we finally do come to a mutual agreement?"

"I keep my word."

"I'll damn well keep mine," he said. "Stop mixing me up with Jeff."

The next number was a fast one and when she turned to leave, he caught her hand.

"I really can't do this—" she protested.

"You're a quick study. Watch my feet and then follow me," he said, pulling her with him.

She did what he said and soon she was dancing with him. He spun her around, caught her and then returned to the quick steps. She studied his feet for a few more minutes and then looked up to find him watching her intently. Her heartbeat skipped and she drew her breath, tossing her head and feeling her hair swing.

"Perfect," he said softly.

"Not really. I've stepped on you twice."

"Never felt it. Accept my offer, Olivia, and have a better life and an easier one," he urged. "We're a mere technicality away from what you want."

She shook her head. "That isn't quite the same."

He spun her around and yanked her up against him, his arm banding her waist instantly and holding her close while he looked down at her. She felt his hard length pressed against her and she wanted to wrap her arms around his neck and kiss him. At the same time, she looked into his eyes and felt the clash with him over their futures. She knew the light moments were gone and the flirting was over.

He spun her away from him and then the music stopped. Gasping for breath, she let him take her hand and she felt the calluses on his palm that indicated he really did do ranch work.

"Let's go back to the hotel and talk things over," he suggested.

Knowing they might as well get back to business, she nodded. At the door she glanced back over her shoulder. In the past couple of hours, she had had the time of her life, the best she could remember.

She was surprised by her own reaction and wondered if she had really been in love with Jeff at all.

In the limo she was as silent as Matt, aware they were each locked in separate worlds. At the hotel as they reached their adjoining suites, Matt shed his coat and tie and unfastened the collar of his shirt. "Let me come in for a while. I'll order tea or lemonade or whatever you'd like," he suggested.

She nodded and opened her door, moving inside. He followed and tossed his coat on a chair. "What would you like to drink?" he asked.

"Hot cocoa," she said, wondering if she could drink anything. Her nervousness had returned, but she didn't want it to show. All evening she had felt as if what she wanted was slipping through her fingers. She could feel his resistance to her offer. When he said no, was she ready to make her decision and stick by it?

He ordered a pot of hot chocolate and a cold beer. Only one lamp burned in the fancy suite and in the soft light, his appeal heightened. It would have been easier to deal with him if she hadn't had this fiery sexual reaction to him. And why the chemistry she couldn't imagine because they fought for opposing goals. She suspected he truly did not like her at all. Facing him, she knew part of his attraction was his rugged good looks and a sexiness that probably drew most females he encountered.

He moved around the room, turning on soft music, dimming the light, rolling back his cuffs, seductive moves, yet she knew seduction wasn't his goal. He wanted her to agree to his offer. His control was admirable because she guessed it was an effort for him. She suspected he usually got his way.

At a knock on the door, she watched Matt cross the room in long strides to let the bellman wheel in a cart with a silver pot, china cups and two cold beers on ice. Olivia sat on a wingback chair and crossed her legs. In minutes, Matt handed her a cup of steaming chocolate.

"It's too hot to drink right now," she said, placing it on a coffee table and then leaning back.

When he sat nearby and gave her a long look, she drew a deep breath. "I feel like the proverbial bug under a microscope," she said.

"An absolutely stunning butterfly, maybe. A bug—no," he answered quietly, his gaze drifting lazily over her while she couldn't avoid being pleased by his compliment. "Are you ready to discuss the terms of my offer?"

She shrugged. "It's not essential because I really do not intend to accept it. I prefer that you accept my proposal."

"Let's just say, 'What if?' and talk about my offer for a while. All right?"

"I suppose, as long as you don't abandon me here in Houston if we don't come to an agreement. I do want to return to Rincon."

"I promise to get you home and I don't intend to reach a decision tonight. I only want to talk things over. When I first approached you, we were complete strangers."

"And the brief time we've been together has made a difference?" she asked in surprise because it hadn't changed her opinions.

He set the bottle on a table. "We'll live in my house, but what happens if you want to go out with someone or start seeing someone regularly?"

She shook her head. "You're assuming we will go with your offer."

"Let's discuss it."

"It's pointless to, but if it makes you happy, all right," she said. "For now, I don't want any man in my life. Not at all. You're still going on the assumption that I'll accept your offer and we won't marry. Or do you intend the same agreement if we marry?"

His eyes narrowed and her heart began to thump faster at the determined expression on his face. "No. If we marry, I don't want sordid gossip floating around Cedar County about this baby's mother or stepfather."

"So what do you propose? A celibate life?" she asked, unable to imagine that he would agree.

"Hardly. If I agree to your marriage proposal, I want sex."

Heat blazed in her, and she could feel the perspiration break out on her forehead. While her emotions boiled, they stared at each other. "That isn't what I intended."

"That's what it would have to be."

"How often?" she shot back, trying to catch her breath and wondering if she could handle sex with Matt Ransome without falling head over heels in love with him—a love that she was certain he would never return. Could there be great sex and no love with a handsome man who was helping her raise her child? Hardly.

Fear curled in her, thick and as palpable as smoke from a fire. Jeff had broken her trust and trampled her feelings. Could she expect anything better from his older brother?

"Let's say after your pregnancy is over, twice a week and then we can go from there."

"And until my pregnancy is over?"

"I don't see any need to be definite except if I marry you, then I want a wedding night with sex."

She was certain he could hear her heart thudding. His demands were making both propositions, his and hers, real to her.

"You know what you want, don't you?" Agitated, she stood and moved to the floor-to-ceiling window to gaze down below at the lights on a sparkling pool. Was she ready for sex with him? Her body was more than ready. His words had set her ablaze, but sex was a fast track to heartbreak. Remembering his spectacular, sizzling kisses that had stormed her senses and had been the beginning of seduction, she knew he would be a fabulous lover. And that was what worried her because Matt Ransome seemed as hardhearted as they came.

"There's always my offer," he said quietly, standing close behind her. She hadn't heard him get up or move across the room. She turned to face him. He stood only a foot away. He had rolled back his sleeves and unfastened one more button on his shirt. All she could think of was sex with him—a wedding night.

"If I increased the amount of money, would you accept my offer? If I changed the hundred thousand dollars to a hundred and fifty thousand, how's that?"

Again, he shocked her and she stared at him while the amount spun in her thoughts. "If you're that willing to raise what you'll pay me, then marriage must be binding enough that you want to avoid it at all costs," she whispered.

Matt stood waiting quietly, letting her think about the money. He could afford what he had offered and he did not want marriage, yet standing so close to her, gazing into her wide green eyes, his pulse raced and he was hot with desire. She was stunning with her new hairdo and clothes. She had been a looker before, but now she was breathtaking. Men had watched her all evening in a restaurant where people would be far more restrained than the honky-tonk at home.

No matter how enticing she was, he didn't want a permanent entanglement. Even with the increase in his offer, he felt to his soul that she was going to hold out for marriage.

He inhaled deeply, his gaze sweeping over her slender bare shoulders and long, graceful throat, the soft curves that the dress hugged and her tiny waist. Her long legs were spectacular. He already knew that from seeing her in the towel and cutoffs. Could he take her to bed, live under the same roof, share a baby with her and still keep his heart locked away?

He had no doubt that once she got her law degree, she would be gone. He hoped by that time, she would feel that her child was part of the Ransome family. In the meantime he better worry about the present. What would he do if she turned down his offer?

"I've made you a damned handsome offer," he said aloud, half to her and half to himself.

"I know you have. It was generous before you raised the amount. It's the long-term commitment I want."

"I'll never love again," he said. "You better believe me because I do what I say."

"I imagine you do," she replied, looking up at him. "Jeff told me about how your father got lost one time when his small plane crashed in the Rocky Mountains and after the searchers gave up hunting for him, you flew up there, trekked into the mountains on your own and found him and brought him out of there on a stretcher you improvised. Jeff said you do what you say and you don't give up. Actually, he said you're stubborn as a mule."

"As if he wasn't. I knew my dad was there and I wasn't going to leave him. He had broken one leg and he couldn't get out on his own and no one else survived the crash. My dad is a tough old codger."

"I suspect you're rather tough yourself."

"If so, I've had to be sometimes," he replied, fighting an urge to reach out and touch her. In spite of the conflict between them and his anger, he wanted her. Desire was a throbbing, hot flame tormenting him. She was beautiful and he couldn't stop wanting to hold and kiss her.

"And stubborn?"

"I suppose. If it's stubborn of me to avoid falling in love

again, then so be it. I believe you have a streak of that trait your-self," he said, and she smiled at him. "So you still plan to move on someday?" he asked.

"We both know marriage will give the baby more," she said, ignoring his question.

Every minute with her he had been torn between anger and attraction and that was still true. They were at an impasse, and his desire was escalating. He knew he needed to get distance between them.

"I'll sleep on it," he said. He strode out the door into the hall, closing her door quietly behind him and going to his room.

Shedding his clothes he moved around his room. Sleep wasn't going to be part of his night. Would she walk away from all he offered simply to hold out for marriage?

He absolutely didn't want to marry again. Not even if the woman was fabulously beautiful and sexy? The question taunted him because he couldn't extinguish memories of holding her in his arms, of her scalding kisses, or how stunning she had looked tonight. How badly he had wanted to peel her out of that scrap of a dress! Marriage would mean sex with her. She had already agreed to it.

He groaned, knowing sleep was impossible. He glared at the door that led to her room. She would give up most of the cash if he would marry her, but that didn't matter because cash was no problem for him.

Coming from the background of poverty, she had a far smaller regard for money than he would have expected.

Feeling hemmed in and wishing they had flown home tonight, he paced his room and then moved to the window to stare outside. It was late and traffic had thinned. He wasn't giving up the baby. Deep down, he still felt that she would disappear if he rejected her proposal. "Dammit!" he swore, knotting his fists, wishing he could walk away. She knew she had what he wanted.

By morning, after a shave and shower, he continued to toss the choices back and forth in his mind. He went around to knock on her door and stood waiting, wondering how she had slept.

She opened the door and gazed up at him. Dressed in a white suit and red blouse, once again, she looked stunning. Her hair was looped and pinned on one side of her head, giving her a more sophisticated appearance. No amount of fancy clothes or cosmopolitan hairdos could extinguish her sultry, sexy aura and there was no stopping his body's immediate response to the sight of her.

Matt drew a deep breath. "Good morning."

"Good morning," she replied and stepped back. "Won't you come in?"

As he entered the room, he inhaled the seductive scent she wore. He wanted to tangle his fingers in her hair and pull it down. At the same time he wanted to send her packing. Never since childhood had he had to battle someone and lose as he was with her. Even when Margo left him, at the end he had been angry, but ready for her to get out of his life. He couldn't handle Olivia. It was the first time in his life he had been in this position and he didn't like it.

Staring at Olivia, he was tempted to tell her to pack and go if she wouldn't accept his terms, but when he thought about losing the baby, he clamped his jaw closed more tightly.

This morning she was gorgeous and looked as self-confident as if she already had her law degree. How much easier all this would have been if she had been as plain as a guinea hen. "You're ready to fly home?"

"Isn't that what we're doing?"

"I'm not in a rush. I'll take you to breakfast." They faced each other in a tense silence. "Have you come to a decision on my offer?" he asked and held his breath.

"I still want more than money," she replied nonchalantly as if they were discussing what to order for breakfast, and his insides clenched.

"Dammit, I don't think you know what you're doing!" he snapped, trying to hold back his fury and hating to meet her terms.

"Indeed, I do," she replied with the coolness of a card shark. "So do you have an answer for my proposal?"

He jammed his fist into his pocket. In the night he had made his decision what he would do if she turned down his offer.

"How can you reject the fortune I'm extending to you? You're not thinking about your baby."

"Oh, yes, I am. I can decline your offer because I think you want my baby in your family to such an extent that sooner or later, you'll agree to my proposal. If you do, you'll make a greater commitment than what you're now suggesting I take."

"You're damn sure of yourself," he grumbled, thinking he had misjudged her by a country mile when he first saw her. She was smart, self-possessed and quickly shedding any rough edges she had from her poverty-stricken upbringing.

She merely shrugged. "I'm more sure of you," she replied softly.

He shook his head and rubbed the back of his neck. "I have to hand it to you. I usually get my way in deals. I've bought land, horses, cattle, took over a drilling company for my dad, etc., etc. and you're the only one who's held my feet to the fire and given me something I couldn't cope with."

"Do tell," she said blithely, and he wanted to grind his teeth. At the same time, he had to hand it to her for holding out for the big deal.

"At least, it's a relief to know this baby's going to inherit some brains."

"Thank you, I think. Unless you're referring solely to your brother."

"You know I'm not talking about him."

They stared at each other while silence once again filled the passing time. She smiled at him and began to move around the room, placing her bag and a sack together in a chair so her things would be ready to go. Finally, she turned to face him. "Still debating? We can go to breakfast while you think it over."

Knowing she wasn't going to change, he shook his head. There was no need in prolonging the moment of decision because he was the only one vacillating about her proposition.

Her eyebrows arched and she slanted her head. "No? That must mean you've come to a conclusion? What are you going to do? Are you going to marry me?"

Five

Olivia's pulse jumped because the fury that burned in his gaze made her think there was a possibility he would acquiesce and do what she wanted. While she waited, she held her breath and watched the battle in his tense expression. His blue eyes flashed with pinpoints of fire.

The tension ripped at her nerves and finally she blurted, "What's your decision?"

"You win. I'll marry you," he snapped in clipped words.

Joy and relief flooded her. Her baby's future had just been sealed. It held a promise for the best possible chance for a family, a caring father-figure and education for her baby. And herself. She fought the urge to throw her arms around Matt and shout her gratitude. Instead, she merely nodded and tried to bottle her bubbling response.

"I have some stipulations." He ground out the words, and she nodded.

Like a wave pounding into shore and then receding, her relief swept away and was replaced by worry over what she had gotten herself into. What was he going to require of her in exchange? One condition he had already told her was sex with him! And soon.

"Thank you," she said quietly, feeling his anger that was almost tangible enough to spark the air around them.

He inhaled deeply and gave her another long look that burned like a streak of fire. "We'll have to work out the prenup agreement," he said.

She nodded while her heart thudded. She tried to bank her excitement and keep a lid on all her expectations of what she would gain when she married into the Ransome family.

"Let's get breakfast and make plans," he suggested. "We don't have to check out of the hotel until after lunch, so while we're here in the city, if you want to shop for a wedding dress, I'll give you a list of the stores where I have accounts and you can charge it to me, or if you prefer, I'll go along and write a check or give you a card."

"It's bad luck for the groom to see the wedding dress before the wedding."

He gave her a withering look. "I don't think that old superstition applies in this case. Business arrangements have little connection to superstition."

"I prefer to shop by myself," she answered with what she hoped was as cold a voice as his.

He nodded. "I've already made an appointment for a meeting with my attorney at three o'clock this afternoon. Right now, let's go to breakfast and negotiate the details."

She nodded. "Fine. Give me one minute here," she said, going into the bedroom. She returned shortly and smiled at him. "There. I quit my job."

"That's one good thing," he said.

Picking up her purse, she walked beside him, trying to keep quiet and let him talk. His face was still flushed and a muscle still worked in his jaw. His voice was tight and she could only guess the depth of his anger. She suspected that except for his divorce, he had rarely had to give in to something he didn't like.

Breakfast was in a solarium in the hotel. She doubted if Matt appreciated or even noticed their sunny glass-covered surroundings and tall potted palms. He drank coffee, but otherwise barely touched his breakfast.

While Matt sipped his coffee and studied notes, she remained silent.

"The first stipulation I have, is if you have an abortion or a miscarriage, the deal's off on everything. We get divorced immediately and you get nothing."

"That's fine," she agreed quickly and was surprised at quirk of his lips in a crooked smile. "What's there to smile about?" she asked.

"You won the war. Now you'll let me win the battles," he observed dryly.

She flashed a smile at him. "I can be agreeable and yes, you're right. I got what I wanted on the big issue. Now I can be cooperative on other things."

His expression softened and he studied her, his gaze roaming slowly over her features as if he were trying to memorize her looks. "I intend to get what I want, too," he drawled, and a tingle spiraled in her because she knew he was no longer referring to the prenup agreement.

"So what do you want?" she asked with a jump in her pulse.

"Forbidden fruit," he answered in a sexy tone that fanned flames of desire. "Seduction," he said, drawing out the word until it became personal and enticing.

In response, her throat went dry. "You want sex and you feel lust, but there won't be any love between us or even the illusion of it."

"That doesn't mean it won't be great sex," he replied, looking at her with blatant desire in his gaze. "Are you getting cold feet and wanting out of this marriage proposal?"

She sipped her water and prayed she looked cool and collected and that he didn't have a clue what a tempest he stirred in her. "Be warned now—no love on your part will guarantee no love on my part."

"Do you really want to fall in love with me?" he asked, leaning forward and if she hadn't known better, she would have thought that there was a trace of honesty and vulnerability in his voice.

"At this point, no, indeed not! No more than you want right now—or could—fall in love with me." She raised her glass of water. "Here's to great sex, Matthew Ransome. And a marriage made at the bargaining table."

One corner of his mouth quirked, and one dark eyebrow lifted wickedly. "You tempt me," he said, leaning even closer, "to go after your heart that you've sealed away. And I would if I didn't want to keep my own heart protected. Risk your heart and you risk heartbreak."

"So we'll both be locked in to living together and trying to resist falling in love. And you think it'll be an easy task."

"I know myself and know what heartbreak is," he said, gruffly. He reached the short distance between then and drew his fingers along her cheek, sending flames of desire to a scalding temperature. "So you're willing to marry me and have sex to get what you want. You're willing to risk your future."

"I'm securing my future. Not risking it," she said, correcting him and failing to keep the breathlessness out of her voice. "The whole point of this is to take care of my baby," she added, unable to look away from his intense gaze that held her now. Her heart pounded and she suspected if there had been no table between them and they hadn't been in public, he would kiss her. And she wanted him to. Unable to resist, she reached up to stroke his cheek just as he had hers. His jaw was clean-shaven and smooth. The moment she touched him, desire enveloped her with the heat of a furnace.

"You're taking risks, too, to get what you want," she whispered. "Your heart may belong to me someday, Matt Ransome." The clash of wills between them was covered with an icing of desire, creating an emotional dessert that held the potential for spicy, red-hot sex. Goaded by his announced intention to resist falling in love when he planned to seduce her, she leaned the last bit of space and placed her lips on his. Before she closed her eyes, she saw the flash of surprise in his.

Then she was lost. His hand went behind her head and her kiss became his kiss. His tongue thrust deeply into her mouth with possessive, demanding strokes that caused her heart to pound. Her body responded fully to him, aching, on fire with wanting him. They were in public, restrained by their surroundings and with an effort she leaned away. Trying to get her breath, she opened her eyes to find him watching her.

"Sex is going to be great," he whispered.

"I'm going to make you open that vault to your heart," she flung back at him, realizing right now that if they had sex, she would want his love that he kept locked and guarded.

"No, you're not," he answered firmly, but she noticed with satisfaction the perspiration that dotted his forehead and his flushed face.

She leaned closer again. "Let's see how long you can resist me, Matt," she challenged, and he inhaled.

"Don't try to work your magic on me."

"I don't have any magic," she rejoined and his eyebrows arched.

"The hell you don't," he said, tracing her jaw with his finger. "No woman should have the effect on men that you do."

"Do I really now?" she asked, surprised that she had any remarkable impact on Matt.

"You know damn well you do! At least this marriage is going to have some real pluses and some challenges."

"And you like a challenge?"

"Of sorts. I'm not happy about being pushed into marriage."

"You're not being pushed. You can say no. You pointed that out to me on your offer."

"Dammit," he said quietly while he glared at her, and she knew even though he had accepted her proposal, he wished he didn't have to marry her. "We might as well get the questions answered and settled."

He sipped his coffee and looked at the notepad he had placed on the table beside his plate. While she ate a delicious bowl of peaches, she watched him scribble notes. The waiter brought golden omelets, but Olivia's appetite had vanished. So had Matt's because he didn't even attempt to eat, merely reading and writing notes and sipping his coffee.

Determined to avoid letting him know what butterflies she had and how uptight she was, she forced herself to take bites of her breakfast and try to get it down.

"It won't go in the prenup, but once we're married, I expect you to stay faithful. I'll do the same."

She nodded. "Our vows will cover that one."

"You said we'd dissolve our marriage after you get your law degree. As far as I'm concerned, this marriage, if we do enter into it, might as well be permanent."

"Permanent! And what do you mean—if we enter into it? I thought we agreed this is what we're doing."

"We did, but a lot of things can happen between now and weeks or months from now."

She wondered what he had in mind and was there something he was going to do to try to get her to back out of the marriage agreement. And permanent was mind-boggling. "I never planned on permanent!"

"If we're getting married, then a lasting marriage is a good business arrangement. I'll get to raise Jeff's baby, and you'll be educated and provided for and have a family for your baby. Neither of us wants an emotional entanglement, yet we'll have sex in our lives. Who knows—by then, we might be in love."

Setting down her fork with her omelet only barely touched, she drew a deep breath, suddenly feeling as if walls were closing in on her. "I can't envision being married to you for the rest of my life."

"You can always file for divorce if you want out. You know that."

"Yes, but I had no intention of going into this with permanency in mind."

"Can't you see where that would be best for your baby?"

She stared at him. Marriage to Matt Ransome. Permanent as in *forever.* Endless with no emotional entanglement, according to him. Impossible to her.

"You can't do forever?" he asked quietly, and she suspected he was pushing this condition to get her to back off from the whole marriage concept, which she had no intention of doing.

"Yes, I can do 'as long as we both shall live'," she answered, stiffening her resolve to see these nuptials through, "if everlasting is what you want." She would deal with that one as time went by.

"I would like to adopt the baby so it's mine and there's none of this stepdad stuff," Matt declared.

Joy bubbled in her over the adoption suggestion that she hadn't dreamed he would make. She nodded. "Great! That's gratifying to hear."

"I think we said the sum I'll settle on you will be one hundred thousand."

"I told you that you can cut it in half if we marry."

He shook his head. "No. We'll leave it at one hundred." His blue eyes got that piercing look that drove into her like knives. He leaned closer over the table. "One hundred thousand is enough money for you to marry, get the Ransome name and then take the money and run. You could disappear."

"I won't do that."

"Damn straight, you won't! I'll find you," he said with steel back in his voice. She had no doubt that he would do exactly as he said, but she had no intention of running out on the deal he was offering. "Part of our bargain is that you don't run out on me. My mother did that to her family. My first wife all but did that with me."

"If I repeat vows, I'll live up to my promises," she said and gazed back at him unflinchingly. He gave her a long, hard look with icy blue eyes, but instead of chilling her, she faced him and noticed his long, thick eyelashes, bedroom eyes. A lock of black hair fell on his forehead. He had thick hair that held a slight wave and a firm jaw that gave him a rugged appearance, yet at the same time, he was handsome with his straight nose and prominent cheekbones.

She wondered if she was sinking herself in a quicksand of heartbreak. How easy it was going to be to fall in love with him! For all his gruffness and reined-in anger, there had been flashes of charm when they had been out on the town last night, as well as a few minutes ago when he was flirting with her. She had vowed she would never again trust a Ransome or get involved with one, yet here she was committing to the closest possible relationship with a Ransome who had his heart locked away.

"I'll draw up a will. I own the ranches with my father, brother and sister and we want them to stay in the family. If something happens to me, my share will go directly to the baby when he or she reaches twenty-one. The money I have will be divided between you and to the baby. Fair enough?"

She nodded. "For a man not in love with me, you're making another generous offer."

As he inhaled deeply, she wondered what was running through his mind because she couldn't possibly guess. Somehow she suspected he was wishing he could have the baby and get rid of her, but then she might be wrong.

He shifted and his knee bumped hers. His eyes narrowed while she felt a tingle from the contact.

"I need to meet your family," she said.

"I know. I'll get them together."

"You're not touching your breakfast," she said quietly.

"I don't have any appetite," he replied, biting off the words abruptly. He fluctuated between flirting with her and then giving way to his suppressed fury over having to acquiesce to her wishes. In the moments when his charm and appeal surfaced, she found him irresistible.

She suspected after marriage he would accept their bargain and then she would have his charm and sex appeal to deal with daily, a possibility that gave her a tingly anticipation and at the same time, sent warnings of heartbreak pounding in her mind.

Where Matt's brother had been an engaging fun-filled boy,

Matt was a devastating man with charm and sex appeal that overwhelmed her.

"I don't think we'll have an issue about the baby's education since you fought so hard to get one," Matt said, scribbling more notes while she nodded.

"I'll still open an account for you with the one hundred thousand in it. That is your money. I'll pay the ranch expenses, etc. and open a joint account for us."

"You continue to surprise me," she said, again amazed by his magnanimity when she knew he was unhappy with her.

"We might as well work together. We're binding our lives together forever," he added and she wondered about her future with him. "Hopefully," he continued, "we'll stop fighting each other."

She laughed. "I wouldn't count on that one," she exclaimed, leaning closer. "You intend to seduce me. You want my body." She placed her hand over his on the table. "If you do, I'll warn you now—I'll seduce you because I'll want your heart."

"I thought you were going to try to avoid another heartbreak."

She shook her head. "We're on a different course since I made that declaration. We're marrying, and you're making it permanent. If that's the case, and we'll be intimate, then I want more than lust and a purely physical relationship for the rest of my life. I want love."

"Once again, you want more," he repeated, smiling at her. "Where have I heard that before? Only this time, you won't have the leverage you did about marriage." He turned his hand to take hers and rub his thumb across her knuckles, stirring tingles. "You're flirting with me, Olivia."

"So I am. Don't deny that you like it."

"Of course, I like for you to flirt and to kiss. As you said, we're stuck with each other now, so we should make—" he paused and desire heated his gaze "— love, as well as the best of it," he finished in a velvety drawl that held its own caress. "I'll have to say that you're damn cooperative now that you've got what you want."

"I try," she said, bestowing a smile.

He laughed and straightened up, releasing her hand. "I'll get you a wedding ring. We need to make some decisions about the wedding first. How about a small wedding?"

She tingled at the prospect and wondered if she could go through with this loveless marriage of convenience—even with Prince Charming, which Matt had been on occasion. "That's fine," she said, but her words were breathless and her head spun. Marriage—and then she would be in Matt's bed. Sex with Matt Ransome! Again she thought about sex with him—over and over she thought of it. Her palms felt sweaty, and she watched him writing in his notebook. If he was disturbed or gave the notion of sex with her any of his attention, he was hiding it well.

"I'll pay the wedding bills, of course," he continued. " If you don't have a particular church, we can be married at the ranch. The only people I want to invite will be our cowboys and my family."

Trying to get back to thinking about what she was doing instead of sex with Matt, she mulled over his suggestions and shook her head. "You're so concerned about my baby—which will soon be our baby. Maybe you should think about inviting a lot of your friends, too. Otherwise, I'm not too likely to be accepted by some people because of my background and where I've worked," she said, and he nodded.

"You're right. Good decision."

"Why do I get the feeling that from the first, you've expected the worst from me?" she asked.

"Maybe I misjudged you. You constantly surprise me. But it's for the good, so that should be all right," he admitted. "We'll have the whole deal, a big wedding and reception."

"Why not a small, private wedding and then the big reception?"

He shook his head. "I'd say the big wedding because I want people to accept you as much as any other member of my family and there will be a reluctance by some locals for the reasons you said and because you were close to my brother who had a reputation for being the wild man of the county."

"I'm three months pregnant."

"Won't matter. You don't look it anyway. I'll hire someone to work with you to plan this wedding."

"If we have a big wedding, it will take time to plan."

"No. I'll hire a wedding planner who can get everything ready. I'll call family and close friends. Word will get around before the invitations. You get your wedding dress right away," he said, starting a new list, writing while he talked. She wondered exactly how much wealth the Ransome family had because Matt didn't seem daunted by anything except her proposal.

She had butterflies dancing a ballet in her stomach at the thought of a big wedding with all his family and friends present. "Matt, I don't have any family and only a few friends."

"Doesn't matter. Most of the county will come to the wedding and lots of people from other counties and from Fort Worth. Matter of fact, guests will come from everywhere because my brother and sister get around. By the way, you have carte blanche on this."

"You already trust my judgment?" she asked.

His gaze drifted down over her as far as he could see with the table blocking his view and then back up in a leisurely, thorough study that curled her toes and made her forget business. "You have good taste. You look like a professional woman this morning—like the lawyer you will be someday. Last night you looked fabulous. I think I can trust you with the wedding decisions. I'll help with the wedding at the ranch because we've had so many catered parties there. I already have a battery of people who can handle all aspects of the reception. We should open an account for you today."

She nodded, growing more dazed with each of his quick decisions. It all seemed like a dream, magical, impossible, yet the man beside her was real enough. And the most fabulous, awesome aspect of all—her baby would officially be a Ransome. Matt would help raise him or her.

What was impossible to put out of mind and ran in an undercurrent of thought all the time they talked was the far more immediate prospect of sex with Matt—getting naked with each other. The thought stirred a burning low in her middle. And would there ever be more than lust and a baby between them?

He pulled out a small black book, flipped it open and scribbled in it, turning to hold it out to her. "How's this date for our wedding?"

Stunned, she stared at the black circle he had drawn and then she looked up at him.

Six

"I couldn't possibly!" she exclaimed while she stared at the date circled—next Saturday. "This is Monday! This week—not even a full week to get ready for the biggest event in my life, a complete life change, an enormous wedding with your relatives and friends. Impossible!" she exclaimed, trying to ignore a feeling of panic that surged while she reminded herself this had been her idea and she was getting what she desired.

Part of her wanted to ask for a year to get ready. The other part would like the wedding as soon as possible, to lock her into the Ransome family before something happened that changed Matt's mind or made the wedding impossible. Next weekend—it sounded the same as tomorrow.

His blue gaze settled on her. "You're quiet. Getting cold feet?"

"Never," she replied emphatically. "I want this with all my heart."

While they looked solemnly at each other, she knew they each had different goals for their futures. And they each would fight for what he or she wanted. She knew that, too.

He glanced at his watch. "We should select invitations today. I'll get a list of guests and get someone at the Ransome office to address the invitations and get them out at once."

"Matt, we can't do this in a few days. Give me another week at least."

"All right. The date will be the following Saturday," he said with assurance in his tone. "Let's go. I have calls to make, and you can shop for your wedding dress. We can meet back at the hotel for a late lunch around one. When we fly home, we'll go to Fort Worth and open a bank account for you. How's that?" As he talked, he fished his billfold out of his pocket, withdrew a credit card and flipped it over on the table so it landed in front of her. "Buy whatever you want," he said casually and she stared at him. "Or if you don't find what you want, we can go to Fort Worth to shop. Or Dallas."

"I'll find something," she said, quietly. "Thank you."

"And you're surprised again, aren't you? You must think I'm a green-headed ogre."

"No. I'm simply amazed you're so generous when you're angry with me. And I didn't know your family had such wealth," she said.

He gave her a dubious look. "C'mon. That's common knowledge in the county. It runs back to the fortune my great-granddaddy made on cattle and land."

She shook her head. "Your brother flashed money, but no more than a lot of other cowboys and until he left for the mountain trek, he didn't do anything that made him look particularly prosperous except play poker. He never took me home with him, so yesterday was the first time I've ever seen the Ransome ranch."

Matt shrugged and gave her a rueful smile. "You get your way on the future for both of us, so why should I stay angry or try to keep things from you when you'll be my wife next week?"

Wife next week. She was glad she was sitting down because her head spun at the thought of becoming Mrs. Matt Ransome so soon.

"We pick up and go on from here," Matt continued. "I don't want revenge because you and I are going to be a unit. From here on, it would be like fighting myself."

"And you're not?" she asked softly, unable to resist flirting with him now that their future together was sealed.

"Not what? Fighting myself?"

She smiled at him. "You don't want to be attracted to me. It aggravates you that you want to kiss me."

"Maybe so," he said, leaning close enough again to start her heart pounding. "Sooner or later, we'll work things out. I just usually manage to get my way and this is one time that I haven't."

"Maybe I can keep you from regretting your decision," she said in a throaty voice. "If we both try, Matt, we can have a good marriage."

He wrapped his fingers around her hand again. "I'd like that," he said and leaned close. "Just remember, I warned you that I'm not going to love again. And remember the old saying: 'All's fair in love and war'. You've had all the forewarning that I need to give."

"And so have you," she said with a smile. With her free hand she stroked his nape lightly.

His eyes darkened, and she knew she was taunting a tiger that could bound to life and devour her heart so easily. "I'm beginning to look forward to this, Olivia," he said softly. "And I look forward to our wedding night and having you in my arms." While he talked he reached up to wind locks of her hair in his fingers, tugging so lightly, yet making her aware of his touch.

Her pulse raced and her mouth was dry. "Twelve days from now, I hope we know each other better."

"You've learned a lot about me already and I know some about you. And I'll answer any question you want."

She tilted her head to think a moment. She was curious about him and had a multitude of questions, but she tried to choose the most urgent. "Are you still in love with your ex?" she asked, and a shake of his head gave her pleasure.

"Not even in the tiniest fraction. If she wanted to come back tomorrow, I wouldn't want her to, but she won't want to. She's in love with her job. And then with herself. When we were married, I made a threesome." He waited expectantly.

"When you were growing up, did you and your siblings get along with your father?"

"Well enough," he answered easily. "Our father can be a dictator and a lot of people are cowed when they deal with him, but we've grown up with him and his fiery temper and determination."

"Are any of you a lot like him?"

"I hope not," Matt replied. "You can ask me more later. Right now, let's go," he said, gathering his papers and standing, coming around to hold her chair.

As soon as they separated, Olivia began shopping for a wedding dress.

When she slipped the cool silk of the first one over her head, her heart thudded at the sight of her image.

The white dress was a dream. Tendrils of her hair had tumbled free and fell around her face and she had to admit that she thought she looked pretty, but it was the wedding dress and what it symbolized that held her speechless. She was dressing for her wedding for a marriage of convenience that she was going to contract to for the rest of her life. With a man who was angry with her, accustomed to getting his own way, and determined to avoid ever falling in love with her.

Would her baby's future be worth what she was willing to sacrifice, Olivia asked herself, because she suspected that no matter what she did or felt, Matt Ransome wasn't going to fall in love with her. The image in the mirror that stared back at her was a wide-eyed woman in a wedding dress about to marry— in less than two weeks—in a loveless marriage.

If she had good sense, she would guard her heart, too, she thought, turning to look over her shoulder at the dress. She guessed it would take a long, long time for Matt to forgive her for pushing him into this marriage of convenience.

Would his family accept her?

She suspected that would be one of the least of her problems.

She removed the dress and tried one that was white satin with a full skirt and cathedral train. Every moment of the past two days had held a dreamlike quality, but seeing herself in wedding dresses was surreal. She was going to marry a week from Saturday!

She ignored the pang that tore at her heart. This wasn't what she had planned for herself, but then nothing had gone as planned since she had met the first Ransome.

An hour later, she found the dress she wanted and knew she needed to look no further. She turned first one way and then another as she studied her reflection while she smoothed the skirt to a white sleeveless silk with a low-cut V-neck and straight, plain lines with a removable train. The simple elegance and flattering style made it the dress she wanted.

In another hour her head spun with her purchases of a veil, shoes and wisps of lacy undergarments. She stopped in a book-store to select some books on pregnancy and baby care. When she glanced at her watch, she realized she would have to race to get back in time to meet Matt at the hotel.

When she arrived, he was in the lobby, seated with papers spread in his lap. At any moment she expected him to back out of their bargain. Soon she would be Mrs. Matthew Ransome. When the time came, would he go through with the ceremony?

As she approached him, his gaze assessed her, and she tucked a wayward tendril of hair behind her ear while her pulse jumped.

Watching her cross the lobby, he waited until she was only yards from him. He gathered his things and stood.

"Sorry I'm late," she said breathlessly. "I have boxes in the cab."

"You should have called," he said, walking beside her to go back outside to retrieve her packages.

"I don't own a cell phone," she replied, amused that he would automatically assume everyone he knew had a phone. He gave her a quick glance and reached into his pocket to hand her a phone.

"Take mine for now. I can get another easily." Matt took her arm and she was aware of his body warmth as she walked close beside him. She could detect a hint of barberry aftershave that was as tangible as his hostility. Yet he had accepted her terms. Marriage to a Ransome. One minute she wanted to kick her heels in the air and shout for joy. The next minute she wanted to pack and run.

He opened the cab door to retrieve her packages and move them to the waiting limo. Looking at an enormous box tied in white ribbon, he remarked: "I see you found a wedding dress."

"Yes, I did and it's bad luck for you to see me in it before the wedding."

Matt gave her a mocking grin. "You're worrying about me seeing your wedding dress?"

"All right, maybe that's foolish."

Their limo driver transferred her packages. "You should have let us pick up your wedding dress," Matt said.

"They placed it in the cab for me and I knew you would get it out," she said.

When she climbed into the waiting limo, Matt slid into the seat facing her. "Did I tell you this morning that you look beautiful?"

"Thank you," she replied.

"Perhaps we can make this arrangement halfway work."

"I hope it works completely," she admitted, wishing momentarily that she really could have it all—including a marriage with love. "It'll be a fraudulent marriage in some ways," she said quietly.

"This morning over breakfast I think we settled that we can make a marriage of convenience more palatable," he said.

"Maybe with time," she replied.

"While you shopped, I got a wedding planner," he said, handing her a slip of paper with a name, address and phone number scrawled on it. "You have an appointment in Fort Worth tomorrow afternoon at one."

"That was quick."

"For parties at the ranch we have a regular caterer and a band, so I've hired them for the wedding."

Olivia stared at him and wondered if she was getting entangled with a dynamo who would try to take charge of every aspect of her life.

"You're giving me a look," he said. "Do you disapprove?" he asked, startling her by guessing what was running through her mind.

She shook her head. "No, I'm a little overwhelmed."

"I doubt that," he remarked drily. "I've contacted our family minister and we'll have the reception at the ranch."

"You've done it all," she said. "Except buy my wedding dress."

He shook his head. "Not quite. We both need to get attendants. The wedding planner will have a florist and a photographer and you can arrange with her for the wedding cake. The big deal is telling my family. I suspect it may be a bombshell. I'll warn you right now, my dad may be difficult. Katherine might be, too, but it's dad who intimidates people. If you want, I'll see to it that you never see him without me until after the wedding."

Amused, she gazed at Matt. "You think he'll scare me out of this? If so, I'm surprised you didn't send him to talk to me before you accepted my proposal."

Matt smiled. "I don't think my dad will frighten you away, but you may not want to deal with him alone. I think you're a match for him which is saying something, believe me. Not many people can hold their own with him, but I bet you will. And if Katherine gives you a hard time, I'll deal with her, too. As soon as we get back to the ranch, I'll call them."

"Fine," Olivia said, wondering what kind of confrontations she would have with his family.

"When you become my wife, you won't need that law degree," he remarked.

Startled, she gazed back at him in silence while she thought about it. "I want to get an education. With the arrangement we have, I don't know what I'll need in the future."

"You can think about it," he said. "I moved my afternoon appointment with my attorney to tomorrow morning at ten. We'll both meet with him to go over the prenuptial agreement."

"That's fine, too."

Soon they boarded the private jet. When the plane taxied down the runway and soared into the air, she looked down at the city spread below and knew she would never forget the past night or today. Her gaze lifted to the expanse of blue sky that stretched endlessly in her view.

Once they were airborne, she heard him writing and turned away from the window to see him poring over his notes. Until he wanted her to talk to him about something specific, she was going to look out the window. It was her second flight in an airplane and she was still dazzled by it.

"Olivia," he said and a tingle spiraled in her.

"Yes?" she replied, giving him her attention.

"I want you to agree now that you'll stay with me. I don't want you to get your law degree and then take your child, divorce me and move away. Of course, if you're going, I can't hold you, but I want in the prenup that you won't get anything of mine if you leave. And I'll want joint custody."

"That's fair enough. I'm sure I can find legal work in this area. I want to practice law when I pass my bar exams."

"I can keep a child with me a lot of the time when I'm on the ranch."

"You don't know the first thing about taking care of a child, do you?" she asked.

"Nope, but I can learn. What kind of experience have you had in child care?" he asked, and her cheeks flushed hotly.

"Maybe none, but this morning I bought some baby books that I intend to study. Also, I think that child care is more likely to come to me innately than to you," she replied with a haughty air.

"We won't argue that one. Time will tell," he replied, drawing circles on her knee with his finger. She was aware of his touch and the warmth of his gaze and she wanted to lean toward him, to brush his lips with hers.

"Later this month I'm in a rodeo in Jet. The event is bronc riding. Will you come watch me ride?"

She nodded. "You always say your brother was the wild one. Seems to me bronc riding is on the wild side."

"Not so much. We do that on the ranch just for the fun of it."

She turned back to look out the window while she thought about the man she was marrying and what an enigma he was.

The rest of the day was dizzying. As soon as they landed in Fort Worth, Matt whisked her to a bank downtown and they were ushered into a thickly carpeted office where she watched with perspiring palms while Matt signed papers and deposited twenty thousand dollars into an account for her and put the remaining amount of money into a savings account. She was stunned to walk out of the bank a wealthy woman with an account and money to spend any way she so desired.

"Matt," she said, placing her hand on his arm while he stopped and looked down at her.

"Thank you. I never dreamed I would have money, not until I'd maybe practiced law forever. When I become a lawyer and pass the bar, I'll repay you," she said.

"Don't be ridiculous. We're getting married. I don't like having my money and your money. It's ours. If you contribute, fine. If you keep what you make for yourself, fine. If I marry you—even in a paper marriage, Olivia, then I'll share my bank account with you unless you go hog wild with it."

Amazed that he would allow her full access to his fortune, she could only stare in speechless wonder.

"Okay?" he asked when she didn't respond.

"Of course it's all right," she replied hastily. "I am constantly taken aback by your generosity. I can't even imagine someone sharing like you're willing to do."

He stopped and turned to her and she felt as if she were drowning in pools of blue. "Olivia, next week you'll become my wife. That's the way you wanted it. We'll have a bargain that I intend to live by for the rest of my life."

For the first time, she realized how permanent the approaching marriage of convenience would be. "Suppose you fall in love with someone?" she asked, wondering again what she had gotten herself into—for that matter, gotten both of them into.

"I won't."

"You can't know that! No one knows what will happen when love is involved."

"I'm not going to fall in love with anyone. My money will be your money as long as you handle it reasonably well. You don't have to repay the money I put in the bank account for you today."

"I'm absolutely stunned over what you're doing," she admitted, knowing every small detail of this moment would be etched in her memory forever. Wind blew locks of his black hair and his blue eyes were intent on her. A faint smile hovered, deepening creases in his cheeks. Besides Matt, the passing crowd, the sound of cars, the heat of sunshine—she would remember this event that in her wildest imaginings she had never dreamed would happen.

"Are you all right?" he asked.

"Yes. Just bowled over by your magnanimity."

"I'm just doing what I want to do. You can show me your gratitude tonight," he drawled in a husky, sensual voice that strummed across her nerves and set them quivering. As the same time, his eyes twinkled, so she didn't know whether he was teasing, goading her into something, or really meant it.

"I'll think about it," she said, giving him a saucy toss of her head.

He chuckled softly as she turned to walk to his car.

Finally they returned to the ranch and when they entered the house, Matt tossed his keys on the kitchen counter. "I'll call my brother and sister tonight. In the meantime, I'll grill steaks and we can make more plans. Where do you want this dress? You can keep it in another bedroom so it won't crowd you."

In minutes they had all her new purchases in another bedroom, and she had agreed as soon as she changed clothing, she would join him for a swim.

While she hurried to get ready for the swim, his words

echoed in her head: "You can show me your gratitude to-night." Had he meant that? Was he going to want sex before the agreed time because of the money he had given her? Or had he been teasing? If sincere, then he was in for a surprise because sex for her new bank account was not part of any bargain they had struck.

Before she left for the pool, she took a long look at herself in the mirror. She had bought a new black two-piece swimsuit that was cut low on her belly, high on her hips. She studied the changes in her body, aware that her breasts were fuller. Her stomach was still flat and she ran her hand over it, thinking about her baby. A girl or a boy? She was beginning to want to know and not wait another six months to be surprised. She wondered whether or not Matt would want to know.

Satisfied with her looks, she twisted her hair and pulled it up in a ponytail. She grabbed her cover-up, a big towel and flip-flops before going to the sparkling blue pool. Matt already had fired up the grill and the smoking mesquite smell was tantalizing.

As she walked across the patio where cool air was piped near the house, Matt bobbed up in the pool, and raked his hair away from his face, giving him a harsher, more rugged look. Water glistened on his broad shoulders, and her pulse began what was becoming a familiar racing.

He watched her approach and her heart thudded at the slow, thorough perusal he gave her from head to toe. His gaze lingered on her breasts and on her stomach, drifting down over her legs and she was on fire by the time she neared the pool.

He pulled himself up out of the water with a splash, sending cold drops sprinkling her. Her pulse was already racing, but now her heart thudded as she looked at him clad in only a scrap of black suit. His skin was tan, glistening with water, muscled, lean and hard. He was studying her, but no more than she was eyeing him and she couldn't resist staring. While her heart pounded, she marveled again that soon—tonight possibly—she would be in bed with him.

"If I hadn't seen the doctor's report myself, I'd never believe you're pregnant. You don't show at all," he said in a husky voice, walking closer.

With each step he took, her drumming pulse beat faster. She barely knew what he said as she looked up at him. They wore only bits of clothing and she knew he was as aware of her bare body as she was of his. And she wanted his lean hard body against hers. She could feel heat creep into her cheeks over the way she had been ogling him.

"How in heaven's name did you get my doctor's report? That's private," she asked, annoyed. "I may call my doctor about that."

He shrugged. "Who knows what my P.I. did, but he had the report. Your doctor may not have known someone looked at your record." Matt jerked his head toward the pool. "Come in. The water's great."

He made a running dive into the pool, swimming away from her. She followed, sliding into the cool water to swim. At the end of the pool she clung to the edge, shook water away from her face and found him beside her.

"You're beautiful, Olivia," he said in a husky voice. "I think we may have made a damn fine bargain."

"Those aren't exactly the magic words that every woman wants to hear two weeks before her wedding."

His eyebrows arched. "We're going into this like any business deal. You surely didn't expect hearts and flowers."

"No. That's not one of my stipulations. Last night was great because it was memorable to go out and not be reminded at every turn that what we have between us is a contract."

"You do want more," he observed and moved closer. "This is one thing we have between us that isn't in the contract."

Seven

He slipped his arm around her waist and drew her up against him. The moment she touched the length of his warm, hard body and legs, her stomach did flip-flops. When her hands went to his shoulders, desire exploded in her.

Sliding her arm around his neck, she looked at his lips and then glanced up to see him looking at her mouth with hungry longing. When he bent his head and covered her mouth with his, her heart pounded. Time and thought stopped. She lost all sense of where she was or what she had been doing. She was in his arms and he was kissing her senseless and she was coming apart at the seams over his kisses.

His arm tightened and his arousal was hard against her belly. Desire shook her. His free hand moved over her shoulders and throat and then slid down her front. While he continued to kiss her into oblivion, he held her away a fraction. His hand unfastened the halter top she wore and peeled it down, baring her breasts.

"Matt!" she exclaimed, ready to protest, remembering that she was going to show some restraint with this Ransome, but his fingers stroked her nipple and her protests melted. Warm and wet, his hand cupped her breast while his thumb circled her nipple slowly, making her moan softly and thrust her hips against him and want him with a need that shocked her. She twisted slightly to give herself access to him, sliding her fingers over his thick rod.

He growled deep in his throat as he kissed her. Then he leaned down to take her nipple in his mouth, teasing with his tongue, stroking and circling her taut bud.

"Matt!" she gasped again, unable to tell him to stop, knowing she was already breaking her promises to herself. How would she resist him twelve more days when she was letting him do what he wanted now? Did she want to wait until after they were married?

Desire surged, and she trembled as she kissed him and responded to his hands playing over her, first on her bare breasts and then sliding down over her belly. His hand slipped into the bottom half of her swimsuit and he found her soft folds, stroking her so lightly, yet setting off more blazing fireworks.

"You're so damn responsive to me," he whispered.

She tangled her legs with his and ran her hands over him, feeling his muscled body and firm bottom.

In minutes she knew there would be no stopping for either one of them. She pushed lightly against his chest and twisted away. He caught her arm to hold her.

"Matt, don't go so fast. I'll be in your bed soon enough."

Desire blazed in his eyes. An intense yearning that made her heart pound as violently as his passionate kisses had. He placed his hands on her waist and lifted her up out of the water and she placed her hands on his shoulders.

His gaze drifted over her bare breasts, slipping lower. "You're beautiful!" he gasped and her heart jumped.

How could she possibly keep from falling head over heels in love with him? He was devilishly handsome, rugged, sexy. He could be charming and she had the feeling that he really hadn't turned his charm and lovemaking on full force as far as she was concerned.

She didn't doubt that he meant what he said about keeping his heart locked away. Could she really scale the walls of that fortress?

She looked into his blue eyes and all she could see was desire so blatant it made her nipples tingle again. The heat low in her body intensified.

With his gaze locked with hers, he lowered her slowly, holding her closer and letting her slick, wet body slide against his. His hard shaft slipped between her legs and she gasped with desire that swept her with the force of a tidal wave. Closing her eyes and clinging to him, she knew she had to stop him right now and she needed to get out of his arms and get some distance between them.

She wasn't going to fall into his arms and into his bed and succumb to his seduction on the third night she had known him.

With an effort, as he leaned forward and his lips brushed hers, she splashed away from him and scrambled to pull her suit back into place. She looked over at him and saw him treading water while he watched her with a faint smile.

"Scared of me? Or scared about your own reactions?" He waved his hand. "Come on back. I can show restraint."

"Sure you can," she teased lightly. "Catch me," she said and turned to swim away as swiftly as possible.

He caught her easily and hauled her into his arms, laughing with her, but as their legs tangled and he held her close, their laughter vanished, replaced swiftly by need.

With pounding pulse, Olivia wriggled away. "Not yet, Matt," she said, wondering how long she could wait.

He swam past her and climbed out, grabbing up a towel and tying it around his middle. He shook water away from his face as he slicked back his hair. "I'll get out the steaks and pour glasses of iced tea."

Getting out of the pool, she watched him cross the patio and her mouth went dry as her gaze drifted over his broad, powerful shoulders and muscled back that tapered to his tiny waist and tight bottom. Abruptly, he halted and glanced at her, catching her staring at his body. He turned around to stroll back to her and each step closer he came to her, the more loudly her pulse pounded until she was certain he could hear it.

He placed his hand under her chin. "Go ahead and look. What you see will be yours to play with whenever you want," he said in a velvety voice. He stroked her cheek and let his fingers lightly slip lower, caressing her throat and pushing open the cover-up to fondle her breasts. "And what I see will be mine to play with and make love to, I hope."

"I believe that was part of our bargain," she whispered, unable to get any firmness in her voice. Was she already falling in love with him even before her wedding?

How disastrous would this bargain be to her heart? A bargain with a demon of her own creation. She could have taken the money, lived with him and waited to see if they fell in love instead of this headlong rush into marriage to get a commitment for her baby.

It was done now and she wasn't backing out, but she should take care and guard her heart more than she had so far. Two days ago she wouldn't have dreamed she would be at risk of heartbreak.

He looked over at her. "Penny for your thoughts."

"I was just mulling over what odd turns life takes and a week ago this time, my life and prospects for the future were entirely different."

"Regrets?"

"Absolutely not. Never! I couldn't possibly regret the changes. What about you? This morning you were filled with anger."

"We'll see what the future brings. Let's sit down and go over some more stipulations."

Amused, she smiled. "You're trying to think of everything. That's impossible."

"Maybe, but I want some requests. I'm in no hurry, but I want a DNA test to determine that there is no question that my brother was the father."

"That's fine," she said. "He was, so test away." She sat at a wrought-iron table on a cushioned iron chair, crossed her legs, catching Matt staring at her bare legs.

He pulled on a T-shirt over his swim trunks and then dropped the towel. The T-shirt hid his swimsuit and it was easy to imagine him without it and she hoped he had no inkling that she was doing so.

"Do I get a say in the baby's name?" he asked, pulling his chair close and stroking her knee, starting more fiery tingles.

She thought about that one. "I think we should both approve the selected name," she said breathlessly, only half aware of what she was replying to him.

He moved closer and placed his hands on her shoulders. "We've already learned that we can get along and the sex promises to be great. We both have mutual goals about the baby. But make no mistake, Olivia. I'll never fall in love again," he reminded her.

Annoyance flashed in her at his stubborn refusal to even give love a chance and then she thought how far she had already come with him. She slanted her head and smiled at him. "At the moment, I'm not after your heart. But when and if I decide I am, you may find that you don't have such a fortress as you thought."

"You've been warned."

"So have you," she said, and interest danced in his eyes. His gaze lowered to her mouth. She started to turn away, but he caught her, kissing her and lifting her onto his lap. Their legs were warm and bare and her pulse thundered while passion possessed her.

Matt leaned down to kiss her possessively. While his tongue stoked a fire in her, his arm banded her waist tightly. His other hand slipped down over her back and across her bottom, heating her desire.

Wrapping her arms around his neck, she twisted to press against him while she kissed him in return, pouring all her need into the kiss. She could feel his arousal hard against her and his free hand roamed over her while his hungry kisses demolished her intentions to resist him.

With desperation, she broke free, gasping for breath and satisfied to see his breathing was as ragged as hers as they both gazed at each other.

"Olivia, I don't think my life will ever be the same again."

"You can bet the ranch on that one," she whispered, standing and wanting to stay in his arms, wanting him to love her the rest of the night. She swept past him. "I'll dress for dinner," she called over her shoulder without looking back at him.

She hurried to her room for a cold shower, lecturing herself about resistance and caution and self-control and gaining his respect. She dressed in a denim sundress, sandals and caught her hair up in a ponytail. There was no way to stop unruly tendrils from escaping and curling around her face. She leaned forward to glare at her reflection.

"Get some control," she whispered. "You're mush when he kisses you." She didn't want to even think about his devastating kisses. But if he was leaping over barriers around her heart, she suspected she might be building bridges over his. "Just you try to resist falling in love with me, Matt Ransome," she declared.

She straightened up. "Yeah, right," she said, reminding herself that the man had iron willpower, and he could probably keep his heart locked away for a lifetime if he chose to. She thought about Jeff's story about Matt rescuing their father when all the professional rescuers had pulled out of the area. Jeff said Matt refused to give up, but he wouldn't let Jeff or Katherine search with him and Nick had a sprained ankle. She was dealing with a man who had a will of iron and would make all kinds of sacrifices to get what he wanted.

Would her heart break over this hard, tough cowboy? And beneath the wealth and sophistication, she suspected there was a cowboy who was a lot of country.

She squared her shoulders and smoothed her skirt. She was willing to take some risks. At this point she had the world to gain—and only a broken heart to lose, she reminded herself.

With a toss of her head she left to join him for dinner.

By the time she strolled onto the patio, he was grilling

steaks. A plume of gray smoke spiraled above the cooker and tantalizing smells made her mouth water, but it was the tall, handsome cook who took her breath and made her pulse jump.

He had dressed in slacks, western boots and a knit shirt, but how easily she could remember the body and muscles beneath those neat clothes. He glanced at her and then turned to give her his full attention, watching her walk toward him.

Tingling and growing hot, she sauntered up to him, stopping only inches from him. "Like what you see?" she asked in a sultry voice.

A faint smile quirked his mouth. "My anticipation about our wedding night is growing," he replied and her pulse jumped another notch.

"It'll be even better than you imagine," she said.

"You're flirting again, Olivia." He ran his finger just above the top of her sundress, drawing a line on her bare skin that made her draw her breath. "But why do I think you have an ulterior motive? I think you want me to fall in love with you so you can steal my heart away and twist me around your little finger." His fingers trailed upward to her nape where he caressed her lightly. "Am I right? Or will you admit the truth?"

"I'll answer honestly," she replied, wanting to kiss him instead of chat with him. "I hadn't thought about twisting you around my little finger and I don't really believe that I possibly can. Maybe I'm just trying to protect my heart so if I do fall in love with you, I won't be rejected."

He propped his foot on an iron chair and placed his arm on his thigh as he leaned closer. She was hemmed in by him and by his leg on one side of her, the cooker on the other and the chair behind her. His blue eyes pierced her as if he were searching for answers in her gaze. "So you're not getting cold feet yet over our deal?"

"Of course not," she said, acutely aware of his proximity and his leg touching her hip lightly. "We need to talk about the wedding. How many attendants will I need to have because you'll have groomsmen."

"Back to business? I'd rather talk about making love."

"We better take care of business if you want this wedding next week."

He smiled at her and traced the curve of her ear. "All right. How many attendants do you want?" he asked in a husky voice and she suspected he was giving little thought to the approaching nuptials.

"You're not thinking about our wedding," she said.

"I'm thinking about making passionate love to you on our wedding night," he answered in a husky voice and leaned down to brush her lips with his.

Her heart thudded, but she fought her impulse to kiss him and stepped back. "Matt, we have to make decisions about the wedding. How many groomsmen? I have three friends here, but I can well imagine that you will have a lot more close friends, plus your brother. I'll be happy to ask your sister to be an attendant."

His heated gaze kept her pulse racing. "All right. We'll discuss the wedding—for now. I've been trying to get in touch with my family to let them know. While you dressed, I tried to call Nick and Katherine. I've left messages for both of them."

"Are they here in Texas?"

"No. I called their cells. Katherine is in Chicago, and Nick is on a rig in the Gulf. I talked to my dad and of course, he wants to meet you. We're having him join us for breakfast in the morning. How's that?"

"Fine," she said, wondering if his entire family would disapprove of her and try to talk Matt out of the marriage. For an instant a surge of panic threatened, but then she reminded herself that Matt had agreed to marry her and he said he would keep his word.

Matt caressed her nape and she stopped thinking about his family. "Three attendants will be fine. If you want her, ask Katherine," he said. "I can't predict what she'll do or say."

"I hope they don't hate me."

"If they do, do you want to call off the marriage?"

"No, I don't."

He tugged on a curling lock of her hair. "Dad will be the most difficult to deal with. He's not the same since Jeff's death. Jeff was his baby and his favorite which is why he let Jeff do just what he damn well pleased."

"If I have a boy, I don't mind if you want to name him after your brother."

Matt traced his finger around the curve of her ear. "That might be a real fine thing. It would mean a lot to the whole family. 'Course you may be having a girl."

"When the time comes, I'll find out what my baby is going to be. When I have an ultrasound, you can even go with me if you want."

His eyes narrowed. "I'd like to go with you," he replied. "I'd really like it," he repeated as if surprised by his own feelings. "Something else—as soon as we marry, I wish you'd refer to this baby as 'our' baby, even though I'm not the blood father. For all intents and purposes, I will be this baby's father."

"That's wonderful!" she exclaimed, delighted with his suggestion. "Our baby," she repeated, the words thrilling her. Then she focused on him again. "You're standing close," she said quietly.

"It bothers you?"

"You know you disturb me," she replied.

"If the steaks weren't going to burn, I'd do more to disturb you right now," he said in a husky voice that was its own caress. He walked to the grill to take the steaks off and set them on the table.

Hunger pangs increased her anticipation, but when she sat down at the table across from Matt, she lost interest in food. Talking to him and making wedding plans took precedence over eating. As they chatted, she couldn't believe her good fortune.

Over dinner Matt charmed her with stories about the ranch and his brothers and sister, yet all the time he talked about them, Olivia couldn't stop wondering how much they would accept her and the approaching marriage.

She barely touched her steak and noticed that Matt didn't either. They talked about a myriad of subjects and she wondered if his life had been lonely before, but then she pushed that notion aside as ridiculous. Matt could do as he pleased and she suspected he kept busy all the time. Looking into his thickly lashed blue eyes, she couldn't imagine, in spite of what he had said, that there weren't women around often. His handsome looks and virility took her breath. If only—she dismissed that thought immediately. She was getting more than she ever dreamed possible. She had to stop looking for love.

The sun set and lights came on automatically in posts scattered around the patio. The pool sparkled with light and she was dazzled by her surroundings, but far more by Matt. He reached across the table to take her hand in his. His fingers were warm and strong. At the intense look in his eyes, her pulse speeded.

He reached into his pocket with his other hand. "I bought a ring for you today while I was waiting," he said and placed a small black velvet box in her hand.

Surprised, she opened it and her heart missed beats when she looked at the dazzling diamond that sparkled against the dark velvet. "Matt!" she gasped, stunned by his gift. She looked up at him. "It's fantastic!"

"You like it?" he asked.

"Of course, I love it!" she said. "It's magnificent! I can't believe you would do this! We barely know each other. I'm astounded—" She realized she was babbling, but she was caught off guard and never had expected any such ring.

"Olivia," he said, cutting short her words and leaning closer to slip his hand beneath her chin. "For this baby's sake, we're entering into a marriage of convenience, but as far as I'm concerned, I think it would be best for our baby if all our friends think we're in love. You'll get a hell of a lot more respect that way, and men will leave you alone. Unless you let them know they don't have to leave you alone."

"Don't worry about that one," she said. "We've already agreed to be faithful to each other."

"At this point that's merely lip service."

"Not for me," she said, solemnly, her excitement diminishing. He took the ring from her and slipped it onto her finger.

"It's a perfect fit," she said, wiggling her fingers slightly and watching the huge diamond sparkle. "This has to be the biggest diamond I've ever seen in my life."

"Good. It's eight carats and that should be big enough to keep guys away and earn you respect from the women."

She looked at the glittering diamond and then at him. He was being generous beyond her wildest dreams. She pushed back her chair and walked around the table and something flickered in the depths of his eyes. As she approached him, he scooted his chair and she sat on his lap and wrapped her arms around his neck. "Thank you," she said and leaned down to kiss him.

His arms enveloped her and he shifted her closer, kissing her in return until she forgot all about the dazzling ring and was lost in Matt's kisses.

His hands brushed her bare shoulders and nape, sliding down to twist free her buttons. He pulled down the front of her sundress to cup her breasts in his hands. When his thumbs drew circles on her nipples, she moaned with pleasure, a sound that was muffled as his tongue plunged deeply into her mouth.

Then his hand was beneath her full skirt, pushing it high while his fingers caressed the inside of her thigh. He turned her on his lap so he could slide his fingers into her lacy panties.

"Matt!" she gasped.

Shifting her over him so she was astride him, he cupped both her breasts and lowered his head to her breasts, to kiss first one and then the other. He drew his tongue in slow circles around her nipple while his thumb continued to circle her other nipple.

Bombarded by sensations and desire, she clung to his shoulders and then let her hand slide down to his hard shaft. With a pounding pulse, she unbuckled his belt and unfastened his trousers, trying to free him from the restraints of clothing. She wanted him totally, yet she clung to her resolution to wait until their wedding night to give herself fully. She refused to fall into his arms and his bed so quickly even though every caress and kiss was fueling the bonfire that consumed her.

Lost to his lovemaking, she moved her hips while trying to fight through the fog of need back to caution and patience.

Catching his wrist, she held his hand. "You're going too fast again." She swung her leg over him and straightened her clothing, trying to pull the top of her dress back in place.

His blue eyes had darkened with passion and the heated look in them made her heart pound. When he fastened his clothes, she returned to her chair and studied her new ring. "I've never dreamed of owning jewelry like this."

She looked at him and her heart missed a beat because the desire in his expression shocked her.

"I want you, Olivia. I want you in my arms in my bed and I want all that passion you have bottled up turned loose."

"You have to wait only a few more days," she reminded him, wondering if either one of them could resist that long. Already, they weren't able to keep their hands to themselves and when they started kissing, they almost lost all restraint.

"Let's clean this up—"

"Nope," he said, standing and taking her hand and crossing the patio to a cushioned glider. "Later. Let's sit and talk."

Olivia moved to a chair close to the glider and received a mocking smile from Matt. She looked at the ring again. "This is absolutely fabulous. Thank you so very much."

He nodded. "Wedding dress, ring, minister, wedding planner, caterer, band and lawyers. We need to get in touch with my family and get our attendants lined up. Your attendants will need to get dresses. As soon as we go to the courthouse tomorrow and take care of the legal stuff with the county, I think we'll have everything else in order."

"I can't believe you're getting all this done this quickly," she said, knowing she could always expect him to try to take charge and go at a gallop to get what he wanted.

"We have parties out here and some of the arrangements aren't that different," he said.

Butterflies flitted in her stomach at the thought of talking to the rest of the Ransome clan.

Matt took her hand, lacing her fingers in his. He raised her hand to brush her knuckles with kisses, his warm breath a caress that made her want back in his lap. As she talked about classes she could take in the fall, Matt scooted his chair against hers. Finally, she stood. "I insist we clean. Mrs. Marley won't be here tonight or tomorrow."

He waved his hand. "Sit and talk. I'll clean. It'll give me something to do because I'm not going to sleep."

She wrinkled her nose at him. "I'm not going to ask why you won't sleep," she said as she sat again.

"You know exactly why," he replied in a low voice. He reached over to lift her into his lap.

She wound her arms around his neck and smiled at him. "I think we did this a short time ago."

"I can't remember," he said, looking at her mouth.

She inhaled and pulled his head down as she placed her mouth on his to kiss him, knowing every kiss made her want more. "Matt," she whispered, kissing him between words, "you're making it harder to wait—"

"Darlin', you're definitely the one making it harder," he drawled in a sexy innuendo that she barely heard over her pounding pulse. Matt's arm tightened around her and his tongue went deep. He kissed her long and thoroughly before she made him stop again. Standing, she moved away. "I'll see you at breakfast."

He gazed at her with a smoldering intensity and she hurried away, knowing a few more seconds and she would have been right back in his arms.

That night she was restless, worrying about Matt's father and how his family would accept her after learning she had talked Matt into a loveless marriage of convenience.

Tuesday morning at breakfast, she could feel the tension in spite of Matt being charming and his father chatting easily. Duke Ransome was a large, powerful-looking man with shoulders as broad as Matt's and a deeply tanned complexion.

Dressed in western shirt, jeans and boots, he still was a handsome man. He had brilliant blue eyes and a scar across his temple that was a testament to his rugged ranch life. He could be as charming as Matt, but his smiles ended before ever reaching his cold blue eyes that continually bored into her.

It was no surprise to her when breakfast was over and they moved to the family room to have Duke look at his son and announce, "Matt, I'd like to talk to Olivia for a few minutes, just the two of us."

"I'd be happy to talk to you, Mr. Ransome," Olivia said, trying to sound collected. She had dressed with care and was thankful in her shopping yesterday that she had bought a new, tailored navy suit and matching silk blouse. Ignoring her churning stomach, she hoped she looked poised with her hair looped and pinned behind her head.

"Dad, I think anything you have to say might be well said with all three of us together," Matt suggested.

"Nope. I want to talk to Olivia. I'm not going to bite her head off," Duke said and smiled at her, but it was a smile that chilled her and she wondered what he intended to say.

"I'm staying to hear whatever you have to say," Matt said in a voice that was as firm and direct as his father's and she knew at this point the decision was between the two males so she remained silent.

"Very well," Duke said and nodded, motioning to her. "Please sit down."

She sat in a leather wingback chair and Matt perched on the arm of the chair beside her.

The moment Duke Ransome turned his steely gaze on her, she braced for trouble. "You know we're all interested in your baby and want the baby in this family because it's a Ransome," he began.

"Yes, sir. Matt has made that clear and that's why we're marrying," she replied, aware that Matt remained silent. She wondered if he and his father had planned this talk together and hoped to get her to back out of the pending marriage.

"Which, of course, was your idea. I know my son doesn't want to wed again, for convenience or any other reason."

Olivia merely smiled and waited. Duke Ransome moved to the window and looked out at the sprawling ranch land. "We've fought for this land and protected it and I've struggled to keep my family together. I miss Jeff. This baby is his child and is a part of him."

"Yes, sir," she said, wondering if he intended to try to stir her sympathy. Questions swirled through her thoughts and curiosity about Matt plagued her. Why was he silent? Was he hoping his father would drive her away?

Duke Ransome turned to face her and his gaze chilled her. "There's no love between you and Matt because a week ago you didn't know each other and I know you haven't fallen in love in the short time you've known each other. Matt is not in love, I'm sure."

"No, sir. We haven't fallen in love," she admitted. "But we think we have a good arrangement."

"Maybe I can give you a better one than Matt can. I don't want you messing up my son's life. And that's what you'll do." She started to speak, but he raised his hand.

"Hear me out. Give us Jeff's baby. You're a beautiful woman and you'll fall in love again. You can have a lot more babies. Give us Jeff's baby and I'll deposit in your account a half of a million dollars to let us have the baby and you get out of Matt's life permanently. You can add this amount to what Matt has offered and you can keep the ring he's given you. In total, my proposition, plus Matt's offer and his ring will be well over half a million."

Eight

Stunned, Olivia stared at him. After surprise shook her, her mind began to function. "Thank you for your generous offer, but my answer is no."

Duke's eyes narrowed. "Did you hear how much I'm willing to give you? You can't turn down that much money."

"I can and I have," she said quietly. Matt's arm curved around her shoulders and he gave her a squeeze.

"You haven't even thought it over," Duke said, scowling at her.

"I've kept quiet, Dad, to hear your offer, as well as to hear Olivia's response," Matt said in a firm voice. "Just now Olivia refused you. That's what I wanted to hear. She's honest and true and up-front about all of this. You and Jeff have both underestimated her and misjudged her just as I did before I met her. In my judgement of her, I was off a country mile and you're even more mistaken about her. Just as Jeff was. Jeff couldn't see beyond a desirable woman."

"Dammit! Neither can you!" Duke snapped, his voice rising. "Don't be taken in again. You married a woman who couldn't wait to dump you. You don't know anything about women, Matt. Stop interfering here."

"I'm not interfering. Olivia just refused your offer."

"You don't think this baby needs its mother?" Olivia asked, her anger increasing by the second.

"No," Duke replied, his attention shifting back to her. "We'll make up for that. My children grew up without their mother and they turned out fine."

"Perhaps they did," Olivia replied. "From what I knew, as charming as he was, Jeff cared about no one but himself." She glanced at Matt who gazed back with an unfathomable expression. "Matt is cynical and talks about his sister and brother being wild," she continued and turned to face Duke again. "All of your children might have benefited from a mother's influence."

"By any standards my family is a fine one," Duke said, and his face flushed a deeper red. His anger was palpable. Olivia regretted she was the cause of it, but she wasn't intimidated by Duke Ransome and she had no intention of giving up her baby for any amount.

"I didn't say they weren't a fine family, Mr. Ransome. I just think a mother might have had an additional positive impact on them. My baby is going to have its mother. Your family puts too high a priority on material things." She tried to bank her own smoldering anger and think clearly because she was making monumental decisions about her future and her baby's and she didn't want to make the wrong choice in an emotional, knee-jerk reaction.

"I think that's a bit difficult to accept coming from a person with your background and your demands on my son. You can't tell me money means nothing to you," Duke said, gruffly.

Matt stood and placed his hand on her shoulder. "That's enough, Dad. A week from Saturday Olivia and I intend to marry. We're working out a good arrangement that will give our baby a father and a mother and a family and financial support."

"Financial support! Like hell!" Duke's fiery gaze bored into Olivia. The room snapped with tension, yet she felt insulated, certain about what she wanted and reassured by Matt's stand against his father.

"The tramp will take you for as much as she can get!" Duke exclaimed, still staring at Olivia.

"Tramp?" Matt put his hands on his hips, clenching his fists and taking a step toward his father. "I don't think so," he said in a chilling tone that made Olivia draw a deep breath. "She turned down your offer of half a million dollars—that's no tramp after money, Dad, and you better face the truth. She's going to be the mother of your first grandchild. You owe Olivia an apology."

"Matt, please," Olivia said, standing and placing her hand on Matt's arm. "I don't want to cause a rift between father and son."

"Like hell you don't," Duke snapped. "In your lifetime you'll never have such wealth as I'm offering. If you marry my son, you won't be able to touch the Ransome money. Matt will see to that."

"I'm not after cash. There are other things in life that are important."

"I think you're after the Ransome fortune and I'll do everything in my power to keep you from getting a dime of it."

Olivia could feel the waves of anger emanating from Duke. His fists were clenched, and his face flushed a deeper red.

"Dad, you're on dangerous ground—" Matt said, stopping when she squeezed his arm.

"Wait, Matt," she said and turned to his father. "Mr. Ransome, it's not the Ransome money that I'm after. I'd like my baby to be part of this family that he or she belongs to by blood, although after the past few minutes, I am having second thoughts about that. From what I know so far, Matt is an honorable man. I would like a father for my child. My baby is a Ransome, therefore, I would like my baby to have the benefits of being a Ransome, but not at a price that will compromise his or her life in any manner. Frankly, you, sir, make me want to walk out of the door and never look back. Your son, on the other hand, has accepted my proposition for a marriage of convenience that will give *our* baby opportunities beyond anything I can ever offer."

"Damn straight, you little—"

"Dad!" Matt snapped in a tough, determined voice as he stepped forward with clenched fists. "Apologize to the woman I intend to marry and to the woman who is the mother of your grandson! You damn well apologize or you'll never know this child. I'll cut you off right here and now."

"Matt. Don't!" Olivia stepped in front of Matt, placing herself between the two angry men. "Stop this! Don't let me tear apart your family," she urged. Her heart pounded and she was cold with worry, wondering if Matt even saw her or knew she was in front of him. His blue eyes flashed with fire and his chest heaved.

"Get out of the way, Olivia," Matt said without taking his gaze from his father.

"No! I won't let you two destroy this family," she said.

"If you reject my offer, you'll regret it all your life," Duke said, lowering his clenched fists and turning to look at her.

"I'll never regret turning down your offer," she declared.

Duke glared at Olivia. "You're a cool customer, Miss Brennan. If you're holding out for a better offer, you won't get it."

"Sir, I've already gotten it," she said softly, and his jaw tightened. Matt stepped beside her and placed his arm around her shoulders.

"Dad, you apologize to my fiancée or don't come back to my house or to our wedding."

Olivia bit back a protest at Matt's threat because she wanted a united front with him, but his ultimatum to his father hurt. She never intended to rip apart a family.

"You have my apologies," Duke snarled in a tone that clearly indicated his insincerity. "There—you have your damned apology." He looked at his son's arm draped across her shoulders. "I hope both of you know what you're doing," Duke said.

"I think we do," Matt answered.

"You give long and thorough consideration to my offer,"

Duke said to her. "It would set you up for life. You know that you can have other babies and you know that we would provide a truly good life for Jeff's child. There's not a shred of love between you and Matt."

Olivia and Duke held each other's gaze for a tense moment. "I won't forget your offer. It was interesting to meet you, Mr. Ransome."

"You watch your step, missy. I'll do everything I can to talk my son out of marrying you."

"I think your son probably makes his own decisions."

Duke nodded. Striding from the room, he slammed the door behind him.

She let out her breath and turned to face Matt. "I hate that you and your dad had such a fight."

Shaking his head, Matt raised his eyebrows. "Dad didn't tell me what he was going to do, although I should have guessed. I'm sure he thought he'd made you an offer that you couldn't possibly refuse."

"Half a million to give you my baby and get out of your life."

"I'm a little amazed you could so quickly and easily turn down that amount."

"None of you get it—you can't hang a dollar sign on a child. I'm not giving up my baby."

"I didn't ask you to with my offer. I wanted you to let us share Jeff's child's life."

"I won't give up my baby for any amount. I didn't have to think about my answer."

Matt studied her and put his hand on her shoulder. "Dad doesn't know you at all and he thinks everyone can be bought."

She ran her hand across her brow and Matt placed his finger beneath her jaw and tilted her face up. "Upset?" he asked.

"This past hour hasn't been the easiest time in my life," she said, trying to lighten the moment, but she felt weak in the knees and anger still smoldered inside. As much as she wanted to ignore Duke Ransome and forget his hurtful words, his "tramp" accusation rang in her ears and it hurt.

"I doubt if your father will attend our wedding."

"Oh, yes, he will. I know my dad. Did it ever occur to you that you could be getting into a union that you'll hate?" Matt asked in a quiet voice while reaching out to trace his fingers along her cheek. "Soon I'll be the legal father and have as much say as you in our child's life."

Our child. The words slipped across her raw nerves, reminding her of all the changes that were soon coming because of her decisions. "I'm willing to take the chance. I think we'll work out an arrangement we can both accept," she said, hoping she sounded cool and Matt didn't have an inkling of the butterflies she had over the thought of her future shared with him and his family.

"If I ever worry about you holding your own with my family or anyone else, remind me to forget my concern," Matt said. "I've seen some tough men that couldn't cope with my dad. You won that round with the old man," Matt added. "There are a lot of people who've had tough times, and they would've taken the money and never looked back. I think Dad lumped you in with that group." Matt studied her, his gaze going slowly over her features and making her pulse drum.

"Thanks for standing up for me."

Matt shrugged. "You gave him your answer. He should've accepted it and his remarks were way out of line, but he's accustomed to getting his way and doing whatever he has to do to succeed. I misjudged you a hell of a lot more than a country mile," Matt admitted. He leaned forward to brush a light kiss on her forehead before glancing at his watch. "We need to go to town to the attorney's office. If we don't leave now, we'll be late."

"I'll get my purse," she said, gratified by Matt's remarks and his support.

"Meet you at the back door," he said and left the room with her, going the opposite direction when they reached the hall. Halfway down the hall, she glanced over her shoulder to find him still standing where she had left him. His hand was on his hip as he watched her. When she looked at him, he turned and disappeared into his office.

Matt went to his desk to get a briefcase that held papers and notes he had made for the prenuptial agreement. Half his thoughts were on the coming appointment. The other half were on Olivia and his father. He was astounded his dad offered her so much money, but by now, he wasn't surprised that Olivia had turned him down. She wanted marriage and all the commitment that went with it, even if it was going to be a business arrangement. A lot of people would have wilted with his dad and given in to him, but also, by now, Matt knew Olivia better. She was a strong woman who would not be intimidated by his dad or outsmarted by him. If the situation hadn't involved such high stakes, it would have been amusing because few people refused his dad.

Matt knew he would hear from his father soon to try to persuade him to back out of the approaching marriage.

Matt had no intention of backing out. Each day it looked like a better proposition. They would have an acceptable arrangement for living together; the baby would be his to share—he would become the adoptive father; and he would have sex on a regular basis with Olivia. If the marriage arrangement worked, he could imagine they might drift into loving each other, but in the meantime, he never wanted to go through heartbreak again.

Later, in the car as he drove into town, Olivia shifted on the seat to face Matt. "I guess your father is never going to accept me," she remarked.

"Once you present Dad with his first grandchild, he'll accept you so quickly that you'll be astounded. Believe me, I know my dad. He's wanted a grandchild, dreamed about one, harassed my sister to get married, harassed me when I was married to give him an heir. No, he's going to love your baby and you won't be able to believe that he offered you a fortune to get out of our lives. You'll see a transformation that will astound you and Dad will act as if nothing disagreeable ever happened."

"I'll believe it when it happens," she said unable to imagine Duke Ransome changing so drastically.

"My dad probably expected you to jump at the chance for a fortune because you didn't grow up in comfort."

"Comfort!" She laughed. "There were nights I slept on buses because it was safer and more peaceful than going home. My parents drank and—" she stopped abruptly. "You know all about my background. When I was in high school, I'd just ride the bus at night so I could study. I always felt education was my passport out of that life and it has been."

"That's what I mean. Dad and I misjudged you badly."

"Now I only have to face your brother and your sister."

"I still haven't been able to get in touch with Nick or with Katherine, but I'll keep leaving messages for them."

"They'll probably try to talk you out of this wedding, too. They know we're not in love." She looked at her ring and wriggled her hand. "I think the rest of the world will be fooled about it."

"Don't be surprised if you get some other kind of offer from my dad. He doesn't give up easily."

"I'm not worried."

"No, I suppose you're not," Matt said. "You continually surprise me."

"For one reason or another, most men I've met have misjudged me," she admitted. "That first night you certainly did, and I'll bet your P.I.'s report about me was not at all what you expected."

"You're right. But then, maybe I've surprised you. Because of my brother you prejudged me." Matt smiled at her. "I haven't had a chance to tell you, but you look like you're worth a million today. You look gorgeous," he said. She could see the warmth in his gaze and his compliment pleased her, taking away some of the tension of the past hour.

"You sweet-talkin' devil. You'll turn my head," she teased, momentarily forgetting the raw differences between them, giving him a mocking, coy look that made him grin.

"The more I know you the less I dread this wedding."

"Just watch out, Matthew Ransome," she said, leaning across the front seat. "First thing you know, you'll be in love with your wife," she said and laughed, straightening up and scooting back into her place.

"You would do that when I'm driving," he remarked,

shooting her a quick glance before his attention returned to the road. "Remind me later what you said. And I'll tell you again. I'm not falling in love with anyone, Olivia. All women are romantics and sometimes they pay a high price for it."

"Is that right?" she asked with such sweetness in her voice that he scowled.

"Time will tell, but you're in for more heartache if you're going into this contract thinking I'm going to fall in love soon."

"I think you've made it quite clear that you're a man with no heart. But no matter how much you declare that, Matt, you have a heart and you've loved before, so there's a chance you'll love again. You won't if you shut yourself off from everyone, and I hope you don't do that with this baby because if you want to be a real dad, then you'll have to open your heart."

"That's different and I will."

"Then just take care that if you get your heart functioning again, it doesn't do things you hoped to avoid."

"I'll take care," he answered with a cynical tone. "You better worry about protecting yourself."

"You sound defensive. You're getting angry and you're a tad beyond the speed limit. I think I see a flashing light behind us," she said, looking in an outside mirror.

"Oh, hell!" Matt snapped, and she had to bite back laughter because she knew she had goaded Matt into losing some of that iron control he had. She remained silent while he pulled off the road. When the patrolman approached the car, Matt greeted him.

"Hey, Ebby," Matt said easily, extending his hand and shaking the patrolman's hand when he leaned down to look into the open window. "Ebby, meet Olivia Brennan, my fiancée."

"You're getting married?" the man asked without hiding the surprise in his voice.

"Sure am. You'll get an invitation to the party soon," Matt said.

"Howdy, Olivia," the trooper said in a friendly voice, and she smiled at him.

"Look, my attention was on my fiancée and I just forgot

what I was doing," Matt explained easily. "You know how it is. You and Tamara just got married what—five months ago?"

"That's right. Five months and one week. Look, just slow down a little and try to think about your driving. I'll give you a warning this time, Matt."

"Thanks. I sure will go slower."

"Nice to meet you," Ebby said to Olivia and she smiled in return and twisted in the seat to watch him walk to his car and soon pull around them.

"You got yourself out of that one," she said as Matt drove onto the highway.

"Remind me to put his name on our invitation list."

"You're driving quite sedately now," she observed. "All we both have to do is to hang on to our cool through the prenup agreement."

She received a crooked grin. "You think I can't do that, don't you?"

"I don't have any idea. I don't even know what you want in the agreement."

"You know most of what I want because I've discussed it with you before."

In a downtown building in Fort Worth, she entered the large reception area and in minutes a short, blond man with lively brown eyes approached them and shook hands in greeting with Matt who then introduced her.

"Vic Waterman, this is Olivia. Olivia, meet Vic."

"Glad to meet you," he said, shaking Olivia's hand while he smiled at her. "Both of you come with me and we'll find a quiet place to work."

In a paneled conference room they sat at an oval table and Vic Waterman produced papers and a legal pad. While Matt opened his briefcase to take out his papers, she waited quietly.

For the next two hours they went over prenuptial details. At one point Matt said that he wanted it clearly stipulated that if she divorced him, she forfeited any claims on the Ransome money for herself. When he gazed directly at her, she nodded.

"I find that quite acceptable," she answered easily, watching Vic Waterman write in his tablet.

Finally they worked out an agreement that was to Matt's satisfaction as well as her own. Trying to contain her excitement, she was thrilled with the contract that would protect her in many ways and provide for her baby.

The closer she came to becoming Matt's wife, the more anticipation she experienced. She wanted the ceremony over and done, her baby's future secured. As she glanced at the handsome man she would soon marry, her pulse jumped. How much was she looking forward to the wedding for her baby and how much for herself?

How many times would she remind herself that she was going into a loveless marriage? Was she a hopeless romantic as Matt had declared? Was she dreaming of the impossible, of a man who would fall in love with her? Did she want him to and would she fall in love with him? She knew she was already doing exactly what she had promised herself she would never do—stop guarding against heartbreak.

If something happened tomorrow and she had to walk away from all this, Matt included, she could do it without hurt, she was certain. Would she feel that way in a month? She glanced at him again. Leaning back in his chair, he had pushed his coat open. His self-confidence was obvious. He was handsome, sexy and exciting. If he dreaded their approaching nuptials, he didn't show it. And she hoped she didn't show her nervousness either.

She looked into Matt's blue eyes. It was impossible to tell what he was thinking—whether he hated her for this or if he expected a satisfactory arrangement. She bent her head to skim over all the points they had thoroughly discussed.

Finally they were finished and told Vic goodbye. In the lobby of the building Matt turned her to face him. "You have the appointment this afternoon with the wedding planner. Let's grab a bite to eat and then we can separate and meet later to go home."

She nodded and walked two blocks with him to a small restaurant that was busy with a lunch crowd.

"Feel like celebrating? You're getting what you wanted," he said as soon as they were alone in their booth.

"Yes, I'll celebrate. And you protected yourself with the agreement we just signed, so you should be satisfied."

"Actually," he said, glancing at his watch, "what is going to satisfy me is my wedding night with you," he said in a husky tone that changed the conversation. He reached across the brown wooden table to draw his fingers along her arm and her heartbeat quickened while she drew a deep breath.

"See, that's what I like. You have an instant response to me." He leaned closer over the table and lowered his voice. "You're the sexiest woman I've ever known."

"I seriously doubt that one," she said, suspecting he flirted without giving it thought.

"I'm telling the truth. You're sexy and you respond to the slightest attention. Right now, you've got me aroused and hopefully, I've done the same to you."

"Please remember that we're out in public."

"Believe me, I wouldn't be sitting over here and you over there if I didn't remember that we're not alone. But that doesn't mean I can't touch you," he added. He slipped his hand beneath the table and caressed her knee, sliding higher along her thigh.

"Matt!" she exclaimed while heat rose from deep within her and her desire intensified.

"No one can see me. We're in a booth and it's dark beneath the table. No one cares what we're doing. I want you alone with me, in my arms, but more than that, I want the night to come when you're in my bed and I can make love to you."

"You stop now," she said breathlessly, knowing she had the firmness of jelly in her tone. His light strokes along her leg were stirring feelings she didn't want to have now, making her want to be in his arms and making her want to reach for him in return.

A waiter approached their table. With a mocking smile, Matt straightened and leaned back in his seat. She ordered a salad and listened to Matt order a burger. Then they made plans for the afternoon, but now she was more aware of Matt than their conversation and it was difficult to concentrate or talk about appointments and buying clothes and running errands.

After lunch they separated, agreeing to meet in three hours. She walked a short distance and turned to look in a store window, but instead of seeing the display, she watched Matt striding away. He was tall enough to spot easily in the crowd of people on the street. Wind caught locks of his black hair and he had a long purposeful stride. Saturday night and seduction. She still wondered if she would last until a week from Saturday without trying to seduce him or letting him entice her into sex.

Fishing in her purse, she produced a list of purchases to make. Her engagement ring flashed with brilliant fire in the afternoon sunshine and she was still amazed that Matt would give her such an expensive gift.

She met with the wedding planner, and then shopped and finally went back eagerly to meet Matt, hurrying because she didn't want to be late and keep him waiting.

That afternoon at the ranch Matt shut himself in his office to take care of business. In her room, she changed to cutoffs while she remembered the last few minutes with Matt. "When your wedding night comes, Matthew Ransome, I'm going to make love to you like you've never been loved before," she said, knowing she wanted this marriage to work. She crossed the room to the mirror to study her image. "Are you falling in love with your fiancé?" she asked her image softly. She looked down at the brilliant diamond he had given her. He was being too good to her, too appealing and his kisses too devastating. Was he seducing her into an illusion of love?

"You knew you were in for heartbreak," she told her image.

She pursed her lips, remembering kissing him. "But so is he," she said softly. "The men in this family have had their way far too long."

She patted her stomach. "I've turned down two fortunes for you, so I hope you know how much I already love you," she said quietly. "*Our* baby." Matt wanted her to refer to the baby as *our* baby. Excitement fluttered in her. She was going to have a family for her baby. A father, grandfather, aunt and uncle.

Staying out of Matt's way, she explored the house. In the library, she roamed around the room, looking at leather-bound volumes that were shelved along with dog-eared children's books that must have been Matt's and his siblings'. She opened cabinets to find more books and then she found a closet with shelves of scrapbooks. She looked at dates on labels on the spines of the books and pulled out some from years earlier to look at pictures of Matt as a child. She enjoyed pictures of his brothers and sister, studying them and able to pick out Jeff's cocky grin and Matt's usually solemn expression.

After she had worked her way through a stack she noticed a large gray metal box on a shelf. The box was dusty and looked as if it hadn't been touched in years. When she tried to open it, she couldn't.

Curious, she lifted it down carefully because it was heavy. She placed it on the floor and sat beside it to try to get it open, but was unable to until she discovered a tiny brass key taped to the bottom of the box. Puzzled, she stared at the key a moment. Why would someone bother to lock a box and then tape the key where anyone could find it?

She pulled the key away and unlocked the box. A chill ran down her spine and she had a premonition of disaster. Shaking away the feeling as ridiculous, she opened the box.

Nine

Four books were in the metal box. Lifting them out, she saw that they were baby books. She glanced through them and found Matt's, then replaced the others in the box. The pages in Matt's book crackled when she opened it and she wondered how long since anyone had looked inside. She read his birth announcement and then she saw baby pictures. Turning a page, Olivia looked at a stunning young woman with black hair and movie-star looks.

This was her baby's grandmother. Olivia turned the pages slowly, looking at Matt's baby pictures and his parents. Duke was thinner, younger and undeniably handsome. Matt's mother was beautiful and Olivia stared at her picture. How could this woman walk out on her four children?

Matt insisted his father would love his new grandchild. What about Matt's mother? Was there a chance she'd had regrets through the years? Would she have changed now and want to know her grandchild?

Olivia scooped up the scrapbook and headed toward Matt's

office. She knocked on the open door. Seated behind a desk with papers spread in front of him, he was talking on the phone. He had shed his coat and tie, unbuttoned his shirt, rolled up his sleeves. Her pulse quickened and she wanted to cross the room and finish unbuttoning his shirt, take it off and run her hands over his muscled chest. Momentarily, she forgot why she had come because Matt was a virile, sexy male. When he motioned her to come in, she tried to stop thinking about his hot kisses or his hard body.

She sat across the desk from him. As soon as he ended his call, he asked, "Getting tired of being on your own?"

"Not in the least."

"I'll knock off in just a few minutes and we can swim and I'll take you into town to dinner."

"Thank you." She went around the desk to place the scrapbook in front of him. Slipping his arm around her waist, he pulled her down on his lap. She arched her brows at him. "If they could see us, people would think that we're really in love."

"In just days we'll be husband and wife for real. We might as well enjoy each other," he said.

"I quite agree," she said softly and leaned forward to kiss him. He wrapped his arm around her waist again to return her kiss that swiftly escalated in passion. She wound her arms around his neck and kissed him hungrily.

His hand slid over her knee and along her thigh. As she moaned with pleasure, he tugged her T-shirt out of the cutoffs and slipped his hand beneath her shirt to cup her breast.

"Matt!" she gasped. Desire was a hot flame low inside her. The seductive onslaught increased as he leaned down to take her nipple in his mouth. He licked slowly with his tongue, circling her bud, sucking and biting lightly, a sweet torment that made her want to spread her legs and give him full access to her.

Winding her fingers in his hair, she pulled his head up so she could return to kissing him.

His arousal pressed against her thigh and she wanted him badly. She ran her hands across his broad shoulders, clinging to him as he cradled her against his shoulder and leaned over her to kiss her hungrily. She was barely aware of his hands at the waist of her cutoffs as he unbuttoned and pushed them away. His hand slid into her lace panties and he touched her intimately.

Desire flashed like fire. Eagerly, she unbuttoned his shirt and ran her tongue over his flat nipple. His fingers stroked and rubbed her, creating a stormy friction that escalated swiftly into a pounding need.

Moving her hips wildly, she twisted against him as he carried her to an edge. He kissed her, thrusting his tongue deep and then slowly withdrawing it, to thrust deeply again, mimicking the act of sex.

Gasping, she cried out, wanting infinitely more of him. "Matt!" she cried, turning to straddle him while she unfastened his belt and trousers to free him. She leaned down to take his thick, throbbing shaft in her mouth.

He closed his eyes and wound his fingers in her hair, groaning as she licked and caressed him.

He started to slide her over him, but she caught his hands. His eyes flew open and desire burned in their depths. "Olivia—"

"We can wait until after our wedding. It's not that far away." She scooted off his lap and pulled on her clothes, straightening them, meeting his hot gaze and turning to walk away from him. "We're waiting," she said again, as if to convince herself.

When she turned around, he had straightened his clothes and was sitting watching her with a smoldering gaze.

"This marriage will be good, Matt."

"Yeah, it will," he replied, but she wondered if his thoughts were on making love instead of what she said to him. "It'll be hot and sexy," he said in a husky voice that made her wonder if she could continue to wait until Saturday.

She moved back near him. "I know something we didn't put in that prenup agreement," she said, leaning one hand on his desk and bending closer to him.

He looked up at her. "Yeah, what's that?" he asked in a husky voice while he slid his fingers slowly up her arm to her throat.

"What if we want to give this baby a brother or a sister? If I want to, will that be acceptable to you?"

"Hell, yes, it would. I never dreamed I'd have a child of my own. Shortly after Margo and I married, she made it plain that she was never having children."

"How awful to not tell you until later!" Olivia exclaimed.

"Yeah. We had some real fights over it because before marriage she hadn't leveled with me about not wanting children." He slanted Olivia a look and his blue eyes filled with curiosity. "So if I want another baby, you'll agree to my getting you pregnant?"

"Yes, I will," she said. "I think it would be wonderful to have more than one."

"How many do you want?" he asked and a suspicious note crept into his voice.

"One more child would be marvelous."

"We agree on something."

She laughed. "We haven't disagreed that much. We got through the prenup without too many battles."

"More or less. What's this?" he asked, turning the baby book around. "Damn, I haven't seen this since I was a kid."

"There are baby books for all of you on a shelf in a closet in the library. They were locked in a box."

"I haven't thought about that in years. They were locked away when we were little kids so we couldn't get to them."

"Why didn't your dad want you to look at your baby books?"

"Probably just didn't want us tearing them up. By the time we were big enough to open the box to look at the pictures, I guess none of us wanted to. I never did."

Olivia opened the book and pointed to a picture. "Matt, that's your mother, isn't it?"

"That's her," he said gruffly.

"Where is she now?"

"How the hell should I know? None of us have seen her since we were little kids."

"She'll be our baby's grandmother."

He looked up and his expression was a storm cloud. "Don't get any sentimental ideas."

"She will be the grandmother. How do you know if she hasn't changed in all these years—"

"Dammit, no! Don't you contact her. She walked out on us. Do you know what that does to a little kid?"

"I can well imagine," Olivia answered solemnly, thinking about her own parents who had been a problem all her life.

"We're not contacting her or even trying to if you possibly could. She could live in Australia for all I know."

"You hired a P.I. to check into my background. Why don't you learn her whereabouts and a little about her? She might deplore what she did, Matt."

"No. And don't you even think about it."

"It doesn't matter to you that she's the grandmother?"

"It does not. She wasn't a mother to us. She's not going to be a grandmother to this baby. Understood?"

Even though she mulled over what he said, she nodded.

"Olivia, I mean it. You forget her. She didn't give a damn about us."

"She's beautiful, Matt."

"What's that got to do with anything?"

"Nothing. I just wondered how long since you've even looked at one of her pictures."

"Actually, not for years, nor do I care to now. I would think you'd understand my attitude because of your own background, although I know your parents never abandoned you."

"They might as well have," she said, looking at the window and remembering her own life. Her gaze swung back to Matt. "Very well. She's your mother, so you have the right to ignore her, but you've never heard her side of the story and your father is a strong-willed man."

"Olivia, if you were married and had four little kids, almost babies, would you walk out on them for another man?"

"Of course I wouldn't. You should know that."

"That's right. So what kind of woman abandons her family?"

"I just thought she might have regretted what she did. Or she might have tried to come back and your father wouldn't let her—have you ever thought of that?"

"I don't think so because he was hurt. As young as I was, I know he changed when she left. He's never been as carefree or good-humored since. I don't think he would have kept her away. You just said you wouldn't walk out on little kids."

"I suppose you're right," Olivia said with a sigh as she picked up the scrapbook. He caught her arm.

"Leave the scrapbook and we'll go swim now."

"I'll put it up and meet you at the pool."

"We could shower together before our swim," he suggested, trailing his fingers along her arm. She looked at him with arched eyebrows.

"I think not."

"We're going to be married soon," he replied. She suspected he was teasing her and didn't have any expectations of showering with her.

"Until then, no." She grabbed the scrapbook and left, hearing him chuckle behind her.

Matt watched the sway of her hips as she left his office. He tossed his pen on the desk and thought about his baby pictures with his mother. He didn't like looking back and remembering the hurt and longing.

"Damn, it's been a long time," he said to himself. He didn't want to contact his mother or have Olivia get in touch with her. His thoughts jumped to Olivia and desire stirred. She was sexy, gorgeous and so self-possessed it continually surprised him. Today, she had been cool, decisive and as far as he could tell, got exactly what she wanted in the prenuptial agreement. She didn't seem to care that he put a stipulation in that if they divorced, she forfeited all rights to any money from him except child support. Her attitude toward money was also amazing, but then it always dealt with her losing control of her baby.

Marriage to Olivia. It was far more palatable today than it had been yesterday. Matt strode out of the room, hurrying to change to swim because he looked forward to being with her. At the thought of her long legs and lush body, he broke out in a sweat. He moved faster, longing to get into cool water and put out the fires his imagination ignited.

When he stepped outside, she was there, stretched on a chaise longue with her eyes closed. As he approached her, his gaze ran over her and he marveled again how flat her stomach was. She didn't look one degree pregnant.

Matt was intrigued by her. Olivia was fascinating, unpredictable and he had to admire and respect her and admit that she had gotten the best of him, as well as his dad, in the contests over their futures. Maybe someday he and Olivia would love each other. It surprised him that he even considered the notion. Was her influence changing him?

Olivia had stretched on the chaise to read, but in minutes she'd shoved the book aside and closed her eyes. It was cool and pleasant by the pool. Then she heard the door slide open and she watched Matt who had changed to his brief swim trunks. A white towel was thrown casually over his broad shoulder. Like flint striking a rock, the moment their gazes locked, sparks flew. Olivia's pulse raced and she inhaled deeply. As he approached her, she could see desire heat his blue gaze.

Looking powerful, too appealing, he strolled toward her until he reached the chaise. His gaze left hers and drifted slowly over her, making every inch of her tingle. When he looked into her eyes again, she was breathless, wanting to reach for him.

Stretching out beside her, he drew her into his arms and turned her on her side to face him. Pressed against his hard length with only tiny scraps of material between them, she ached with desire. Each encounter, every hour, her need for him grew. His body was warm, hard. She could feel the rough texture of his thighs with the short dark hairs as her legs pressed against his.

"Let's swim in the nude," he suggested, unfastening her swim top to shove it away and then pushing down the skimpy scrap of material that only partially covered her bottom. With eager, trembling hands, she shoved down his trunks and pressed against his arousal. She twisted away from his kiss. "We're waiting until our wedding night."

"Sure," he whispered gruffly and covered her mouth with his again until she wriggled away and stood.

As she retrieved her suit, he watched her, his eyes taking in every naked inch of her. "I want to kiss you from head to toe and love you until you're senseless," he whispered.

She turned her head to slant him a look. Beneath his watchful gaze, she pulled on her suit. He was stretched back on the chaise, his arousal hard and ready for her. Her heart pounded and she longed to go right back into his arms.

Even though he wasn't touching her, she was in flames. Unable to resist, she walked closer and then she leaned down over him, brushing her breasts against his bare chest and raising slightly to look him straight in the eye. "Next Saturday, I'm going to love you until you're too exhausted to move," she whispered and bent down again to draw a line down his chest with her tongue, sliding lower over his flat, washboard stomach, tasting his slightly salty skin. She looked up. "I want you to want me until you're crazy with desire."

She drew the tip of her tongue lower, over his thick manhood.

He groaned and sat up, sweeping her into his arms to kiss her passionately, pulling her into his embrace. Her heart thudded and she kissed him in a dizzying spiral that momentarily made everything else between them insignificant. Surroundings and circumstances vanished. His kisses changed her to a quivering, boneless mass of jelly. She wanted him as she had never wanted a man. He could drive her to a point of need that made her lose all reason.

"Later, later," she whispered, pulling her top back in place and turning to walk away from him toward the pool.

Without looking back, she went down the steps into the pool, letting the water swirl around her. As she cooled down, her racing pulse slowed to a normal beat. She swam in long strokes, in no hurry, just wanting to relax and cope with scalding desire. And try to get a wall of resistance between Matt and her.

He followed, diving into the water, swimming to catch up with her. He bobbed up beside her and moved them both where they could touch bottom and stand. He slid his arm around her waist to pull her close.

"Next Saturday, you're mine," he said, sliding his hand over her hip.

Her eyebrow arched. "It's mutual that day."

She kicked away from him, and for the next half hour any time he swam close, she turned to swim away. She kept distance between them, enjoying the water, wanting to be in his arms, excited to be with him.

Finally she climbed out. "I'll go dress for dinner," she called, hurrying to slip into her cover-up.

"As far as I'm concerned, you can eat dressed the way you are right now," he said, climbing out behind her. Water splashed off his body and her pulse jumped while she assessed him thoroughly.

She gave him an amused look. "I think I better put some clothes between us," she said and left, her back tingling because she was certain that his gaze followed her across the patio until she was out of his sight.

She let out her breath. By next Saturday night, they would be wild with desire and she intended to make love to him until he never wanted to let her out of his life.

When she returned to the patio, he was in jeans and a fresh T-shirt that clung to his muscles and revealed his powerful shoulders and biceps. Wind lifted locks of his black hair and she thought about how it felt to run her fingers through his thick hair. His gaze drifted over her T-shirt and cutoffs and as she walked up to him, she saw the approving warmth in his eyes.

"You look great," he said.

"Thank you," she answered, smiling at him. "I'm glad you approve."

"I approve except I'd like to peel you out of your T-shirt and cutoffs."

"Maybe later," she said. He smiled, but his eyes sparkled with anticipation that matched her bubbling excitement.

While a thin column of gray smoke drifted skyward, steaks sizzled on the grill. The tantalizing smell whetted her appetite. "I'm starving," she said.

"The feeling is mutual," he said in such a husky voice, she turned to look at him. "I could eat you for dinner," he said, and her pulse jumped.

"No, that comes later," she replied softly, and his chest expanded as he inhaled.

"I'm ready to cool down with some tea," she said, seeing that he had two glasses of iced tea poured. He handed one to her and in minutes they sat at the table with thick steaks and baked potatoes.

"Here's to our future together," he said, raising his glass of iced tea and she touched her glass against his with a faint clink.

"May it be less stormy than our past," she added, and he smiled. "Soon I'll enroll in the university for the fall. It's a dream come true for me to be able to do that. I'll carry a full course load. Thank you, Matt, for your generosity."

"I have to thank you in return. I'm getting a baby in my life."

"You'll be a good dad, I imagine."

He shrugged. "I don't know until I try and see how I do. At least I'll love the little boy or girl."

"Now that the prenup agreement is out of the way, I need to concentrate on the wedding arrangements. The wedding planner will be here in the morning at ten."

"All that is up to you. I'll take care of the honeymoon arrangements," he said.

"We're taking a honeymoon?" she asked, surprised. "I'm amazed we're going on a honeymoon."

"Why not take a honeymoon?" he asked and the corner of his mouth lifted slightly.

"Since we're not in love—"

"We're going to have great sex," he said, lowering his voice and leaning closer, leaving his steak untouched. "I want you all to myself. Super sex is a good reason for a honeymoon."

"I suppose," she said, but she had a pang of longing for more than lust and great sex. She wanted a honeymoon where they cared about each other, but she knew that wasn't going to be the situation and she better not delude herself. "I like surprises," she said carefully.

"Good. You'll have to wait until next Saturday to find out where we'll honeymoon."

She laughed, and he drew his finger along her cheek. "I like your laughter, Olivia. We're going to have a workable arrangement."

As she gazed into his blue eyes, desire filled his expression. She put down her fork and got up, walking around to him to sit in his lap. When she approached him, he pushed back his chair and the moment she sat down he wrapped his arms around her.

"I intend for it to be better than a 'workable arrangement,'" she said. She leaned forward to kiss him, sliding her tongue into his mouth and drawing it slowly over his. His arms went around her and he held her close, kissing her hard until she leaned back.

"How's that for 'workable'?" she whispered. "Or this?" she asked, tugging up his T-shirt so she could slide her tongue over his flat nipple and then shed kisses lower. "Or this?" she asked.

"Dammit," he said, winding his fingers in her hair and tilting her head back to give him full access to her mouth. He bent over her, molding her to him. His hand cupped her body, pulling her hips closer while he kissed her.

She pushed against him and twisted away and they gazed at each other. "It'll be workable, all right," she said, sliding off his lap and standing. "And we're waiting because it won't be many more days."

He stood to embrace her. "You're going to be mine, Olivia," he said in a raspy voice that played like a soft wind across her raw nerves.

"Be warned, Matt. Soon I may find your heart, and it'll be mine."

His eyes clouded and his jaw firmed. "You're a romantic, a

dreamer and an optimist. Watch out because I don't want to hurt you. What we're going to have will be great, but it won't be love."

She smiled at him, hiding the stab of pain his words caused and surprised by the intensity of hurt. "We'll see," she said, wondering if she was deluding herself about him. What would it take to make him fall in love with her?

"In the meantime, let's clear things up and sit down and do some wedding planning," she said, trying to keep her voice light and casual.

Matt's cell phone rang and he pulled it out of his pocket to answer. "It's Nick," he whispered. "Hi," he said. "I've got news and I know this is short notice. Olivia Brennan and I want you to come home next weekend. We're getting married."

Olivia walked away to give Matt privacy even though he was quiet and his brother had to be doing all the talking. She wondered if Nick was trying to talk Matt out of marrying her. Olivia picked up dishes to carry them to the kitchen. She knew his family didn't want him to marry her. Was she insisting on something that was going to be a disaster for all concerned, and most of all, for her?

She knew she better decide for certain because next Saturday would soon be here.

Friday evening a week later, Olivia had another attack of butterflies. Within the hour Matt's brother was arriving and in an hour and a half his sister would get in. The wedding planner had assistants getting the house ready and tonight they would have a rehearsal and then all go to Rincon to a country club for dinner. The closer the wedding, the more nervous Olivia became, assailed with doubts and last-minute jitters. Was she doing the right thing? she asked herself for what seemed like the hundredth time. Yet she was falling in love with Matt and she prayed that with this marriage, love would come to him. Then doubts would bombard her. Was she locking herself into a loveless union that would grow more difficult with time?

If she thought about walking out, though, she knew that wasn't what she wanted to do.

She slipped her red dress over her head, feeling the silky lining that was cool against her skin. Her wispy underclothes were red lace, a luxury she'd never before been able to afford. She looked around the bedroom and was reassured by the life she was giving her baby.

The moment she walked into the family room and looked at Matt in a charcoal suit and red tie, her qualms fled. When his blue eyes met her gaze, her heart thudded and her concerns about marriage vanished.

Another tall, handsome man stood beside him and they both crossed the room to her. "Olivia, meet my brother, Nick."

Extending her hand, she looked at a man with curly brown hair who stood an inch taller than Matt, as broad through the shoulders with the same straight nose and firm jaw. There the resemblances ended. Nick's dark brown eyes flashed with curiosity as she shook his hand.

"Welcome to the family," Nick said and smiled, his teeth looking a dazzling white against his dark tan.

"Thank you," she replied, relieved that he was friendly because Matt's father still was not and he had declined to join them tonight. "I'm glad you could get here and be with us for the wedding."

"Wouldn't have missed it," Nick said. "Now if we can just get my wandering sister home. Dad will come around eventually."

Unable to agree with him, Olivia nodded, but she didn't want to say so.

"Ahh, here she is," Matt said, looking over Olivia's head. She turned to see a tall, striking blonde in a sleeveless beige silk dress.

"I think all three of you had different mothers," Olivia remarked to Matt and he flashed a grin. "You don't look alike at all."

Without answering her, he was gone, crossing the room in long strides with his brother as both of them welcomed their sister. Olivia watched them hug and kiss, thinking all three could have been models. But then Duke Ransome was a handsome man and Olivia remembered the pictures in Matt's baby book of his mother who had been stunning. Why wouldn't their offspring be handsome and beautiful?

Matt approached her with his sister and brother. "Olivia, meet my sister, Katherine. Katherine, this is my fiancée, Olivia Brennan."

Gazing into crystal-blue eyes, Olivia smiled and shook Katherine's hand.

"So you're the woman who has shaken up this family? As least it put an end to mourning Jeff so much because now there's a new worry."

"And I'm the new worry?" Olivia asked with amusement.

Suddenly Katherine smiled. "I believe you are, but maybe it's not warranted. Goodness knows, this family can use new blood. And a baby is fantastic! I was beginning to give up on ever having a baby in our midst. You two didn't help the cause," she teased, looking at first Matt and then Nick.

"I don't see you helping the cause either," Matt told her in a good-natured tone.

"Don't ever hold your breath on that one," Katherine responded, turning her attention back to Olivia. "So you're going to law school?"

Olivia nodded. "I have to get my undergrad degree first." All the time she talked to Matt's brother and sister, she was aware of Matt at her side. He was friendly enough, but it should be obvious to everyone that he wasn't in love.

Within the hour the wedding party and the minister arrived and they went through a rehearsal. While they received instructions, Olivia felt a pang over the sham marriage. Yet each time she was besieged with qualms, she looked at Matt and knew she was making the best possible choice. If only…she blanked that out. Tomorrow she would be Mrs. Matthew Ransome, for better or for worse. How she wished she had his love.

As soon as they finished the brief rehearsal, they left for the Rincon country club and a catered barbecue dinner.

It was midnight before they returned to the ranch. Nick and

Katherine were staying at their father's house, so they told Matt and Olivia good-night and drove on down the road.

As Olivia walked across the porch and into the house, Matt draped his arm across her shoulders.

"Your brother and sister were wonderful to me. The way they treated me, you'd think we were in love and having a real marriage."

"Nick and Katherine are all right."

"I'm sorry for your sake that your father hasn't had a change of heart."

They entered the kitchen where only one small light was on. Matt turned to face her and put his hands on her shoulders. "Dad doesn't change easily, and he thinks I'm getting into something that's going to make me unhappy."

"I hope that isn't the case," she said, "and I'm truly sorry that he didn't join us. I know it was difficult for the three of you without him present."

"Oh, no. Dad just cut himself out of an evening with all of us. He'll be there tomorrow. You'll see."

She doubted it, but at the moment she was far more aware of Matt running his hands along her arms up to her shoulders.

"Your brother and sister were really great. I wish they stayed here."

"Got butterflies?" he asked, changing the subject abruptly and looking intently at her.

"Not badly," she replied, not wanting to admit how bad a case of nerves she had.

"C'mon. We'll sit in the kitchen and have hot chocolate. Or we could do something else," he said, leaning down to brush her lips with his.

Her heart thudded, but she held him away. "Until tomorrow night," she whispered and stood on tiptoe to kiss him long and passionately.

Finally she twisted away and gazed at him. "I'll pass on the hot chocolate and see you in the morning," she said.

She went upstairs to her room and closed the door.

Tomorrow she would get married to a man who didn't love her. She shook her head. Every time she questioned herself about the ceremony, she knew she wanted to go through with it.

The next morning Olivia could hardly believe that the time had come. This day she would become Mrs. Matthew Ransome. She still half expected his father to do something to stop the wedding.

When Olivia entered the kitchen for breakfast, she heard a knock at the back door and opened it to face Katherine who was in a T-shirt and cutoffs with her hair caught up in a clip. She carried a dress bag and Olivia knew it held the dress that Katherine would wear as one of her attendants.

"Come in. I was just starting to fix breakfast, so why don't you join me?" Olivia asked.

"Sure. That's why I came and left the men behind. Matt can go join them if he wants." She followed Olivia into the kitchen. "I'll hang up my dress in a bedroom," she said, carrying a yellow sheath encased in a clear bag.

In minutes she returned and looked around. "What can I do?"

"I guess fix coffee if you want some. Or pour orange juice."

As Katherine got out the coffeepot, she glanced at Olivia. "So no cold feet?"

"No. Maybe a few jitters, but I'm delighted with our agreement and I think we can make a good marriage of this union."

Katherine continued to study Olivia. "Just don't break my brother's heart. He's already been through that once."

"I have no intention of hurting him," Olivia replied. "Just the opposite is much more likely to happen."

Katherine's brows arched. "You're in love with my brother?"

Olivia could feel her cheeks flush. "I'm beginning to care about him," she replied cautiously.

Katherine nodded, looking lost in thought. "Well then, I hope you both fall in love. Whatever happens, I hope you have a good arrangement. I don't want to see Matt hurt. I don't want to see you hurt." Katherine studied Olivia. "I watched you two last night. You may be good for my brother."

Olivia smiled. "I hope I am," she replied, wondering if Katherine had ever been in love. Matt had talked very little about his brother or sister. She broke eggs into a skillet and stirred them. "We've been so busy all week making wedding arrangements and getting a prenuptial agreement finished that we haven't had a chance to talk about much else."

"Matt's reliable and he keeps his word," Katherine said. "And we're all thrilled about the baby. You don't look pregnant in the least."

"I definitely am," Olivia said, remembering that Jeff wasn't thrilled and hated learning that he would be a father, but she saw no point in telling Katherine. She dropped slices of bread into a toaster and returned to scrambling the eggs. In a few minutes she sat at the table across from Katherine.

"Olivia, Matt told me what Dad offered you."

"Your father may never like me or speak to me."

"He'll come around when your baby is born. That took some guts to stand up to him and it took something special to turn him down."

"You'd have turned him down, wouldn't you, Katherine?" Olivia asked, suddenly certain that Katherine would have.

"Yes. I wouldn't give up a baby of mine for money. I'm glad you didn't either. You may be really good for our family."

"Thanks," Olivia said, feeling as if she had found a friend she could trust in Matt's sister.

"Good morning," Matt said, striding into the kitchen, his gaze going to Olivia as he crossed the room to her and leaned down to brush a light kiss on her lips. He squeezed her shoulder lightly. "Do you want to get married today?" he asked, smiling at her.

"Yes, I do. I hope you're not having second thoughts," she said.

"Nope. Not at all." He turned to his sister. "Good morning, Kat," he said, crossing the kitchen to get toast and eggs.

"You can join Dad and Nick at Dad's house," she said and Matt set down the plate he held.

"I'll go do that and leave you ladies to your wedding talk." He winked at Olivia and left the room.

Katherine turned a speculative gaze on Olivia. "Maybe you're closer to Matt loving you than you think."

Olivia merely nodded because she knew she was a long way from having his love now.

By the time she and Katherine had finished breakfast and she had showed Katherine her wedding dress, the wedding planner and entourage arrived followed by the caterer and soon the house bustled with people. Katherine left to dress and in minutes Olivia's friends who would be attendants arrived to help her.

The band arrived and while they set up on the patio, Katherine joined Olivia and Olivia's friends who would be attendants.

Still caught in a dreamlike quality, Olivia dressed in the white silk. She wore white rosebuds in her hair, which was pinned on top of her head with a few locks tumbling free. Looking at herself in the mirror, she couldn't keep from staring, dazed by her reflection. Her wedding day. Marriage to Matt.

"You look beautiful," Katherine said with a cloudy look in her eyes, and Olivia wondered what had happened to Katherine in the past.

The moment was gone and it was time for the ceremony to begin.

Folding chairs had been placed in the large living room and banks of white roses were placed along the walls. As the piano player began, the groomsmen and the bridegroom entered the front of the room. Then the bridesmaids went down the aisle and finally, with a flourish of a trumpeter, Olivia knew it was time for her to proceed.

The guests stood, turning toward her. While her heart drummed, she walked with Nick who would accompany her down the aisle and then take his place beside Matt as best man.

She saw only Matt, whose blue-eyed gaze was locked with hers. And then she began walking down the aisle toward him.

Ten

Matt's blue eyes bored into her. Tall and devastatingly handsome in his black tux, he smiled at her. She smiled in return while her heart raced.

She was barely aware when Nick moved away after placing her hand in Matt's. His strong, warm fingers closed around her hand and they faced the minister.

She watched Matt as she repeated her vows. His blue eyes were brilliant, yet she couldn't guess what he was thinking—whether he was happy or angry now that the moment was actually here and he was making what they had planned to be a lifetime commitment.

"I, Olivia, take thee, Matt, to be my lawful, wedded husband," she said, dazzled by what was happening. She was marrying Matt Ransome. It was real. The whole marriage agreement had seemed a dream until this moment, but now it was coming true.

Then they were finished and the minister introduced them to the guests as Mr. and Mrs. Matthew Ransome.

"You may kiss the bride," he said to Matt and she looked up as Matt slipped his arms lightly around her and leaned close. His lips brushed hers and then were firm as they met hers in a way that seemed as binding to her heart as the vows they had just spoken. Her heart thudded and the amazement of actually being married to him rocked her. When he released her, she opened her eyes to find him watching her. He smiled and enveloped her hand in his before they turned. Hurrying beside him, she still tingled from his kiss.

As they walked up the aisle, she looked at the guests. With his jaw clamped shut Duke Ransome stared at her. He appeared as angry as he had the last time she had seen him, but her happiness was a solid wall around her emotions this day. Matt whisked her through the house to circle back to the living room for pictures.

Dressed in the pale yellow silk sheath, Katherine walked up to hug her lightly. "Welcome to our family, Mrs. Ransome," she said and smiled at Olivia.

"Thanks, Katherine. I intend for this union to last," Olivia said and Katherine nodded.

"If you ever want to talk, just call me. I know Matt pretty well. Give him time. He was hurt badly before."

Olivia nodded.

"Welcome, Olivia," Nick said, hugging her, his brown eyes twinkling. "I hope for the very best for both of you. May your future be grand."

"Thanks, Nick. You and Katherine were great to drop everything and come home on such short notice."

"I wouldn't have missed this for anything," Katherine said with a smile. Then Matt was beside her again and Katherine turned to hug him.

"You be good to her, y'hear," she said, poking her brother in the chest with her finger.

"What else would I be?" he asked Katherine with a smile.

"Bride and groom, please," the photographer called and they broke up, stepping back as Olivia and Matt posed for the first picture. As Olivia stood with Matt's arm around her waist, she saw Duke watching from the far side of the room, a scowl still on his face. Was he going to give her trouble in the future, she wondered. Then she forgot him as the photographer began giving her instructions on a pose for the next picture.

It was half an hour before they joined the guests on the patio for the reception. She unfastened and removed her train and in minutes Matt removed his coat. The sunny morning would be carved in her memory forever, more garlands of white roses, the tempting smell of roasting beef and pork, and a crowd of friends of Matt and his family. The band played, the splash of the fountain added to the festive ambience. Yet surroundings and friends faded from her notice when Olivia looked at her handsome husband.

She gazed across the patio at him as he laughed at something one of his friends said. Tall, rugged and handsome, he took her breath. The week had drawn them closer—or had she been the only one to feel that way? Would she ever look at him without a jump in her pulse?

As she watched him, he turned his head and gazed into her eyes and even across the crowd and space that separated them, sparks flew. He watched her, yet he was talking to the man beside him. Without taking his gaze from hers, Matt laughed and said something to his friend. As she watched, Matt crossed the patio and strolled toward her.

With each step closer, her pulse accelerated. He stopped only inches away, smiling down at her with that crooked, inviting smile that made her weak in the knees.

"Hi, Mrs. Ransome."

"I don't know if I'll ever become accustomed to that."

"You will someday. You look gorgeous, Olivia," he said seriously.

"Thank you. You look rather nice yourself."

"Thanks," he said and touched a lock of her hair. "I'm about ready to leave."

"We can't leave now!" she exclaimed. "Not with all these

friends you have and your sister and brother here. We have to stay for an hour or two at least."

The corner of his mouth lifted in a smile, but she could see desire burning in his blue eyes. "The very first moment we can get out of here without being rude, you come get me. Promise?"

"All right, I will. In the meantime, we should circulate." Before she could say anything else, well-wishers came up and Matt introduced her to three of his friends who were friendly, polite and respectful and made her realize how much her life had already changed.

When the band director announced that the groom would have the first dance with the bride, Matt turned her into his arms as the band began to play. He held her close, her hand wrapped in his with her other hand on his broad shoulder. He was clean-shaven, his hair slightly windblown now, so handsome she couldn't stop staring.

"I think time has stopped. I've been waiting forever to get you off to myself."

She smiled. "Not a lot longer."

"I could whisk you away after this dance," he said.

"No, you can't. We have to cut the cake and talk to more guests. Patience, patience."

"What saves me is the realization that it's going to be worth the wait," he drawled in a deep voice and she gave him another smile.

"Soon enough we will be naked in bed together and you'll forget how long you had to wait."

He inhaled deeply and his eyes darkened. "That just makes me want to get out of here more than ever."

"Think about something else." She tilted her head to study him. "I don't even know what you like to do for entertainment or what you want out of life."

"Right now, it's you."

Laughing, she glanced across the patio to see his father talking to a group of men. Duke Ransome laughed at something one of the men said to him.

"I see your father has loosened up."

"He's already had a couple of drinks so that took off the edge and now he's with some of his cronies. He's not thinking about us. At this point, it's a done deal. He'll probably settle back and accept life the way it is. When the baby comes, you'll wonder if he's the same man you know now. He'll be nuts about this grandchild."

"That's what Katherine said."

"As a matter of fact, don't be surprised if he doesn't appear with a peace offering. I heard him talking to Katherine and I think he's beginning to plan on having a couple of rooms in his house redone for a nursery and a playroom."

She glanced again at Duke. "I'll believe it when I see it. He predicted disaster if I married you and he wanted desperately to run me off."

"You'll see. He'll thaw fast now because you're family."

She looked up at Matt. "Family. That's one of the most wonderful things anyone has ever said to me."

He laughed and spun her around. His arm tightened around her waist to hold her close while they danced.

"Everyone is watching," she said.

"That's because you're beautiful."

"Thank you, but I don't think that's why." She clung to him, following his lead and thought they danced as if they had been dancing together for years. He twirled her around again and then pulled her close and she smiled up at him. He gazed down with a hungry look that increased her heartbeat. She wrapped her arms around his neck and danced with him, smiling up at him.

"This is going to be a good marriage," he said.

"Trying to convince yourself?" she asked, feeling a bubbling undercurrent of excitement.

"I think it will be good. Don't you?"

"I hope so, but who knows what the future will bring? You and I barely know each other."

He looked over her head. "I think we've got everyone convinced otherwise, except my family and whoever you've told."

The band finished and commenced a slow number. She heard a deep voice behind her.

"May I have this dance?"

She turned to face Nick, who glanced at his brother. "Get lost," he said to Matt and took her in his arms lightly.

"I'm glad you came for the wedding and Matt is glad to see you," she said, looking into his dark brown eyes and marveling how different the brothers looked.

"I wanted to come see for myself. I don't want my brother hurt," Nick said solemnly. "I didn't have a chance to talk to you alone last night. Don't hurt him, Olivia. He said that the two of you aren't in love, but seeing you together last night made me feel better."

"I don't intend to hurt him. I hope neither one of us hurts the other," she said, looking up at Nick. "Matt was the one who approached me and who wanted my baby in the Ransome family. Always remember that. I didn't come to your family or ask your family for money."

"I know. Matt told me that Jeff didn't want his baby. That's sad news for the rest of us. We need this baby in our family. I'm not the marrying kind. Jeff is gone. God knows, Katherine won't marry. Matt keeps his heart under lock and key. Your baby is the only hope for the next generation for our family."

"That's sort of a bleak outlook about you and Katherine and Matt."

"Nope. That's just the way it is. Just be good to him. He'll be good to you."

"I'm glad to hear that," she replied.

"You ever want to talk, you can call me."

"Thanks. Katherine made the same offer."

"In spite of us traveling and not seeing each other constantly, we're all close. We care about each other."

"Good. That's important."

He spun around and she saw Matt standing in a group of people while he watched her dance.

Matt dimly heard the conversation going on beside him, but

his attention was on Olivia. She was gorgeous today. As she had walked down the aisle, he thought his heart would pound out of his chest. She still exuded that earthy, sexy air, but today, she was stunning. He couldn't stop watching her, devouring her with his gaze and wanting her in his arms more than ever. He had made a bargain that just got better with each day. It was a loveless marriage of convenience, but it was a fantastic arrangement in a lot of ways and one of them was the sex he was going to have with Olivia.

His temperature climbed at the thought and he tried to focus on what was being said by friends. In minutes though, his attention was right back on his new wife. He glanced at his watch. He couldn't wait to get her out of here and off to himself.

They hadn't even cut the cake yet and the afternoon threatened to drag on forever. He suspected she was enjoying herself because her eyes sparkled and her face was flushed and she continually smiled.

He was tempted to get her away from Nick to dance with her himself, but he curbed the impulse, even though he ached to hold her. Was she becoming important to him? The notion surprised him because he didn't expect that to happen.

It was only a short leap from being essential to him to being in love with her. Was she going to slip past the barriers around his heart?

In the brief time she had known them she had charmed his brother and sister.

His gaze ran over Olivia in the long, white dress and he imagined her without it, his mouth going dry and his temperature rising again. He glanced at his watch. Time seemed to stand still. He realized the number was ending and he could go claim his bride from his brother.

He threaded his way past couples who wished him well and congratulated him and wanted to talk and finally he was there behind her and he couldn't resist reaching for her.

"Olivia."

When Olivia heard her name, she turned as Matt slipped his

arm around her waist and pulled her close against him. Katherine approached them.

"Come on, you two, before you start dancing again. They're ready for you to cut the cake and the photographer is waiting."

"Gladly," Matt said and Olivia laughed as he took her hand and they followed Katherine across the patio.

Olivia was aware of Matt's hand lightly on hers as they cut into the seven-tier cake together. She had been as dazzled by the cake as all the other details of this wedding where cost was not a problem. The entire day had seemed a dream and she couldn't get used to being Mrs. Matt Ransome. She looked up at her handsome new husband and felt a pang. Only one thing was missing to make the day perfect, but that one thing was the most important of all.

It was three in the afternoon when Matt found her. "We can get out of here now," he said, taking her arm. She smiled at him.

"Let's tell everyone goodbye," she said, and waved at his sister. He groaned and followed her across the patio to Katherine where she stood by the pool.

"We're leaving, Katherine. Thanks so much for coming for the wedding. You take care of yourself," he said and hugged his sister.

"You, too, Matt. I'm happy for you and I hope this works out for you and Olivia."

She turned to hug Olivia. "Be patient with my brother," she said, giving a toss of her head that sent her blond hair swirling across her shoulders. Olivia smiled.

"I'll try. Thanks for coming, Katherine. It meant a lot and I'm so glad to get to know you," Olivia said.

"Hey, I want a hug, too," Nick said, joining them and turning to Olivia who hugged him lightly.

"Thanks for coming to the wedding and I'm glad to meet you, Nick."

"We're happy to have you in the family, Olivia. You're the best thing that's happened to us in years and years."

"I hope so," she replied, wondering how long Nick would feel that way and wondering how much Matt shared the sentiment.

Matt embraced Katherine and then as the two brothers hugged, Matt thanked Nick for coming again. "Don't wait so long to come home, you two," he said to both of them. "Now we're getting the hell out of Dodge," he said, taking Olivia's arm and striding across the patio to a back gate. She stretched out her legs to keep up with him, her excitement mounting.

"I have a car stashed out here. A plane is waiting and we're on our way."

The moment they were in the car she turned to him. "Where are we going? You have to tell me now."

"To Ariel."

"I've never heard of it. Where is that?"

"It's a tiny island off the Yucatan Peninsula. I own it. When I bought the place, it already had a name, but it's not big enough for you to have ever heard of it. We have an airstrip on Ariel so I can fly in and out of there. It's isolated, peaceful and beautiful. I think you'll like it. I have a staff who keep it maintained when I'm there. They were there all last week getting everything ready, but we'll have the house to ourselves. Two couples live on the island who work for me and they'll come in to clean and cook part of the time."

"Aren't they isolated out there by themselves?"

"They like living there and have their own planes on the island. The Thorensons are retired stockbrokers doing just what they want. The demands of the job I hired them for aren't great. The other couple, the Ellisons, had their own business that went belly up, and they've said this job is perfect. A small paradise and a plane to get them out of there whenever they want. So far we've been fortunate during hurricane seasons. We've been hit, but most structures have weathered the storms. I've had to replace roofs and windows, but it's been worth it. You'll see."

She stared at him, amazed that he would own an island. He glanced at her. "You're staring."

"You just surprise me."

He smiled. "Good, because you've been one surprise after

another to me. We're all amazed you turned down my dad—by all, I mean Nick and Katherine and me."

"Katherine said now that she knows me a little, she wasn't so surprised. And she said she understood. She would have turned him down."

"Katherine probably would, but that's different. Katherine is unpredictable. She's grown up with a life of ease and wealth and what she wanted, most of the time. Not so with you. You've had a life of poverty and hardship. That should make my dad's offer much more attractive and far more difficult to resist."

"No, it didn't. I didn't have to think about it."

"Nick couldn't imagine you turning so much down because he had the same impression I did until I told him about you and our first meeting. They like you."

While he talked, Olivia ran her hand over the elegant leather seat and was amazed how swiftly her life had changed. Never had she dreamed of living the life she was now. Even more astounding was her handsome new husband. As she studied his profile, her mouth went dry. She wanted to touch him and kiss him.

"How long?" she asked in a breathless, throaty voice that made him glance at her and then back to his driving.

"How long *what?*"

"How long until we're on that island and alone?" she asked softly, sliding her hand along his muscled thigh.

His fingers wrapped around hers tightly. "Not soon enough," he replied and his voice thickened. While he watched his driving, he raised her hand to brush a kiss along her knuckles.

They sped to the airport in Fort Worth and soon were aboard the Ransome jet.

When they reached cruising speed and she could move around the plane, she unbuckled her seat belt. "I'll change out of this dress."

"Just stay the way you are," Matt said, catching her wrist. "We'll be there before you know it."

She sat back and buckled up again. "All right, but will I step off the plane into sand?"

"Nope, and you can hold up your skirt. I've got a high wall around my place so soon you can go completely naked and no one will see you except me which is exactly what I intend. That's one reason I bought this particular island. Privacy and peace and I can get to it quickly and easily."

Olivia looked below at the lush green fields and then she turned back to her husband.

"Your dad congratulated me on my marriage to you today," she said.

"I saw him talking to you and would have joined you if I'd thought you needed to be rescued, but after last week, I know you can hold your own with my dad."

"I think he's just making the most of a bad situation right now."

"He'll accept you. He probably has more respect for you than he did before."

She laughed. "Like father, like son. All of you must have thought your brother got tangled with a real bimbo."

"It was easy to jump to conclusions and make hasty judgments."

"Just remember that in the future," she said, thinking again about the scrapbook of pictures of his mother. "I think there's a remote possibility you might have done that concerning your mother."

His smile vanished, and he leaned forward, catching her chin in his hand. "You leave that alone, Olivia. You're getting into something that doesn't concern you and none of us wants any contact with her. She walked out on us. Get it?"

"Yes, I do, but it was decades ago and the little I've seen of your father, you could have been told a twisted version of the truth. After all, you were little kids. How difficult would it be to bend the truth and convince all of you that you were hearing facts?"

"If you didn't know me and we weren't married, would you try to cultivate my dad's friendship because he's the grandfather of your baby?"

Startled, she gazed at Matt while she mulled over his question and she shook her head. "No, I wouldn't."

"All right. She may be a hell of a lot worse than Dad. Leave it alone. At least my dad raised all of us and he cares deeply about this grandbaby."

She could see Matt's point and she nodded. She smiled at him and leaned forward to place her hands on his knees and brush a kiss lightly on his lips. "Let's not have any cross words mar this day that has been a dream-come-true event so far. It's perfect, Matt, and I want to make you smile and then I want to kiss and love you until you will never want to let me go."

"Do tell, Mrs. Ransome," he drawled softly, leaning inches from her face. "Sounds like the best plan possible to me. We'll have our own private beach and we can stay naked. Food is already cooked, and no one is coming in to do anything unless I call and ask them to." His voice lowered while he drew his finger along the V of her neckline, stirring tingles. "I'm going to love you senseless, Olivia. I feel as if I've been waiting forever for this night."

He slipped his hand behind her head and kissed her long and passionately. As he started to unbuckle her seat belt to pick her up, she caught his hands to stop him and she pulled away. "Wait. Not here and not now."

He looked amused as he leaned back. "I'll wait, but no one is going to disturb us here."

"Just wait until we're alone."

"It already seems like I've waited eons."

She smiled at him and nodded in agreement.

When they began to fly over the Gulf, she looked out at bright blue water with an occasional boat creating a white wake. She spotted a dazzling white cruise ship and pointed each thing out to him even though he was right beside her and could see for himself.

She knew when they approached the island and at first she was astounded how small it looked but when the plane lost altitude to land, she forgot size. Her breath caught and she stared in wonder at white sand that was as dazzling in the sunshine as the cruise ship had been. Palms swayed gently and the water was a brilliant blue, lapping at the shore with tiny whitecaps. She saw the landing strip and two planes tied down and a hangar with a tin roof.

The pilot helped Matt transfer their bags to the waiting car and then Matt held the door for her. As she watched him stride around the car, she knew she was hopelessly in love with him already.

He was too sexy, too appealing, too handsome, too generous, too likeable to keep her heart sealed away. When he circled the car, wind blew locks of his black hair. How had she ever thought she could resist falling in love with him?

Sliding into the car beside her, he leaned over to brush another light kiss on her lips. "Welcome to Ariel, Mrs. Ransome."

"Thank you, Mr. Ransome," she said, trying to keep from being too solemn and losing the joy and excitement she had experienced all day, yet it was sobering to face that fact that she was in love with her virile new husband and know that he not only did not love her in return, but he might not ever stop guarding his heart.

She had locked herself into a loveless marriage. She reminded herself that this loveless marriage was going to be a far better future than she had ever dreamed of before.

She clung to that thought as they swept along a road that was made of broken shells with lush green jungle crowding them.

They rounded a bend and drove into a clearing and her heart jumped at the beauty of the house. Made of white stucco, it was a sharp contrast with the blue waters beyond it. The lawn was well tended with palms and masses of bright red hibiscus, a blooming yellow poui, red chenille plants and masses of pink oleander. Climbing yellow bougainvillea ran up porch columns and over the roof.

"It's paradise, Matt!" she gasped.

"Good. I think so, too, and I'm glad you like it. Wait until you see our ranch in Argentina. We're going to stay here four days and then fly to the ranch."

"Argentina?"

"When I met you, I told you we were buying another

ranch—it's in Argentina. We've leased it for the past five years so it won't be new to our family."

He parked and came around to open the door. As she stepped out, Matt swept her into his arms. Shrieking with surprise, she wrapped her arms around his neck.

"I'll carry my bride over the threshold," he said, going up the steps easily and crossing the porch to enter a house with a wide hallway and a gleaming plank floor. Ceiling fans turned lazily. Matt carried her to the bedroom where he slowly lowered her, letting her slide down his muscled body while he set her on her feet.

"Oh, this is fantastic!" she said, looking through floor-to-ceiling glass doors that opened onto a flower-and-palm-covered patio. White sand ran a hundred yards down to the water.

"You're what's fantastic," he said, catching her wrist and pulling her to him. Removing her veil, he tossed it aside and tugged pins out of her hair. When her hair tumbled over her shoulders, he wound his fingers in it, then tightened his fist and tilted her head to give him access to her mouth.

Her heart thudded, and she forgot their glorious surroundings.

"You're the most beautiful bride in the whole world," he said softly right behind her as he brushed a kiss on her nape and then turned her to face him. "I've been waiting for this moment far too long," he said and his voice lowered another notch.

Eleven

Olivia trembled at the sight of the blatant desire in Matt's intense gaze that lowered to her mouth and made her lips tingle. She stood on tiptoe, wrapping her arms around his neck and pulling him closer while she brushed her lips across his mouth.

With a groan he leaned down. "You'll never know how much I want you," he said, grinding out the words. His arm circled her waist, and he pulled her against him while his mouth covered hers. His tongue stroked hers, sending streaks of fire in its wake. Desire became a white-hot need as she thrust her hips against him.

Kissing her deeply, he leaned over her. Her heart thundered, drowning the sounds of the waves on the beach. She wound her fingers in his hair at his nape and then let her hand slide down to twist free the studs on his shirt. She leaned back to catch his wrist. While she watched him intently, she removed a cuff link so he could slip off his shirt. "I've waited all week, Matt," she whispered.

"I've waited a lifetime. You're what a man fantasizes and dreams about."

"I don't know that I want to be anyone's fantasy," she whispered. "I want you to desire me because I'm Olivia—my own person. One way or another, Matt, I'll get to you. You can't guard your heart against love. You may not be able to guard it against my loving. We'll see." She picked up his other wrist to remove that cuff link. He caressed her nape with his free hand and as soon as she had his shirt off, she tossed it aside.

She drank in the sight of his muscled chest, running her hands over him lightly. "I could look at and touch you forever," she whispered, trembling, on fire with longing, yet wanting to savor every moment of this night. She leaned forward to kiss his nipple while she continued to explore his chest and smooth back with her fingers.

He inhaled deeply and tangled his fingers in her hair. "Ahh, Olivia. You'll burn me to a crisp," he whispered. "I've wanted you since the first moment I saw you."

She leaned down, tracing the tip of her tongue across his flat stomach above his belt while she unfastened his belt and pushed away his trousers.

His hands slipped beneath her arms to pull her up and they looked into each other's eyes, his hungry desire blasting into her like a whirlwind. He hauled her into his embrace, holding her tightly and leaning over her while he kissed her.

In minutes or hours—time was gone and she had no idea, he turned her around and drew his tongue along her nape. His breath was warm, sexy.

He brushed his hands so lightly across the front of her dress and she gasped, feeling the faint contact on her sensitive nipples.

She inhaled and closed her eyes, reaching behind her to slide her hands along his strong thighs.

Cool air spilled across her shoulders and down her back when he unzipped her wedding dress. It fell around her ankles with a swish of silk that she barely noticed, but she was awed to see that his fingers trembled as he turned her to face him.

His burning gaze consumed her as he pushed away the

white scrap of lacy panties she wore and the thigh-high dark hose. He rested his hands on her hips and looked at her in a gaze so filled with need, it was like fingers drifting down over her and caressing her. Then he cupped her breasts, his thumbs circling her nipples leisurely in an exquisite torment that made her clutch his arms and close her eyes and try to draw him closer.

"You're beautiful!" he said in a raspy voice. "So responsive. So beautiful."

"Matt! I want you," she gasped, trembling with desire and melting from his touch. When he covered her mouth with his, kissing her hard, she shoved down his briefs. His strong arm banded her, pulling her against his hard length.

With a desperate hunger for his loving, she moaned softly, wanting all of him now. His thick shaft pressed against her belly, hot and hard for her. He picked her up while he continued to kiss her and carried her to the bed where he placed his knee and lowered her.

While she wound her arms around his neck, his hands were everywhere, exploring her body with a thoroughness that heightened her insatiable need.

His tongue traced from her ear to her breasts and he took a nipple into his mouth to bite lightly. His tongue drew slow, hot wet circles in a delicious torment around her taut bud. At the same time, he caressed her other breast, stroking her in a tantalizing feathery touch that ignited more flames. And then his hand slipped between her legs. When he kissed her inner thighs, she spread her legs for him.

Slowly, thoroughly, he trailed kisses down her legs to her ankles and then turned her over to explore the backs of her legs, kissing her behind her knees, moving higher until he reached her nape. "Every inch of you is sexy and beautiful," he whispered.

Wanting him beyond measure, she rolled over to push him onto his back and then she returned his kisses, working her way down his chest, letting her tongue circle his flat nipples. Excited by his response as he wound his hands in her hair and groaned, she kissed his muscled, washboard belly. When he started to sit up, she pushed him down. She rubbed her pouty nipples against him and then ran her tongue around his shaft, letting her warm breath tantalize while her hands stroked his thighs. When she moved between his legs, he reached for her again, but she pushed his chest.

"You have to let me kiss you the way you kissed me," she whispered, shoving him down and continuing her rain of kisses until she rolled him over and worked her way along his back. When she kissed his inner thighs and played with his hard bottom, he twisted onto his back. She took his shaft into her mouth to stroke him with her tongue, slipping her hand between his legs to caress him.

"Olivia," he whispered, grinding out her name in a voice that was gravelly and thick. He was beaded with perspiration, aroused with his shaft rock hard and ready. He stood and held her in front of him while he stepped before a full-length mirror.

"Look how beautiful you are," he whispered, playing with her breasts, his hands dark against her pale skin. He kissed her nape and rubbed his shaft against her bottom and slid it between her legs to rub her.

She moaned with desire, whirling around to hold him. "I want you!" she cried, pulling his head down to kiss him passionately.

She hadn't thought it possible to want anyone to the degree she wanted Matt. She wanted to feel him inside her, to wrap her legs around him and love him through the night. Desire enveloped her, taking her breath and making her nerves raw. How could she want anyone this badly? Her hands swept over him in a feverish need.

"You're gorgeous," he whispered in her ear. "Look at us, Olivia."

Twisting around, she opened her eyes to meet his burning gaze in the mirror. The hunger in his expression took her breath and left no doubts that he wanted her. As he turned her to face him again, his blue eyes devoured her.

"I didn't know I could ever want a woman this badly," he said, and she didn't tell him she felt the same way about him. Words were lost as he swept her into his embrace, leaned over her and kissed her with such hunger she wondered exactly what he did feel for her.

How could he kiss her so wildly and not be falling in love?

She knew that he could do exactly that and still guard his heart. His hands and mouth and hot shaft drove everything from her mind except desire.

His kisses set off fireworks low inside her and sent flashes of light bursting behind her closed eyelids while every nerve tingled. She thrust her hips against his and closed her hand around his manhood, hoping to drive him beyond control.

He picked her up and carried her to bed, lowering her gently and then moving over her.

Spreading her legs for him, she opened her eyes to feast on the sight of him while her heart thudded. She ran her hands along his rock-hard thighs and then took his shaft in one hand as she sat up to run her tongue in slow circles around the velvet tip.

His hands wound in her hair again, shaking away the last of the pins and he groaned, letting her kiss and fondle him for a moment. With a groan he pushed her down.

Watching her, he moved between her thighs and then lifted her legs over his shoulders. His dark shaft throbbed with need. She looked up to meet his fiery gaze and then he lowered his head and his tongue stroked her most intimate places while his hands slipped over her bottom and between her legs.

Closing her eyes, she cried out with passion and arched her hips, thrashing wildly as need built to a raging inferno.

"Matt, love me! I want you to make love with me now. I can't wait longer," she cried out.

He leaned down and flicked his tongue around the curve of her ear. "Yes, you can wait," he whispered and let the tip of his tongue toy with her ear. "I want you really wild with no control at all, begging for love."

She wriggled away and sat up between his legs. "Two can do that," she whispered fiercely. She took his shaft in her mouth again, sliding it in and out and stroking him with her tongue.

He gasped and shoved her down, lowering himself. "Now," he whispered and she held him as the thick tip of his hard rod touched her.

She cried out and arched her hips, trying to pull him closer and wrapping her long legs tightly around him. "Love me, Matt!" she cried. "I want you! You don't know—"

He entered her slowly, filling her, hot and hard and driving her to wild abandon. Her head thrashed and her hips undulated in a rhythm to match his in an ageless dance of passion.

She was one with him, joined in body and now in marriage, falling more and more in love by the moment and devastated by his lovemaking.

Need burned her to cinders. "Matt, love me!" she gasped as he continued his slow torment, drawing his shaft out and then sliding into her in a scalding loving that heightened desire with each stroke.

Tension wound in her like a spring coiled tighter and tighter until she felt as if she would burst with the longing that drummed through her veins.

Sweat poured off him while she cried out and thrashed and nipped his shoulder. She clung to him, her hands sliding down his back, squeezing his hard buttocks. In abandon, she rocked with him.

Knowing that she was in love with this strong, sexy man who was taking her to paradise, she wanted to declare her love, but she bit back the words. She wasn't going to let him know that she had fallen in love with him when she was certain it would not be mutual and might not ever be returned. She didn't want his pity or sympathy.

Yet how difficult it was now, in the throes of the most passionate moment of her life, to avoid crying out her feelings and being totally open and honest with him.

His control vanished and he pumped into her, filling her hot and thick as they rocked together and spun to a blinding climax.

"Matt!" she cried, unaware of anything except his manhood and the sensations exploding from his loving.

"Olivia!" he gasped and covered her mouth, devouring her with another kiss that was a storm of passion.

All she knew was Matt, his body, his arms holding her, his thick rod inside her, filling her and joining them. She held him tightly as they finally slowed and then were still.

She caressed his damp back, sliding her hands down over the curve of his buttocks, down over the backs of his thighs, feeling the short dark hairs curl against her palms.

"You demolished me," she finally whispered.

He turned his head and she looked into his eyes. When she did, he leaned forward to kiss her. In seconds he pulled away. "You're fantastic,"

"Thank you," she answered quietly. "I'll say the same for you. We're a mutual admiration couple."

"One half of this couple is boneless and unable to move," he said, placing his head down on her bare shoulder and turning her on her side to face him. Their legs were tangled together and she toyed with locks of his hair with her free hand.

"It is great sex between us," she observed.

"You think so?" he asked solemnly.

"Yes," she answered in surprise. "You don't think so?"

"I don't know," he answered carefully. "In a few minutes we'll try again and see."

She hit his shoulder lightly. "You were teasing!" she exclaimed. "And I fell for it."

He chuckled softly. "We will try again, but not until I can move and lift my head."

"Lift your what?"

He laughed in a deep, throaty chuckle that conveyed his satisfaction. "Wildcat. You're trying to arouse me again."

"No, I'm not," she protested lightly. "When I try to arouse you again, you'll know it and it won't be just 'try'."

He nuzzled her neck and pulled her more closely against him. "This is good, Olivia. Better than I dreamed possible and I had high expectations."

"'High expectations' translates into you thought I was a bawdy wench," she remarked dryly, amused.

"Could be," he admitted, trailing kisses along her ear and throat. "We're not getting out of bed the rest of the week."

"That's what you think. Hunger will soon set in. I'm eating for two, you know. Now, I want to check out the beach. The water looks like the most inviting thing around here right now."

He hugged her. "I'm beginning to think you had a very good idea when you proposed to me. I should have thought of this."

Her heart leaped even though she knew he wasn't thinking about falling in love.

"Good! I don't have to have a guilty conscience about finagling you into marriage."

"I don't know. I like you to have a guilty conscience because then you'll do more to please me."

"Is that so? I better start learning what pleases you. Let's see—how's this?" she asked, kissing his neck lightly.

He groaned and pulled her close against him. "You give me a moment to catch my breath. I don't have a bone in my body that will function now. I can't stand. I can't even move." He smiled at her and raked her damp hair away from her face. "This is good, Olivia. It's a hell of a lot better than what I had planned for us."

"Good. I quite agree, but remember that when times get tough."

"So what's going to make times get tough?" he asked, arching his eyebrows. The humor had gone from his tone of voice.

"I don't know now, but you know there will be moments we won't agree. There have been a few already and we barely know each other."

"This is a fine arrangement for both of us. You'll get your law degree, I get to be a father and we'll give our baby a family. You couldn't ask for more."

She kept her mouth closed, but she knew she wanted a whole

lot more. She wanted his heart. She wanted him to fall in love because she was falling in love. She ran her hand along his muscled shoulder and the strong column of his neck, feeling the damp sweat still at his hairline. She couldn't get enough of touching him, kissing him and she wanted so much more from him than merely a fine, workable arrangement. Maybe with time, she thought, running her finger along his jaw and then so lightly across his lips. He bit her fingers gently and then kissed her forehead.

"Later, you can practice law in Rincon or even in Fort Worth which isn't a bad commute," he said.

"I'm not worrying about that now," she said. "I have to get through years of school before that time comes."

"If there are more babies, you may change your mind completely." She smiled at him, and they gazed at each other in satisfaction. To her surprise, he rolled away, stood and picked her up.

"I thought you were weak-kneed and all that," she exclaimed.

"I'm getting my strength back," he said. "Touching and looking at you is doing all sorts of things to revive me."

"Where are we going?" she asked, alarmed as he strode outside.

"This is a very private beach, remember? The only people here are on the other side of the island, so don't worry. Unless there's a low-flying plane, which there isn't, we have this strictly to ourselves."

He carried her into the water and finally it was deep enough that he let her legs down and slowly let her slide down the length of him to stand facing him. She felt his arousal, hot and hard against her in spite of the cold water.

"You're oversexed," she accused, teasing him.

"Only because of you," he rejoined and pulled her to him to kiss her. His hands slipped over her, tantalizing strokes that rekindled her desire and she caressed his smooth, wet body, finally slipping away from him.

"Come here," she said, laughing up at him and catching his hand.

He splashed back to the beach with her where she turned to wrap her arms around him and kiss him hungrily.

As if they hadn't made love, he swept her into his arms again and walked to a chaise. He sat and put her astride him. His hands cupped her breasts and his thumbs circled her nipples as his thick rod slid into her and filled her. She closed her eyes and gasped with pleasure, moving her hips.

Need built, driving her to move faster, tension coiling with each stroke of his manhood. She felt his fingers between her legs, rubbing her and creating more fires.

"Matt!" she cried out, moving wildly, pumping him until release burst in her with her climax. His hands held her hips as he still thrust and then he clutched her more tightly.

"Olivia! I want you!" he exclaimed deeply. He thrust rapidly, shuddering and she knew he had reached his climax.

She fell across him, gasping for breath. His breathing was as ragged as hers and she could hear her pounding pulse. Sunshine was hot on her back and he was hot beneath her.

"We need to get into the water to cool down again."

His arm circled her waist and he held her tightly against him. "Not quite yet. I want to hold you."

She smiled and raised her head to look down at him. He was bathed in sweat and his hair was a tangle of black locks across his forehead. Satisfaction filled his blue eyes and made her heart drum.

"I married a most handsome, sexy man," she said lightly, tracing her finger along his jaw.

He rolled her beside him, turning to face her. "And you're gorgeous and I don't want you to even open those bags you brought. I want you naked all week."

She laughed. "I think not! I carefully bought two new swimsuits—"

"I'll get them off you faster than you can get them on," he said, brushing hair away from her face. The ends were damp, but she hadn't done any swimming so the rest was dry.

"I've bought new clothes for this week."

"Show them to me back in Texas next week," he said.

"I'm not sitting around and eating in the nude."

"Shall we take bets?" he asked wickedly and she had to laugh.

"I'm perfectly willing to stay naked all week," he offered.

"I'll bet you are. Now that's not a bad thought but if you do, it'll mean we'll never get far from the bed or this chaise."

"I'll make that sacrifice," he teased. "It's good between us, Olivia."

She nodded. "It may just get better and better. Had you ever thought of that?"

He studied her and ran his finger down her cheek. "Maybe I can stagger into the water now if you keep me from drowning if I slide under."

"I'll keep you from drowning," she remarked and stood, walking toward the water and turning to see him sitting on the chaise watching her.

"You're not coming?"

"I was enjoying the view."

"Matt! Stop ogling me and come swim."

"I'd rather ogle," he said, standing and her gaze raked over him before she turned to go into the water. Her back tingled and her cheeks heated because she knew he was watching her closely. As soon as she was in waist deep water, she sank down to cool and turn to watch him stride casually into the water.

His body was muscled, male perfection, well-sculpted, tan. Just the sight of him made her pulse pound and rekindled her desire. "Come on in," she said.

Matt strolled leisurely out to her. He was exhausted and satisfied, but watching her just now, he knew that wasn't a condition that would last. Not with Olivia going around nude. He marveled at his good fortune. She was a fantastic lover with a body beyond belief. But he knew it was more than her body. She had a sexual air about her that was seduction just being around her.

The beach had a gradual slope and Olivia had walked out to a point where only her head and shoulders were above water. He joined her, reaching out to slip his arm around her narrow waist.

"I thought all this water would cool you down," she said, slanting him a saucy look.

"It should, but your naked body is a lot stronger influence and it heats me up. Touching you excites me," he said softly. "Looking at you excites me," he added. He gazed at her, infinitely thankful he hadn't gotten his way and settled for living under the same roof and nothing more.

And then he wondered if he was falling in love? Had she gotten past his barriers and reached his heart?

The idea startled him and he stared at her, wondering what he truly did feel for her and what it could develop into. Was he already in love with his new wife? Even when he had thought he was guarding his heart so well.

"Give me a few minutes," she said. "I recognize that look in your eye."

"You bring it on with your sexy walk and your bare bottom and long legs. Want to see?" he asked, stepping closer and rubbing against her, amazed himself at how easily she turned him on.

"I know there's something wrong with you," she remarked. "Duck yourself under the water and cool down." She turned to swim away from him and he followed, catching her and pulling her into his arms to kiss her while he treaded water and kept them both afloat.

"Don't you ever get enough?"

"I don't know," he answered. "This making love to you is all new to me, so we'll just have to see," he said before ducking his head to kiss her again.

To his surprise, he discovered that he couldn't get enough of her. They made love leisurely, and then quickly with a hungry passion that he wouldn't have thought possible when they had already loved so much.

That night, long after she had fallen asleep in his arms, he stirred and looked down at her, combing long locks of her hair away from her face while satisfaction filled him. She was sexy, beautiful and intelligent. She was going to give him babies and a marriage and solid family life. Gratitude filled him and he wondered how long it would take before he did fall in love with her. Or was he already there? Was he in love with his new wife?

They had barely eaten dinner and he was ravenous, but as he rolled over to kiss her awake, her warm, soft body aroused him and soon he was making love to her again and he forgot all about his stomach and food.

The next morning Olivia woke and shifted. She looked around, momentarily disoriented and then a strong, brown arm tightened around her waist and memories tumbled back. She looked at her sleeping husband who held her tightly. They had made love off and on since arriving and now her stomach was growling with hunger.

She slipped out of his embrace and went inside, switching on a small lamp and looking around at an inviting large bedroom with a king-size bed, bamboo furniture and a polished plank floor. She retrieved her bag, showered and pulled on a sheer black negligee she had bought and then went to the kitchen. She discovered it was fully stocked with food and dishes that had been cooked and were ready to heat. A fruit platter was in the refrigerator and she removed it, taking off the wrap that protected it and eating a thick chunk of delicious pineapple.

"There you are," Matt said and she turned to see him standing in the doorway.

He had showered and slicked back his wet hair and tied a white towel around his middle. Her pulse began to drum, but she picked up a strawberry and waved it at him.

"We are going to eat before I faint."

His mouth curved in a crooked smile as his gaze drifted down over her and she wished she had simply pulled on cutoffs and a T-shirt instead of the sheer, sexy negligee.

"Matt, we're going to eat. Did you hear me?"

"Sure. We'll eat, but you didn't dress like that and expect me to not notice, did you?" he said, strolling to her and her heart began a drumroll.

"You stay right here," she said, placing a hand against his

chest as she passed him and hurried from the room. She dashed to the bedroom, gathered clothes and changed.

Shortly she returned to the kitchen to find him getting out skewers with chunks of steak, mushrooms, onions and small tomatoes.

He placed them on plates and he already had glasses of water poured. "I heated these in the microwave. They've already been cooked and they should still be tasty."

"They'll be a feast," she said, trying to resist falling on it and devouring it as hunger tore at her. "I'm starved."

He studied her. "I liked the black thing better."

"I'll bet you did," she said, smiling at him and wondering how long the towel would stay tied around his middle, knowing if it lasted through breakfast, then she would remove it.

They were halfway through breakfast when she looked up to meet his smoldering blue gaze. She realized he was no longer eating, but looking at her with as much desire as if they had never made love. She lost all appetite and lowered her fork as he pushed away his chair and came around the table to take her into his arms.

"I feel like it's been a day instead of an hour since we made love," he said, kissing her throat.

She turned her head to kiss him, winding her arms around his neck and all thoughts of breakfast were forgotten.

Three days later Olivia was stretched beside him on a chaise after making love. "It may be difficult to return to reality."

"If you'd like to stay longer, we can, but you'll love the Argentine ranch. It's spectacular. We can stay here or on the ranch as long as we want.

"Don't you have to get back?"

"I told you that we're buying the ranch in Argentina. I stay there or on the California ranch a good part of the year."

She sat up to look at him. "What about the Texas ranch?"

He gave her a crooked smile and toyed with locks of her hair. He was stretched out with a towel across his middle and she wore a two-piece red swimsuit. "We have a foreman, but usually I go back after a few months to keep Dad happy. He wants me to run the ranch and as long as he's alive, I don't stay away more than a couple of months at a time."

Surprised, she studied him. "What do you mean by, 'As long as he's alive'?"

"After Dad's gone, I'll probably turn the Texas ranch over to Sandy full-time and move to Argentina. I love that ranch— it's beautiful country. I'll go home for board meetings for Ransome Energy, but I don't have to live there."

"You didn't tell me this," she said stiffly.

His eyes narrowed. "I think I mentioned the ranches. Besides, Dad will be around, probably until our baby is grown, so it really doesn't matter."

"It matters a lot," she said. "And you never know what tomorrow will bring. You told me about buying a ranch in Argentina, but you didn't tell me that that's where you prefer to live."

His hand stilled. "This is going to be a problem?"

"Indeed, it is," she said, her temper rising. "You should have told me."

"This won't happen for years. Look, Dad's alive. It would hurt him if I didn't run the Texas ranch, so as long as he's living, I'm not going to stay away any great length of time. He should be around many more years. You're conjuring up something that doesn't exist at the present."

"Your father has had one heart attack and you can't say what will happen to any of us on any given day. A vacation now and then would be fabulous. To live there—no way."

"It's as good a life as in Texas," he said in a cold, quiet tone that chilled her even more.

She shook her head. "No, it isn't. I want a regular life and regular school in the U.S."

"Okay, Olivia. We can settle it when the time comes."

"Somehow that's not much reassurance," she said, trying to curb her anger.

"I'm redoing an eight-bedroom ranch house in Argentina right now. Even with Dad alive and at the ranch, I intend to stay in the new ranch house, once it's finished, at least two months out of the year. I want my child to go with me. Dad knows I do this every year and that's all right. I do a couple of months on that ranch and it brings in a hell of an income so Dad's fine with it."

"That's disruptive and I can't leave school and later I can't leave a job."

"Look, we're married. You don't even have to go to school any longer and you sure as hell don't have to practice law or work for someone else."

She stood up. "You should have told me. I'm not letting you take my baby off to Argentina for months and I'm not giving up law school because you prefer that ranch to the three others that you own."

"So what the hell are you going to do?"

She stared at him with her anger boiling and hurt simmering that he hadn't told her about his preference in ranches or his plans for the future. "I'll have to figure that one out, Matt, but I'm ready to get out of here." She swept past him and into the house, going straight to get her bags, feeling she should pack and get someone to fly her away from the island before she really lost it and said things to Matt she would regret. How could he possibly think she would take her child to go live in South America, isolated on a ranch for a large part of the year? She steamed with anger because he hadn't leveled with her about his plans.

Tossing her clothes into the bag, she turned to gather more and saw Matt standing in the doorway watching her. He had tied the towel around his middle.

"Can you get a plane for me?" she asked stiffly, gathering more of her things. "I don't want to stay here any longer."

Anger flashed in his eyes and a muscle worked in his jaw. "I'll fly you back myself." He turned away and in minutes she saw him on the patio talking on his cell phone.

She wasn't giving up getting her education. She had seen the anger in his expression and she didn't think he was going to change one aspect of his life either and she realized they should have spent more time talking about their lives. She tossed her shirts and shorts into her bag. She had spent time talking to him. He knew about her law school plans and her desire to practice law. She just hadn't known anything about his goals for his future.

Anger made her shake. She didn't think he had been up-front and straight with her. She didn't know what she would do when they reached Texas. Was she walking out of this marriage already?

She knew she wouldn't do that if he went to Argentina to live forever and she never saw him again. Marriage still gave her baby a future and it gave her a chance for law school that she might not ever have worked out otherwise. No, she would stay, but she could see all hopes for love or a happy marriage smashing into a million pieces that couldn't be put together again.

Matt had acquiesced to her wishes to get the baby into the Ransome family, but he wouldn't consent to her wishes on this. She had no illusions about that. He wouldn't care what she did at this point.

She dressed in emerald slacks and a matching emerald linen top and caught her hair behind her head in a ponytail, tying it with a bright emerald scarf.

"The plane will be ready in an hour, Olivia," Matt said from the doorway.

She nodded. "Sorry, but I know what I want," she said quietly.

"You always have," he replied and they stared at each other and she could feel the clash of wills that was as strong as that first night they had met. She picked up her bag and swept past him.

"I'm out of the bedroom if you want it to yourself," she said.

She went to the front to set down her bag. Hurting, she paced the room, looking around her and suspecting she would never be back here again.

A little over an hour later, she was buckled into a seat in the plane and Matt was up front at the controls. She wondered how good a pilot he was, but then guessed that he was probably quite good. He had hardly spoken on the way to the airport and she could feel the waves of anger that buffeted her.

Tears threatened, but no matter how she looked at it, she

didn't see changing her mind about her future and tossing aside her education. If she didn't get one and Matt sent her packing one day, without an education, she would be back at jobs like she'd had in the past.

And she knew without question she wasn't letting him take her baby out of the country for months at a time, no matter how productive the ranch was or how beautiful. Not during a school year when a child would have to be tutored.

When they landed, she was no closer to solving the problems facing them and she could see he wasn't either or he wouldn't look as if he were trying to bank his fury.

At the ranch house he took the bags and she went on to her room so she could be alone.

Matt set his bag in his room and then carried hers to knock on her door. When she called to come in, he stepped inside and faced her. The tension was thick between them. His anger was palpable and she raised her chin, ready for a fight with him. She hurt and could feel something precious and vital slipping out of her life.

"Here's your bag. Where do we go from here, Olivia?"

"I don't know. I'll have to give it thought. I want to stay married."

"I'm sure you do. Well, we have a deal, and I'll stick by it," he said gruffly and then left abruptly.

Matt strode down the hall and outside, beginning to jog to work off his frustration. He wondered if she really would stay. He expected her to walk out. It hadn't ever occurred to him to talk to her about the ranch in Argentina. His dad was alive and well and Argentina on a permanent basis was far in the future. Too far to give much thought to now. She could get her degree and practice law. He hadn't foreseen that his plans to live in Argentina years from now would be a problem. To stay a couple of months a year hadn't seemed unreasonable either.

She could go on with her life and he with his, but he wanted to take the baby with him a lot of the time and she obviously was going to try to block that every way she could.

Was he wrong? He didn't think he was being unreasonable and a lot of women would have loved it if they had the opportunities that he was providing for Olivia.

"Dammit!" he snapped and kicked a rock as he jogged. Let her go and to hell with her, he told himself, but even as he did, he thought about the past days since the wedding and how great life had been with her. He hurt badly and he had to admit that he wanted her in his life.

He ran for over two hours and finally returned to the house. He had no idea where she was, but he wasn't going to pursue her when she wouldn't want him to.

For the next two days he didn't see any sign of her until he began to wonder if she had packed and moved out without telling him, but at night he could hear her moving around in her room. He had no idea where she ate or what she was doing.

Then Saturday morning, a week after their wedding, he was walking down the hall when her door swung open. She was white and her eyes were round. She grasped the doorjamb and clung to it.

"Olivia! What's wrong?" he asked, forgetting their argument.

"I'm going to the emergency room," she answered weakly and then her knees buckled.

Twelve

His heart thudded as Matt swept her up in his arms. He carried her downstairs to his car where he placed her on the backseat. With rising panic, he dashed around to climb behind the wheel and race down the drive. Terror made him cold as he picked up his cell phone and punched numbers with one hand while he steered the car with the other.

"Who's your doctor, Olivia?"

"Dr. Porter. I've called him and he's meeting me at Rincon General."

Matt called 911 and talked to the dispatcher, giving directions to the ranch.

"We're headed to town. Send an ambulance to meet us. I'll see it coming. I'm driving a black four-door." He replaced the receiver and gripped the wheel glancing in the rearview mirror.

"How're you doing?" he asked her. "What's wrong?"

"I don't know. I have cramps and I'm faint and woozy," she answered. His heart thudded. He was frightened for the baby, frightened for Olivia. He prayed they would both be all right.

He sped down the ranch road and spun out on the highway, heading into town and listening for an ambulance. He saw it coming long before he heard it and he slowed, pulling off the road and getting out to flag it down. As it approached he stepped into the road and waved his arms.

Slowing, the ambulance pulled off and in minutes they were loading Olivia into the back. Matt held her hand. "Hang on, darlin'," he said, giving her hand a squeeze. "I'll follow and I'll be there with you."

The ambulance made a slow, careful U-turn and headed back the way it had come at a much slower speed.

With a pounding heart, Matt hunched over the wheel and followed, wanting to step on the gas and get her where she would have help.

At the emergency entrance, he watched helplessly while they wheeled her inside and then directed him to a waiting room. Rubbing his neck, praying she and the baby were all right, he paced the room. Fear gripped him. It was over an hour before a nurse called his name and he hurried across the room.

"Dr. Porter can talk to you and you can go see your wife. It's the third room on the right through those double doors."

"Thanks," he called over his shoulder, already jogging the direction she had pointed. Matt found the tall, thin, brown-haired doctor coming out of a room and he introduced himself.

"She's fine," Dr. Porter said. "Or she will be."

"She didn't look or feel fine," Matt snapped, wondering if she had received the care she should have.

The physician smiled. "She hasn't been eating right. It's a matter of getting the right fluids back in her. We'll keep her tonight and release her in the morning and if she'll take care of herself—or you take care of her—she'll be back to normal in no time."

As relief poured through him, Matt felt weak in the knees. "Thanks," he said. "Can I see her?"

"Yes, but she's dozed off. She's malnourished and what-ever's been bothering her, I told her she needs to stop worrying about it until after this baby arrives," he said and Matt realized the talk was directed at him.

"I understand. Thanks," Matt repeated. He moved past the doctor and went inside, walking quietly. Olivia had an IV dripping a solution that went into her arm and she lay still with her eyes closed. Matt wanted to kick himself.

He felt as if he had caused this as much as if he had withheld food and water from her. He knew that wasn't the case, she had done this to herself, but he felt responsible. And he realized she was important to him. She had given him a dreadful scare, both for her and the baby, but he had been terrified for her and he realized she was far more important to him than he had admitted to himself.

And she was more important than living on their Argentina ranch or any other damn thing like that in his life. He'd stuck it out on the Texas ranch the majority of the time for his dad. He could do that for Olivia and the baby. They were the most important people in his life now.

That thought startled him, but he realized it was true. He moved a chair beside the bed and sat down, taking her hand in his. "I love you," he said quietly, knowing she couldn't hear him, but he wanted to say it. He raised her hand to his lips and brushed a feathery kiss across her knuckles. "Get well, darlin'," he whispered.

She turned her head and opened her eyes to look at him. "Matt?"

"I'm here," he said. "Go back to sleep."

She stared at him and he leaned over the bed to kiss her lightly on the mouth. He sat down again, still holding her hand. "Go to sleep. You and the baby are going to be fine."

She nodded and closed her eyes.

Matt called the ranch and settled in the vinyl chair, watching her breathe and thinking she looked weak and vulnerable. He wanted to pull her into his arms and hold her, but he knew that wouldn't help her.

That night he slept in the chair by her bed and when he stirred the next morning, Olivia was gazing at him with curiosity.

"Hi," he said, leaning forward to kiss on her forehead. He took her hand in his.

"Hi," she answered. "You were here all night?"

"Yep. How're you feeling?"

"Better. I guess they've been giving me something."

"Your doc said you haven't been eating right."

"I suppose not."

"We'll remedy that," he said quietly. "I'll start cooking for you. But then, maybe my cooking will be an improvement and maybe it won't be," he said, and she smiled.

"I want to get out of here."

"They said you could go this morning."

The door opened and a nurse appeared and Matt stood. "I'll come back, Olivia. I'll wait in the hall." He stepped outside, going to get a cup of coffee.

The morning seemed long and tedious but by half past ten, Olivia was dismissed. They brought her down to his car in a wheelchair. She moved to the car to buckle herself into the passenger seat.

"I'm better," she said as soon as he pulled away from the hospital entrance. "Thanks for going with me."

He reached over to take her hand. "You're not going to skip any meals after this."

"No, I won't."

"Do you want something to eat now?"

"Goodness no. They removed the IV and then brought me breakfast. I couldn't eat another bite."

He glanced at her and saw to his relief, that her color was good and she looked like herself except thinner and he wondered if she had eaten at all since returning from Ariel.

He turned in the park and drove beneath a tall live oak that provided cool shade beneath it's arching branches. He cut the motor and turned to Olivia who looked at him with curiosity. "What are you doing?"

He lowered the windows to let in a morning breeze and turned in the seat to take her hand. "You gave me a hell of a scare."

"I've been eating, but I guess not enough. I thought I was taking care of myself."

He kissed her knuckles and ran them along his cheek.

Olivia could feel the rough stubble on his jaw. He hadn't shaved and his clothes were rumpled, his hair tangled. She thought she had heard him tell her that he loved her, but she wondered if she had imagined it or it had been medication they had given her that caused a delusion. Worry clouded Matt's blue eyes and she wondered what was on his mind. She wished she knew whether he had really declared his love or not.

As if reading her mind, he slipped his arm around her waist. "I love you."

She closed her eyes. How she had dreamed of him saying that! Now it didn't matter because they couldn't work out a future together. Tears threatened and she had received a lecture from her doctor about her attitude.

"Olivia," Matt said in a husky voice, "will you marry me?"

Surprised, she opened her eyes wide and stared at him. "We're married, remember?"

He gave her a faint smile. "I remember, but you proposed and I wasn't in love."

Her heart started drumming as she stared at him.

"This time, I'm proposing to the woman I love."

"What about living in Argentina on your family ranch instead of the Texas one?"

"I've always given that up for Dad. I can give it up for you and our baby. It won't mean much to me without you there. Will you marry me?"

Stunned and overwhelmed, she stared at him while tears spilled down her cheeks. He wiped them away. "Don't cry, darlin'. I didn't intend to make you cry."

She smiled and put her arms around his neck. "They're tears of joy, Matt. Of course, I'll marry you, but we don't need to do that. Your declaration of love is the world to me! I don't want to plan another wedding."

"Whatever you want. If you do, okay. If you don't, okay. I just want you to know that I love you and I want you to be my wife."

She hugged him again, feeling as if weights had been lifted from her heart. "Matt, you've just made me the happiest woman in the world!" she cried, tears spilling down her cheeks.

"You don't act happy, darlin'. You're crying—"

"I told you, they're tears of joy, believe me. I love you, too, Matt Ransome. I'm going to make you the happiest man on earth."

He chuckled. "Maybe in bed. Sometimes, though, I suspect you're going to worry the socks off me the way you've done in the short time I've known you. Since meeting you, darlin', my peaceful life has gone out the window."

She smiled at him. "I'm worth it," she said, and he laughed.

"Yes, you are," he said and then bent his head to kiss her.

Overjoyed, Olivia clung to him while her heart thudded with so much joy she felt as if she would burst. "Let's go back for another honeymoon that won't be cut short," she whispered.

"Sounds like a deal to me," he said and smiled, leaning down to kiss her again.

Epilogue

The following January as wind howled and snow swirled, blanketing Rincon, inside a hospital delivery room, a baby's cry filled the air. "Here's your boy," Dr. Porter said, placing a small baby on Olivia's stomach.

Matt leaned over the baby. "He's perfect!"

Olivia smiled. "I think so, too."

The nurse picked up the baby to clean him up.

"Jefferson Matthew Ransome," Olivia said.

Matt grinned broadly and bent to kiss his wife. "You have a perfect baby," he said softly.

"We have a perfect baby," she reminded him, and he gazed at her with love in his eyes.

He straightened up. "I've got to tell the family. They're all coming to see little Jeff Ransome."

"You'd think no one ever had a baby before," Olivia said, looking at banks of flowers that had already arrived from Matt's father and Katherine and Nick. "Look at all these flowers, and that was before Jeff was born."

"Dad's outside and can't wait to get in here to see you."

"Phooey, Matt. He doesn't want to see me. He wants to see Jeff."

"He'll be happy with you for giving him Jeff."

Olivia smiled at her tall, handsome husband and thought how good life had become for her. Now she had a baby son that she and Matt could love. Matt took Olivia's hand.

"I'm leaving for a few minutes, but I'll be back soon," he said.

She nodded and watched him stride out of the room and joy filled her over her baby and over Matt being in her life. Thirty minutes later he returned and crossed the room to her bed. "Are they finished working on you?"

"Yes, they are."

"Then Dad wants to see you. Sandy and some of the guys are here, and Katherine's flying in if the blizzard doesn't ground planes. Nick will arrive tonight."

"That's great. I'm glad Jeff has arrived in a family that will love him."

"We're going to love him so much, it'll make your head spin."

"You're not going to spoil him to pieces," Olivia said, and Matt grinned. His blue eyes twinkled as he pulled a box from his pocket and placed it in Olivia's hand.

"This is for you, darlin'," he said, and she opened a black velvet box. She gasped with surprise and delight when she lifted out a diamond and emerald bracelet.

"It's beautiful, Matt!" she exclaimed. "Just gorgeous."

He leaned down to take her in his arms and she hugged him. "Not half as beautiful as my wife," he said quietly. "I love you, Olivia. You're my world and my life now."

His words thrilled her, and Olivia clung to his broad shoulders as she turned her face up for his kiss. Her love for him made her heart pound with joy and she held him tightly, eager to be home in his arms again, knowing when she married him, she had made the best choice of her life.

* * * * *

In July 2007, look for
Revenge of the Second Son,
Nick Ransome's provocative story.

On sale 18th May 2007

LOVE LESSONS
by Gina Wilkins

Catherine Travis had all the trappings of the good life –
except someone special to share it with. Could it be that
gorgeous maintenance man and part-time student
Mike Clancy would fix her, too?

A WEDDING IN WILLOW VALLEY
by Joan Elliott Pickart

Ten years ago Laurel Windsong had left, cancelling
marriage plans with Sheriff Ben Skeeter. But now she's come
home – and discovered that it's never too late for true love.

THE RUNAWAY AND THE CATTLEMAN
by Lilian Darcy

Jacinda fled to Callan Woods' remote cattle station in the
Australian outback to protect her child. She found Callan
attractive and protective, a man she could depend on.

Available at WHSmith, Tesco, ASDA, and all good bookshops
www.millsandboon.co.uk

0507/23a

0507/23b

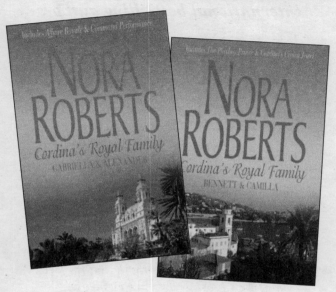

Queens of Romance

An outstanding collection by international bestselling authors

EMMA DARCY
Hot-Blooded Affairs

16th March 2007

CAROLE MORTIMER
Meant to Wed

20th April 2007

NICOLA CORNICK
Regency Weddings

18th May 2007

MARGARET WAY
Outback Marriages

15th June 2007

Collect all 4 superb books!

M&B

www.millsandboon.co.uk

Three timeless tales of love and marriage from international bestseller Betty Neels

Featuring

Heidelberg Wedding

When surgeon Gerard Grenfell offered her the chance to work with him in Europe, Eugenia Smith went happily, but that was before she realised she was falling in love with a man who already had wedding plans.

Wedding Bells for Beatrice

Beatrice told single father Gijs van der Eekerk to marry again, but she hadn't bargained on him offering her the position! Especially when love didn't appear to be part of the deal...

Making Sure of Sarah

Having fallen in love with Sarah at first sight, Litrik ter Breukel vowed to go slowly because of her youth and innocence. But perhaps he simply needed to propose!

Available 4th May 2007

FREE

2 BOOKS AND A SURPRISE GIFT!

We would like to take this opportunity to thank you for reading this Mills & Boon® book by offering you the chance to take TWO more specially selected 2-in-1 volumes from the Desire™ series absolutely FREE! We're also making this offer to introduce you to the benefits of the Mills & Boon® Reader Service™—

- ★ **FREE home delivery**
- ★ **FREE gifts and competitions**
- ★ **FREE monthly Newsletter**
- ★ **Books available before they're in the shops**
- ★ **Exclusive Reader Service offers**

Accepting these FREE books and gift places you under no obligation to buy; you may cancel at any time, even after receiving your free shipment. Simply complete your details below and return the entire page to the address below. You don't even need a stamp!

YES! Please send me 2 free Desire volumes and a surprise gift. I understand that unless you hear from me, I will receive 3 superb new volumes every month for just £4.99 each, postage and packing free. I am under no obligation to purchase any books and may cancel my subscription at any time. The free books and gift will be mine to keep in any case.

D7ZEE

Ms/Mrs/Miss/Mr..........................Initials ....
BLOCK CAPITALS PLEASE

Surname ....

Address ....

....

....Postcode ....

Send this whole page to:
The Reader Service, FREEPOST CN81, Croydon, CR9 3WZ